EMPIRE
OF DESIRE

RINA KENT

To those who didn't only dare to hope,
But also went for it,
And grabbed that motherfucker by the throat.

AUTHOR NOTE

Hello reader friend,

This book isn't dark as the rest of my books, but it's filled with a lot of angst and contains tropes such as age gap, father's best friend, marriage of convenience, unrequited love, and office romance.

Empire of Desire is a complete STANDALONE.

Sign up to Rina Kent's Newsletter for news about future releases and an exclusive gift.

My forbidden husband.

I kissed my father's best friend and it kind of didn't go well.

Not only because he's eighteen years older than me—but he also didn't like it.

Not one bit.

In my defense, I didn't mean to fall for him. It just happened.

Nathaniel Weaver is the most attractive man I've ever seen with enough charisma to blind the sun.

He's bigger than the world, owns half of it and conquered the other half.

He was forbidden.

Wrong.

So I totally got over him. Or so I told myself.

Until we're forced to get married.

Now I'm trapped.

But maybe he's trapped too.

Because we're both reaching for that forbidden fruit dangling between us.

PLAYLIST

"Car Radio" – Twenty One Pilots

"Trees" – Twenty One Pilots

"Doubt" – Twenty One Pilots

"The Hype" – Twenty One Pilots

"Fall Away" – Twenty One Pilots

"Chlorine" – Twenty One Pilots

"Intro III" – NF

"Intro 2" – NF

"The Search" – NF

"Just Like You" – NF

You can find the complete playlist on Spotify.

EMPIRE
OF DESIRE

I'm reminded of my "privileged" upbringing and all the shackles that came with it. Isn't it said that no worthwhile benefits come without sacrifices?

Still, this isn't the time to have such images or thoughts. After all, this is supposed to be a cheerful occasion. The keyword being *supposed*.

Coming to my friend's place to celebrate his daughter's eighteenth birthday is the last thing I wanted to do. Not only do I have countless case files sitting on my desk, but I also have a structural planning meeting at the firm. However, if I told my best friend/partner that I prefer the firm over attending his little princess's birthday, he'd have my balls on a platter. The fact that it's also his firm means nothing on the sacred day of her birthday.

Fifteen minutes. I tell myself as I step out of my car and button my jacket. *I will only stay around for that amount of time and then make up an excuse to leave.*

My partner inherited his mansion from his father after he kicked his "evil" stepmom out with all sorts of legal suits. I've never seen the appeal of this ancient property. Yes, it's vast and has two pools, but he spent a fortune to renovate it and bring it to its current shape.

The house is white with a prim and proper porch that's decorated with colorful exotic plants and extends to the large garden where the birthday party is being held.

There's a long table near the pool that's surrounded by countless people. Some of them are partners and associates from our firm. They're all over the occasion, not missing a chance to kiss Kingsley's ass.

The man himself, the rogue bastard—whom I often bloodied my knuckles fighting when we were in high school—steps out of the house, wheeling a huge pink cake that's almost taller than he is, and when he starts singing *Happy Birthday*, everyone else joins in.

I stop near the house's entrance, waiting for the whole charade to end. Yes, I came to the fucking birthday, but that doesn't mean I'll enjoy the happy-go-lucky crowd.

PROLOGUE

Nathaniel

THE THING ABOUT AMBITION IS THAT IT CAN'T BE STOPPED, measured, or contained.

There's always something to do and a power to pursue. No matter which direction I take, there's a goal to reach and a situation to conquer. However, ambition can't be blind or else it'll become destructive.

I'm currently toying with that line.

The need for more and the fear of less.

The constant pulses of energy and the downfall of the subsequent emptiness.

Truth remains, ambition is my driving force, and yet I still have no clue how I ended up standing on its edge, staring into a dark, foggy abyss.

Its smoky tendrils swirl around me, waiting to drag me under. This isn't the first time I've stared into that abyss and it's stared back. Whenever I'm at a crossroads, I'm reminded of how I ended up here.

Happiness isn't my scene.

Neither are birthdays. Not when mine was supposed to be a funeral.

Gwyneth, Kingsley's only daughter, grins wide as tears gather in her lids and she quickly wipes them away with the backs of her hands. She has a soft smile that's nothing like her father's—in fact, she barely resembles him. His hair is dark, hers is auburn with streaks of lighter strands. His eyes are blue-gray, hers have a rare heterochromia, where the insides are green and the outsides are a mixture of blue and gray.

Now that she's all grown up, she looks more like she's his sister, not his daughter. But then again, he's barely aged with all the physical activities he takes part in.

The song comes to an end as King reaches her, and they both blow out the eighteen candles among cheers and random shouts of "Happy birthday" from the crowd before he pulls his daughter in for a hug. They stay like that for long moments, then he steps back and kisses her forehead.

If someone had told me the ruthless King who used to street fight like a champ would grow up into a mushy father, I would've gone the blasphemy route.

But the evidence is right in front of me. He's wrapped around that girl's finger and the worst part is he's well aware of it.

It could be because he had her when we were in our final year of high school and was clueless as fuck about the meaning of having a child—he still is sometimes. Or because he always called her his second chance at life.

I remain near a tree and check my emails, replying to the urgent ones while I wait for the whole scene to be over.

It takes more than ten minutes—five minutes away from my self-imposed deadline—and I haven't even shown my face yet. After Gwyneth finally goes to accept birthday wishes and King disappears into the house, probably to get more drinks, I make my way toward him.

Going unnoticed is hard as fuck when most of the people

present either work for me or used to work with me, but the cake—and the birthday girl herself—has them preoccupied. I'm safe. For now.

I find King in his kitchen, rummaging for beer bottles in the fridge and giving distinct, methodical orders to the catering staff. Now, that's the King I know. Clear-cut and precise. Which is one of the reasons I got along with him in the first place.

After all, devils recognize each other.

Or maybe he's an ex-devil now, considering all the mushy shit he does whenever his daughter is involved.

I lean against the counter and cross my legs at the ankles. "You're only short a maid's outfit to complete the role."

King turns around holding two cases of beer and his expression immediately sharpens. Gone is the soft man who was singing *Happy Birthday* not too long ago.

He straightens to his full height, but no matter how much he tries to get more on me, his six-foot-two is still an inch shorter than me. But he's more buff.

Aside from boxing with him for old times' sake and doing some hiking, I'm not as obsessed as he is with sports.

"You can go." He hands the beer to one of the staff and they all scurry out of the kitchen at his order.

After slamming the fridge shut, he retrieves a Zippo from his pocket and flicks it open, then closed. He quit smoking a long time ago, soon after Gwyneth's birth, but he's never lost the need to have that lighter. "I thought you weren't coming."

"I'm here, aren't I?"

"Nice save, because I was planning to kick your ass."

"You can't win against me. Not in this lifetime, at least."

"Last week's match says otherwise."

"In last week's match, you cheated by throwing the towel in my face."

"It's called street fighting, not noble martial arts. I'll let you win this week."

"Fuck you. Don't act benevolent when you're going down."

"We'll see about that. Now, why are you late?"

"It's just a birthday, King. I don't see what the big deal is."

"My daughter's birthday. That's the big deal, Nate."

I resist the urge to tell him it's still just a birthday since those words will definitely get me punched. My face is kind of real estate now and can't be bruised in any way. King's, too. Which is why the face is a red zone in our fights.

King flicks his lighter shut, slips it back in his pocket, and reaches into the cabinet. He retrieves a bottle of The Balvenie 21 Year Old Port Wood Finish and pours two glasses, then slides one across the counter to me.

"Drinking this early?" I swirl the contents.

"It's a special occasion."

I take a sip to hide whatever grimace my mouth was about to make. "Because it's her birthday or because it reminds you of her mother?"

"Her mother can go fuck herself. That woman doesn't exist." He downs the whole glass.

"Clearly. Judging by the million PIs you've hired over the last eighteen years."

"There's no harm in knowing one's enemies' whereabouts."

"You want me to believe that you won't do anything once you find her? Really, King?"

The corner of his lips curve in a smirk as he pours himself another drink. "I never said that."

"Keep me and the firm out of this mess."

"The firm, maybe. But you, my friend, will definitely go down with me."

He steps to my side and leans against the counter. We drink in silence, which was our ritual after we fought in high school. Back then, we were bloody, bruised, and barely breathing, but we sat on the school's rooftop that overlooked New York City and shared a beer. It was also around that time when we vowed to conquer this city.

Almost two decades later, we have branches all over the States and in London and France.

And it still doesn't feel like enough.

Nothing does.

"She's growing up so fast." King sighs, watching Gwyneth help the catering staff. "I want her to go back into being my little angel."

"Kids aren't constant."

"Don't I fucking know it. The other day, she was having a virginity talk with her friend."

"Why the fuck are you talking about your daughter's virginity to me? Or at all?"

He waves me off and continues, "I should've known this was coming, but I still had dark thoughts about all the ways someone could take her away. Then I started to seriously consider the option of becoming a killer to protect her."

"Just so we're clear, I won't be your attorney."

"Fuck you, Nate."

"For abandoning you when you do something stupid?"

"For being a jealous motherfucker because I always win, not only in the street fights and with my higher grades, but I also had a child before you."

"First of all, you didn't win all the fights and the ones you did were always by some dirty play. Second of all, grades are subjective. I still win more cases than you do and my methods are smart and efficient, unlike your hard, ruthless ways that are more trouble than necessary. As for children, no thanks. I practically raised my nephew and he's enough children for a lifetime." I check my watch. Twenty minutes since I arrived. Five minutes more than I'd planned to stay. I place my glass on the counter. "I'm out."

"Where to?"

"A meeting with a client."

"On a weekend?"

"No rest for the wicked." I turn and start to leave, but his voice stops me.

"Wait."

"What?" I glance at him over my shoulder.

"You didn't wish Gwen a happy birthday."

"Do it on my behalf. I'll leave you the gift."

"Fuck no. You'll go over there and do it yourself. I don't want to see the disappointment on my angel's face when she learns that her uncle Nate completely ignored her on her special day."

Five minutes. I won't stay any longer than that.

Gwyneth

I'm officially an adult now.

Or that's what I like to think. Dad definitely still considers me a little girl that he needs to protect at all times.

I can sense him watching me, even when he's out of sight. Especially during the moments when I plan to do something he doesn't approve of.

Ever since I showed up at his door when I was less than one day old, Kingsley Shaw has made it his mission to protect me at all costs. It didn't matter that he was seventeen going on eighteen and in high school at the time and had no damn clue how to raise a kid.

Especially a naughty, active one like me.

He still singlehandedly raised me while he went to college and then law school and passed the bar. Let's just say that toddler me didn't exactly make Dad's college life easy, but he never once made me feel like he was absent.

I've always been a well-loved daughter, albeit lonely, with a brain that suddenly becomes blank for no apparent reason. The therapist Dad took me to says it's depression. I call it an empty brain that no therapist can cure, but that's not the point. The point is that I was loved but never spoiled or treated as if I were royalty just because my grandpa was rich or Dad owns a law firm.

He's still strict as fuck and gives me a curfew—that I will hopefully get rid of today.

I tell my dad's friends that I'm going to grab something to

drink. I don't really have many of my own friends, so Dad usually brings his. When I do invite my classmates, they get super intimidated by all the hotshot businessmen and political figures that are present, so I stopped making them and myself flustered.

I don't like my birthday anyway. It reminds me of the day when my empty brain was born.

And the woman who gave it to me.

Anyway, I walk among the crowd, forcing smiles. They don't come naturally to me, not like they do for Dad. Many things he excels at are my weaknesses, such as physical activities, charisma, and a complete brain, I guess.

What I'm good at, though, is multitasking, so I don't have any trouble running my gaze over all the people present while smiling and playing my birthday girl role—the role I play every year for Dad.

My dark red dress clings to my skin, but that has nothing to do with the perspiration after so much moving around. I resist the urge to wipe my sweaty hands on the material. Not only is it designer, but I also chose it carefully, so I'd look like an adult.

It molds to my curves and shows off my waist, and it also has a deep V-neckline, accentuating my breasts and teasing some cleavage. I even sacrificed my favorite white sneakers for the black high heels that are currently murdering my poor feet.

But it's all for nothing if I can't find him.

My nape heats and strands of my long hair stick to my neck and temples. The more distance I cross, the more I clink my nails together.

Almost everyone Dad knows is here, *almost*, because my step-grandma is never welcome in Grandpa's house, per Dad's words.

And *him*.

The man I've started to look for in a crowd when I have no right to.

After what seems like forever, I throw my weight on the swing Dad made for me and put in the backyard near the second pool when I was a kid. My gaze gets lost in the lights shining from the water, and I release a long breath.

The area is lit by lanterns and countless strips of fairy lights hanging between the trees, but it's still dim compared to the front of the house.

My heart feels a little bit bruised, stomped upon, even though I have no actual logical reason to feel this way.

But what is logic anyway? Dad says all the good things are a little jaded, imperfect.

Illogical, even.

I'm not supposed to wallow in misery on my long-awaited eighteenth birthday, but here I am. Swinging back and forth in the wake of the destruction that's happening in my chest.

I had great plans for today. Not because I like birthdays, but because this one is special. This one means I'm officially no longer a child.

But my most important plan was aborted before it was even implemented.

I retrieve my phone from my bra and scroll to the photo album named "Memories." I find a picture from my first birthday, where I was squealing in Dad's arms while Uncle Nate was trying to grab me.

Nate.

Not Uncle Nate. He's Nate.

I run my fingers over his face and pause at the jolt that zips through my entire body.

It's been some time since I started feeling these weird zaps whenever I see him or think of him. He even started appearing in naughty dreams that made me sweaty and wet and I had to relieve myself in the middle of the night.

That's why he can't be Uncle Nate anymore.

He's not even Dad's friend or the man who's more powerful than the world. He might be a senator's son, but he's so much more than that.

He owns half of the world and eats the rest of it for breakfast.

"There you are."

I freeze, my hand tightening on the phone. Did I maybe gain wizard abilities for my birthday and conjure him up?

That's stupid, of course, because I can feel the warmth his body always emanates and smell his cologne. A little bit musky, a little bit spicy. A little bit…wrong.

I shouldn't know him by his smell alone or be able to recognize him among the dozens of people crowding our house. I shouldn't have heated ears and a throbbing neck just because I heard the deep, rough tenor of his voice that's only meant to say firm, serious things.

A voice that I've started to dream about despite my damn self.

And now, he's behind me.

And that means he can see my phone.

I jolt, hugging it to my chest, and in hindsight, that's such a bad idea, because now I'm thinking about him between my breasts, and my heart kind of explodes all over the place.

My reaction goes downhill from there and there's no way to stop it. My lips part, and my expression must be frozen like a deer caught in the headlights.

But instead of commenting on his picture on my phone, he steps in front of my swing, towering over me like a fucking god.

One with Adonis looks and as cold as the statue.

That's what one of the magazines compared him to. They called Senator Brian Weaver's son—that's Nate, by the way—one of the most sought-after bachelors and the most apathetic of them all.

But I've never received the frigid treatment everyone talks about. For me, he has always been warm. Well, *somewhat* warm. Because Uncle Nate is too businesslike to ever be warm in the traditional sense.

Nate. I chastise myself. *It's Nate.*

"Don't worry. I won't peek at your conversations with your boyfriend."

My heart does that flippy thing that makes me feel as if I'm going to vomit or faint or maybe both.

While it does have something to do with his presence when I thought he wouldn't come, it's more about what he said.

Boyfriend.

As in, he's my boyfriend since I was staring at him. Well, that's not exactly what he meant, but in my twisted brain, it sure as hell counts.

I tilt my head back to see the entirety of him. Though I doubt there's any picture frame that can contain him.

His face is all sharp lines and defined cheekbones, which become shadowed depending on where the light is coming from. He has the type of features that communicate with the slightest twitch and the merest of movements. Nate has always had immaculate control over his body language and facial expressions, and it shows in each of his movements.

The older I've gotten, the more aware I've become of his imposing, silent character that speaks through actions more than words. I've also begun to see why he's the perfect partner for Dad. They're alike in a way, but Nate is still harder to read. Due to his rigid demeanor, I have to be extra careful in deciphering any change in his facial expressions.

It's blank now, which could mean a lot of things. Is he angry, disapproving?

Or maybe he's just indifferent as he is most of the time.

I can't stop looking at him, studying him, getting my fill of his face as if I won't see him for a while. I'm engraving everything into my memory, like how he fills his suit or how he appears majestic in it.

I can't stop staring at his thick brows and lashes, at the slight stubble covering his jaw, and at how a few strays of dark blond hair kiss his forehead with each gust of wind.

And for a tiny moment, I wish I was a stray hair or the air. Either would do.

But what I really can't stop staring at are his dark eyes that appear almost black right now. Those eyes have a language of their own that no one is allowed to learn, no matter how much they attempt to.

A language that I've been desperately trying to speak for a while now.

I grip the phone harder, needing the courage it provides as I speak, "I don't have a boyfriend."

"One less thing for King to worry about."

I bite my lower lip, unable to hide the disappointment at how he blatantly ignores my statement and pushes it all to Dad.

It'd be better if I stopped.

Usually, I would.

Nate isn't the type of man anyone likes to push—and I'm no exception.

But if I did, how would I accomplish what I've strived for? I waited for my eighteenth birthday to shout that I'm a woman now.

That I want him to see me as one.

That's probably why I ask, "Do you think I should have a boyfriend?"

"That's none of my business, kiddo."

"I-I'm not a kiddo."

His lips twitch. "You just pouted like one."

Damn it. I knew he still thought of me as if I were a little girl. Can't he see I'm all grown up now? That I'm looking at him?

That I can't *stop* looking at him?

"I'm making it your business," I insist. "So what do you think?"

"About?"

"Should I get a boyfriend?"

"No."

My heart nearly rips my ribcage open and hops out to dance at his feet. He said I shouldn't get a boyfriend. That can't be meaningless, right?

"Why not?" I try to sound cool, but I can't control the tremor at the end.

"King wouldn't like it."

Oh.

So it's back to my dad again.

Seems I'm out for blood, though, because I still refuse to drop it. "How about you?"

"How about me?"

"Would you like it if I had a boyfriend?"

He pauses, then says, "I would be neutral."

Right.

Of course, he would.

Why would the king of the jungle look in the direction of a stray cub when he has countless lionesses by his side?

The breaking sound in my chest that I felt when I thought he didn't show up returns and I dig the edge of my phone into my ribcage as I struggle to maintain a neutral façade.

This would be the perfect time for me to stuff myself with some vanilla ice cream or a milkshake while I hide in the closet.

"Happy birthday, Gwyneth." He reaches into his pocket and produces a small blue box and tosses it my way.

I let the phone fall to my lap so I can catch it. Receiving a gift from him is almost enough to make me forget about his words. About the apathy everyone in the media talks about.

Almost.

"Can I open it?"

"Sure."

I didn't even open my other presents, but the ones that I have from Nate are always first on my list. In the past, he's always gotten me toys and books. This isn't the packaging of either of those.

Inside, I find a gold link bracelet with a scale charm hanging from the chain. I let it dangle between my fingers and smile. "It's so beautiful."

"My assistant picked it out."

I drag my gaze from the bracelet to him.

He's letting me know that he would never pick something like this for me, but whatever, he's the one who bought it and that's all that matters.

"It's still beautiful. Thank you."

"King said you want to study law."

"Yeah. He's my role model." *And you.*

I don't say that, though, because in some way, it feels like he's put up walls in the span of seconds. The tightening in his jaw and face scare me.

But apparently, they don't scare me enough, because I blurt out, "Can you help me put it on?"

"No."

It's a point-blank refusal that makes me wince. Usually, he doesn't refuse my requests, not that I make them often. Even though I've known Nate all my life, I was always intimidated by him one way or another.

Like people are intimidated by my dad, I guess.

"Why not?"

"You can do it on your own." His expression closes and I know he's done with any type of conversation and will leave, shutting all the doors in my face.

And if he goes, my plan for today will be an epic failure.

If he goes, I will have nothing.

He still doesn't see me as an adult. He still thinks I'm a kid, and if I don't do something about it, that will never change.

If I don't do something about it, I know, I just know that I will regret it for the rest of my life.

So I gather the remnants of my courage and let my phone and the box fall to the swing as I stand up.

Thanks to Dad's genes, I'm not short by any means, but I still barely reach Nate's shoulders, even with heels on. Oh, and I'm so tiny compared to his broad build and mass of toned muscles.

But I don't let that stop me and I step closer until my heaving breasts nearly graze his chest. Until the fabric of my dress is mere inches away from his tailored jacket.

It's not the first time I've been this close to him, but it is the first time under these new circumstances and in the midst of all the zaps and jolts and dreams that he's always the main character of.

Dreams that leave me soaked and aching for a single touch.

"What do you think you're doing?" His voice is as stiff as his body, but he doesn't step back or push me away.

He remains there like a sturdy wall that I always want to climb.

"Can't you help me put the bracelet on?"

"I said no."

"What's wrong with doing it?"

I pause at my own words.

Doing it.

Me and Nate.

Nate and me doing it.

Shit. I need to rinse my mind with bleach and hope all the dirty thoughts disappear.

"Go back to your party, Gwyneth."

I twist my lips in disapproval. He never calls me by the nickname everyone uses for me, and I hate it.

Gwyneth sounds impersonal and detached.

Putting distance between us is the last thing I want, so I push my body forward, toying with an invisible line where his world is separated from mine.

I'm crushing that line, decimating it, burning it to ashes.

Because I'm an adult now and I can do that.

"I want to be right here, Nate."

His thick brows dip in the middle. "What did you just call me?"

"Nate," I say, lower this time, a little bit uncertain, a little bit scared. Because, holy shit, his deep, rough voice and the tightness in his body can be terrifying.

My thoughts are confirmed when he says firmly, with an authoritativeness that strikes me straight in my bones, "It's Uncle Nate."

"I don't want to call you that anymore."

"It's not up to you to decide. It's Uncle Nate, got it?"

I swallow at his non-negotiable tone and the firm edge to it.

No wonder he's a force to be reckoned with in the courtroom. If I were a criminal, I'd be on my knees right now.

Hell, I'd be on my knees even without the criminal part.

"Answer me, Gwyneth."

"Yeah. Okay. Got it."

He narrows his eyes at that and I know he hates it, my using two or three different terms for the same thing. He told me so once, to measure my words before letting them loose, but I'm not as disciplined or as assertive as he is. Never was and probably never will be.

But a part of me longs to be, because if I am, he'll see me as a woman, not a kid.

A woman.

But instead of commenting on my words, he says, "Now go back to your birthday party."

"I don't want to."

"Gwyneth," he warns.

"I want a birthday present."

"I already gave you one."

"The bracelet doesn't count, because it was picked out by your assistant." I don't actually think that at all, but he doesn't need to know that.

He releases a breath. "What do you want?"

"Can I have anything?"

"Within reason."

"You told me once that reason is subjective. That means what you see as reason is entirely different from what I do."

"Correct."

"Then don't say I acted unreasonably, okay?"

Before he can form thoughts or theories, I grab the lapel of his jacket, flatten my breasts against his chest, and get on my tiptoes.

The moment my lips touch his, I think I've reached another level of existence—one I had no idea existed. They're so soft and warm but have an underlying hardness like the rest of him.

I move my mouth against his closed one and even dart my

tall and broad and has an eight-pack. No kidding. He's the health-iest man I know. But he also has a few age lines that make him the wisest ever—aside from a certain someone.

Also, the look in his blue-gray eyes, the same eyes that now look at me with love, can kill. I can tell why many people find him intimidating and absolutely brutal. When someone has his fortune, looks, and personality, people either bow or stay away.

But once again, I have the superpower of being his only flesh and blood.

"You forgot your phone." I wave it in front of him and take a slurp of my vanilla milkshake—which is my version of a morn-ing coffee.

Dad sighs as he takes the phone. He's not the type who for-gets, *ever*—his memory is like an elephant's, but it feels as if he's been preoccupied more than usual lately.

Maybe it's an important case. Or his unending legal battles with my step-grandmother, Susan. I swear, neither of them will let go and it'll just go on forever in court until one of them dies.

After he tucks the phone in his pocket, he pinches my cheek. "What would I do without you, my little angel?"

I pull back. "Hey! I'm not little anymore. We celebrated my twentieth birthday a month ago."

"You'll always be little to me. Besides, a vanilla milkshake is still your favorite drink, which proves my theory."

"It's my happy drink."

"Uh-huh."

"I've really grown up. See how tall I am?"

"How tall or old you are doesn't matter. You'll always be lit-tle to me."

"Even when I'm old and wrinkly and taking care of you?"

"Even then. Deal with it."

"You're hopeless, Dad."

"Gwyneth Catherine Shaw, who are you calling hopeless?"

I fix his crooked tie and feign sadness. "A certain Kingsley who's getting old yet refuses to settle down with someone."

"I have my little angel and, therefore, I need no one else."

"I'll leave one day, Dad."

"Not if I have a say in it."

"Are you going to keep me single forever?"

"Hmm." He stares at me thoughtfully, as if he's trying to figure out the ending to humanity's misery. "Hypothetically, no, because I want grandchildren—eventually. But I don't like the journey that leads to that outcome."

"There could always be a surprise pregnancy."

Dad stiffens and I internally curse myself for not keeping my mouth shut. This, of all subjects, isn't something he's a fan of—because of my mother, I guess.

He hid it from me until I was eight. Up until that time, he used to tell me that she'd died, but then I overheard him talking to Nate and that's when he told me the sad reality.

Ever since then, we made a pact to never lie to each other.

"Are you pregnant?" His voice loses all humor.

"What? No, of course not, Dad."

He grabs my shoulders and leans down so his eyes are level with mine. "Gwen, if you are, just tell me."

"No…"

"Is it that kid with the bike? I'm going to fucking murder him."

"It's not Chris. I was just kidding. I'm sorry."

"Are you sure? Because that motherfucker is going to have a surprise visit from me and his Grim Reaper."

"Don't, Dad. I'm really not pregnant. I promise."

He releases a breath, then staggers backward as if he's been punched.

What I just said must have reminded him of how I ended up at his door. My mystery mother—who's a taboo subject around here—abandoned me in front of Grandpa's house when Dad was still in high school with a measly note that read "She's yours, Kingsley. Do whatever you want with her."

And that's how I came to life. Abandoned. Discarded.

She didn't even tell him to take care of me. Just "whatever he wanted."

"Don't joke about things like that, Gwen," Dad tells me in his no-nonsense voice.

"I know. I didn't mean to." I grin up at him in an attempt to change the mood. "Aren't you forgetting something else?"

He places his briefcase on the floor and opens his arms. "Come here."

I dive in, wrapping my arms around him. "I love you, Dad."

"Love you, too, Angel. You're the best gift I've ever received."

Moisture gathers in my lids and it takes everything in me not to be all emotional and tell him stupid things like how it hurts that I'm not Mom's gift, too. That she considered me trash to be discarded. That she's a coward who abandoned both of us.

Because, in a way, I've always had a hunch that he was waiting for her. Twenty years later and he must be exhausted. He must be at his limit.

Maybe I'm at my limit, too. Despite all Dad's love, I've always felt that a piece of me was missing, lost somewhere I can never reach.

That could be the reason I grew up to be a hollow person with barely anything at my core. Someone sweet on the outside, but completely and utterly empty on the inside.

Someone with a dysfunctional brain.

Someone who needs lists and coping mechanisms to stay afloat.

"Did you change your shampoo, Gwen? It's still vanilla, but is it a different brand?"

I roll my eyes as I pull back. He has a super sensitive nose, like he can smell when I've had a drink behind his back, even after I brush my teeth and consume copious amounts of mouthwash.

"I mixed two brands together. Seriously, Dad, you have a weird sense of smell."

"It's for when my angel decides to drink when she's not supposed to."

I make a face and Dad ruffles my hair, sending the auburn strands flying.

"Not the hair!" I jerk away and smooth the stubborn thing down.

"You still look beautiful."

"You're only saying that because you're my father."

"You got my genes, Angel, and that's not something trivial. Anyone would find you beautiful."

Not Nate.

A jolt rushes through me for just thinking his name. It takes all my resolve to say goodbye to Dad without turning a furious shade of red.

After he leaves, I sit on the steps, place my milkshake beside me, and grab my bracelet. The one he gave me for my birthday two years ago.

The same birthday where I kissed him and he rejected me so cruelly, I still feel flushed to my bones thinking about it.

If I thought Nate was turning cold around my eighteenth birthday, he's now as hard as granite. He doesn't speak to me unless it's absolutely necessary. We rarely see each other, and when I go to the firm at the pretense of getting my father lunch, he just ignores me.

He doesn't do it in a rude way that would make Dad notice. He's subtle yet efficient. I can now count the number of times I've seen him over the last couple of years.

Crossing paths—about twenty.

Conversations—zero. Aside from the stray "How are you?" that's detached and without warmth.

It's not like he was always present when he was Uncle Nate. He was there for Dad mostly and didn't pay me much attention, as if I were background noise.

A wallflower, maybe.

A kid.

But I could at least exist in his vicinity without feeling like I'd detonate from the inside out.

After I kissed him, I ruined the easygoing relationship we'd had for eighteen years.

But I don't regret it.

Because I'd hoped I would be more than a kid to him. I'd hoped that he'd see me in a different light.

All my hopes are up in the air now.

But I need to plan Dad's birthday in the next few weeks, and that means he'll be there.

I gulp, my heart hammering in my chest.

Though it shouldn't be, because I got over him, you know. It's for the best, anyway, since Dad would go berserk, so everything is fine.

I'm *fine.*

I've been telling myself that for two years, but it's never felt true. I guess that's because he's Nate.

The same Nate who taught me to control the emptiness inside me and turn it into a strength.

"That hollowness never goes away. It's part of who you are now, whether you like it or not," he said on my fifteenth birthday when he found me hiding in Dad's wine cellar. That's what I do when it gets to be too much and I don't want to upset Dad—I hide.

That day was one of those overwhelming days. I hated it, my birthday, and myself. I felt like that abandoned newborn baby on the side of the road again, even though I remembered none of it. I felt like an unwanted presence and it made me empty. So empty that I couldn't breathe and had to hold in the tears when Dad sang me *Happy Birthday.*

It was the day I realized that despite having the best father in the world, I didn't feel complete. I thought I was weird because all I kept wishing for was a mother.

On every birthday, that's the only thing I wished for. A mother. *My* mother. I wished she'd come back and explain why she did that to me.

But Dad was so happy that day, like on all of my birthdays. He always made them an event that he planned for weeks in advance.

So I couldn't be an ungrateful bitch and start bawling in front of him.

That's why I sneaked into the wine cellar and did it alone, in silence.

Until the door opened and he appeared. Uncle Nate. He was still an uncle at the time, an intimidating one who would put a bully's parent in their place with a few words. He'd done that once, when I was ten and a girl called me uneducated because my mother was a whore. It's been an ongoing rumor; Kingsley Shaw fucked a whore and had to become a single parent when said whore disappeared.

I didn't tell my dad, because I knew he'd be loud and cause drama, but Nate picked me up from school that day on his behalf and noticed something was wrong. He interrogated me until I confessed everything while ugly crying. That same evening, he visited the girl's home and told the mother she would either keep her daughter under control or he'd sue her for everything she owned.

"You don't cover up for people who hurt you, Gwyneth, do you hear me? That's the exact attitude that will encourage them to continue hurting you and others. If you don't want King involved, you come to me. Understand?"

I remained silent in his car, still a bit stunned about how the bully and her mother looked genuinely scared. At that moment, I almost idolized Nate as much as I did Dad.

"Do you understand?" he insisted in that firm voice, and I finally nodded.

"Good. Now, let's go somewhere you can forget about all of this."

He took me to the amusement park and bought me vanilla ice cream. It was one of the happiest days of my life.

The following morning, the bully apologized to me. That's when I realized people fear Nate not only because of who his father is but also because he always keeps his promises.

What happened on my fifteenth birthday was a bit similar

to the bully incident. Nate found me and crouched by my side, but he didn't touch me.

"But I hate it." I hid my face with my hands. "I hate that something is missing inside me."

"Are you going to let it rule you or are you going to bring it to its knees in front of you? Because those are your only two options, Gwyneth. It's up to you what you decide to fill it with. Strength or weakness."

I chose neither.

I chose to fill it up with him.

TWO

Kingsley

I USE THE VOICE COMMAND TO CALL NATE.

The sound of ringing fills the car, but there's no answer.

"Fuck." I hit one of my fists against the steering wheel as I take a sharp turn to the right.

I zigzag between cars, ignoring their honking and the occasional name-calling.

Right now, I'm on a mission.

One that will only be fulfilled once I'm at the firm and talking to that low-fucking-life.

When I first saw the document this morning, I thought something was wrong. Surely, the name and the fucking proof that lay in front of me were some sort of a mistake.

A miscalculation.

A *coincidence*.

A fucking anomaly in the system.

But it wasn't.

And neither were the facts that I learned from the private

investigator. Neither were the records that I had to stoop low and call in favors to acquire.

The truth was sitting squarely in front of me all this time, hiding in plain fucking sight and I was too blind to see it.

Was it arrogance?

Ignorance?

After all, I've grown so fast in so little time. Not only that, but I've also taken on unnecessary and endless battles for the sake of my pride. My bitch of a stepmother who nearly got me killed would attest to my ruthlessness. I'm out to destroy that woman, but only in small doses until she'll consider taking a rope to her own fucking throat. But then again, she's too narcissistic to ever consider that option.

All this time, I've thought myself above being manipulated or toyed with. After all, I'm Kingsley fucking Shaw, owner and cofounder of Weaver & Shaw, which has grown tremendously in only a couple of years.

That's what happens when two geniuses leave their fighting days behind them and decide to take over the world. We once wondered what would happen if Nate's ambition and my power collided. What would happen if he chose to crawl out of his senator father's shadow and become a force to be reckoned with?

What if I used the fortune Dad left behind and I fed off my best friend's ambition?

The answer was simple. No limits.

That's what I've always loved the most about Nate, even back when we used to punch each other, race cars, and compete about who got the hottest girls. Even when I win, he bounces back stronger and on the verge of breaking all hell loose.

His tenacity is endless.

Like a loop or an infinity sign.

Like a fucking horizon.

If you give Nathaniel Weaver the right resources, he'll build one castle, then more, and then a whole fucking city of them. Other people may dream big, but he dreams of taking over the world.

Not in a political way like his father, but in a discreet type of way. From the shadows, where no one can see or hurt him.

Just the way I prefer it.

That's why we're like yin and yang.

When we first met in high school, it was hate at first sight. We were both driven, him more inwardly, me outwardly, and it was only a matter of time before we clashed. That happened in one of the underground fighting rings since we often participated in matches. I box to stop myself from killing. He does it to blow off steam.

Back then, I beat him within an inch of his life. But he never fell down and he refused to forfeit, even when his blood painted the floor red. The organizers had to stop the fight before I killed him.

It was the first time I'd seen a worthy opponent. I can still remember the sheer force of his determination when he stared at me, coughed up blood, and bounced back to his feet.

That's when I knew he wasn't a spoiled senator's son after all. He was more.

I beat him to pulp a few times after that, but he still came back for a redo, over and over, until he was able to win against me. Then it became some sort of a ritual.

We were rivals but often saved each other's asses from the principal, our parents, and even the police.

We had our own world and no outsiders were allowed inside. Many women tried to get in; they wanted to play on both sides, but we dropped them within a fucking minute. We could fight over anything—opinions, strategy, employees—but never over women.

It's not worth jeopardizing our partnership and friendship for it. Though friendship might not be entirely accurate; we're still rivals in a way. We still compete and fight and call each other on our shit.

But like yin and yang, we complete each other. Where he's quiet, I'm loud. Where he's cold, I can be hot-blooded, which makes our partnership extremely profitable.

When Nate and I are on a mission, nothing can stop us.

Or at least, I thought so until this morning.

Until the fucking phone call I had not so long ago.

Until I realized the actual danger to my daughter's life.

The daughter I didn't think I wanted when she showed up at my door. But one look into her innocent rainbow eyes made me fall in love when I thought I wasn't capable of the emotion. I never even considered giving her away, I couldn't. She was a part of me and I knew I had to protect her. It didn't matter that I was young and reckless at the time. It didn't matter that I knew shit about raising a child.

Living with a strict father who kicked Mom out to marry his mistress turned me into an unfeeling motherfucker whose sole purpose is destruction—my own included. And when that same mother killed herself, I swore to never forgive my father, his wife, or the fucking world that made my mother end her life.

That's why I took a reckless path as a teen and nearly ruined everything.

But that was before this tiny baby with little hands and a rosy face bulldozed through my fucked-up existence. Even before I did the DNA test, I knew she was my flesh and blood. I knew she belonged with me.

She's the blessing I never thought myself worthy of. Which is the reason behind her name. Gwyneth.

Her existence gave me a new purpose that was entirely different from wrecking my life. I've always been addicted to power, but she's the reason I did everything to acquire it.

Because those with power can protect their family.

And Gwen is the only family I have.

The family I'll slaughter everyone in my path for, just so she'll remain safe.

But there was a miscalculation on my part.

I didn't look close enough at my surroundings and, therefore, I didn't identify the one person who could threaten her. The one person who could take her away from me after I'd raised her for twenty years.

"Fuck!" I hit the gas and call Nate again.

He finally picks up and speaks with a bored tone. "What is it, King? I have a meeting."

"Fuck meetings. This is an emergency."

"What is it?" His voice sobers up.

I open my mouth to rain hell down on him, but the blaring of horns interrupts me. A car cuts in front of me and I hit the brakes hard, the loud screech echoing in the air.

But it's useless.

A haunting sound of metal against metal fills my ears and I'm swung back by the airbag until my neck nearly cracks.

My eyes are half-open as liquid streams down my forehead and forms a red haze in my vision.

In a fraction of a second, I'm disconnected from my body as if I've somehow left its confinements and am now existing someplace else.

My ears buzz long and hard and my body doesn't feel like mine anymore. I'm floating somewhere, motionless, unblinking, but there's movement.

Not from me.

Sounds, colors, and sensations blur together as a commotion from outside slowly filters in, and with it comes Nate's voice. "King! Kingsley…say something. What the fuck happened?"

"Gwen…" I croak. "Take…care of…her…"

I want to say more.

I want to curse him for what he brought into our fucking lives. It's all because of him and his safe and strategic plans that everything is going to hell.

But no words come out.

My vision slowly darkens, and invisible hands drag me under.

I'm so sorry, my little angel.

THREE

Gwyneth

THE GLASS OF WATER SLIPS FROM MY HAND AND HITS THE sink with a loud *crash*, splintering all over the surface.

The sound collides with the climax of *Car Radio* by Twenty One Pilots that's playing from Alexa.

I wince while I carefully grab the tiny pieces and throw them in the trash and simultaneously scroll through my phone.

Aside from the memes and mindless conversations in my group chat with my college friends, there's nothing of importance. Though calling them friends is an exaggeration. Colleagues would be more appropriate.

Chris, Jenny, Alex and I all take pre-law at the same college, so we kind of flocked toward each other. It's hard for me to consider anyone an actual friend, because most of the people I've met since I was in elementary school were either interested in my super successful father or our family drama, namely the drama between Dad and my step-grandma. It got worse in pre-law since everyone is gunning to snatch an internship at Weaver & Shaw.

The screening process of interns is so strict and thorough that I'm not sure if even I'll get in. Dad made it clear that there would be no preferential treatment and if I wanted to intern at one of the best law firms in the world, I needed to prove my worth.

But not to him. Nate's the one I'd have to impress, because he's the managing partner of the New York branch. He also holds the key to Weaver & Shaw's entry gate, and besides being a perfectionist, he's also stern.

Everything about Nate is, whether it's with work or in personal relationships.

I ignore the group chat and scroll to my contacts until I find the name *Susan*.

Okay, so Dad definitely doesn't know that I secretly got his stepmom's number. Or maybe not so secretly, since I asked her for it when we bumped into each other at a restaurant.

I don't know why I did it, and she must've been as surprised as I was, because she gave me that hawk-eyed stare that made me kind of squirm. Or maybe I knew exactly why I wanted the number. For something like today. I'm planning Dad's birthday and I hope they somehow get along.

When Grandpa died, he left this house, which he bought when he married Dad's biological mother, to Susan, and Dad was livid, like absolutely furious in a way I've never seen before. It didn't matter that he'd inherited the shares Grandpa previously owned in Weaver & Shaw; the house was his number one priority. He went as far as proving that Grandpa was senile and not in a sound state of mind when he wrote his will. He won and the will became null and void. Then they had another long case about his inheriting the house because of the sentimental value it holds to him, and although Susan fought tooth and nail, she didn't stand a chance. But she's appealing now. Not only for the house, but also for shares of W&S. Her argument is that since the will is null and void, she should receive a percentage of them, if not all. Dad said she'll never win, not in a million years.

I hate all their legal battles.

I don't want Dad to keep fighting her in court until either of them dies. I know this might not be the most logical idea since she stole his mother's place and drove her to suicide, but I do believe in making peace.

And most of all, I believe in making Dad less stressed, even if he still has to deal with a million other things.

I hit Call before I chicken out and lose my resolve. My forefinger swirls between the pieces of glass in the sink as I listen to the ringing of the phone.

Susan picks up and I pause moving my finger and stare through the window at the garden.

"Who is this?" she asks in her usual closed off, slightly snobby, slightly judgmental tone.

"It's me. Gwen."

There's a long pause that almost extends to a minute. "What do you want?"

"It'll be Dad's birthday soon, and I've been wondering if you want to come."

"The only thing I want for your father's birthday is his death." *Beep.*

I gulp, letting my hand holding the phone drop to my side.

Well, I can't say I didn't expect that. While I'd hoped there might be a way to bring them together, maybe that's not possible, after all.

Does that mean I have to watch them go at each other's throats for the rest of my life?

I stare at the flowers and trees outside as if they'll provide an answer. Maybe it's clearer than I actually thought and I just need to stop meddling in things that don't concern me.

Or people who don't pay attention to me.

My phone vibrates with a text.

Chris: Wanna go out later?

I bite my lower lip. Chris and I have been sort of dating. Sort of, as in, going out on weekends and making out on the back of his Harley. Jenny says I'm more attracted to his bike than him, and that might be true. I like the thrill of doing things I shouldn't be doing, like stealing sips from Dad's liquor, coming home after curfew, and kissing Dad's best friend.

It's a character flaw.

Anyway, Chris and I still haven't gone all the way and I don't want to. I feel like if I do, I'll be letting myself down or something. Not that he's been pressuring me or anything, but he can't be patient forever, no matter how much he enjoys the make-out and groping sessions.

It isn't right to lead him on, though, which is why I need to make a decision. Either end this or go all the way in.

The main reason I said yes to Chris in the first place, aside from his negotiating skills, is because I needed to move on.

I needed to find someone else to fill up the emptiness.

There's one tiny problem, though. I hadn't thought that the previous occupier of that spot, Nate, would refuse to leave his place for someone else.

But I've been pushing him out gradually. Soon, I'll get completely rid of him and maybe someone who actually likes me, like Chris, will fill it.

So I type with shaky hands.

Me: Sure!

Chris: Can I come to your house or will your father rearrange my features?

I smile, remembering Dad's actual threats when Chris thought it was a good idea to pick me up on his bike.

Me: He's working over the weekend and won't be home until late. We're safe.

Chris: Can't wait to see you, beautiful.

My heart shrinks at that word.

Beautiful.

Why does it hurt so much to hear Chris say it? Probably because he's not the one I want to hear it from.

Yeah, no. I'm not going there.

I go back to picking up the shards of glass when movement outside catches in my peripheral vision.

It can't be.

I lift my head so fast, I'm surprised I don't snap a tendon. My eyes track him as he makes his way from the garden to the front door.

It's him.

It's really him.

Nate.

My fingers falter and something stings my skin. I must've cut myself on the glass, but I don't pay attention to it as I stare at the man whose long legs eat up the distance in no time.

Even the way he walks is unique. Only, he doesn't walk, he strides, always with some sort of purpose. His movements are purposeful, confident, and so damn masculine. Everything about him is manly, hard, and tenacious. It's present in every line of his face, every flutter of his lashes.

It's in the way his broad shoulders stretch his tailored black jacket. The put-together look doesn't fool me, though, because I'm well aware of what lurks beneath it.

Muscles. Whether it's his chest, abdomen, biceps, or strong thighs. I know because I've watched him box with Dad many times, half-naked, and he gave me my first view of male beauty. I've seen his cut abdomen and bulging muscles. I've seen his fluid movements and quick reflexes.

Young girls my age only have eyes for teenage boys and jocks, but I've seen better.

I've seen grown-up beauty that only comes with a lot of physical activity and age. And unfortunately for me, nothing can top that anymore. Not the jocks back in high school and definitely not college boys.

Because that's what they will always be in my eyes. Boys.

The man who's approaching my house, however, is the definition of masculinity. It's what those romance novels I read behind Dad's back talk about.

"Alexa, stop," I say, putting a halt to my favorite playlist, and slowly turn around, ignoring the droplets of blood streaming from my forefinger. I need to see him when he walks in through the door. I'm not doing anything wrong, okay? I just want to watch him up close.

It's not a crime.

And I'm *totally* over him.

I don't even want to think about why he's here in the middle of a workday. Nate rarely comes to our house since the kiss two years ago, and when he does, it's only when I'm not around, and then I have to hear about it from Martha and wallow in misery by eating a shitload of vanilla ice cream.

Yeah, I'm boring that way.

Anyhow, Nate shouldn't be here when Dad isn't, and definitely not alone. Is this a trap?

Oh, maybe he knows I'm planning Dad's birthday and wants to help.

"Where's Gwyneth?"

My heart jumps at hearing my name in that deep voice of his that always gets me tingly and a bit warm.

He's asking Martha about me. *Me*, not my dad. So that means he's here for me.

Oh, God.

This is bad for my fragile heart. I want to scream that I'm in here, but my voice refuses to come out. Turns out, I don't need to, because Martha directs him to the kitchen.

I remind myself to breathe as the sound of his strong footsteps echoes through the hall.

You need air, Gwen. Freaking breathe.

It doesn't work. The breathing part, I mean. Because the moment he steps into the kitchen, he sucks up all the oxygen and leaves me floundering for a taste of air.

Even if it is intoxicated with him.

But the expression on his face makes me pause. Whether it's my gulping for air or anything really.

I just stop.

Nate has always been a hard man of a few words and a no-nonsense personality. I felt it—breathed it, actually—when I made that reckless decision to kiss him.

But this is the first time I've seen his face darkened and his fists clenched. Fists with bruised knuckles as if he hit something solid. That's rarely happened in all the years he's boxed with Dad since they're careful about safety. Or at least, Nate is.

Are you hurt? I want to ask, but the words are stuck in my dry throat, unable to find a way out.

I lost my air and now, my voice, and apparently my motor activity, too, because I'm stuck in place, powerless to move.

"You need to come with me, Gwyneth."

It's one sentence. One single sentence, yet I know something is terribly wrong. Nate doesn't take me anywhere with him.

Ever.

I grab a piece of glass and press it against my cut forefinger, causing droplets of blood to stain the kitchen floor.

Drip.

Drip.

Drip.

I focus on that and the sting of pain instead of the ominous feeling lurking in the space surrounding us.

"W-where are we going?" I hate the stammer in my voice, but I can't help it.

Something's wrong, and I just want to run and hide in a closet.

Maybe sleep there for a while and never come out.

"It's Kingsley. He had an accident and it's critical."

My world tilts off its axis and splinters into bloody pieces.

FOUR

Nathaniel

A COMA.

The doctor is telling us that Kingsley is in a vegetative state. He's saying things about swelling in the brain due to the impact and that he might wake up in the next few days, weeks, or never.

This hotshot surgeon spent hours working on my friend with his people, and yet he still couldn't bring him back.

He was in the operating room for hours, just to tell us that King might or might not wake up. I don't miss the fake sympathy or his attempts not to give hope.

But even if I grab and shake him, then punch him in the face, it won't bring King back, and it sure as fuck won't serve any purpose. Except for maybe getting rid of some of my pent-up frustration.

Gwyneth listens to the doctor's words with her lips slightly parted. They're lifeless and pale, like the rest of her face. She clinks the nails of her thumbs and forefingers together in a frantic, almost manic type of way. It's a nervous habit she's had since she was a kid—since she learned the truth about her mother.

She flinches slightly with each of the doctor's explanations, and I can see the exact moment hope starts dimming from her colorful eyes.

Because she has a tell.

Whenever she's sad or under the weather, the blue-gray will dim out the green, nearly eating it out like a storm would swallow a bright sky. And just like that, the signs of rain condense in the form of moisture in her reddening lids.

She doesn't cry, though.

No clue if it's due to Kingsley's upbringing or the missing piece she's been searching for since she learned about her mother, but Gwyneth doesn't cry in public.

At least, not since she was a pre-teen.

She just keeps jamming her nails against each other, irritating the cut on her forefinger over and over again.

Clink. Clink. Clink.

And with each clink, she's burying something inside. A needle, a knife, or something sharper and way deadlier. She's swallowing the poison while being well aware of its lethality.

Due to my line of work, I've seen countless people's reactions to grief. Some have mental breakdowns, others express it in any physical form possible, whether it's screaming, crying, hitting, or sometimes, straight out murder.

The emotion is so strong that reactions differ from one human to another. But the ones who suffer from it the most are those who pretend everything is fine. Those who stand tall and treat the occurrence like any ordinary day.

Unless they're psychopaths or have lost their sense of empathy, that's not normal. Gwyneth sure as hell doesn't have any antisocial tendencies, so she's digging her own grave with those bloodied nails right now.

As soon as the doctor finishes his dialogue, he says we can see Kingsley, but only through a window since he's still in the ICU.

Gwyneth steps in the direction of her father's room, but her feet falter and she sways. I catch her by the upper arm before she falls, my hand flexing around it to steady her.

"I'm fine." Her voice is low, lethargic even.

I release her as soon as she's able to keep her balance. The last thing I want to do is touch her.

Or be near her.

But her state is abnormal and needs to be monitored. It's safe to say that Kingsley was—is—her world, not just her father. He's her mother, brother, and best friend, so no, I don't believe for one second that she's fine.

Gwyneth's steps are stiff and unnatural as she crosses the way to the room. She stands in front of the glass and freezes. Completely. She's not even blinking—or breathing properly. Her chest rises and falls in a strange manner that leaves her in a near-panting state.

I stride to where she is and observe the scene that's responsible for her reaction.

The view of the hospital bed is as ominous as the liquid that's slowly trickling into his veins from the IV.

King's arm is in a cast and his chest is all bandaged up, but that's not the worst part. It's the galaxy of blue, violet, and pink covering his face and temples. It's the cuts across his forehead and on his neck. The gruesome scene stands out in minuscule ugly details against the whiteness of the sheets and the bandages.

"Dad…" Gwyneth's chin trembles as she slams both her hands against the glass. "Hey, wake up. You said we'd have lunch together tomorrow. I even picked out my outfit for the day. It took me a long time, you know, so you can't just bail on me."

I step back, not wanting to interrupt her moment, but I can still hear her voice. The quiver in it, the desperation behind it, the denial lacing it.

Everything.

"Dad…stop pretending to be asleep. You're a morning person, remember? You hate sleeping too much." She digs her nails in the glass. "Daddy…you promised to never leave me alone. You said you're not her, right? You're not irresponsible like Mom, not cruel like her, or as heartless. You're…you're my dad. My best friend and everything. Best friends don't go to sleep without notice, so wake up! Wake up, Dad!"

She bangs her fists against the glass with an increasing strength that shakes her slim shoulders.

Her voice turns hoarse and bitter the longer she calls for King. The denial is evident in each of her screams and bangs.

I walk up to her and reach out but then pause. I'm not supposed to be touching Gwyneth. Not for any reason.

But if I don't stop her, she'll break her hands or slip into a hole in which no one will be able to find her.

That's what she does when she's overwhelmed. She hides. And she does it so well that it's impossible to get through to her unless she's the one who makes herself visible again.

I don't allow myself to think as I grab her by the shoulder. "You need to stop, Gwyneth."

"Let me go. I'm fine." She rotates her shoulder in an attempt to loosen my grip on her, but I only tighten it.

"Your father is in a coma. You're allowed to not be fine."

"He's not in a coma. He will wake up." She bangs her palm on the window again. "Wake up, Dad. This isn't true. Wake up!"

She starts flailing her arms, and I recognize the signs of a panic attack as they slowly materialize in her. The shortness of her breath, the beads of sweat on her forehead, and the trembling of her lips. She probably doesn't even realize that her psyche is hanging off the edge.

I grab her other shoulder and jerk her around to face me. "Gwyneth, *stop*."

She flinches, a tremor seizing her whole body. I probably shouldn't have been that stern, but it worked.

Her hands fall to her sides, but the shaking doesn't stop. If anything, it's stronger, more subconscious and without any apparent pattern. She stares up at me with those mesmerizing eyes that are stuck in the blue-gray mode, suffocating all the green that's trying to peek through.

Fuck the way she looks at me.

As if I'm a god with all the answers and solutions. As if I'm the only one who can make everything right.

I've always hated the way Gwyneth looks at me. Correction, I've loathed it since her eighteenth birthday party when she demolished the brick wall that separated us.

Because the god she sees in me? That one is most definitely a demon in disguise.

"It's not true. Tell me it's not true, Nate."

I should reprimand her for not calling me Uncle like I usually do, but this is neither the time nor the place.

"Denial won't help you. The sooner you accept reality, the faster you can deal with it."

"No." She grits her teeth, then lets out another haunted, "No…"

"Let go, Gwyneth." I try to soften my tone, as much as I'm able to, but it still comes out firm. Like an order.

She shakes her head again, but it's meek, weak, just like she is beneath my touch. Until now, I've never noticed how small she actually is compared to me.

How fragile.

Actually, I did once. When she was pressed up against me with her lips on mine.

But I shouldn't be thinking about that. I shouldn't be thinking about how small my best friend's daughter is or how she feels in my hold when we're in front of his hospital room.

A muscle clenches in my jaw and I loosen my hold on her shoulders, starting to step away from her.

I'm unprepared for what she does, though.

Completely and utterly taken off guard.

Just like two fucking years ago.

Gwyneth lunges at me and wraps both arms around my waist.

And as if that isn't enough, she stuffs her face in my chest—her damp face.

I can feel the moisture clinging to my shirt and seeping onto my skin. But it doesn't stop there, no. It's like acid, melting away the flesh and bones and reaching for an organ I thought only functioned to pump blood.

If my jaw was clenching earlier, I now feel like it's going to dislocate from how hard I'm gritting my teeth.

"Gwyneth, let go of me."

She sinks her nails into the material of my jacket, grazing my back, and shakes her head against my shirt. More moisture, more shaking.

She's like a leaf that's about to be blown away and destroyed into pieces.

"One minute…" she whispers against my chest.

"Gwyneth," I warn, my voice guttural and strong, and I can tell she feels it coming from where her face is hiding.

"Please…I have no one but you."

Her statement makes me pause. The truth behind her words strikes me deep in that little nook she's been digging for herself since she was eighteen.

Fuck. It's true.

With Kingsley gone, she has no one but me.

I let that information sink in, recalling his last words to me over the phone. The fact that I should take care of her.

Take care of his fucking daughter.

I forget that I should be pushing her away, throwing her off me. So Gwyneth interprets my silence as approval and does what Gwyneth does best.

Takes liberties.

She presses her body against mine, sniffling into my chest. And the scent of vanilla hits me in my bones. The sound of her weeping is low, haunted, and I know it's not every day that she shows this side of her to anyone. Especially me.

I let her grieve, I let her get the excess energy off her chest, because if she doesn't, she'll explode.

But I don't touch her, don't hug her back, and I sure as fuck don't comfort her. I keep my hands on either side of me, and my body is stiff, giving off unwelcoming vibes.

Either she doesn't catch on to them or she doesn't give a fuck, because she hugs me tighter. This girl has zero understanding of the word *boundaries*.

I stare over her head and through the window at Kingsley's inert body and sigh deeply, but even that is mixed with her low sniffles.

Everything is muddied with her pained voice, her soft body, and the smell of fucking vanilla. But my attention remains on the man lying on what seems like a deathbed.

For someone so smart, you did something so fucking stupid, King. You should've never entrusted her to me.

FIVE

Nathaniel

GWYNETH FALLS ASLEEP.

After so much struggle and standing for hours in front of Kingsley's room, she lost the physical battle and slumped over on one of the chairs in the waiting area.

I told her that she could go home, but she vehemently shook her head, pulled her knees to her chest, and closed her eyes.

Which is why she's about to fall forward.

I place a finger on her forehead and push her back so she doesn't hit the ground. It's light contact, only a damn finger, and yet it feels as if my skin has caught fire and the flames are now extending to the rest of my body.

In hindsight, I shouldn't have let her hug me. Or I should've pushed her away sooner. Because now, even a mere touch brings back memories of her body pressed up against my chest.

Her slender body that I can't stop thinking about how small it is compared to mine.

I clench my fist and close my eyes to chase away the haze.

It doesn't work. Because even though she's out of view, her scent clings to me as stubbornly as its owner.

Vanilla was never my thing—in anything. And yet, it's the one thing I'm able to smell.

When I've made sure she won't drop, I release her. She falls sideways on the chair, still hugging her knees to her chest in some sort of self-comfort.

"Dad…" she murmurs in her sleep, a tear sliding down her cheek.

After all the crying she did earlier, one would think she doesn't have any tears left, but grief works in mysterious ways. Maybe she'll never stop crying. Maybe this event will change the life she knew up to this point.

It sure as fuck is making dents into my own.

I remove my jacket and place it on her. It's supposed to be a single motion, but I'm cut off guard. Again.

Her hand reaches for mine and she grabs it in a steel-like hold, even though her eyes remain shut.

"Don't go…"

The haunted murmur is packed with so much pain and heart-break. Maybe it's a plea, maybe this is her begging like she did earlier.

This is why I don't like seeing Gwyneth and have done everything in my power to make her as invisible as possible for the past two years.

She's no longer the innocent little kid I've known all her life, though the innocence is still there. She's not the child who asked me to hide things from her father because she didn't want to hurt him.

All that stopped when she stopped acting like a kid—toward me, at least.

She has a way of worming herself into any armor, no matter how solid and apparently impenetrable it might seem. She doesn't even use brute force. Her methods are soft, innocent, un-coordinated even.

I wish it was a tactic or that she was being cunning. I would've recognized that and put an end to it accordingly. The most dooming part is that it's genuine fucking determination.

She takes after King in that department. Just like him, she won't stop until she gets what she wants. It doesn't matter how many times I push her away, she dusts herself off and slips back in.

If I make her invisible, she just flips the switch back on and glows brighter than before.

If I ignore her, she still stands out with her small body, colorful eyes, and fucking vanilla scent.

A strand of her fiery hair sticks to her forehead, nearly going into her eyes. I reach a hand out to remove it, even though I shouldn't be touching her.

Even if touching her means walking through fire and knowing exactly how I will burn.

And for a moment, that doesn't matter.

Just one moment. One second in time. The consequences blur and my savage instinct takes over.

When I was younger, I relied on that instinct to score clients, win cases, and get to the top. My instinct is one of my most valued assets. It tells no lies and always sees ahead before my mind can catch up.

But right now, it's impulsive, lacking its usual coolness. Because, fuck no, I'm not supposed to ignore the consequences. I'm not supposed to give in to whatever demon is rearing his head from the depths of my soul.

And yet, I am. I'm letting it guide my actions.

One touch.

One second.

One—

"There you are."

I retract my hand, inhaling deeply before I turn around to face the source of the voice.

Aspen.

She's my only friend aside from Kingsley. We share ambition

and a no-nonsense personality. Everyone at the firm calls her my strategist because she's not afraid to use unconventional methods to get things done.

I should be thankful that she put a halt to an impulsive moment, but the exact opposite emotion lurks in my veins.

Aspen's sharp hazel eyes slide from me to Gwyneth before landing on me again. "Are there any updates on Kingsley?"

I place a forefinger to my lips. The last thing I want is for Gwyneth to wake up and have another meltdown. So I motion at Aspen to follow me down the hall. Once we're out of view and earshot, I tell her about the situation.

She leans against the wall and crosses her arms over her dark blue tailored jacket as she listens to every detail with keen interest. If there's anything I'm sure that Aspen will always have, it's her attention to detail.

"So this leaves only you at the head of Weaver & Shaw," she says when I'm done.

"He could wake up."

"You don't believe that, Nate."

I don't. I'm practical enough to know that we've probably lost him for good. But admitting it out loud is similar to punching my own gut, so I don't say it.

"How about his little princess?" she asks, and even though she'd normally say it in a condescending manner, she doesn't now.

Aspen has never shied away from going for Kingsley's throat, proving to have a temper that matches her red hair. She usually doesn't agree with his reckless ways since she's more methodical, like I am.

And he's never liked the fact that she earned her place as a senior partner and he couldn't kick her out if he wanted to. Not that I would let him. Aspen is an asset to the firm and she's been a pillar in my life ever since I stole her from another firm and convinced her to join me and Kingsley in our new endeavors.

I lean against the wall and cross my ankles. "What about her?"

"With Kingsley gone, she'll be in over her head. Surely, you know that his stepmother will use this chance to strike in court."

"We'll represent Gwyneth and keep things as they are."

"Even if you personally take the case, there's no way Susan will come out of this empty-handed. Gwyneth can't touch her inheritance or trust fund until she's twenty-one. That's a whole year for Susan to demand the house and shares of the firm. She'll have a leg to stand on, too, since Kingsley made his father's will null and void. Because he used his father's money for Weaver & Shaw's capital, she can sue for her husband's shares that Kingsley inherited. Not to mention that she'll be up against a girl who can't touch her money yet. And before you suggest it, yes, we can stall in court, but considering all of Susan and Kingsley's legal battles in the past, I say Gwyneth doesn't stand a chance. She doesn't have her father's legal experience, revenge spirit, or ruthlessness. She'll be eaten alive by Susan."

I want to disagree, but I can't. Aspen is right. Kingsley's lawsuits against Susan were fueled by pure spite. He hated her and was out to destroy her. Gwyneth doesn't share her father's feelings about Susan, so even if we represented her, there's no telling how it would go.

Not to mention that the fight could last forever and would cause her emotional damage in the long run.

"Susan could take shares of the firm, Nate." Aspen insists on that point, staring me in the eye. "The same shares Kingsley inherited from his father are up for grabs now that the will has no standing in court."

"Like fuck she can."

"Exactly. Which is why you need to take the whole matter in your hands."

I pause, recognizing the glint in her eyes. "What are you suggesting?"

"In a few days, we can have the doctor announce that Kingsley isn't likely to get his functions back. We can't process his will since he's not dead, but thankfully, he already signed documentation that makes Gwyneth the executive of the estate in the event that he gets incapacitated. As soon as she has control of his assets, make her sell the shares to you."

"What?"

"She trusts you and wouldn't question you. This is the best solution to keep the firm out of greedy hands. If you have a crushing majority instead of the fifty percent you own, then Susan wouldn't even dare to go against you or demand anything."

"Are you hearing yourself, Aspen? You're telling me to gain full ownership of Weaver & Shaw at the expense of taking advantage of my friend's only fucking daughter."

She throws a dismissive hand in the air. "She's still a kid and knows nothing about managing a law firm. You can return it to her later if she proves herself worthy, but we both know she's only an inexperienced pre-law student who barely understands how the world works. You can't possibly be thinking about leaving anything in her hands, are you?"

"No, but I'm not betraying King's trust either."

"He's in a coma, Nate."

"Which makes me more of a lowlife if I stab him in the back."

"You're not. You're simply protecting both your assets."

"By taking advantage of his state and using his daughter?"

"Yes."

"No, Aspen. That option is out of the question and that's final."

Her brows furrow but soon return to normal. She knows me better than to argue with me on this. I might be a bastard, but I have my own set of principles that nothing and no one would touch or change.

"What are you going to do then, Nate?"

I release a breath, loosen my tie, and focus on my train brain. That's what my father called it, a train brain, because once it's moving, there's no stopping it or reversing. Not for any reason.

"Let me think about it."

She narrows her eyes and taps her foot on the floor. "Is there something I don't know about?"

"What are you talking about?"

"Such as your jacket covering her or your hand reaching out for her, maybe. You don't do that, not even with the women you sleep with."

Of course Aspen saw that and stored it in her eidetic memory. She doesn't forget anything, so I have no clue why I thought she would let that slide.

"Gwyneth isn't a woman I fuck, Aspen. She's King's daughter and she just learned that her father might not wake up."

"That's all?"

I nod, but I don't voice the fucking lie. The words burn in my throat and it's impossible to let them out, so I swallow them down with their blood.

Aspen still watches me peculiarly, but she says, "In that case, think fast. We don't have time to waste."

I'm more aware of that than anyone. Time is never on our side in these types of situations. Which is why I need to act fast.

I don't want to entertain the idea forming loud and clear in my head, but even I know that it's the most logical thing to do.

Despite the fact that it doesn't make sense on so many levels.

SIX

Gwyneth

WHEN I WAS A KID, I HAD A PROBLEM LEARNING WORDS. I don't know why. I have a high IQ, and I can figure out my way around things, but memorizing words was a bit difficult.

The professionals my dad took me to thought I had some form of dyslexia, but it's not like I couldn't read or recognize words. It's not that they all appeared the same. They just appeared alive.

You know that feeling when you're reading something and it nearly jumps off the page at you? For me, it was literal, and that's exactly how it felt. As if the words were coming after me.

Turns out, I didn't have a problem with all the words. Just the negative ones. The words that make my skin itchy and my vision turn hazy. The words that I felt instead of only reading them.

Anxiety made my skin crawl and my nose tingle.

Cruel turned my cheeks hot and my body tight with the need to defend the one who was subjugated to it.

Fear made my teeth clench and my heart shrink in anticipation for what was to come.

Sad erased my smile and had me on the verge of crying.

It's one of the reasons why I don't watch tragic movies—or any movies that display emotions that can trigger me. I relate to that stuff so much.

Someone might be wondering why this crazy person would choose to pursue law when she's dangerously empathetic. Good question. I mean, I shouldn't have, logically. I probably should've been a social worker, someone who takes care of children and young adults.

But here's the thing, I don't think all lawyers need to be detached to do their job. I don't think they need to kill their humanity to climb up the corporate ladder. Those who do that aren't real lawyers according to yours truly.

Lawyers can be empathetic, because that enables us to understand our clients and help them in the best way possible. Empathetic lawyers are people's favorites according to a study performed by yours truly again. They like it when we understand them, listen to them, and aren't impersonal.

Anyway, back to my empath problem. It's especially hard with words. I guess that's because that's what started it for me. Simple negative words.

They trigger me. As in, they really put me in a funk and I have to step away and hide and wish for whatever those words did to end.

So I had to come up with a coping mechanism. You know, something that doesn't make me want to lose my mind the moment I read *murder* or *insane*.

I had this genius idea that practice makes perfect. I mean, if I'm exposed to those words a lot, surely I'll be desensitized. There will be a day when I'll see them and be like, "Meh," then ride my white unicorn toward the rainbows.

So I made a list of them, in alphabetical order. The notebook is called "The No Words."

Each letter has negative words underneath it, sorted by color. The yellow ones are easier, the orange words are a bit harder, and the red ones? Jeez, the red ones took me on a trip to hell when even writing them.

It didn't work at first. I would look at the closed notebook with all the negative words in it, shudder, then jam it back into my drawer.

Which defied the whole purpose of making myself desensitized.

So, during my teenage years, I'd get that list out and read it aloud, throw up a little, feel more nauseous, hide in my closet for an hour, and then take a cold shower and eat vanilla ice cream.

It was a process. A long one that nearly drove me to want to kill myself and ask Dad for help.

But I didn't. I needed to do that shit myself because it was around that time I decided to be a lawyer like my dad, and there's no way in hell it's normal for a lawyer to flinch at the words *crime scene*, *stab*, or *killer*. That would be embarrassing to my study of empathetic lawyers.

So, anyway, after a battle against words, I came out as a winner.

Well, almost. I started reading my notebook without feeling the immediate need to hide, throw up, or drive my car into a tree.

Almost, because even to this day, I still have problems with one letter of the alphabet. *D*. Fun fact: that damn letter has most of the negative words underneath it, and many of them are in red.

Damage.

Decay.

Dirt.

Distress.

Disgust.

Depression.

Disease.

And my most dreaded of all. *Deadly*. *Dead*. *Death*.

I couldn't really cope with it, no matter how much I tried. It gets stuck every time I say it, pushing against my vocal cords and slashing my voice down. So I made that letter *D* my bitch. I wrote each word a thousand times. I wrote *death*, a few thousand.

My wrists screamed, my heart jackhammered in my throat, and I nearly stabbed myself and bled out on the floor.

When Grandpa died five years ago, I didn't collapse or cry. I just got all my shit together and was there for Dad as he and Susan slashed each other down.

So I was over it, right?

Wrong.

My eyes open as the true reality of death slowly forms in my awareness.

The possibility that my father could die.

As in, my only family member. The only person that kept me together and flipped the world the middle finger while he raised me on his own.

A salty taste explodes in my mouth and I realize it's because I'm drinking my own tears.

Ever since I desensitized the letter C and its words—*cry* included—I don't do that anymore. Well, I don't do it much.

But it's like these tears have a mind of their own. They're not due to the word itself. This isn't my irrational reaction to a random word. This is pulled from a place so deep within me, I have no clue where it's located.

It doesn't matter that my neck hurts and my body is all stiff from the uncomfortable position I slept in. All my psyche is able to process is that Dad could be gone.

I'll be all alone without my father.

The man who painted the world in bright colors and then laid it at my feet.

The man who scowled at the world but only smiled at me.

Now, I won't have anyone to sing me *Happy Birthday* off tune. No one will hug me goodbye every morning or have dinners with me every night.

There won't be anyone who'll slowly open my door late at night to make sure I didn't fall asleep at my desk again because I got so consumed with whatever project I was working on. No one will bring me my favorite green tea infused with vanilla when I can't sleep.

He won't be there to pull me inside when I dance in the rain because I could catch a cold.

He'll just disappear like he never existed. And unlike when Grandpa died, I don't think I can survive this.

I can't go back to the house we called ours and pick up non-existent pieces of myself.

How can I when everything in there bears witness to how well and hard he raised me and how much he sacrificed himself for me?

I didn't even consider moving out after high school. People my age want to get away from their parents, but I didn't. It's where home is.

A sudden shiver jolts me upright when the jacket that's been covering me falls down my arms and to my lap.

My fingers trace the material and I'm surprised they don't catch fire. It doesn't matter that I don't remember him putting it on me, or how I even ended up lying in the chair. The smell gives it away. A little bit spicy and woodsy with an undertone of musk, but it's still strong and manly and so much like him.

The man I hugged and whose chest I cried into.

The man whose shirt I probably messed up.

He didn't touch me back, didn't console me, but having him there, even immobile, was enough for me.

He still had his body tight and rigid like the day of the kiss. He still refused any contact with me, just like back then, but that's okay.

He covered me with his jacket. And maybe I can keep it like I've kept a lot of him with me.

Like his notebook, his shirt when he once forgot it, his hoodies from when he runs with Dad. Most of them were my father's, but if Nate wore them even once, then they became his. Don't ask me why. It's the law. Then there's a scarf that he gave me because it got cold. A book about law. Make that plural. A pen. Okay, pens, plural again.

And no, I'm not a stalker. I just like collecting. And by collecting, I mean the things that belong to him.

But he's not here now.

And there's a hole the size of a continent in the pit of my stomach because now I'm thinking he's abandoned me and I need to deal with these jumbled feelings on my own.

I came on too strong again, didn't I? Now, he really thinks I'm an unstoppable pervert who'll keep touching him whenever I can.

I wasn't supposed to. I wouldn't have if he hadn't touched me first and told me those words that just triggered everything. The fact that I needed to deal with it to get over it.

But he was supposed to be there for when I did deal with it. He shouldn't have left me another memento of himself and then disappeared.

I stagger to my unsteady feet, rubbing at my face with the back of my hands and wiping them on my denim shorts before I neatly lay the jacket on my forearm. It needs to be all prim and proper like him. Though I probably smudged it with my snot and tears earlier.

Yikes.

My fingers graze the bracelet he gave me as I tiptoe around the corner, searching for a very familiar tall man with eyes that could send someone to hell.

Specifically me.

Still, I forge on because I can't do this on my own. I can't stare at Dad's bruised, lifeless body and remain standing. No amount of lists or desensitizing or empty brain syndrome could have prepared me for this.

My sneakers make an inaudible sound on the floor as I look for him. It doesn't take me long to find him, but before I can rejoice, my heart clenches.

He's not alone. He's with the witch. Aspen.

Dad calls her that. The witch. I haven't used that name for her in the past, but now I do because maybe she's enchanting Nate with black magic. After all, she's the only woman he pays any attention to. The only woman he relaxes around and shows that slight twitch in his lips to.

Some would call it a smile. But I've always considered it half a smile. Almost there, but not really.

Anyway, he only shows it to her and I hate it and her. I hate how put-together she is. How she wears high heels and walks comfortably in them, as if they're nonexistent, and has the best collection of pant and skirt suits ever, not like my dull jean shorts and favorite white sneakers. I hate how her hair is bright red like her lipstick, not coppery and rusty like mine.

But what I hate the most is how compatible she is with Nate. How effortlessly they flow, how good they look together without even trying. She's successful, cunning, and a boss bitch in their firm. The exact type of woman I imagine Nate being attracted to.

I overheard him say it to Dad once, that he likes women who go after their careers as aggressively as men do. He likes intelligent women with fire, like Aspen.

It's not a surprise that the king likes a queen.

Because that's the thing, right? The king doesn't look in the direction of damsels in distress, doesn't like doing any saving.

Suddenly, I'm hyperaware of what I am to him. A hurdle that's pulling him down. An obligation left behind by his best friend.

My nails dig into the jacket and I can feel the spicy scent in it rising to my throat and suffocating me. I can feel the woodsy smell turning into high trees that I'm unable to see through or climb over.

I step back and sprint to the chair he left me in. I'll just return his jacket and stop being a pain in his ass. The last thing I want is to become the annoying kid he has to take care of on his friend's behalf.

I'm not a kid anymore. I'm twenty and I can take care of myself. I can handle everything, from Dad's coma to the house to whatever he left behind.

My chest squeezes when I recall Dad's state. I don't even have anyone I can turn to anymore.

My feet come to a halt when I find a familiar face standing in front of the window of Dad's room.

She's wearing a flamboyant pink dress that has a cocktail of colors in it. A feathered hat with the shades of the rainbow sits snuggly on her head, allowing her bleached strands to peek through.

I approach her slowly, struck by how old she actually appears, despite all the Botox and things she's done to her face. It's like it has turned into a mask. Not to mention how swollen and big her lips are, as if they've been stung by dozens of bees.

"Susan?"

She doesn't break eye contact with Dad, and I'm not strong enough to look at him again in his state, but I can see the way she observes him.

How her eyes take in the entirety of him, flicking back and forth as she runs her gloved hand over her leather bag. Also pink.

"Susan," I try again, not sure if she heard me the first time.

"He's in such bad shape," she says quietly, without any expression.

I fight the tears trying to escape and clink my thumb against my forefinger beneath Nate's jacket. So it's my nails against his jacket. In a way, he's here with me.

Also, there's a bandage around my finger that I didn't notice before. Was he the one who put it there?

My thoughts are scattered when Susan faces me, her snobbish expression strapped firmly in place. "The bastard finally got what he deserves."

I reel back from the force of her words, my chin trembling. "How…how could you say that? Even if you guys fought, he's facing death right now."

"As he should have a long time ago. His type of evil needed to be punished sooner rather than later."

"Susan!"

"I'm going to give you a piece of advice, even though you're that devil's spawn." She steps closer until all I can smell is the strong notes of her dizzying perfume. "It'd be better if you drop all the cases and move out of the house. My lawyer said I can win the house back and also the shares in Weaver & Shaw that my husband owned before they were reverted back to your conniving father."

I'm shaking my head despite my attempts to appear unfazed. Dad spent a lot of time, effort, and money to secure the house and the firm. There's no way in hell she can take everything, right? Surely, there's something I can do.

Susan reaches her gloved hand out and clutches my chin between her thumb and forefinger and gives it a little shake. "I'd hate to squash a little girl like you, so why don't you save us both the trouble and drop everything? You'll have your trust fund when you're twenty-one and that's enough to keep you wealthy for a lifetime. I'm having my lawyer draw up a contract so all you have to do is sign."

"No," I murmur, my nails digging into the jacket.

Her swollen lips twist. "What did you just say?"

"No!" I push away from her, my body trembling. "I won't allow you to take Dad's hard-earned things. Never! And he isn't dead, Susan! He'll come back and make you regret ever suggesting that to me."

"You're talking big, but you've got nothing, little girl. Be ready to be crushed in court."

My heart hammers hard and fast in my ribcage as I search for the right words to throw back in her face. I'll never allow this woman to take away what Dad worked for, even if it's the last thing I do.

"That should go to you, Mrs. Shaw."

I startle, my chest doing that squeezing thing coupled with a zap at the sound of his voice.

Nate.

He strides to where we are, and before I can allow myself to bask in relief, his arm wraps around my shoulder.

Nate's arm is on my shoulder.

Is this some sort of a dream? Or maybe it's a dream coupled with a nightmare.

Susan raises her chin, still twisting her lips. "You can't do anything, even if you represent her. The law is on my side this time."

"That might be so if you were talking to her lawyer, but you're now addressing a member of her family. Her future husband, to be more specific."

SEVEN

Nathaniel

NECESSITY.

I've never liked that word. It's because of necessity that my brother decided to leave the country, and that got him killed.

It's because of necessity that people vote for the likes of my father to represent them in spite of the fact that he only cares about himself.

In a way, necessity is the root of all evil. Decisions based on it are a bit impulsive and almost always have dire consequences down the line. Ones that could be dangerous, lethal even.

Of all people, I'm well aware of the dangerous repercussions of hasty actions. I never decide anything unless I have a 360-degree view of the entire situation as well as all of its possible results. This is the first time I've taken a step into territory that hasn't been carefully plotted. It's like walking through a minefield with a blindfold on.

But just like earlier, I don't think about the possible repercussions. I shove them to the back of my mind and focus on the now. On the present and its own sets of cause and effect. What I'm doing is out of necessity. The urgency to keep Kingsley's legacy alive. The burden to protect what he left behind.

However, as I wrap my arm around Gwyneth's shoulder, *burden* is the last thing I feel. There's the usual fire, the scorching hot fucking flames that resemble the color of her hair. There's the softness of her body, the parting of her rosebud lips, and that fucking vanilla scent that's starting to grow on me despite myself.

But a burden is not in the picture.

Not even a little.

Not even fucking close.

If anything, there's a tinge of relief. It's tiny, almost lost in the midst of the persistent chaos, but it's there. The knowledge that this is the only way to actually honor King's last words. That there isn't any other way to efficiently handle the situation besides this method.

She trembles in my hold. It's different than when she was struggling to express her grief. This time is more potent, as if her body is unable to convey whatever is lurking inside except through the tremors that take hold of it.

This entire situation must be too much. Sometimes, I fail to see that other people aren't made for pressure-filled situations. That, unlike me, their feelings are in the forefront, not forgotten somewhere no one can find—or reach.

If Susan hadn't shown her vicious face, I would've attempted to prepare Gwyneth for the decision I made while I was talking to Aspen. I probably wouldn't have announced it the way I did, like some sort of a bomb whose fallout she's currently unable to process.

Susan, the stepmother from hell, as King sometimes calls her, stares me down, even though she's way shorter than me. Her lips twitch and twist and I don't think she's even aware of it.

"What are you talking about?" she asks in that condescending manner that's always pissed King off. He used to say her voice alone put him in the mood to commit a crime, and I'm starting to see why. She has a general grating existence that you can't wait to get rid of and disinfect it from the air.

"Exactly what I just said. Gwyneth and I are getting married."

Two pairs of eyes stare at me blankly, coldly even. I don't focus on Gwyneth's, not fully at least. If I do, I'll lose sight of the reason why I dropped the news now—to get rid of Susan, once and for all.

"You can't possibly mean that. Aren't you twice her age or something? She's only twenty."

As if I don't know her age. I do, very well. Perfectly so. I've been there since she was born.

But instead of giving Susan the opening she's looking for, I squeeze Gwyneth's shoulder. "That makes her an adult, capable of making her own decisions. One of which being that she'll marry me, we'll have joint property, and she'll grant me power of attorney. So you might want to call your lawyer and tell him that any legal—or illegal—fight you have with her will go through me."

The twitching in Susan's lips increases as she glares at me, but she doesn't maintain eye contact for too long. My nephew tells me I have a look that makes people uncomfortable in their own skin even without my having to glare.

And like any weakling who can't stand up to those stronger than her, she latches onto those she believes are weaker and steps toward Gwyneth, jamming a finger at her shoulder. "Is this what you've been plotting all along, you devil's spawn?"

I'm about to break her fucking hand and risk an assault charge, but I don't need to. Gwyneth grabs her step-grandmother's finger and throws it away as if it's disgusting. "I told you I'll protect Dad's assets until my last breath. Now, leave and don't show your face here again. I'm filing a restraining order for reasons of aggressive, threatening behavior so you can never get near Dad."

Susan jerks back as if she's been burned. For someone who practically lives in court and pays a fortune to her lawyer, she has a poor sense of knowing when she should stop.

Which should've been after her husband died.

Or better yet, a few decades ago when she decided to kick King's mother out and thought he'd forget about it.

But she doesn't matter now, or ever, because I can't help feeling a sensation of pride at how Gwyneth put the woman in her place. She's King's daughter, after all, even if she is more empathetic than he's ever been.

"This isn't over." Susan clicks her tongue and turns and leaves in a swish of blinding, annoying pink and loud clicks of her shoes.

I track her movements, making sure she doesn't try anything funny. Aspen is with the doctor in case Susan goes there to attempt to get a legal document out of him. Not that he'd hand over anything if he doesn't want to risk losing his license. But I don't trust people like Susan.

They might use the law to fight, but they wouldn't hesitate to resort to illegal, immoral methods to get what they want.

"Is it true? Do you want to marry me?"

My attention slides back to the woman who's snuggled to my side, looking up at me in that fucking way that stabs my guts and twists my damn insides.

Her eyes spark in a myriad of blue, gray, and green. Bright fucking green that I thought wouldn't make an appearance again after King's accident.

I hate the way she looks at me. I fucking loathe it.

Because it's not just a gaze, it's not mere eye contact. It's words and phrases I don't want to decipher.

I let her go and she staggers a little, as if she's been floating on air and her feet are finally touching the ground. It's where she's supposed to always be—on the ground—not in the clouds she sometimes ascends to.

But even though I'm not touching her anymore, she's still touching a part of me. My jacket is held snugly to her chest as if it's some sort of armor—one she won't let go of.

And I need to stop thinking about what that jacket is touching, because that's just fucked up.

"It's not that I want to marry you."

A swallow, a clink of nails, a slight jump in her shoulders. I've always hated how expressive she is but that she can still hide more than she shows.

"Then why did you say that to Susan? Oh, was it a lie? A smokescreen to scare her away?"

"It was to scare her away and it is a smokescreen in a way, but it's not a lie."

"I...don't understand."

"I meant what I said. We need the joint property for the house and the shares since you now control them, and you have to give me power of attorney. That way, I can manage your assets until you can touch them when you're twenty-one. I'll draw up a contract that joins both our assets, even those owned prior to the marriage. The only way you can do that is with a husband. Hence the marriage idea."

"So...you do want to marry me." The spark returns, turning the green bright, the blue light, and the gray almost nonexistent.

"Did you hear a word I said, Gwyneth?"

"Yeah, you want to marry me."

"Aside from that."

"To protect my and Dad's assets from Susan, which, of course, I want to do but don't have the power to due to my stupid age."

Her nose scrunches at that last bit. *My stupid age.* Her brows dip, too, like whenever King tried to make her eat any flavor of ice cream aside from vanilla and she told him, "I love you, Dad, but I don't like you all the time."

To which he'd buy her unhealthy gallons of ice cream. Vanilla, naturally.

And because she's a bit of a sheltered princess, she has a lot of things to learn. Things King was too soft-hearted to teach her.

Softheartedness is the last thing anyone could accuse me of.

"Shouldn't you be wondering about the joint property part? With that, and the power of attorney, I'll be able to strip you of every last penny and toss you aside."

"You wouldn't." No hesitation. She doesn't even stop to think about it.

"What if I do?"

"No. You're a lot of things, but you're not a backstabber. Also, I trust you."

"You shouldn't. Blind trust is plain stupidity."

"It's not blind. I carefully built it up over time. Besides, there needs to be some sort of trust if we're going to get married."

"This marriage is only for convenience. Do you understand, Gwyneth?"

"Oh."

"It's a yes or no question. Do you understand?"

"Does…does this mean you won't touch me?"

My jaw clenches in two rapid tics and I shake my head. "No. It'll be on paper only."

The gray gains dominance in her chameleon eyes, but I can't tell what she's thinking. Not even when her clinking stops and she steps closer. "What if you do touch me?"

"It won't happen."

"But it happened before. Two years ago, remember? Though I was the one who touched you, but it still counts, right?"

"Gwyneth," I grind out through my teeth.

She flinches, but she forges on, "What I'm trying to say is that it could happen again. You can't stop it."

"I can."

She purses her lips, a frown creasing her forehead.

"No touching, Gwyneth, I mean it."

She lifts a shoulder. "Fine."

"Really?" For some reason, I don't believe that she'd give up so easily. She has the frustrating type of determination that's impossible to break.

"Yeah. It's not like you won't change your mind."

"Gwyneth," I warn.

She jumps again, startled. And I realize I do that a lot to her.

Scare her by being strict and firm and generally harsh. But she's the foolish one who doesn't stay away.

She takes a step back. "I…uh…I'm going to ask the doctor if I can go inside."

She turns around and runs as fast as she can from me. Her shorts ride up her pale thighs and her top stretches against her back. I try to look away, but I can't.

I tell myself it's to see what she'll do as I openly watch the swish of her hair down her back and her legs that don't seem so short now that she's not standing in front of me.

She's not a small person. Just small compared to me.

My fist clenches at that image and it takes everything in me to remain calm and focused on what's to come.

Before rounding the corner, she comes to a screeching halt and spins to face me, motioning at my jacket that she's been hugging to her chest all this time. "I'm going to keep this."

And then she disappears down the hall.

I release a sigh, slowly closing my eyes.

Necessity.

I want to blame it, to shove this entire situation down its throat, but who the fuck am I kidding?

Necessity might have started this, but I'm the one who will pursue it until the end.

EIGHT

Nathaniel

"**D**O YOU HAVE ANY FUCKING IDEA WHAT YOU'RE DOING?"

I sigh for the thousandth time today and face my nephew—the source of the unnecessary question.

"He does," Aspen tells him with her usual assertiveness.

The three of us are standing near City Hall, ignoring the people buzzing around us, and focusing on the time. Or I'm probably the only one who's having an unhealthy obsession with my watch.

Gwyneth is twenty minutes late.

Surely there's a reason behind her tardiness. She's never been the type who's late to appointments. Or irresponsible.

Though it's true that getting married only five days after her father's accident isn't a normal situation, it's not like we have time. The sooner she gives me power of attorney, the easier I can stop Susan's moves. Because she's plotting them as we speak. I made calls, talked to judges, and I know about the subpoenas her lawyer is trying to file. I can only ward her off for so long before I run out of options.

Time isn't on our side, which is the reason behind the hasty marriage.

I stare at my watch again, then at the unanswered phone calls I made. Maybe she needs more time for what girls do when they get married. Though I told her it would be a simple ceremony so we could get to the next step. Nothing fancy. Nothing for her to get ready for.

But this is Gwyneth. The dreamy-looking, chameleon-eyed Gwyneth. She probably had plans for her wedding day. Most girls do. And they certainly don't want to imagine it as an ordinary event during a workday, where each of us will go back to our respective worlds right after.

Because that's what will happen. No one will know about this marriage unless it's absolutely necessary. Like the two witnesses I brought with me. Though I only need one, it's safer to have both so that if one of them can't testify, the other can.

After all, this marriage is purely a formality. Something to use in court. Nothing more, nothing less. She can save her girlhood dreams about marriage for her next one.

"It still doesn't make sense," Sebastian, my nephew, says.

My jaw tics and I don't know if it's because of his words or my earlier thoughts.

"What part of *I need power of attorney* do you not understand, Rascal?"

He stares at me funny, like when he used to want to hit someone but knew he had to reel it in. But he wouldn't normally direct that gaze at me, so maybe he does want to hit me.

Sebastian is ten years younger than me and the only person I consider family. My parents don't count. They're already dead in my mind.

The day he decided to follow my path instead of taking after my father's corruption-smudged politics, I felt a sense of accomplishment I never have before. As if my existence had meaning all along.

"She could've given you power of attorney without the marriage part."

"It's the community property part that matters more. She already signed the contract that says our assets will be jointly owned after marriage, which will give me a strong standing in court."

"And he won't have to worry about her wandering off to God knows where." Aspen steps to my side.

She wasn't a big fan of the marriage idea herself, but like me, she understands that we need to do it in order to protect Weaver & Shaw. Despite the fact that we haven't properly processed King's accident.

Or, I haven't processed it. Aspen couldn't care less about him; her sole concern is the firm's best interest.

As for myself, I don't think I'll ever be able to consider him gone.

So I shove that thought to the back of my mind. It's crowded with all the unnecessary things—things that don't keep the train moving forward.

Sebastian leans against his car and crosses his legs at the ankles. Sometimes it feels as if I'm looking at his father, Nicholas. Another person my parents stole away from me because of their assholish behavior.

His hair is a lighter blond, though, like his mother. One more person to add to the list of people who disappeared because of the Weaver power couple.

That's what they call my parents in the media—a power couple.

Destructive couple suits them better.

"I just feel bad for Gwen," he says, and I resist the urge to smash him against his car—and I never fantasize about hurting my own nephew.

But hearing him use her nickname sits wrong with me. Very wrong. In fact, it's so wrong that I don't even like to think about the reasons behind it.

Yes, Sebastian has met her a few times, and surprisingly, they get along, but the nickname is still off. It's blazing red alerts in my head.

I stand to my full height, but he's oblivious to that and to the rigidness of my body, when I ask, "Why do you pity her?"

"Why do you think?" He juts his chin in my direction. "Because she'll be stuck with you."

"And that's a problem because?"

"Aside from the fact that you and dear Aspen here are using her for the firm, hmm. Let me think." He grins like the little bastard he is. "Oh, you're cold, stiff, and will suck her soul into a black hole of no return."

I grind my teeth and he must notice my body language this time since he throws his hands in the air. "Hey, you're my uncle and all, but I'm not going to lie or sugarcoat shit for you. That's what you taught me, remember?"

"Shut up, Sebastian." Aspen shakes her head at him with a slight tap of her foot and a flip of her hair.

"You don't get an opinion on this since you're his accomplice, Aspen. Hello? Conflict of interest, anyone?"

"Then do you suggest we let go of our work and focus on Kingsley's thousand pending cases instead? Do you want to lose your job at the firm, Sebastian? Right, that wouldn't matter since you're a rich boy from a prestigious family and your senator grandpa can find you another job, maybe even help you open your own firm. But how about the hundred others whose living depends on us, huh? Do we send them to your granddaddy, too, or do we take the most logical route with less hassle? Come on, you're supposed to be smart. Which choice makes more sense?"

Sebastian doesn't move a muscle at her calmly spoken words. It's like she's delivering a closing argument. She's always precise and to the point. Scathing, too. Which is the reason she's a lonely soul; no one can handle her.

I expect Sebastian to come back with his own retort, because my parents raised him to always have the last word. But he just says, "The choice where Gwen doesn't need to sacrifice herself days after her father—and only family, might I add—had a deadly accident."

My fist clenches so hard, I'm surprised a tendon doesn't snap.

That's what I've been thinking about since I made this decision but still came up empty-handed about another option.

"If you don't want to be here, leave," I say casually, with barely any emotion, ignoring the bright, hot feeling burning inside me.

I check my watch again.

Thirty minutes.

It's been a whole thirty minutes and she still hasn't shown up.

Maybe she wanted to doll up, after all. I can imagine her in her princess room trying on one thing after the other.

Or maybe…

I dial her number again and it goes straight to voicemail.

My alerts go up and I try again. When there's no response, I call King's house. Martha picks up after a few beeps. "Hello?"

"It's me. Nathaniel. Is Gwyneth there?"

"She left about two hours ago, said she was meeting you at City Hall."

Fuck. Fuck!

Something hot and furious wraps a noose around my neck as the ominous feeling I experienced this morning rises from the background and fills the horizon. It's red now—the horizon, my vision, the entire fucking scene.

I loosen my tie. "Did you check her room, Martha? How about the wine cellar? The closets? Plural."

"She got into her car and left, sir."

"Did you see her? Are you sure?"

"Yes, I did. I even gave her a water bottle so she could stay hydrated." She hesitates, her voice dropping a little. "Is something the matter?"

Yes, something's the fucking matter. If she left two hours ago, she should've been here a long time ago.

A thousand scenarios explode in my head, none of them

pleasant. In fact, each one is more dangerous than the previous, bloodier, uglier.

I ask Martha to call me if Gwyneth returns and then hang up.

When Kingsley had an accident, I suspected this would happen. I just knew that she'd somehow be too overwhelmed and would do what she does best.

But I saw her talk to Susan like she owned the world. I saw the determination and the need to protect her father at all costs and that blurred my vision, in a way. It blurred my vision of who Gwyneth actually is and what she does.

She hides.

She goes in so deep that it's impossible to find her unless she crawls out of whatever hideout spot she's in. And something tells me she doesn't want to be found right now.

My hand flexes around the phone and I curse under my breath.

But I will fix it.

I will find her.

I'll make Gwyneth visible.

NINE

Gwyneth

HAVEN'T SLEPT ALL NIGHT.

And that's sort of a problem because I become jittery and a bit neurotic when I don't sleep.

Insomnia and I aren't strangers, especially since I didn't manage to completely desensitize myself to that word. It might be written in a red Sharpie because it's one of the words I struggle with the most.

Along with *death*.

I think I also need to add *moving on* to the red list because I can't do that. I'm supposed to, I *have* to, but my mind is stuck in a different type of loop that I can't escape.

So I spent the night in the closet. I wanted to stay with Dad, but Nate said in that stern voice of his to "go home and get some sleep" because tomorrow—today—is a big day. He didn't voice the last part, but I figured it out on my own.

However, I couldn't just get some sleep. Not even after I blasted Twenty One Pilots on my headphones and exhausted myself by dancing. Not even when I swallowed like three sleeping pills. Or maybe it was five. I lost count somewhere.

My mind was definitely not shutting down. Usually, Dad makes me some herbal tea—with vanilla flavor—and reads me a story as if I'm a little girl. He puts on some soothing music and stays by my side until I fall asleep.

But he wasn't there in the ghostly house that, with the lack of his presence, felt like the set of a horror movie. And maybe that's why I couldn't sleep. I couldn't stop thinking about what I'd do if something happened to him while I was under. What if I couldn't get to him in time?

What if death strikes him like it did Grandpa?

So I hurried here first thing this morning. I had to see him for myself and make sure the stupid machines are beeping. That he's alive and didn't leave me.

They moved him out of the ICU because he can breathe on his own and the swelling has nearly disappeared. However, they need to keep a close eye on him, so he's now in a private wing of the hospital, where he has a special nurse, a special room, and everything. But nothing is special enough to heal the bruises on his face or breathe life back into his unmoving body.

I fall to my knees beside the bed and hold his hand. It's scraped and appears lifeless like the rest of him.

When I try to speak, a crushing wave of emotions clog my throat, making the words strangled, closed off. "Dad...you always say to tell you everything because you're my best friend, right? You're the only friend I trust enough to pour my heart out to without worrying that I'll be used down the line. The only friend who won't judge me, even if I'm a little weird and have a strange phobia of words and people and I can be empty sometimes. I feel that way again, Dad. Empty. And unlike the other times, I can't find a silver lining. It's just off and wrong and many other negative words. I thought about it last night like you tell me to whenever I'm stuck. You said I should take a deep breath and think about the root of the issue, because once that's solved, everything else will be as well.

"I think I found it, Dad. The source. It's agreeing to marry Nate. I'm not supposed to do that, right? Even if it means protecting your legacy and what you left me. I'm not supposed to latch onto him like a pest. I don't want to be a burden, Dad. I don't want Nate to baby me or treat me like a delicate flower just because I'm your daughter."

I lick my lips, tasting the saltiness that seeps into my mouth. "So please wake up. If you do, I won't have to feel shitty because I'm using him. I won't have to force his hand and make him do something he dislikes. I did that before and he reacted badly to it. I don't think you noticed it, but he was avoiding me, plastering me to the background as if I never existed. And that hurts, but it's okay because I'm over him now. I *think*. So please open your eyes and come back. Please don't let me be a burden, Dad."

I drop my head to his hand as if that will make him move or acknowledge me. As if that will hasten the process of bringing him back.

Because what I said? Yeah, I've been thinking about it for five days, letting it fester inside me until it's killed all the good words and left only negative ones. Like the red list that I have trouble with.

I'm torn between a sense of duty and common sense—that includes not being a pain in the ass.

"Who said you're a burden?"

My head whips up fast. So fast that I'm a bit disoriented and a sudden sound slips from my lips. It's small, but it's there, like a squeal.

It's him.

My dad's best friend and my future husband.

The man I had a hopeless crush on for years before I destroyed it all on my birthday and then got over him because my pride is a thing.

I'm definitely over him.

And yet, I can't help noticing the way his muscular chest stretches the jacket of his suit or how his eyes darken with each second he watches me. I can't stop myself from looking at that damn stubborn jaw of his and the way it's currently tightening until a muscle tics. Or the way his long legs eat up the distance between us in no time, injecting some sort of a thrilling potion into my bloodstream with each powerful stride.

When he stops beside me, I have to crane my neck to stare up at him because he's so big. Big and strong and a god.

And I don't want to miss a second of witnessing it firsthand. That's why religion exists, right? Because a god is so dazzling, he automatically gains followers and prayers and sacrifices.

Lots of sacrifices.

"Get up."

I want to close my eyes and memorize that voice, the deep tenor of it, the slight humming in it. All of it. But something stops me—the continuous ticking in his jaw. He's mad about something.

Or maybe it's some *things*. Plural. Because he's glaring at me with those darkened eyes that almost look black right now.

"I said, get up from the floor, Gwyneth." This time, he doesn't wait for me to comply and grabs me by the elbow, hauling me to my feet.

I let out a small sound again, a gasp mixed with that stupid juvenile squeal. But that's not important right now. His skin on mine is. His hot skin and his large, veiny hand that's fit for a god.

The place where he's touching me burns and then tingles in rapid succession, and no amount of deep breathing drives it away. Maybe *touching* should be on the negative list, too, because I totally need to desensitize myself to it.

Or maybe just limit it to touching Nate.

He tilts his head to the side, watching me in that harsh, critical way that befits a criminal. Am I one now because I chose the wrong god?

"Did you hear what I said?"

"About what?" I totally wasn't listening, because he's still touching me. He still has his warm hand on my elbow. Nate doesn't do that, you know. He doesn't touch me. Ever. I'm the one who tries it and fails miserably every time.

But he's doing it right now.

And it's hard to focus when I'm floating in the clouds.

"About how you're not a burden."

My heart jolts and I can't control the tremor that shoots through my limbs. It's a knee-jerk reaction that gives away my emotions and I hate it. Especially in front of him. The man who's the reason behind it every damn time.

"I am." I lower my head, staring at my white sneakers, and that automatically makes me look at his prim leather shoes. And the difference between his and mine is so striking that it helps to anchor me in the moment, even if temporarily. "I know you're marrying me because you want to protect Dad's assets and that's okay, but it still makes me a burden. Because I'm not old enough to take care of things myself and I didn't even graduate or pass the bar yet, so I can't practice law or stand against Susan in court and—"

"Look at me."

I shake my head, swallowing after all the rambling I've done. What if he sees the shame on my face—or worse, the things I'm trying to hide? That would be a disaster no one needs.

"Gwyneth."

I flinch, my heart hammering in my chest, but it's not because I'm scared. Not even close. It's due to how he just spoke.

How can someone pack so much command in one single word? In the simple way he says my name? And is it creepy that I want him to keep talking to me in that tone?

For that reason alone, I contemplate disobeying him just to hear it again. But at the same time, I can't ignore the warning, the severity of it.

So I slowly meet his gaze, and I wish I hadn't, because he releases my elbow and I feel like I'm drowning in nonexistent water.

"Do you honestly believe that I chose to do this just to be

there for you or because I'm a knight in shining armor? I'm not, Gwyneth. Far from it."

"Then what are you?"

"Whatever knights in shining armor fight. And that means there's not one noble, sacrificing bone in my body. The reason I'm marrying you isn't because I want to protect you or King's legacy. I'm protecting my firm. My own legacy. So the fact that you feel like a burden is needless and unnecessary. We're using each other. Do you understand?"

My chest deflates and a strong whoosh of air escapes me. It's not relief, though. It's due to being so focused on the way he spoke that I kind of forgot to breathe.

Happens all the time.

But before now, I barely saw him—like once a month or something—and he hardly spoke to me. Now that I've seen him every day since Dad's accident, spoken to him, been close to him, I think I'm having some sort of an overdose. A deadly one at that.

I'll get used to it, right? If I see him constantly, I'll totally be desensitized to his presence.

"Answer my question. Do you understand?" he repeats in that stiff tone, the strictness in it touching places within me that should remain untouched.

"Yeah."

"Don't let your mind wander to places it shouldn't. The next time you have a doubt or a thought, you come to me and say it. You don't hide, and you sure as fuck don't turn off your phone."

I flinch again, and it's crazy, but this time I think I do it because hearing him curse is as rare as seeing a flying unicorn. And it's hot—him cursing. It's masculine and fits his authoritativeness so well.

"My battery died," I offer lamely, because yeah, it did, but I also let it run down on purpose.

"Make sure it never does again. The next time I call, you pick up."

"You're not my keeper, Nate." I need to put that out there somehow so that I don't still feel like a burden.

He pauses, watches me intently with that savage gaze of his—that I now know why people are afraid to make eye contact with. By using a mere look, he can make a person doubt their life. It would be safer to avoid those dark eyes and the twisted promise in them, but I don't.

I never liked safe, anyway.

"Then what am I?"

"Huh?" I'm so completely taken aback that no other words come out.

"If I'm not your keeper, what am I?"

My dad's best friend. But I don't want to say that, because I hate it. I hate that it's all he'll ever be.

"A friend?" I try.

"I don't do friends."

"But you have Aspen."

"Aspen and I work together and we're close in age. Do you fall into that category?"

I twist my lips, wiping my clammy palm against my denim shorts.

"Do you, Gwyneth?"

Damn it and him and Aspen. And what's with his need to have an answer to every question he poses? The dictator.

"No, I don't. But age is only a number, you know. Just because I'm younger doesn't mean I can't work or be friends with you. Those things can be changed."

"No, they can't."

"Yes, they can." I plant my feet wide apart.

"Let's say they can. That won't be happening in the near future. So what does it make me now?"

"You."

"Me?"

"Yeah, just you. I don't need a category to stuff you into. You're just Nate."

"That's not true, though, is it?" He motions at my smartwatch and I stare at it, thinking maybe it melted by being in his presence, because that's how it feels sometimes. Like I'm the helpless star in the sun's orbit and my only destiny is to burn.

"What time is it?"

"Eleven, why?"

"Where were you supposed to be an hour ago, Gwyneth?"

"Oh."

"Oh isn't a place. Where were you supposed to be?"

"At City Hall."

"Why?"

"To get married."

"And were you there?"

"You know the answer to that."

"I need you to say it. Were you there?"

"No, but that's because I came here and forgot about the time…"

"Stop."

My insides jolt and I swear something is being rearranged near my gut, because that single word holds so much authority that it strikes me to my bones.

"Don't do that again," he says.

"Do what?"

"Blurt out words without thinking. Excuses are for the weak, especially if they're not backed up by evidence or valid reasons."

"I did have a valid reason."

"I'm listening."

"I told you earlier. I didn't want to be a burden."

"And I told you that's not the case. So that's all cleared up."

"I guess."

"I guess is neither a yes nor a no."

"The world isn't only yes or no. There are "I guess" moments— maybes, the unsure. Nuances and all of that."

"And all of that, huh?" he repeats with a slight twitch in his lips. It's the unicorn half-smile. The one he never offered me after I stupidly thought I could kiss him and get away with it.

"Uh-huh, and I have a lot of them."

"A lot of what?"

"Nuances and all of that."

"I'll keep that in mind." He tips his chin toward the door. "Now, let's go. We're late."

The wedding ceremony.

Ours. Mine and Nate's.

My cheeks burn so hot, I'm surprised I don't go up in flames or explode or something equally embarrassing. Because, holy shit, this is actually happening.

How does someone react to being married to their one-time crush, who they kind of got over—but not really—and who also happens to be their dad's best friend?

Because I think I need a manual or something. One that doesn't make me act like the age he so obviously disregards.

"Yeah, okay. Sure."

"Those are three words for the same thing."

"So?" My voice sounds a little bit squeaky and kind of breathy.

He pauses, that line returning to his forehead. "Are you nervous?"

"No! I can handle this."

"Are you sure? Because if you're not feeling well, we can—"

"I'm not a child, Nate. I stopped being that a long time ago, and do you know what that means? It means I can make my own decisions and function under stress. It means I know this marriage is important, not only to protect Dad's assets, but also those of everyone at W&S and their clients. So I can do this, okay?"

"Okay."

He says it calmly, casually, like he believes my words wholeheartedly, even more than I do.

"Okay," I repeat, releasing a puff of air. "Let's go."

"You still didn't answer my question."

"What question?"

"What am I to you?"

It comes to me then, the answer he's been fishing for since he asked the question. Or maybe it's my own twisted brain that comes up with it and refuses to let it go. Because once the thought was planted there, it's been impossible to get rid of it.

So I say the one thing that makes sense. "After today? My husband."

The husband I'm not allowed to touch.

TEN

Gwyneth

THE GETTING MARRIED PART DIDN'T MAKE ME WANT TO throw my guts up.

I mean, it should've been simple, but it really wasn't.

Probably because I was half-dazed and half-fuming at Aspen's presence. Yes, I knew she was going to be there. She's close to Nate's age and works with him, after all. *Gag.*

But yeah, seeing her there might've brought out the temper I usually try to bury inside. It's toxic, you know. Like, super toxic, and I don't want to be that person in front of Nate on our wedding day.

Aspen didn't do anything either. Her mere existence is enough to push me to my limit.

Anyway, it's over. We're married. We put on rings in front of the judge, but we removed them as soon as the ceremony ended because Nate made it clear that this whole marriage is a secret and no one but the four of us, and Susan, will know about it. He has those rings now, in his pocket, and he'll probably throw them away the minute he's out of view.

We'll have our certificate soon and then everything will fall into place like a domino effect. And yeah, I still can't believe it, but I'll get used to it. I guess.

After we get home—without Aspen—and I pinch myself a few times, I'll add her name to the *A* section of negative words.

Because why is she so close to him? And only him? Dad can't stand her—same, Dad, same—and it's mutual. She's not interested in the social game, so why is she interested in Nate of all people? Why is she relaxed around him and why does she talk to him when she's usually stuck up and mean and witchy?

Then it hits me when we're leaving City Hall. Does she…love him? Or maybe they're sleeping together.

I steal a peek at them since they went out first and are now descending the stairs in front of me. They're talking in hushed whispers because the world can't know their secrets. They're so in tune, so comfortable with each other that I think I'm really going to throw up now.

Shit. They're definitely sleeping together, aren't they?

My hand finds my bracelet and I squeeze it so tight, I nearly rip it off.

"You okay?"

I slowly break eye contact with the scene to focus on Sebastian, Nate's much more approachable nephew whom I might be following all over social media just to see glimpses of his uncle in his updates.

Since Sebastian's parents died when he was young, his grandparents adopted him, but it was Nate who basically brought him up. They have an easy-going, heartwarming relationship in which Sebastian basically tries to annoy his uncle and usually fails. He can be a stone, that way, Nate. But when his nephew chose to follow in his footsteps by becoming a lawyer, Nate looked the proudest I've ever seen him.

Sebastian is probably the only person I've witnessed Nate care for closely and monitor every chance he got.

And I might have been a tiny bit jealous about that.

Anyway, Sebastian is the heartthrob of the media and has been since he was a star quarterback in college. The Weavers are kind of a big deal around here.

Brian Weaver is a successful senator. His wife, Debra, is an influential woman, and together, they're a famous couple.

Sebastian is the intelligent grandson who was an athlete and is now one of the youngest people to acquire a junior partner position in a law firm.

And Nathaniel Weaver, well, he's the cold Greek god who rebelled against his parents but is still the most eligible bachelor. Aside from my dad.

Not anymore. He's married now, even if no one will actually know about it.

"Yeah, I'm fine," I tell Sebastian. He's watching me with light green eyes that are nothing like his uncle's darker ones. His hair is too blond, too bright.

But he's beautiful. Like, "superhot" as Jenny always says. And I see his charm, I really do. But I don't feel it.

I don't feel tingly and hot, with a need to control my damn face and emotions for just being in his presence.

"Are you sure, Gwen?"

"Yeah."

He stares at Nate, who's still busy talking to Aspen, still plotting whatever those two plot when they're together, then lowers his voice. "If you have a hard time with him, let me know."

My attention shifts to Sebastian and I watch him closely. "And what are you going to do?"

"Stop him, of course."

"He's your uncle."

"Doesn't mean I'll blindly take his side."

"Really?"

"Really."

"So you're, like, my ally now?"

"If you need one."

Warmth floods me and I let a smile break on my lips as I touch his arm. "Thanks, Bastian."

He's about to say something when a shadow falls over us. Or me, to be more specific, because Sebastian is tall enough to escape it.

Me, though? I'm caught right underneath it, in the center of Nate's overwhelming scrutiny. His gaze is so hard and sharp that I unconsciously squirm.

"Didn't you say you were going back home?" Nate asks in that voice specifically designed to make people feel uncomfortable.

I did say that I wanted to sleep a little before I go back to see Dad. I'm skipping classes at this point because, what if something happens to him while I'm studying and I can't get there fast enough? What if he stops sleeping and decides to go into that *D*-word phase?

"What's the rush?" It's Sebastian who asks with a shiny glint in his eyes. "Gwen and I were going to have coffee and catch up."

We were? Not that I mind, but I'm really about to collapse. Insomnia and copious amounts of stress and anxiety and overthinking will do that to you. I'd go out with Sebastian under different circumstances, but I don't think that's physically possible right now.

"*Gwyneth* needs to rest and you have work to do." Is it just me or is his voice harsher, stronger, almost like a whip?

Also, how does he know I'm at my physical limits? Does he see it in my sickly pale skin or my unfocused eyes? It's the dark circles, isn't it? Those suckers appear with a vengeance after white nights.

"In that case, I'll take a rain check." Sebastian pats my hand, which is still on his arm because I got distracted by Nate.

"Give me a ride, Sebastian," Aspen says from the bottom of the stairs. I almost forgot she was there. *Almost.*

Nate grabs me by the elbow and pulls me back from his nephew. The act is so effortless that I feel like I'm floating on air as we leave the scene without another word.

Aspen gives me a look that I don't know how to perceive. Is

it pity? An apology? But why would she pity me or apologize to me? She's not the type. She's a witch.

Right, Dad?

"Where are we going?" I ask Nate once I'm a bit out of my daze. Only a bit, though, because I think those pills I crunched on like candy are starting to take effect.

"I'll drive you home."

"Why?"

"Because you're a few minutes away from collapsing."

So he did know about my exhaustion. Yikes. Am I that obvious to everyone else?

"I can take a cab. You said you were going back to the firm."

"Since you were late, I rescheduled my morning meetings, so I don't have anything until the afternoon." He unlocks his car and steps to the driver's side.

I roll my eyes. "Sorry for messing up your morning meetings, husband."

He pauses with his hand on his door's handle. "What did you just call me?"

"Husband. You know, when people get married, they become husband and wife."

"Lose it."

"Lose what?"

"That word. Lose it."

"No." I cross my arms over my chest. "What I call you is up to me. Besides, we need to keep things authentic if we want Susan to believe it. She's cunning, you know. It's not by coincidence that Dad has been battling a lifetime of court cases against her."

"Gwyneth," he warns.

"You need to start calling me Gwen or something else for this whole thing to work."

A cold smile paints his lips and I know I won't like his next words even before he says them. He's cruel that way, with absolutely no regard for others' feelings. "How about kiddo?"

"I'm not a kid."

"If you say so."

"Is that what you still see me as? A kid?" I storm from my side of the car to stand in front of him. "Would a kid be able to marry you?"

"It's a fake marriage."

"Fake is an illusion, but this is real, tangible, *touchable*."

I don't miss the way his jaw clenches at that word. Touchable. One he made so clear that he doesn't want to be part of this relationship.

"Step back."

My cheeks must be hot crimson, because it's only then that I realize I'm close to him. So close that I taste him on my tongue, so close that his warmth is wrapping around me like a blanket. Or, more accurately, a noose, because it's suffocating me with each passing second.

Ordinarily, I'd give him back his safe space and go hide in mine, because isn't that the right thing to do?

However, I also thought that the right thing was Dad being safe until he's old and gray. But he isn't, and everything I've taken for granted is changing, evolving, and spiraling out of control.

So I don't follow Nate's order.

I stand there in the path of his hurricane, under the scrutiny of those dark eyes and in the shadow of his body.

I stay.

I stare.

And I remind myself to breathe.

"Gwyneth, I told you to step back."

"And I'm obviously refusing to."

"Did you just say you refuse to?"

"Yeah. Why? Are you scared of something?"

He steps forward and I startle, jumping away so suddenly that my back hits hard metal. It's the car, I realize. I'm plastered against the door, and I mean glued to it, like it's my lifeline, because it suddenly feels like it now that he's close.

Like as close as when I kissed him. When I got on my

tiptoes and just went for it. And now, I'm staring at his sinfully-proportioned lips. At how they're only a breath away because he's hovering—looming over me and blocking the sun and the air and every natural element.

He's a god, after all. And gods can totally control the elements and leave me gasping on nonexistent oxygen.

He's not touching me, but I'm full of those little tingles, those sharp needle-like stings, and I can't help it. Just like I can't help the blood that came out after that prick from the glass. It's natural.

It's chemical.

It's how it's supposed to be.

"Do you truly think that, Gwyneth? That I'm scared?"

"Well, aren't you?"

"Do I look scared to you?"

I study him then, like really look at him and the strong lines of his face and how lethally handsome he is, because he takes his god image seriously. He's always groomed to perfection, beautiful to the point it hurts in my non-desensitized heart. Because I didn't add that word to the negative notebook.

Heart.

But yeah, he definitely doesn't look scared. I've never seen Nate scared or anxious or any of the things that we humans are plagued with. But his face isn't stuck in that rigid aloof expression either.

There's a tightness in his body, a tic in his jaw, and a look in his eyes that I don't recognize. I've never seen it before. I've never seen that lowering of his lids or the dilating of his pupils.

And it's a bit scary.

Or maybe a lot scary, because I'm shivering uncontrollably. Is he trying to scare me? Trying to make me out as some sort of a criminal that he has to break down just because I talked back?

"Answer the question, Gwyneth."

"No."

"No, what?"

"No, you don't look scared."

"Then how do I look?"

Scary. But I don't say that, because that would mean I can't hold my own, and I can totally do that. Hold my own. Now, I just need to convince my unreliable brain of that fact.

"I don't know," I say instead.

"You don't, huh?"

I shake my head once.

"Let me enlighten you then. This is what I look like when I'm holding back. When I'm not acting on what I'm thinking and dragging you to a corner where no one will see you flinch or hear you release those small noises you do when you're out of your element. So you should be the one who's scared, not me."

I don't think I'm breathing anymore.

Otherwise, why am I wheezing and why is the back of my throat so dry that it feels like I'm stuck in the desert?

I swallow.

I inhale deeply.

But it still doesn't give me my sanity back. The sanity he confiscated with his hot, strong words.

"Why should I be scared?" I can't help it, okay? I want to know why, because maybe that will give me back the air I lost as collateral damage from being near him.

There's a bang when he hits the top of the car next to my head, and I jump, my heart doing a strange jolt that freezes me in place.

That and the way he hardens his jaw and darkens his eyes, then directs them at me like daggers.

Holy shit. Why does he get to be so damn hot when he's angry? Doesn't that defy the whole purpose behind it?

"Were you listening to a word I said?"

"Yeah, and that's why I asked. Why should I be scared?"

His hand reaches for me—well, not for me, but for my hair, for a stubborn rusty strand that's been flying in my face for the past twenty years. I can't tame it into submission, no matter what I try.

Nate has a hold of that strand now, and my throat pulses,

then something between my thighs pulses, too, because they're jealous of that strand. But they'll never admit it.

I'm jealous of that strand, of the way it has the sole attention of his dark eyes. But I don't have to be jealous for long, because he tucks it behind my ear, slowly but not sensually. That cold edge is still covering his face, still tightening his jaw and turning the veins in his neck rigid.

"You should be scared, because…" his thumb slides from behind my ear to the hollow of my throat, to the insane pulse that's currently self-destructing me. "If you don't stop flaunting yourself around, if you keep provoking me and don't stay in your lane, I'll be inclined to take action. I'll swallow you down so fast, there'll be nothing left of you, let alone your sarcasm and naïveté. You'll stare in the mirror and not recognize yourself anymore. This is my last warning and the only courtesy I will give you. *Stop*, Gwyneth. You don't know what the fuck you're dealing with. So go back to college, to your safe boys and vanilla milkshakes and boring little life."

Is it possible for a heart to leave the ribcage and still beat? Because it feels like it's spilling out of my chest with each word from his mouth.

I should probably listen. He does look terrifying, and I don't know if I can really handle it when he takes action while in this mode.

But what's the point if I don't find out for myself? If I don't take the step and see it personally. All of it.

So even though I'm having some sort of a heart attack and I still can't breathe properly, I say, "But I don't want safe and boring."

I want you.

I almost say that. Almost, but I don't get to, because his next words knock the living breath out of my lungs.

"You're well and truly fucked, baby girl."

ELEVEN

Nathaniel

WHEN MY FATHER SAID THAT I HAVE A TRAIN BRAIN, IT had absolutely nothing to do with how much I actually love trains.

My train brain doesn't reverse. Ever. Once it's moving forward, it just keeps going. There are no regrets. No going back and definitely no retracting what I fucking said or did.

So now, I have a train life, one that's only focused on getting shit done and moving on to the next thing, then the one after that, and so on. That's how my train brain works.

Forward.

Outward.

Nothing is kept inward. Otherwise, it'll rot and cause my downfall.

Now is no different. The present and the past are only a step for the future. A stop, a station. They're not what I should be focused on and I certainly shouldn't be thinking about her fucking words. The words that she shouldn't have said in that sultry voice that I want to hear say fucked-up things.

I don't want safe and boring.

That's what started it all. That's what brought us to this moment where she's staring at me as if I'm the big bad wolf from her favorite fairy tale. Even though it used to scare her, she wanted to hear the story over and over again, because that's what Gwyneth does. Instead of running away like normal people do, she stands in front of what scares her and looks at it—or him—with those chameleon eyes.

I want to see what makes them that way, she used to say. *Everyone has a reason, right?*

And now, I'm the one she's focused on. The one she obviously fears—or is at least apprehensive of. But she still willingly stands in the path of my destruction.

When I drove her back to the house, she didn't stop her scrutinizing either. Her inquisitive eyes kept watching, observing, as if waiting for some sort of a sign.

What exactly, I have no fucking clue.

We're now in front of King's house. We agreed that I'll be moving in, not only because we can't leave this place empty, but I also don't want her alone after everything that's happened.

However, she doesn't know that piece of information, and she never will.

"Go get some sleep," I tell her.

She faces me with a slight furrow in her brows. "How do you know I didn't sleep last night? I looked at myself in the rearview mirror, and I don't have dark circles."

"You have tremors."

"Tremors?"

I tip my chin at her hands. Her fingers are shaking slightly, even though they're lying inert at either side of her.

She lifts them up and stares at them under the sun, her lips falling open the slightest bit. And I want to jam my fingers in there, open her mouth wide with them and order her to suck on them.

I clench my fist.

What the fuck am I thinking about? In King's house? About his daughter?

It's those damn words. She shouldn't have said them. She shouldn't have confessed that she doesn't want safe and boring. That's what girls like her are supposed to want. Fucking safe and fucking boring. It's predictable and with a known result.

This whole new thing isn't.

"Oh. I didn't notice that." She lets her arms fall. "How did you?"

"How did I what?"

"Notice my tremors when I haven't?"

"Because you were doing it when we were at City Hall." *Lie.* It's barely noticeable unless you look close—really fucking close.

"I was?"

I nod but don't say anything else. She keeps watching me, though, as if waiting for my words. When they don't come, she wipes her palm on her denim shorts.

"So what happens now?" she asks in that tone again, in that fucking bright and lively and damn curious tone.

"Now you go to sleep and I go back to the firm."

"And after that?"

"After that, you'll wake up and eat something. Actually, do that now. Eat before you sleep."

"You give a lot of orders, did you know that?"

"And you do a lot of talking back."

"Because you're so inflexible. Someone has to lighten up the mood a little."

"Is that supposed to be funny?"

"If you want."

"Do you see me laughing?"

She throws a dismissive hand in the air. "I never see you laugh, Nate. So the problem is you, not me. Anyway, what happens after I wake up and eat and go to visit Dad and you come back from work?"

"What do you think will happen?" I'm treading on dangerously thin ice, but I can't ignore the light shining through the greenish part of her eyes, the playfulness in it. But even that is darkening now as she gulps audibly, the sound carrying through the air.

"I...don't know."

"You don't, huh?"

"No."

"That should mean nothing will happen."

"But you said something about me being fucked. I heard it. And I also heard the other thing."

"The other thing?"

She bites her lower lip. Hard. I'm surprised it doesn't start bleeding. "You know."

"Say it."

"I...can't."

"See. This is why I told you to go back to safe and boring."

"I said I don't want that. If I did, I wouldn't have kissed you two years ago."

At the mention of that, memories of her lips against mine rush back in. It's a myriad of hazy things, like her body against mine and her scent bleeding beneath my flesh.

I don't even like kissing, but now, I can't stop staring at her fucking lips. The lips that started it all when they shouldn't have.

"That's not a moment to be proud of, Gwyneth."

"I know. I should've grabbed you harder so you wouldn't have been able to push me away. But you're strong. I've seen the way you work out with Dad, so I don't think I stood a chance either way."

I can feel the muscles clenching in my jaw and upper chest. With every word out of her mouth, she's digging a knife into places that shouldn't be disturbed.

"For once, you said something accurate."

"Which part?"

"The part where you wouldn't have stood a chance. You didn't. You *don't*. So stop playing with fire."

"Or...what?"

I approach her predatory-like, deliberately taking my time. At first, she stands her ground, looking up at me with those ever-changing eyes. Eyes that the longer I stare into them, the stronger I'm pulled closer. It's a fucking trance that I have no chance of warding off.

When I'm within touching distance, she steps back, one foot behind the other, matching my pace, but she's not fast enough and trips. I catch her by the elbow and pull her toward me.

She crashes into my chest. And it's a full-body fucking crash, where her soft curves are molded to me, her thighs touch mine, and her head is nestled against my shirt.

And is that her heartbeat or mine that's about to rip flesh and bone?

She stares up at me as if hearing the same rhythm—the pulsing, the pulling, the tugging—and her lips are parted again. There's a blush in her cheeks, a pink color that extends to the hollow of her throat and the shells of her ears.

And because I can't fucking help it, I lift her chin with my thumb and forefinger, angling her head back. I do it because I want to watch her mystic eyes, the changing in them, the mixture of emotions swirling in them. But maybe I also do it because I want to touch her.

Put my hands on her.

She's soft and small and that does fucked-up shit to me.

It shouldn't.

It can't happen.

But fuck if I understand that right now.

Because this, right here, this moment suspended in the middle of nowhere feels like the truest thing I've experienced in a very long fucking time.

But then something happens.

A full body shake takes hold of her.

And it's not just one of the side effects of her insomnia; it's a violent type, as if she's about to combust. Her chin trembles, too, like when she's scared.

Like right before she goes to hide.

What the fuck am I doing?

I release her and step back. I need to get away from her before I do something I'll regret.

Under King's own fucking roof.

TWELVE

Gwyneth

TWO WEEKS LATER, I'M FORCED BACK TO REALITY.

I'm forced to let go of the hope I held on to so tightly when Dad had his accident. Because the truth is, he's not waking up and probably won't. The doctor said that the more time he spends in a coma, the slimmer his chances are of coming out of it.

And even though I've been visiting him every day, I can feel the gloomy cloud that hovers over his hospital bed. I can tell that my dad is probably not there anymore, no matter how much I talk to him and read to him and everything in between.

And that's just been too painful to think about, so I distracted myself with school before the summer break. And cleaning. I do that a lot when I'm anxious or stressed. I scrub floors and counters and dishes and the bathroom.

In my head, I'm scrubbing my mind clean. Does it work? For a while, maybe, but not in the long term. Because the problems far outweigh the solutions. I thought myself strong enough to take it all—let it soak in and then vanish—but maybe it's been disintegrating me from the inside out.

The thought of the *D*-word happening to Dad makes me shake uncontrollably in my closet.

That's why I need to be distracted. Summer vacation has officially started, and if I don't keep myself occupied, I'll go mad. I'll live in my closet, scrubbing the floor and eating ice cream until I have some sort of a crisis.

A mental breakdown. Meltdown. Or something else that ends with *down*.

It doesn't help that Susan isn't backing off. Not even an inch. She's still throwing suits left and right, trying to get the house back because it was her husband's and should've belonged to her, but my father "stole" it.

Despite my efforts to get involved, Nate doesn't give me many updates about her.

"I'll handle everything," is his signature response whenever I ask about anything.

He's taking care of the legal side, the firm, and Dad's hospital procedures.

Everything.

Except for me, obviously.

Ever since the day we got married, he hasn't touched me. Not even a brush of his hand or fingers or whatever. It's like two years ago all over again. I can recognize it when he's pulling away from me, you know. He only speaks to me when it's necessary, in monosyllables, and won't stay in my company for long.

He chose a guest room on the ground floor that's as far away from mine as physically possible while still living in the same house.

But it's different this time.

I didn't kiss him. I didn't do anything, actually. He's the one who touched me, set me on damn fire, told me I'm truly fucked and called me baby girl.

He called me baby girl.

No matter how active my imagination is, it couldn't, even in its wildest form, have made that up.

And then he just went back to his workaholic life and left me wondering if maybe I'm losing my mind and all the tension I felt on the wedding day wasn't there. Maybe I was too sleep-deprived to think straight. Maybe the pills made me go whacko.

But no, that can't be true, because even after, I could taste it. The tension, I mean. It's been thick and large and has been seeping into my lungs with every breath I take.

And that's another reason why I'm nearing the edge. I can feel it when it happens. I find no pleasure in doing things. I hide in the closet more and even my vanilla ice cream and milkshake don't taste the same.

Oh, and I hear the emptiness tapping at the insides of my brain.

I can't be on the edge. The edge is where all disasters start to happen. Like insomnia and depressive thoughts and every negative word in my notebook.

So I came here.

To Weaver & Shaw's law firm.

The main prestigious branch that's situated in New York. Maybe going to one of the other countless ones scattered around the States and Europe would've been safer. The managing partners have been calling and asking about my dad and they actually like me. Which can't be said about the person in charge of this one.

But that would mean leaving Dad's side, and that's not going to happen.

Anyway, I've been inside the building countless times before, but this is the first time that it's felt huge and intimidating. This must be how the new applicants feel when they walk the long halls and ride the elevator to the towers.

The bright white floors and walls and the spotless glass doors and windows give it a clean, businesslike look. The setting is done this way as a psychological trick to make it trustworthy. If I were a client and walked through this place, I'd feel a sense of assurance.

But I'm not, and assurance is the last thing bleeding into my veins right now.

I catch a glimpse of my reflection in one of the glass doors and my feet falter for a second. I'm wearing a black pencil skirt and a white shirt. My rusty hair is pulled into a ponytail and my makeup is light, professional.

It killed me to not wear my denim shorts, but at least I kept the white sneakers. I just chose the simplest ones I've got that go with the setting.

And I'm also carrying a box of bribes.

So, the thing is, Nate doesn't know I'm coming here today. And he'll probably be mad. But whatever, he's always mad in a way—and hopefully, by the time I get what I came here for, it'll be too late for him to kick me out.

Because he's a jerk. A few days ago, I asked him to let me intern at the firm for the summer and he said no. Point-blank. When I asked why, he ignored me.

Asshole.

So I'm taking things into my own hands. I'm interning here in spite of him and his assholish behavior. It's the only way to keep myself occupied during the summer.

Besides, he's not the only hotshot lawyer here. I've been between W&S's walls for years and I know the best attorneys who can keep me distracted and busy enough to stop my overthinking altogether.

"You can do this," I mutter under my breath and stride down the hall to the open space where junior assistants and interns have their desks.

But I'm not after them. They're small fish that would never in a million years stand up to Nate.

The ones I'm after are sitting in the break area, drinking coffee and chatting among themselves. The partners.

They have enough power to stand up to Nate and not lose their jobs—hopefully.

Sebastian is one of them.

But he does corporate law, and uh, I don't really like that. So I'm more interested in the other two. Knox Van Doren and Daniel Sterling. Criminal and international law, respectively.

Both of them are British, have stellar reputations, and are certified playboys.

I keep a low profile as I head to where the three of them are sitting. They usually have these coffee breaks around this time, and Nate has his administrative meetings in the morning, which is why I came in now.

Everything is calculated to give my plan further chance to succeed. I'm taking things into my own hands and it's all going to be fine.

"Hi!" I say too cheerfully, making three pairs of eyes slide to me. Sebastian smiles and so does Daniel. He has a charming presence that's similar to Sebastian's when he was in college—Nate's nephew is a bit more serious now.

Daniel is pretty in a model type of way with his piercing turquoise eyes, light hair, and fit physique. It's one of the reasons why magazines love putting him on their covers. That and his shrewd ways in the law circuit. "Gwen! Did you bring us some of your cupcakes?"

"Yeah." I grin, waving my bribes box. "I stayed up all night making them."

"You're a doll." Daniel takes the box, opens it, but pauses before eating. "Sorry about Kingsley. That must be hard."

"I'm fine." *Totally.* Like I'm not on the verge of mentally collapsing or anything.

But I've always thought saying I'm fine, even when I'm not, works. At least people will leave me alone and I don't have to be the subject of their pity.

"What are you doing here?" Sebastian asks. "For Nate?"

"Nope."

"Then?" It's Knox who asks, staring at me over the rim of his cup. I don't know if it has something to do with the fact that he deals with many dangerous criminals, but he has a gaze that could make a sinner confess his deepest, darkest secrets.

Which contradicts his Prince Charming image. But then again, Dad always said Knox was never the Prince Charming type. He just gives off those vibes.

"I want to intern here this summer."

There's a brief silence, and I'm tempted to fill it, but I don't. I can't be rambling in a professional setting. These men aren't Dad's colleagues anymore. They're lawyers I need to impress.

"What did Nate say?" Sebastian asks. I know he didn't tell them about the wedding, but he knows, and that means he'll constantly refer back to him. Nate is his uncle, after all.

"He doesn't know." I pause. "Technically, he refused."

"Technically?" Daniel grins and that causes his cheeks to crease with gorgeous dimples. "Tell us more."

"Nate doesn't think I should intern, but that doesn't make sense, right? I'm taking pre-law and need the experience to apply for law school, so I can't just do nothing during the summer."

"You can." Knox grabs a cupcake and rotates it between his fingers but doesn't eat take a bite. "Dan and I didn't do any pre-law internships and we're doing just fine."

"That's because you guys are geniuses. I'm not. But I'm a super hard worker and a fast learner and I'm definitely not lazy, so I can get all sorts of things done."

"Nice." Sebastian raises his mug in my direction. "Continue selling yourself that way and it'll work."

"Listen to our Weaver Prince here. He's worked with enough corporations to know what marketing is," Knox says, referring to Sebastian—that's what they call him, prince, because Nate is his uncle and he's the king.

They called me Shaw Princess, too, when they first met me, but I told them it's just Gwen. Sometimes, it's hard to live in the shadow of an otherworldly man such as my dad and to be seen as just an extension of him.

"Does that mean I'm in?" I ask hopefully.

"We don't personally approve interns, love." Daniel snatches his third cupcake. "HR does and we just pick."

"I can't submit to HR."

"Why not?"

"Nate, right?" Sebastian asks.

"Yeah." I clink my nails. "He'll know I went against his order, and I'd rather he doesn't find out until I'm in."

"Now that you mention it, I want to see the look on his face, so we should make this happen." Sebastian grins.

"My, Weaver Prince. Is this a rebellion?" Daniel smirks.

"You both love it."

"I'm a good fucking citizen." Daniel chews his cupcake. "Knox, however…"

The latter sips from his coffee, a gleam shining in his eyes. "If we do this, will there be some fun, Sebastian?"

"I can assure you of that." He gives me a knowing look and I try my hardest not to blush. "I can't take you in, though, Gwen. I have enough interns for a lifetime. How about you, Dan?"

"Me, too, I'm afraid. Aspen, however, doesn't have any interns."

"Not her." I twist my lips.

"Why not?" Knox pushes his mug away and focuses on me. Well, shit. I can't be badmouthing a senior partner in front of the lawyer that I want to work with the most.

"She's Nate's friend and she doesn't like Dad." I step toward Knox. "So you're all I've got."

"You're telling me to go against Nate for you, and that's such a bad idea, Gwen."

"I know, but I promise to make it up to you with hard work. Criminal law is my passion."

Daniel grins, shaking his head. "You're not listening to him, love."

"Huh?"

"He said it's a bad idea."

"Yeah…I know."

Knox stands and smiles down at me, his features becoming

hard with the motion. "What you don't know is that I love bad ideas."

"Does that mean you're taking me in?"

I'm waiting for a nod or a yes to do my happy dance, but Knox goes quiet and the atmosphere changes from light and playful to completely suffocating.

I recognize it so well since this is what my life's been like for the past couple of weeks. Breathing is a chore and everything in between is too charged and asphyxiating.

My heart thunders as I slowly turn around and catch a glimpse of the man who's been torturing my days and nights.

The man I wasn't supposed to see now.

He has a hand in his pocket as he strides to us in the midst of onlookers. That's what Nate does—he steals attention.

He's a thief.

Because every time he's in sight, I'm robbed of breath and other things I don't want to put a name to.

And now, I feel like he'll rob me of something else. Something I really don't want to give away.

So I won't.

Because I'm taking things into my own hands now.

THIRTEEN

Nathaniel

MY WORKPLACE IS SACRED.

After all, it's where my ambition thrives. Where my plans are made and my strategies are conducted.

This is where I come to focus and forget about the girl I leave behind and go back late so that I don't see her. Only, she's not a girl, is she?

I want to call her that to stop my dick from having ideas, but she was never that—a girl. At least, not for some time.

She's a woman now. A grown-up fucking woman with legs that go for miles and a tiny waist that can almost fit in only one of my palms.

And she's currently in the place where I'm supposed to be focused, not sidetracked.

Gwyneth is right here, at W&S, and while it's not her first time, she doesn't usually dress like she's at a business meeting.

And definitely not with these three fuckers—my nephew included. Kingsley made it his mission to keep her away from them and their whoring ways. So I'm just taking care of it on his behalf. Like I promised him.

It's definitely not because of how I want to jam their faces into the table. I shouldn't be thinking about hurting three of my best attorneys. I shouldn't, and yet that's the only fucking urge that's rushing through my veins instead of blood.

"Who's taking whom in?" I ask all of them, not bothering to cool down my tone.

I don't have the frame of mind to, because she's here. In my focus zone. And she needs to be fucking gone.

"Me." Knox places an arm around her shoulder. "Gwen will be interning with me."

She smiles up at him with those bright, bright eyes, all green and with barely any gray or even blue. She's happy, ecstatic, and the thought of murder becomes more and more appealing.

And that's an anomaly for a lawyer. A fucking error in the matrix that shouldn't exist.

But it does, and the more she smiles at him, the more he has his hands on her, the redder and hotter that thought becomes.

"Remove your hand if you don't want a harassment suit, Van Doren," I say with enough nonchalance that doesn't betray my disturbing inner thoughts.

Sebastian grins and I glare at him, so he pretends to be sipping from his coffee and going through his phone. Daniel stands, hugs a box of pastries to his chest, then grabs my nephew by the shoulder and drags him out. "We're out of here, but we're rooting for you, Gwen. Welcome to the dark side." He winks at her and Sebastian gives me a knowing, taunting look before they're both out of the break area.

It's only the three of us. Me, Gwyneth, and Knox, who still has his fucking arm around her shoulder.

"Nah, you wouldn't do that. Right, Gwen?" Knox shows her his dreamy smile, the one I've seen him use to charm women. "We get along, don't we?"

"Yeah," she says readily, cheerfully, with that energy that I don't like others to see. I don't like others to see anything about her. Period.

"No."

At my closed off tone, her smile falls and her lips purse before she steps away from Knox and marches to me with hard, determined steps.

But they're for me. Her entire attention and those ever-changing eyes are only focused on me and me alone.

"I have the right to apply for an internship."

"And I have the right to refuse your nonexistent application."

"But why? I have the grades to be accepted here. This is discrimination."

"And you can sue for it," Knox tells her. "With the right arguments."

"You shut up before I call a board meeting about your malpractices."

"Hear that, Gwen?" He steps beside her. "I can sue him for that threat, too. You'll be my witness, won't you?"

"If he doesn't let me intern, I will be." She's talking to Knox, but her entire attention is on me, her eyes digging holes into my face.

I've had countless opponents and most of them didn't dare to even look at me, but Gwyneth doesn't only stare, she also glares and talks back, among a lot of other fucking things.

"You can't win against me in court, Van Doren. Maybe in a couple of decades, and only if I'm suffering from some form of dementia. And you, Gwyneth, do you honestly believe threatening me is the right way to handle this?"

"Well, I asked nicely and you didn't listen."

"That's because I didn't want to."

"He's not the boss of you, Gwen," Knox says. "If you want an internship in your dad's firm, you just have to take it."

She squares her shoulders. "That's right. You're not the boss of me, Uncle Nate."

I grind my teeth, and it's not only because she called me that after so long, but also because she said it in a taunting way. In a "you're my father's best friend, so you're supposed to give me what I want" kind of way.

It takes all my self-restraint not to catch those words and jam them back down her throat so she doesn't utter them again. Maybe make her choke on my fingers at the same time. Or another part of me.

"Yet," I say.

"What?"

"I'm not the boss of you yet, considering that you do want to intern for me."

"Not for you," she says slowly. "For Knox."

"That won't be happening, so it's either with me or you're out of here."

Her lips fall open and she swallows, then clamps them shut before they open again.

Knox releases a tsking sound. "Like uncle, like nephew, all you and Sebastian ever do is steal my interns."

"But...I want to intern with Knox," she says with more conviction.

"Then leave."

She purses those lips again, her body getting rigid and her nostrils flaring. She's clinking her nails against each other, too.

Clink. Clink. Clink.

"Or follow me." I turn around, not waiting to see if she follows. She will.

Not only did she come over here with one intention, but she's also not the type who gives up, not even if she has to make compromises.

I'm the one who's supposed to push her away, not offer her an internship or even invite her to my office.

This is my focus zone, after all, and having her in it will fuck everything up. But it's not like she disappears from my mind when she's out of sight.

Whoever said that is a fucking moron.

Besides, either she's with me or with someone else. And there's no way in fuck I was going to let her be with Knox, Daniel, or even Sebastian.

I've been hit by the same haze that took over me when Aspen told me that my "wife" brought cupcakes and was talking with the three fuckers. Logical thoughts were the last thing on my mind when I barged in there. I knew she didn't like it when I refused the internship, but I didn't think she'd show up and negotiate her way into one.

Behind my back.

I'm well aware of her half-jogging behind me as I march to my office, but I don't look at her. I'm charged up enough as it is without being distracted by the sight of her.

If I had enough decency, I would slow down and let her catch up, but that term doesn't fucking exist in my dictionary.

As soon as we're inside, I shut the door, lean against it, and face her.

Gwyneth stands in the middle of the office, catching her breath. But then she glares at me with her arms crossed over her chest. "I don't want to intern with you."

"Good thing you don't have a say in it."

"But you said no the other time. What made you change your mind?"

Her going to someone else.

Knox's hand on her.

The fucking cupcakes she brought.

Any. All.

"Why do you want to intern here?" I ask instead of answering her question.

"I want the experience."

"Why now?"

"It's summer and pre-law students intern during the summer."

"That's all?"

"And…to keep busy, okay? I can't afford to feel empty right now, so don't stop me from doing this."

It's about Kingsley. *Fuck.*

I should've known that the happy façade she puts on in front of Martha and the world is just that. A façade. A disguise to hide what she's feeling inside.

She's excellent at that. Hiding. Whether physically or emotionally. Especially when it comes to the emotional pain, because she's far more open in other areas.

I push off the door and approach her slowly. I don't miss the way her eyes widen a little or how she watches my every move. She does it all the time back at the house, which is one more reason why I keep my fucking distance.

"Why didn't you say that when you first talked to me about the internship? When asking for something, you're supposed to back it up with all the right arguments."

"You didn't really give me a chance. You said no, and that's final. And the discussion is over. Your three favorite expressions, remember?"

"Watch the tone, Gwyneth."

"I'm sure Knox wouldn't mind it if you just let me intern with him."

"That's out of the question and that's final."

"See? You said it again! It's final this and final that. I'm not a robot, you know. There's this little thing called emotions, and I'm not desensitized to them. I don't have that word on my negative list."

"Your what?"

"It's a thing. You don't need to know about it." Then she mutters under her breath, "Maybe I should add you to the list."

"Are you calling me names, Gwyneth?"

She fakes an innocent smile. "I can't do that to my new boss."

"How about your husband?"

Her lips fall open again, and I revel in that, probably more than I should.

I love taking her off guard, making her bothered in her own fucking skin. It's a small taste of what she does all the time.

"I can call you names," she whispers.

"Such as Uncle Nate?"

"That was because I wanted to…"

"What? Get attention? Provoke me? What exactly were you thinking about?"

"I don't know."

"I'll call you kiddo until you figure it out then."

"Not that! I…just wanted to provoke you, I think."

"Will you be repeating it?"

"No."

"Good, or else you'll be back to being kiddo."

Her lips part again and a bright fucking light shines in her gaze. But instead of focusing on the happiness she's projecting in waves, on how pleased she is about not being a kiddo anymore, I march to my desk, retrieve a thick case file, and push it at her chest.

"Go through the previous case records and find me something I can use."

She remains there, fingers wrapped around the file. "That's all?"

"What else should there be? You asked for an internship and this is it. I won't take it easy on you, Gwyneth. In fact, it'll just get more difficult going forward. So if you don't have the will to go through this, walk away now."

"I can do it. I *will* do it."

"If you say so."

"You don't believe me?"

"I don't believe things I don't see."

"You're so cynical, you know that?"

"And you're still standing here. Go work and behave."

Her hold on the file falters and I lean forward in case she drops it.

She bites her lower lip and I don't take my eyes off it, watching her wet it, her teeth nibbling on the plump cushion before she finally releases it. "B-behave?"

It's like we're playing a game of cat and mouse, and I don't think I have the will to stop where this game is going anymore.

Or maybe I lost control of it a while ago and I'm only just admitting it now.

Either way, this is heading in a dangerous fucking direction, and I'm letting it.

Because fuck this. Fuck whatever is left of my conscience. I've never had one anyway, so I might as well stop pretending it's there.

"Yes, Gwyneth. Behave or you'll pay."

FOURTEEN

Gwyneth

BEHAVE OR YOU'LL PAY.

Behave. Or. You. Will. Pay.

He can't say things like that and then walk away—or more like kick me out—because I have questions. Lots of them. How am I going to pay? Why? Where? When?

So many questions.

Like everything when it comes to Nate, I guess. And I don't know why I want to pay, or maybe I do know. Because I'm a masochist, in a way, and masochists like pain, especially when it's a result of something we've done.

I think that's why I kissed him back then, because my masochistic tendencies took hold of me and I couldn't escape them. And God forbid I tell Dad about them, because what would I say? Dad, I think I have masochistic tendencies toward your friend and I'm unable to stop them. Yeah, I wouldn't be able to look him in the eye again.

Anyway, because of what Nate said, I'm unable to focus on

the file. I read a few lines and then I go back to thinking about all the words he said to me.

Baby girl.

Behave.

Pay.

Oh, and truly fucked. That one is the most important.

They're just measly words, but they're digging beneath my skin and jamming themselves against my bones. Maybe I should make a list for them, too, like the negative words, because they're triggering something a lot worse than my empathetic reactions.

"Hey, new girl."

I lift my head abruptly and kind of bite my lip in the process. *Ow.*

But that's not the issue here. It's that someone called for me. I'm the only new girl in the intern area today and every single one of the other interns is avoiding me like the plague. That's what happens when they know I'm Kingsley Shaw's daughter. As in, the Shaw of Weaver & Shaw. They either kiss my ass or avoid me.

The ass-kissing isn't necessary now that they have the internship and my dad is out of the picture. It's the first time I'm glad no one knows about my marriage to Nate. That could get too complicated too fast.

Anyhow, the partners like me, but the interns don't. I think they may even hate me because they don't think I've worked as hard as they have to get the internship.

Try impressing Nate, assholes.

So being called out of nowhere and referred to as "new girl" instead of Ms. Shaw is coming out of left field. I look up and find the person behind the name-calling. A short woman who's wearing khaki slacks and a shirt that are both maybe a few sizes too big. Her thick, black hair frames her small face and she's wearing black-framed glasses. She must have bad eyesight, because I can barely see her eyes—they look like tiny brown dots.

And she's looming over my desk, even though her height doesn't really give her that luxury. Her aura does, though. It's dark, like pitch-black. And her poker face doesn't help.

"You called for me?" I ask.

"Yes. Follow me."

"To where?"

"Less talking and more working, would you?"

I want to ask her who she is, but she's already walking away and I have no choice but to go after her. What's with people telling me to follow them today?

We take the elevator to the IT department. I squint, absolutely clueless about all the machines and things lying around. Jeez. If I get lost in this place, I'll never find my way out.

There are a few guys typing away and staring at a million screens. I guess a big firm like W&S does need this much protection. I'm kind of impressed by their support work. The lawyers get all the credit, but without the IT techs, the firm will crumble.

The short girl leads me to a computer off to the side and sits in front of it, then motions at a chair beside her. "Sit down."

I do, still unsure about what's going on. Now that I study her closer, she looks younger than I thought. Maybe a few years older than me, but she's definitely in her twenties.

She retrieves a log and drops it on the table in front of me. Despite her outside demeanor, she has a very soft, feminine voice. "Help me sort through those case dates. I'm creating a chart."

"Uh, I think you got the wrong person. I'm interning for—"

She types away at rapid speed, her full attention on the screen. "I don't care who you intern for. You're interning, and that means you can help instead of daydreaming."

She saw me daydreaming. Yikes. That must be why she picked me.

"I'm a pre-law, though. I really don't know how I can help with IT."

"They teach you how to read in college, right? The time you've spent complaining could've been used to get some work done."

"Fine, you don't have to be so snarky." I open the log. "I'm Gwen. What's your name?"

"Jane. Now, work."

It's actually a lot more fun than I thought. I help her in making lists of cases by year and she makes charts for them that can be sorted alphabetically, by lawyer, by nature, by docket number, and even by judge.

And she does it so fast that I'm a little ashamed it took me hours to go through the files Nate gave me. It was the hostile looks from the other interns, maybe. Jane, however, makes me motivated to work.

"That is so beautiful." I motion at the result on the screen, but Jane doesn't even crack a smile, just continues on as if her fingers are fluid and all they know is the colorful keyboard.

"Doing needless things again, Plain Jane?" a guy with frameless glasses asks as he stands beside us. He's one of the techs who were sitting in front of the screens earlier.

His friend, who's wearing a tacky flannel shirt, joins him, laughing.

"I get bored when I finish my tasks earlier than you, boys," she says without looking at them, and I can tell it pisses them off, because they're not smiling anymore.

"Screw you," the flannel shirt guy says.

"You might want to pick your dignity up off the floor before you say that," I say. Standing up for injustice is instinct for me. No clue who I take after for that. It sure as hell isn't my dad, though, because he only believes in merciless justice. He thinks normal justice is weak and useless.

"And who the fuck are you?" frameless glasses guy asks.

I guess no one in IT really knows what's going on in the rest of W&S. Because all the junior associates and interns recognized me. Or, at least, most of them did.

I lift my chin. "Jane's friend."

"Whatever." He rolls his eyes and leaves.

"Assholes." I punch the air after them.

Jane's manic tapping stops for a second and she tilts her head to stare at me. It's a bit creepy with how her hair drops to one side as well. "Why did you say that?"

"Say what?"

"That I'm your friend."

"Because they were being jerks. I'm allergic to those." *Even though I married one.*

"I don't need you to stand up for me."

"Sorry, but I can't stay quiet when things like that happen."

"If you keep it up, you'll end up getting hurt one day."

"One day isn't today." I stand and twist my neck, then move my legs to get the blood circulating to my toes. "Let's go get lunch."

She opens a drawer and retrieves one of those sandwiches you get from the convenience store. "I have my lunch right here."

"That's not called lunch. Let's get a real one." I reach for it and she catches my hand so fast, I flinch.

"Don't touch my computer."

"I was going for the sandwich."

Her hold slowly eases from around my wrist. I massage the skin as it quickly turns red.

"Wow, you guys are super possessive of your computers, huh?"

She pushes her glasses back with the heel of her palm. "I'm sorry. I didn't mean to hurt you."

"It's fine." I grin, even though it does really hurt. It's as if she's a trained ninja. "Lunch?"

She pushes the button on her screen, making it go black, and begrudgingly stands up. I intertwine my arm with hers, and she looks at me funny, but she doesn't pull away as we head to the elevator and take it to the intern area.

"Do you like home-cooked food better? Because I can cook. I love it sometimes, though I love baking more. I brought cupcakes this morning, but I don't think there will be any left, because Daniel stole them all. Do you know him? He's funny and has a dreamy accent and dimples. Jeez, they shouldn't be legal. Anyway, I'll bring you new cupcakes tomorrow—"

"Hey."

"Yeah?"

"Lawyers aren't usually this chatty."

"But we're supposed to be. Talking is what wins cases, Jane."

"And here I thought it was actually studying law."

"Hey! Rude."

She lifts a shoulder as if she couldn't care less.

I can't help the smile that pulls my lips. "You're funny."

"I'm sarcastic. There's a difference."

"I'll go with funny." I grab my bag from my desk, trying to ignore the interns' cutting gazes. Jane doesn't even pay them any attention and keeps studying her black nails.

Soon after, we take the elevator to the parking garage. "Hey, Jane."

"What?"

"You really don't know who I am?"

"You said you were Gwen."

"Yeah, right." I don't know why I feel giddy because some-one actually doesn't associate me with Dad, the firm, or anything.

I'm just Gwen. And that's liberating.

The moment the elevator opens, my smile drops and so does my heart. Because Aspen is getting in Nate's car and she's smiling. No, she's laughing, and *he's* smiling.

Aspen is in Nate's car and she's happy and it's lunchtime.

But that's wrong.

Yes, I know they're close, but she's not supposed to be with him during lunch and be happy about it. Or maybe this is normal, but my head doesn't understand that logic right now.

I'm not thinking as I let my legs take over and start walking toward the car. The same car he picked me up in on our wedding day. The same car that Aspen shouldn't be getting into while she's all smiles like that.

But I'm late, because the car has already left the parking ga-rage. It's already out and I'm standing here, staring at the exit with the sound of the tires and Aspen's laugh echoing in my ears.

And I want to chop off my ears and feed them to the nearest dog.

"Gwen?"

I slowly look away from the exit to focus on Jane. For a second, I forgot she was there, that she almost saw me make a fool out of myself.

Because I shouldn't. I'm fine, right? It doesn't matter who Nate spends his lunch with or that he returns her smile or that she only laughs with him.

"Are you okay?" Jane runs a hand in front of my face. "You look like you're having a stroke."

"I'm fine. *Fiiiine*. Yeah, totally fine."

"You don't look fine. If you were a PC, I'd run a malware check. But I can't, so I'm lost here."

That earns a smile from me. "I don't think any malware checks can fix me or what I saw."

"What you saw? You mean Aspen?"

"You know her?"

"Who doesn't? She's the only woman around here with balls bigger than some men."

"So you *like* her?"

"Not specifically. But I like what she does. We need more women like her."

"I heard Kingsley Shaw hates her, like, loathes and despises her because she's witch." God, I'm stooping so low, even using Dad like this—sorry, Dad—but it's because of what I saw that I can't help it.

"I heard he's an egotistical jerk."

"Hey!" My voice cracks, feeling the jab on behalf of my father.

She lifts a shoulder. "All I'm saying is there are always two sides to every story. Just because Kingsley hates her doesn't mean she's bad. Besides, Nathaniel is more important and he likes her."

"He...doesn't."

"Of course, he does. I recently joined the firm and even I know that everyone is betting on when they'll get married."

They won't, because he's married to me. I want to shout that, but I can't. And what's the point anyway? When everyone at the firm believes that Nate and Aspen suit each other.

My opinion doesn't matter.

Then why does it feel like my heart is about to splinter into a million pieces?

My mood takes a sharp dive for the rest of the day.

Instead of working at my desk amid the hostility, I take the case files and hang with Jane. And by hang, I mean that I work while she types away at her computer.

All the time, I can't stop thinking about the scene I saw in the parking lot. The synergy between them, the laughs and smiles, and I clink my nails against each other so hard, I break one.

Then I accidentally get a paper cut and my thumb bleeds, and it's supposed to hurt, but I don't feel the pain. Because the real pain is banging on the walls of my ribcage.

So I review the case files. *All* of them. That's what I do when I'm stressed. I enter high-functioning mode.

And I needed to finish them so I could see him again. I couldn't just go to his office without having done my work. But now, I have.

So I reorganize the files and the Post-it Notes I made for each detail that could be used as a weakness, as well as my observations through some research I did myself and any advanced research I asked Jane to help with.

I'm feeling confident when I'm carrying them to his office. I did a great job.

My phone vibrates and I juggle the files in one hand and check the text with the other.

Chris: Hey, stranger.

I clink my nails under the papers. After everything that happened over the last couple of weeks, I kind of ghosted my college friends, Chris included. He came by the house soon after Dad's accident and I told him I needed time to wrap my head around things.

And I did.

The result is that I can't keep dragging him into my mess anymore. I guess I was just too hopeful when I thought he could make me forget.

I realize now that no one can.

So I type with one hand.

Me: Hey! Sorry I haven't been around.

Chris: And here I thought you forgot about me.

Me: I haven't. We need to talk.

Chris: Now?

Me: In a bit.

Chris: Where are you? I'll pick you up.

Me: I'll send you the address.

He really doesn't need to since I have my car, but I forget all about that because I'm in front of Nate's office and I have all the work done.

So I send him my current location and hide the phone.

"Miss Shaw," Nate's assistant, Grace, greets me. She's a middle-aged woman with a kind smile that I've always found heartwarming.

"Is Nate in there? I finished the case files and I think I have solid footing on some weaknesses."

"He went home for the day."

"He...what?"

"He went out for lunch and said he wouldn't be coming back for the rest of the day. I'll hand them to him tomorrow morning."

The world starts spinning and it takes superhuman control to place the files on Grace's desk.

I didn't hear it wrong.

Nate went out to lunch and called it a day.

With Aspen.

He's been with Aspen all this time.

The shards that splintered in my chest earlier are digging their way into my heart and I can't fucking breathe.

But I have to. I need to breathe.

So I go outside to do just that.

FIFTEEN

Gwyneth

"**A**RE YOU LISTENING, GWEN?"

I slide my attention from my assaulted vanilla milkshake that I've been jamming the straw in and out of to Chris, who's staring at me with a furrowed brow.

He came to pick me up earlier and we've been sitting in a coffee shop and talking. Well, he's ended up doing all the talking while I've been thinking about other things.

Like what was Nate doing with Aspen the entire afternoon?

For hours.

Alone.

She didn't even leave in her car.

Logically, I shouldn't be this affected, because I have no hold on him, right? Except maybe I do. After all, there's a marriage certificate that says he's married to me, and it should go without saying that he doesn't leave with a woman who isn't me.

It's only on paper. The marriage isn't real.

"Are you still upset about your dad?" Chris tries again.

He's such a gentleman. Like the best ever, and he's hot, too, with his leather jacket, medium-length hair, and his pouty lips that are good at kissing.

But I don't think kissing should feel good. There needs to be a shattering quality to it. Maybe something like the feeling that's now taking asylum in my chest.

It's supposed to hurt. To tear someone from the inside out and make them bleed out.

But is being hurt and shredded to pieces the correct thing to do?

Maybe Nate's right. Maybe safe is what I should choose. Because who wants to be ripped apart with no hopes of ever pulling themselves together again?

Me, apparently, because the longer I stare at Chris, the surer I am that he isn't who will give me what I wish for.

"It's not about Dad." I stare at my milkshake, following the swirl of my straw before looking up at him. "I'm sorry, Chris."

"For what?"

"For leading you on. I promise I didn't mean to, but…"

"You're just not that into me, huh?"

I wince.

"It's okay, though my pride is a bit wounded. Now, I think Jen is right and you used me for the Harley."

"If it's any consolation, I think you're perfect."

"Just not perfect for you?"

"Yeah, I guess. If I weren't crazy, I would've chosen you."

"It's because you're a little crazy that I like you, Gwen. People who don't appreciate that about you don't deserve you."

"They don't?"

"Nope and you need to cut them off from your life."

"But what if I can't? What if they already made a snuggly place for themselves in there and it's impossible to find them, let alone remove them?"

He relaxes back in his seat, crossing one ankle over the other, and takes a sip of his iced coffee. His favorite drink is similar to his personality—cool, delicious, and definitely soothing. "I guess that means you're in too deep."

"Nope, no. You're supposed to tell me I should find a way to push them away, even if I'll get hurt in the process."

He tilts his head to the side. "Why do you have to get hurt in the process? If anyone should be in pain, it's them."

"I don't like that—hurting people, I mean. I feel horrible doing it to you."

"Never mind me. I'll just be your practice, babe. Now, tell me, who's the asshole?"

"You…don't know him."

Of course, he does.

Everyone in the country knows about the Weavers and their power. Besides, Chris studies pre-law, so he's more than aware of W&S.

But I'm a coward, okay? I don't want him to judge me for being so hopelessly and stupidly into Dad's best friend. I usually wouldn't care, but Chris is special. He likes my weirdness, and people like him are keepers. I don't want him to run for the hills because I'm upset that someone who's way older than me is out with someone more suitable. Someone close to his age and who works with him.

I scoff, slurping half of the milkshake without the straw to soothe my burning throat.

"Whoever he is, he's a jerk who doesn't deserve your time."

"Yeah, he's a fucking asshole."

"A motherfucker."

"A cold bastard with no feelings."

"Get it off your chest, Gwen."

"And…and he's never even stopped to ask me things, you know, even though I've learned everything about him. He thinks I'm a kid, because he likes to remind me that I'm *young*. He likes bringing up the age part because I can't fight it. So he's like the biggest jerk to ever exist and I hate him sometimes. I wish I could hate him all the time."

Chris smiles a little. "It'll take practice, but you'll get there."

I sigh, feeling a little relieved after my outburst. "Thanks for listening to me blabber even though I was a bitch to you."

"You were never a bitch, Gwen. You gave enough signs to push me away, but I wanted to stay close. It's my choice and I still stand by it."

"You still want to be friends?"

"Of course. Besides, you're stuck with me for the summer."

"What?"

"I got accepted for an internship at W&S."

"Oh my God, Chris! Why didn't you tell me?"

"I just did." He grins in that charming, lighthearted way and I'm so happy for that. I'm happy that I didn't hurt him to the point of taking away his beautiful smile.

"I'm so glad we get to spend time together."

"I thought you'd be all over getting rid of me."

"Of course not! We can be friends, right?"

He clinks his iced coffee against my drink. "Sure thing."

We fall into an easy conversation, which isn't anything new. Chris and I have always gotten along, which is why he asked me out, saying he wanted to take it to the next level. That obviously didn't work, so I'm thankful that we can still have a friendly relationship.

We talk about college and exams and where our colleagues are doing their internships. He tells me about the interviewing process at W&S and how hard it was, but he passed because he impressed them and he's a genius.

It's great to know that I won't be a lonely face in the midst of all the hostile interns. With Chris around, I'll have a more tolerable summer.

We go shopping for a few suits since he can't just show up in his leather jacket, though it's a killer look. Then I end up buying a few things for myself. I lose track of time in all the shopping we do, but I don't mind.

Being preoccupied is nice. I'm the type who shouldn't be given too much free time, because it'll all be spent on overthinking until I drive myself insane.

By the time Chris drops me off at home, it's late. I take a few moments to pull my pencil skirt down my thighs. I had to hitch it up so that I could ride behind him, and used the bags to cover up. Apparently, pencil skirts and Harleys aren't best friends.

My hair is enemies with the helmet, too, because it gets stuck inside it. For the third time today.

"Stupid hair." I groan as I struggle to untangle it without ripping it from the roots.

Chris chuckles and slides down from his bike to take over the task. He's gentler than I am and manages to remove the helmet without pulling out my hair.

"You're supposed to be patient, Gwen."

"Isn't that another word for boring?"

He shakes his head as he smooths down my hair.

"Thanks, Chris. For everything."

He wraps his arms around me. "I've got you."

I hug him back. "Now I'm feeling like I'm using you."

"I'm the one who's using you so that you'll give me a permanent job when you own W&S."

I push back, laughing. "They'll be lucky to have you."

"I'm holding you to that." He ruffles my hair before he hops on his bike. The sound of the revving engine echoes in the air as he leaves, and I remain there, waving, until he disappears out of sight.

Then I tiptoe to the entrance because Dad will totally have my ass for being late and riding on a bike.

My shoulders hunch when I open the front door.

Right. Dad isn't here anymore. I think I'm still in denial about it all, because every day, I wake up thinking I'll find him in the kitchen or that he'll be banging on my door, telling me I'm late for school.

In my mind, my dad's still here. He'll come back, because that's what dads do. They stay.

They don't leave like moms do.

My dad won't abandon me like she did.

"What time is it?"

I jump, letting the bags fall from my fingers and hit the ground with a resounding thud.

The entry hall is dark aside from the garden lights slipping through the windows. But some of it is camouflaged by a tall, broad figure who's standing there, blocking the soft hues, massacring and turning them into a shadow.

I can't see his features clearly, but I can feel the harshness in them. It's hanging in the air and shooting imaginary daggers at my chest.

"I asked what time is it, Gwyneth."

My spine jerks in a line at the cold edge of his voice and the blunt authority in it. He's always been firm, stern, but this is the first time it's sounded so angry, and that pushes me to talk.

"Uh, eleven, I think."

"You think? Is that the best reply you can come up with after disappearing, not answering your phone, and returning on the back of a fucking bike?"

"You called me?" I reach into my bag that's in the middle of all the shopping items and rummage through it until I find my phone.

Sure enough, there are three missed calls from Nate.

"It was on silent mode," I say slowly, and it sounds like a lame excuse.

"What did I say about answering your phone?"

"I was working and forgot to turn it back on…"

"Answer the fucking question, Gwyneth."

The force of his anger slams straight into mine, dragging it out in all of its chaotic glory.

You know what? *Fuck him.*

He doesn't get to talk to me this way after he was the one who hurt me. So what if I wanted to forget about him for a few hours by hanging out with a friend? Why is he trying to make me feel guilty about that?

I raise my chin. "You don't get to tell me what to do, okay? I can choose not to answer my phone and to go out on a bike and come back late and you have no say in it. You're not my dad, Nate!"

The silence that falls between us is deafening and that makes me hyperaware of the sound of my own breathing, of the pulsing in my neck and the thundering in my chest.

The pause stretches for so long that I don't think it'll ever end. Or maybe I'm just imagining things and it's only been a few seconds.

Nate strides toward me, the sound of his footsteps is sure and strong and I can almost hear them stomping on something inside me. I don't realize I'm moving back until my sneakers skid on the floor, because holy shit, how can I be so equally terrified and excited at the same time?

I think the fear part wins, because the shadows on his face keep multiplying with each passing second.

I squeal when my back hits something. It's only a wall, but I'm so rattled that I'm sucking in air through my nostrils, which makes me breathe in his spicy, woodsy scent.

He's close.

So close that I have to stare up at his punishing dark eyes.

"W-what are you doing?" I don't mean to stutter or speak in such an airy voice, I really don't, but he's kind of robbed something from me.

Because he's a thief. All he does is steal things from me.

First, my respect.

Then my girlhood dreams.

And now, he's coming after my body.

"From now on, I'll have a say in it."

"In...what?"

"The curfew. Answering your damn phone. Not getting on the back of a fucking kid's bike."

"You...can't. You're not my dad."

"No, but I am your husband."

"On paper, remember? No touching, remember? It'll be all

over when I'm twenty-one. Do you remember all of those? Because I do. And this marriage means nothing."

There's a tic in his jaw. It's small and barely-there, but I notice it because I notice everything about him. It's my only superpower.

"It means nothing, huh?" He draws out the words, speaking slowly, but it's downright menacing.

"Yeah, nothing."

"Is that why you pulled up your skirt and hopped on the back of a bike with a kid? Because it means nothing?"

"Chris is not a kid, okay? And he can drive that Harley like nobody's business. That's what it's called, by the way, a Harley, not some normal bike."

"And why did you get on that not-some-normal bike?"

I cross my arms over my chest. "None of your business."

"Watch your fucking tone. Don't go on the defensive in front of me or I promise it'll end ugly—for you, not me. So drop the attitude and your fucking arms."

I don't want to, I really don't, but my arms seem to have a mind of their own as they fall limply to my sides.

"I don't see why you should care who gives me a ride or who I spend my time with."

"Is he your boyfriend?"

The question catches me off guard, or the tone does. It's calm but with a deep, nefarious undertone that makes me curl my toes in my white sneakers.

"What if he is?" I feign nonchalance.

"Answer the question. Is he?"

"I'm not allowed to have one? I'm twenty, you know, and that means I have crushes, boyfriends, and urges. It means I go out and ride motorcycles and do whatever the hell I wish."

"What type of urges?"

"Huh?"

"You said you have crushes, boyfriends, and urges. What are the urges?"

Shit. Of course he'd focus on that part of my word vomit. I

EMPIRE OF DESIRE | 133

should backpedal, pretend it means nothing, but I'm feeling extra ballsy. I feel like being extra bad.

Maybe it'll hurt worse afterward, but I don't care. The pain is worth it sometimes.

"Sexual urges," I whisper in a breathy voice that surprises me.

Apparently, it surprises Nate, too, or maybe my words do, because he goes so tight, I think he's going to auto-combust or something.

Even his voice is as stiff as the rest of him. "Sexual urges like what?"

"You know."

"I don't know. Tell me, Gwyneth, what are the sexual urges you need the not-some-normal bike kid for?"

"K-kissing, for starters."

"Kissing."

"Yeah, with tongue and groping."

"And?"

I can feel the fire spreading all over my neck and ears, but I don't stop. I can't. "Then he'd finger me."

"How?"

"Huh?"

"How would he do it? Would his fingers be deep inside you, making you all full?"

Holy shit. I am now. All full, I mean, and it only took his words. They're not really words anymore. They've gained a dimension and are now living inside me, touching me, making me all stuffed with him.

"Yeah...and they feel so good, too."

"They do, huh?"

Everything in me clenches—my chest, my stomach, and my pussy. It's clenching so hard, as if I'm trying to keep his fingers there.

"How good?" The rigidness in his voice and posture doesn't go away. He sounds like he's on the verge of something. What, I have no clue.

"Very."

"Describe it."

"I…can't."

"Why not?"

"Because I can only feel it. And that only happens in the moment." This moment, apparently, because I'm so hot and bothered, I'd only need to touch myself for a few seconds to get my much-needed relief.

"Show me then."

My head whips up so fast, it hits the wall. But I don't feel the pain, because his words are still swirling around my head.

"What did you just say?"

I don't get to see his face or focus on his reaction, because my feet give out and the world turns upside down. No, it's not my feet or the world. It's him as he picks me up and throws me over his shoulder.

"You'll show me all those sexual urges. Now."

SIXTEEN

Gwyneth

GRAVITY SEEMS TO HAVE LEFT THE BUILDING.

Or maybe it's my sanity.

Maybe it's both.

Because I don't feel either of them—neither gravity nor my sanity. I'm floating on air and unable to land.

Or more accurately, I'm floating on Nate's shoulder. His broad shoulder that I've always looked at and might have dreamt about touching it, but not with my stomach. I wasn't that crazy.

Apparently, I am now, though, because that's all I can think about—my stomach on his shoulder. Okay, that's a lie. I'm thinking about a lot of things, like how his strong arm is looped around my calves and the way my head is hitting his powerful back with each step up the stairs.

He's carrying me like I'm a weightless feather. The effortlessness of the act does things to me. His strength. His brutishness. His domination.

All of it.

And I soak it in, allow it to tear me open and seep inside me. Isn't that what masochists do? Not only do we seek the pain, but we also wallow in it and allow it to grow roots so deep, it's impossible to dissociate from it.

I don't even stop to think about the blood that's rushing to my head or how my eyes feel like they'll pop out of my skull. I should probably close them, but if I do, I'll miss what's happening. No, thanks.

Before long, however, I'm forced out of the brief phase of hanging between the loss of gravity and sanity.

And he's the one who yanks me out.

Just like he did earlier when he pulled the ground from beneath my feet.

He returns it now by throwing me on the bed not so gently, because he doesn't do gentle. Actually, Nate is the furthest thing from gentle. He's coarse and harsh and strict.

So damn strict that my thighs clench in remembrance of his authoritarian, lusty questions from when he trapped me against the wall.

He's trapping me again now, but not with his body. It's his eyes that do the job and they're even more severe than earlier.

They're dark now.

So dark that I think they'll turn into a black hole and suck me in.

I should be scared at the thought of being stuck in a bottomless well, especially since my empty brain pulls that move on me sometimes. But I'm a bit crazy, just like Chris said, and all I can think about is how it'll look in there. In Nate's eyes that are as strict as he is. As authoritative as his voice without him having to use it.

I wonder how it would feel, too. Maybe it will be not-so-gentle, like when he threw me on the bed, or maybe it'll be effortless and sudden, like when he carried me over his shoulder.

And I think he'll do just that when he moves his hand. I think he'll reach for me and suck me into his darkness. But he doesn't. He just places a hand in his pocket and leans against the wall. My vanilla-orchid-and-roses wallpaper looks so girly when his broad shoulders rest against it.

My whole room with its fluffy bedsheets and endless pillows is suddenly so small and suffocating. It's the first time he's been in here and he's managed to steal the entire atmosphere.

Just like he's stolen everything else.

"Show me."

"W-what?"

"What you mentioned earlier, Gwyneth. I want to see what it's like when you have sexual urges."

My cheeks must be flushed a deep shade of red, or maybe my entire body is. Talking about it is one thing, but action is something else completely.

Besides, this is Nate. I...I've never been remotely naked or in such a position around Nate.

I'm leaning back on my elbows with my legs outstretched in front of me—in his direct view—and it feels so different, new, and wrong.

Yet it's right at the same time.

It's the rightest thing I've felt in a while.

"Didn't you say you have urges, plural, and that you need fingers inside you to feel full?"

I gulp. Shit.

I think hearing Nate's dirty talk is going to cause me to have a heart attack and then they'll write his name as the cause of death on my tombstone.

"Answer the question, Gwyneth. Didn't you say that?"

"Yeah."

"You also said it's in the moment and you can't describe it."

"I did."

"Then open your legs and show me."

My elbows can barely hold me up anymore from how much they're shaking, how much my pussy is tingling from his words and the command in them.

But I'm helpless in front of that dominance, so while I remain on one elbow, I reach the other hand to the zipper of my skirt and pull it down as I tremble uncontrollably. Then I fumble to kick it down my legs that are so hot and sensitive that I can feel the sheet scraping against them.

I let my thighs fall open, exposing my vanilla-colored panties. They're lace and see-through and so soaked that another wave of heat covers my body when I realize he can see it.

He can see the arousal and the stickiness.

This is different from anything I've experienced before. Because he's looking at me.

He's looking at my wet panties and my shaking legs and my fingers that are sneaking beneath the lace. But he's not only looking. His nostrils are flaring, too, and the veins in his hand that's at his side appear to be more defined and masculine. The thought of that same hand on me, touching me, nearly drives me to the edge.

My nipples harden and push against my bra and shirt, making them ache, but not as much as where my fingers are heading. That's where it hurts the most, because his eyes are there.

So I sink my fingers between my folds, using him as an anchor. And it feels different with him watching like I'm building up an explosion, not an orgasm.

But my hand is too soft and it's not enough, even when I twist my clit and roll my hips.

I think it's because he's there and he's watching with his jaw set in a line. Although I want him to watch me, to see me, so what's wrong?

I can't reach that peak, no matter how much I try, and it's not due to my lack of arousal, because I'm so soaked that there are probably wet spots on the sheet.

"What's wrong, baby girl? Having trouble?"

My fingers pause at that. *Baby girl.*

I think I became wetter, too, but that might be because he's pushed off the wall and is stalking toward me. And it's downright stalking, with his shoulders squared and his steps slow and measured.

And I can't help feeling the sensation that I'm the prey who caught the attention of the big, bad wolf, but unlike in the fairy tale, I won't be able to escape.

Damn how beautiful he is. And it's not only about his face that seems to be cut from solid marble or his physique that could crush me as effortlessly as he carried me. It's about everything else. It's about the masculinity that oozes from each of his movements. It's about that delicious authoritativeness that I can't get enough of.

Before I can think of anything to say to make him call me "baby girl" again, he does something.

He gets on his knees. At the foot of the bed. In direct view of the apex of my thighs.

My hand freezes, and I don't realize it until he motions at it. "You can't get yourself off?"

"I…can."

"Doesn't seem like it."

"I do…usually."

"Not today, apparently." He reaches a hand to where my panties meet my hip and I stop breathing when it makes contact. When his skin kisses mine and then drags them down my thighs.

They're in his hands now, my lace panties that I'm thankful I chose this morning.

And then they're in his pocket. Not on the floor, not somewhere no one would care about. They're with him.

"Open your legs wide. Let me see."

My fingers tremble on my folds and I do as he tells me, parting my thighs, letting him observe how drenched I am because he's been watching me.

He grabs my ankle and pulls. My elbow gives out, and I squeal when my back hits the mattress as he drags me to the foot of the bed. But that's not all.

My legs are on his shoulders. They're hanging loosely on those broad, hard shoulders and he's so close that I'm intoxicated with his scent. I feel like those spices from his scent now, hot and tingly and unable to cool down, even if there was water.

"Did I say you could remove your hand from your pussy, Gwyneth?"

It's then I realize my hand has fallen to the side. "No."

"No, I didn't, and that means you put it back in and you don't remove it until I say so."

God. Why the hell does he sound so hot when he's dishing out orders as if this were a war and I'm a soldier in his battalion?

Because there's something else his orders do. They make me even hotter with a chance of melting right beneath his gaze.

When I take my time to comply with his order, he grabs my hand and places it back on my core. I'm burning now, blushing something furious beneath his touch. But it doesn't end there, because he jams my middle finger inside me.

Just like that.

Like he's had the right to do that for a long time. My back arches off the bed and I bite my lower lip to keep from moaning or screaming like a whore.

But maybe that's what I am right now.

I'm a whore in his hands, and all I want is more.

"Is this how it felt inside? With his fingers filling you?"

"There needs to be another one for them to be fingers. Now it's just one finger," I breathe out, trying to be as coherent as possible to not make a fool out of myself.

"The fucking talking back." He grabs my other finger and I'm ready for the intrusion. It's the only way I'm able to get myself off. Two fingers and teasing my clit."

I can't help staring down at where his hooded eyes are focused on how he's still holding my hand.

But it's not my finger that enters me. This one is thicker, harder, and makes me gasp.

It's inside me now, his middle finger, and it's stroking mine that's also in there. The friction is strange and unbearable and so damn new that I nearly black out.

"Oh, God…"

"Is this how full it felt, baby girl?"

Stroke.

Up.

Down.

Thrust.

"Or was it less satisfying because you couldn't feel his limp fingers?"

He sounds angry, but I can't focus on that, because there's a fire consuming me from the inside and it is so wild and big that I can't breathe.

Any attempts of sucking in oxygen vanish when he slips another finger—his, not mine—into my tight channel. Both of his fingers imprison mine and he moves the three of them in a maddening rhythm. The friction builds hard and fast and *rough*. I can feel it deep inside me and I want to throw up or maybe I want to come, because I think that's what the shaking means.

"Or perhaps it's full like this. So full that you want to burst."

"Yes, oh, fuck…"

"Tsk. Language."

"Oh, please. As if you don't say it yourself."

"Are you sure you want to talk back to me when I can leave you unsatisfied?"

"No, no…please…please…"

I'm almost there, I can feel it deep inside me. The more he strokes and curls his fingers, the more he spreads my inner juices over our fingers.

He pumps them in me and I'm clenching him—us—in a choke-like hold.

"Fuck. Do you feel how your tight pussy is strangling me?"

"Yeah…"

He groans deep in his throat and it does things to me, things like making me tighten around him harder, swallowing him deeper.

And I can't help moaning. I don't have the space of mind to control it or the rest of the sounds that come out of me.

I'm a mess of chaotic emotions and sensations, and there's no way I can mute myself anymore.

"Is it because it feels full?"

"Yeah, full and good and…and…I'm…"

"And you're what?" He pumps harder faster, pressing the heel of my palm against my clit.

The sureness in his movements, the pure dominance of it, drags me under in one swift movement.

"I'm coming!"

I clench around him the hardest yet as that wave crashes into me. The orgasm is neither gentle nor soft. It's callous and demanding, just like him. My legs shake over his shoulders and my head is a fog of mixed emotions—emotions I can't get hold of, so I let them swirl around me like a halo.

Or maybe I'm the one in the halo, floating in a dreamless land where everything feels so good.

After what seems like forever, I'm brought back to the present, suddenly and without warning, when he removes the fingers from inside me—his and mine. And I grab onto him, not wanting to let him or this feeling go.

What if this is a dream and I'll never feel this way again? What if I'll wake up and never find my way back?

But his next words erase any misconception I had about how real this is. "From now on, if you have any sexual urges, I'll be the only one who satisfies them."

SEVENTEEN

Nathaniel

A MISTAKE.

That's what it should be.

Every second from the moment she walked inside and I lost my fucking cool to when she detonated in my hold as if she's waited her entire life for me to come along.

As if she's been saving up for me, for the moment she'd explode all around me, strangle my fingers, and refuse to let them go.

And it all started with when I saw her hopping off the kid's motorcycle. Her lips were red and her hair was blown by the wind and she was smiling. Wide.

I should've looked the other way and kept my distance, as usual—that's what I've done ever since I moved in. I make sure she has everything she needs from afar. Like her stock of vanilla ice cream, her milkshakes—vanilla again—and her favorite fruit, bananas, just because there isn't a version of vanilla fruit.

Martha has specific orders to let me know when those things run out so one of us can take care of getting more.

It's all because of Kingsley, I told myself. If it were him, he would've made sure she had her comfort food if she was feeling down.

In my head, I used that excuse again when I stood there in the middle of the fucking darkness and watched her knee-length skirt barely covering her ass because she was on a *not-some-normal* bike, clinging to the kid.

The safe, *boring* kid that she said she didn't fucking want but was with him anyway.

Then he had his hands on her, touching her hair, pulling her to him, and hugging her. And I was about to go out there, using King as an excuse again, since I know for a fact that he hates it when she rides on a motorcycle. He was anal about removing anything dangerous from her life.

But fuck that, it wasn't because of King.

It was because of me.

A grown man thought about beating up a kid. It was as bad as that and I had to take a moment to not act out on the thought.

And that's when she came inside. Everything after that was a chain of events. As illogical as they were, they just came together naturally.

I've never liked anything as illogical as when she was moaning the house down because her tight pussy could barely take in my fingers. The thought of my dick inside that narrow opening has been plaguing me since I left her room as she watched me with those droopy chameleon eyes that were mostly green.

That's how they look when she's aroused. When she's talking about fingers and being full and fucking urges.

Sexual. Plural.

And now I'm having urges myself, but they're not sexual. They're violent, like when I saw her climbing off the bastard's bike.

Because she's with him right now.

The reason she left early this morning, without having breakfast, is because she was eager to get to the firm and meet with him.

He somehow got an internship. *Somehow*, as in, I didn't even know he was applying at W&S. Though I should've seen it coming and offed him from the beginning.

Christoph is his name. And no, I don't make it my mission to know the name of every intern, but I needed to get this Christoph's file.

And yes, I might've wanted to find a loophole to kick him out of the program.

I study the files HR sent me while I stare at the intern area from my position around the corner.

Gwyneth and the not-some-normal bike kid are sitting together, bumping shoulders and laughing with one another.

I glare at the associate attorney who's supposed to scold them for slacking off. Or Knox—who took Christoph in, no surprise there—to tell his intern to get back to work.

Neither of those happen, obviously.

I stare back at Christoph's file and my jaw tightens with each piece of information I read. Grades, interview questions, and attendance are ticked high. *Extremely promising* is the note HR left about him.

Maybe I can send him to another branch and get rid of him, once and for all.

My conspiracies are put on a halt when my phone vibrates with a call, blocking my view of the email, and *Mrs. Weaver* flashes on the screen.

That's how Sebastian and I refer to Mom behind her back. She's the last person I want to talk to right now. Or ever.

As soon as I hit Ignore, she sends a text.

Mrs. Weaver: Did you just ignore me, Nathaniel?

Obviously.

Mrs. Weaver: You can play hard to get all you want, but I heard something alarming and I need confirmation before I break all hell loose. Call me back immediately.

Something alarming, as in, someone probably asked her if I'm gay. That's what her socialite friends spout off about me when I refuse to meet their prim and proper daughters. That I'm gay.

I ignore Mom and her shallow entourage. The thought of her and Dad brings forward nausea I've been trying to get rid of for fucking decades.

But Gwyneth and the not-some-normal bike kid are still talking and laughing. They're still trapped in their own world as if the rest of their surroundings don't exist.

So I pick up my phone and call her.

Her smile drops when she sees my name on the screen, and she swallows a few times before she picks up.

"Hello?"

"Have you finished the report I sent you this morning?"

"I'm getting there."

"Getting there doesn't mean it's done, Gwyneth."

"I'll be finished in a few."

"My office. Now." I hang up and take the elevator to the highest floor, then head to my office and sit behind my desk.

Soon after, there's a knock on the door before Gwyneth comes inside.

There's a slight blush on her face, probably from all the laughing with Christoph. The thought of him listening to the musical-like quality of her voice and the cheerfulness in it tightens my jaw and fills me with sudden yet potent rage.

She stops in the middle of the office and wipes her hand on her skirt. It's shorter today and her shirt is tighter with the first two buttons undone. But her white sneakers are still the same, as if she can't part with them.

And in a way, she can't. Ever since she started having a defined taste, her obsession with things slowly began to take shape, too. I remember the first time she had a milkshake, when she was three or something.

King and I were studying for our college exams in his small apartment that he moved into after high school. At that time, he shot himself in the foot by firing the thousandth sitter because he didn't trust them around her—not that he trusted anyone. As a result, he had to study, feed her, change her, and play with her.

Needless to say, I was dragged into it and had to indulge her so she'd stop fidgeting and being generally irritable. Not only was she especially demanding but she also refused to nap and give us a break.

"Stop whining and go to bed, Gwyneth," I scolded when she kept hanging onto King's leg.

Her chin trembled and she started crying so hard as if the world was ending. King gave me a dirty look, kicked me in the chin, then held his little princess and started comforting her.

She wouldn't stop fucking crying, though. Because she needed to sleep but refused to. Whenever I glared at her, she hid her face in her father's neck and clung to him as if he were a shield.

In search of a solution, I recalled that Sebastian liked stuffing his face with milk when he was younger, so I went to the kitchen to heat some but stopped. King did heat her a bottle, but it wasn't doing any good.

So I improvised and made a milkshake instead, then added a random flavor available—vanilla.

When I gave her the baby cup, she clung to King, sniffling like the most wronged person on earth.

"It's okay, Gwen, you can take it," King said in the nice voice that he only used with his daughter. "If Uncle Nate yells at you, I'll punch him in the face."

"No, Daddy," she whispered. "Don't hurt him."

I smiled at that and she returned it before carefully taking the cup. The moment she took her first sip, she froze, her eyes gleaming with all three colors before she grinned widely and finished it in record time.

Three minutes later, she was finally out and let us study properly.

It's crazy to think she's now a student herself, about our age back then.

Her gaze meets mine, still as bright and innocent as when she was a kid, though it's a bit sadder now. "You asked for me?"

"Why do you think I did?"

"Because of the report?"

"Correct. Why isn't it finished?"

"I'm still working on it."

"Are you sure you're doing that or are you flirting during work time?"

"I wasn't flirting."

I stand up and stride toward her. She visibly shudders, her cheeks turning a deep shade of red.

"What did I say yesterday?"

"W-what?"

"After you came all over my fingers, what did I say?" I extend a hand and she closes her eyes, her lips shaking before they press together, but I reach around her and click the door shut.

At that, she startles, her eyes opening and moving up to look at me. There's an expectation etched on her delicate features mixed with polar opposite uncertainty. She's always been a spectrum of wild, uncontained emotions.

"What did I say, Gwyneth?"

"That you will…take care of my sexual urges."

"And do you know what that means?"

She shakes her head slowly.

"It means you'll break up with that boyfriend, effective immediately. You'll stop flirting with him or getting on his bike."

Her lips tremble, but there's a fire in her eyes, the blue trying to overthrow the green and smother the gray. "No."

I grab her by the chin and use it to lift her head. "What the fuck did you just say to me?"

"I like the back of Chris's Harley and you're not going to take that away from me."

"You will end it and that's final."

"No."

"You don't want me to fucking make you, Gwyneth."

I can tell she's equal part scared and excited by the way she flinches a little.

"Do you want me to make you? Is that it?" My voice lowers

as I rake my gaze over her modest curves and those legs that have been over my shoulder not twenty-four hours ago.

She watches me intently but doesn't say anything, so I continue, "Do you want me to pound my fingers into that tight pussy of yours again until you scream? Or maybe I will use my cock this time and fuck you so thoroughly, you won't have the space of mind to think about any kid."

Her lips part open and she sucks in a sharp breath before she says, "If you want me to stop, then you stop as well."

"Stop what?"

"Picking up Aspen." She clinks her nails hard, the sound escalating with every second. "Stop smiling at her, flirting with her, all of it."

"What the hell are you talking about?"

"I saw you yesterday. You went out together for lunch and never came back."

"Because we had meetings with judges."

She scrunches her nose like she used to do whenever Martha made the mistake of not including her favorite drink with her meal. "I still don't like it—her in your car, I mean. So if you don't want me on the Harley, don't let her in your Mercedes."

I can't resist smiling at how she negotiates. She's all uptight and serious, too, making a mountain out of a molehill. All her assumptions about me and Aspen are unfounded, but I don't correct her, because she looks weirdly adorable right now.

"And then what?"

That catches her off guard, causing a frown to crease her forehead. "Then?"

"What happens after Aspen isn't in my car and you're not on the back of the bike?"

"I…don't know."

"Are you going to behave?"

I hear the sound of gulping as she stares up at me with wild eyes. "Should I?"

"Good girls do."

"But I'm not."

"You're not?"

"Yeah, I'm a bit crazy. You know, like when I kissed you that day. So I don't think I can be a good girl."

"No, you can't."

"I'm a bad girl, though."

Fuck me, the way she talks in that aroused tone makes my dick so hard, it's painful.

"You are?"

"Yeah."

"We have to do something about that. I can't have my wife and intern be a bad girl."

"I agree. You should do something."

I let go of her and her shoulders hunch, in disappointment, I believe, but she has no fucking idea what I have planned for her.

Because I crushed the last log of guilt I have and I'm going to swallow her, consume her until she realizes she shouldn't have messed with me in the first fucking place.

Until she regrets not choosing safe and boring.

I stride back to behind my desk, not missing the way her eyes follow me, then sit down and beckon her over. "Come here."

She approaches me slowly, like a scared kitten, but she isn't. Scared, that is. Not in the least.

Her eyes have brightened and her clinking has stopped.

I open my legs and tip my chin at the space between them and she complies, her cheeks hollowing with how she sucks on their insides. "What are you going to do to me?"

"I'm going to teach you to behave."

EIGHTEEN

Gwyneth

HE'LL TEACH ME HOW TO BEHAVE.

That's what he said. That's what I heard, and yet I still can't believe it.

I can't believe a lot of things since last night.

When I woke up this morning, I thought maybe, just maybe, it was all a dream and I was still stuck in it, but then I smelled him. Those notes of spice and woods lingered on my sheets and on me long after he left my bedroom.

So it couldn't have been a dream, because Nate never goes into my room. *Never.*

Oh, and my panties were missing. Yup. I slept all night without underwear and kept rubbing my thighs together in a desperate attempt to recreate the friction but failed miserably.

So I left early this morning because I didn't know what would happen if I saw him hovering over me at breakfast. That's what he does sometimes since he moved in. He hovers, leaning against the counter with his legs crossed at the ankles and drinking from his coffee until he makes sure I've eaten something. Because apparently, drinking my milkshake doesn't count as breakfast.

And I didn't want to be babied by him. I also didn't want to be faced with his strict features and punishing eyes or the fact that he might pretend nothing happened.

It would have killed me slowly, and I wasn't ready for the D-word yet. But here I am. Once again under his scrutiny, and he isn't pretending that nothing happened.

Hell, he even called me his wife. In his office. During working hours. And why is that so hot? Because I feel myself on the verge of hyperventilating even as I step between his thighs. His strong, powerful thighs that can squeeze and bend me with ease.

"And now what?" I breathe out.

That's how my voice becomes when he's so close that I can soak in his warmth, so close that I can see the line of his jaw and trace the contours of his face, with my gaze, of course, because I don't think I have the courage to touch him. Or if I'm allowed to. So I grip the desk behind me and lean against my hands so that I won't have the chance to act on that compulsion.

"Not a word, Gwyneth."

"Why?"

"You're a bad girl, right?"

"I am. So, so bad."

"Bad girls don't get to talk, so when I tell you to shut up, you do."

"Okay."

"You're still talking."

I purse my lips, leaning further into my hands until my knuckles dig into the hollow of my back. And it's tingling, my back or my spine, I'm not sure. The explosion of sensations is more than I can take or fathom.

"Now get on the desk." The order in his voice is coupled with the gradual darkening of his irises.

My limbs shake as I use my hands to hop onto the desk until

my feet are dangling and I can glance down and get a direct view of his erection.

Holy. Hell.

I hadn't noticed it earlier—I didn't get the chance when I was looking at his face—but now, there's no mistaking the bulge in his dark pants. And I can't take my eyes off of it. I can't focus on anything *but* it, not even on my shaking insides.

"Do you like what you see?"

"Yeah…" I say absentmindedly.

"Why do you like it?"

"Because you want me." The words leave me in a whoosh and my fractured breaths follow soon after when I finally meet his gaze.

A shadow crosses his face and a muscle tics in his jaw. The hardness in his expression robs me of air and leaves me heaving.

"I never thought you'd want me," I confess in a low voice, urging whatever upset him to go away. But it gets worse. The veins in his neck tighten and bulge and his chest muscles expand so wide that I think it'll explode out of his shirt and jacket.

"Who said I want you? Maybe I only want to play with you."

"You'd have to want me to want to play with me, Nate."

He narrows his eyes on me. "You're supposed to say you're not a toy and I shouldn't want to play with you."

I lift a shoulder. "I don't care."

"You don't?"

"A normal person probably would, but I'm a little weird and a very bad girl, so you can play with me all you want. I'll be your toy." At least that way he's not putting a thousand walls up between us.

That way, I can get close, even if only by sex. I'm fine with sex. I like the feelings it brings and the surrender of it all. And if what happened last night is any indication, sex with Nate will probably bulldoze through all my thoughts and expectations.

As if to prove that it'll go way different than I've fantasized, Nate reaches a hand to the waistband of my skirt and toys with the zipper, his thumb grazing my hipbone beneath my shirt. "You'll be my toy, huh?"

"Yeah."

"I can play with you?"

"You can."

"Do you let boys play with you often, Gwyneth?"

"Sometimes…"

He doesn't like that. He doesn't like it one bit, and that translates through the crowding tension in his shoulders and the way his touch turns from explorative to downright dominating. He grips me by the hip, hard, even though his tone is still calm. "You do, huh?"

"Uh…"

"Answer the question."

"Yeah."

I thought he was seeking confirmation of my earlier words, but his hold is tightening by the second. "What do you let them do?"

"I let them touch me, grope me, and take my nipples into their mouths." I'm not sure why I'm saying this, but I like how it drags out the harsh dominance from inside him, so I don't stop. "It feels good, when my nipples are between their teeth, when they're tugging and pulling and biting."

Still gripping me by the hip, he rips my shirt from inside my skirt and I jolt with the movement, sliding over his desk. I nearly squeal when his hand shoots up my bare stomach and beneath my bra.

When his thumb and forefinger grab hold of my nipple, my mouth falls open in a wordless whimper. He squeezes it, pressing his thumb on the tight bud that's been aching ever since he touched me yesterday.

"These felt good when the boys played with them, huh?"

"Uh-huh. They did."

He presses harder until pleasure pools between my thighs, and I clamp them shut in a helpless attempt to keep the wetness from leaking.

"Open your legs, Gwyneth."

"But…"

"*Open.*"

My pulse roars in my ears at the non-negotiable order and I do. I let my legs part, releasing the friction I've been fruitlessly attempting to keep there.

"Now place your feet on the desk, bend your knees, and keep your legs wide apart." With each order, he strokes and squeezes my nipple until I'm gasping for air.

But I do as I'm told, stretching my skirt up and opening my legs.

"Wider. Let me look at that pussy."

Holy shit.

I've never felt as exposed as I do when he's watching me intently, as if he didn't get a full view of me only last night. As if his fingers didn't wreak havoc inside me and leave me spent.

Still torturing my nipple, he reaches a hand up and cups me through my panties, and I shudder, head lolling to the side because I want to watch him watch me.

"Mmm. You're wet, baby girl."

"I am?"

"You are. Very, *very* wet." He slides his fingers up and down my folds, and even though it's only through the material, my pussy pulses with need.

"Nate…"

"Yes?"

"I need…I need…"

"What do you need? Tell me."

"More…just more."

"But you're a bad girl. You let boys touch you, grope you, put their hands on these nipples and this pussy, don't you?"

"I…won't anymore…"

"You won't, huh?"

"No."

"Why not?"

"Because I don't want them… I want you."

He stills at that, both his hands halting their assault for a fraction of a second, and I look at him then.

I wish I hadn't.

His expression knocks the living breath out of my lungs.

His jaw is clenched tight, but it's not with displeasure, it's with an emotion I've never seen on his face, or maybe he's never allowed me to see.

Possession. Raw and deep and so damn dangerous.

But instead of running away from it, I barge straight toward it. I bare my soul and body for it. I want it. His possessiveness.

I want every last drop of it.

"Fuck, Gwyneth. Since when did you learn to say shit like that?"

"Since you."

"Me?"

"Uh-huh. Because you made me want to be a woman."

"You wanted to be a woman for me?"

"Yeah."

"Why?"

"Because you'd touch me. You'd want me."

"That means these nipples belong to me, don't they?" He squeezes one roughly, sternly, and I whimper, but it breaks into a moan when he cups my core just as hard. "This pussy is mine, too. It's my pussy, isn't it?"

"Oh, fuck…"

"Language."

"Mmm."

"Answer me, Gwyneth. Whose pussy is this?"

"Yours."

"That's right. Mine. So why did you give it to someone else? Why did another fucker look at my pussy, let alone touch it?"

God. If he keeps talking this dirty, I might come here and now.

"Because you weren't there…you weren't touching me, so I had to let the boys do it, but you know what?"

"What?" He's pulling my panties down my legs, and I don't

focus on the trail of wetness that's coating my thighs. I don't focus on how shamelessly I'm drenching his fingers, because I'm preoccupied with something else.

His face holds me hostage. His beautiful, ethereal face that's been stealing my dreams since I started seeing him as a man.

I drop my voice, staring at him from beneath my lashes. "I was thinking about you the whole time they were touching me. I imagined your fingers inside me and your tongue licking me. Your hands were on me too, and they were so powerful and masculine that I can't stop thinking about them."

He pauses with my panties in his hand, his eyes turning a raging shade of delicious brown. "Fuck. You'll be the death of me."

"Is that a bad thing?"

"It's a fucking disaster."

"Will I pay for that too?"

"You fucking will." He lets go of my nipple and I release a noisy, disappointed sound at the loss of contact.

But I don't have to wait on his next move for long, because he stuffs my panties in his pocket—again—and pulls my legs wide, wider than I thought was possible while my feet are still planted on his desk. And then he yanks the hem of my skirt up and jams it in my mouth. "Bite and don't let go."

I do, my teeth digging into the black material, but I don't realize why he's telling me not to let go until he lowers his head.

Until his mouth is on my throbbing pussy. And holy shit, if I thought his fingers were weapons of mass pleasure, his mouth is in an entirely different league.

He laps his tongue over my wet folds, making them wetter, sloppier, and my head rolls so far back, I'm surprised it doesn't snap my neck. The pleasure is so damn strong that I can't focus on anything except for where his body meets mine.

Where he's closing his mouth on me and sucking *hard*. So hard that I'm shaking all over, so hard that I think he's exorcising my soul.

The skirt falls from my teeth. I can't help it. It just does. "Holy…shit…fuck…"

"What did I say about language?" He speaks against me and it's like a rumble on my oversensitive skin.

"I can't…can't control it."

"Because you're close?"

"Yeah." And because it's him. But I don't get to say that, because he sucks on something else.

My clit.

Holy shit. *Shit*!

The spasms take over me without warning and I'm falling. I'm falling so hard that I think it'll never stop.

The fall.

The pleasure.

The depravity of it all.

It does, though, leaving me in a haze, and I think it's over. But his stubble glides over the sensitive flesh of my thighs and he's still lapping at me, sucking, nibbling, torturing my sensitive clit.

For some reason, I'm so much more tender now than when he fingered me. And it hurts. It hurts so good.

"Nate…I can't…take it…" I reach a hand for his hair in an attempt to touch those strands, to push him back.

"Hands and feet on the desk, Gwyneth."

I snap back into position, even though my thighs are clenching and I feel like I'm being set on fire. "It's too much. I don't think I can take it."

He lifts his head from between my thighs and I'm a tiny bit disappointed, not sure why.

"Should I stop, baby girl?"

I don't even think about it as I shake my head.

"Good, because I wasn't planning to. Now bite the skirt before you bring the whole floor down."

Oh, God. I forgot that this is a workplace and someone could hear. Please tell me he has some type of soundproof system here, because I can't control the noises that spill free—even with the skirt between my lips—when he goes back to sucking and licking. But this time, it's different. This time, he's teaching me a lesson, he's teaching me how to behave.

So when his mouth slides to my opening, I'm on the verge again. But he doesn't stop there. He thrusts his tongue inside my tight opening, and it's so narrow, I can't believe it took three fingers in it only last night.

I'm a mumbling mess, my saliva pooling around my skirt as he fucks me with his tongue, in and out in a rhythm that turns me breathless and absolutely delirious.

If he fucks this way with his mouth, how will it feel with his cock? And the thought of his cock inside me makes me come.

Just like that, I'm spasming on the table, my legs falling and my heart lurching in my chest.

Nate continues sucking, licking, fucking, drawing out the wave over and over again until I'm on the verge of collapsing.

When he finally lifts his head from between my legs that have turned to Jell-O, I don't really focus on that, because he licks his lips. The same lips that were sucking and nibbling and fucking my pussy.

I'm entranced by that view, by the way he makes a show of how he ate me, how he's savoring me on his tongue. I'm unable to look away. Unable to even get air into my starved lungs.

"You do taste like a very bad girl."

Well, fuck.

I think something just left me and jumped to him. I don't know what that something is, but it feels important.

Vital.

And now, I can't get it back.

NINETEEN

Nathaniel

I'VE NEVER BEEN ONE TO PLAY GAMES.

They're a waste of time and lack purpose—something that fools do to feel cunning or important. That type of affirmation means absolutely nothing to me.

If anything, I'm the one who makes the games and sets the rules that everyone needs to follow.

So imagine my fucking surprise when I find myself dragged into a game I didn't sign up for. A game that shouldn't have existed in the first place.

I'm in the middle of it now. Right there where the game—Gwyneth—is.

You can play with me all you want. I'll be your toy.

Those mere words turned me into a fucking insatiable beast. I didn't only win her in the middle of the game, but I also had every right to play with her, torture her, torment her.

A week now. It's been a week since the day I broke my own

protocol and brought sex to my workplace. When I ate her out and tasted her sweet cunt.

I don't mix business with pleasure. *Ever.* It's unprofessional, bothersome, and fucking distracting.

Or that's what I thought before her, Gwyneth, my unwanted game. Because I sure as fuck didn't think about the risks when I told her to open her legs, then proceeded to have her for lunch.

And like an addict, the need for more kept multiplying with each day.

Now, I'm the one who seeks that fucking distraction.

I tell her to behave and she doesn't. Gwyneth *really* doesn't know how to. She'll either drop something and bend over to pick it up, putting her ass on display, or she'll flirt with Christoph.

We're only talking, she tells me. *We're friends and we talk. I wasn't flirting with him.* But fuck that, if she's laughing with him and he's the only intern she talks to, then it's fucking flirting.

So I call her into my office, bend her over the table and eat her out. Sometimes I finger her until she's screaming and writhing and begging. I love it when she begs, when her little body is so much at my mercy that she knows she won't be able to escape my wrath unless she begs.

Then when I get home, I go up to her room and have her for dinner. I teach her how she should behave at the firm, how she should be focused on her work, not on anything else. That she's not allowed to have lunches with Sebastian, Daniel, and Knox. Yes, one of them is my nephew, but still. She's too easygoing around them, too vibrant, too alive, and I fucking hate that.

I also hate that everyone seems to be expecting cupcakes from her now. She's been religiously bringing them to everyone, especially the IT girl and fucking Christoph.

She either stays up late or wakes up early to bake them while singing off-tune as Alexa plays her favorite band, Twenty One Pilots. She never told me they were her favorite, but she listens to them all the time, whether she's in the shower, baking, or helping Martha in the kitchen. Anytime, anywhere. They're her auditory vanilla milkshakes and ice cream, I now realize. They're what keeps her at peace, even though her peace is loud.

All of it is too much. From her and the music to her body language. Because she doesn't just sing and listen and bake, she dances, too, and it's as off-rhythm as her off-pitch voice.

Gwyneth is a loud person when she's alone. So loud that it's hard to tune her out. So loud that she interrupts my violent silence. I used to prefer that simple nothingness, the lack of sounds, and the clearance of mind that helps me concentrate and work, but ever since she's been killing that violent peace, whenever I hear her damn "Alexa, play Gwen's playlist," I can't resist coming out to watch the show.

Like right now.

I lean against the kitchen's entryway and cross my legs at the ankles. After I got home a while ago, I took a shower and then went to get some water while wearing a towel. Something that made Gwen stare at me bug-eyed as her cheeks, ears, and neck turned red. So I changed into sweatpants and a gray T-shirt. Sometimes, I forget I'm not on my own now and that there's a woman who looks at me as if I'm the most beautiful and frustrating thing she's ever seen.

In the past, I didn't give a fuck about how women saw me. Yes, King and I often attracted attention for our looks and athletic bodies, but it was all a game. A shallow, meaningless game that had no effect on my life whatsoever. So why the fuck do I feel a tinge of pride whenever Gwyneth looks at me as if I'm the only man she sees?

Back to the present—I usually stay outside so she doesn't notice me, but fuck it, I'm watching her up close and personal today.

Holding a spatula as a microphone, she plays the role of a backup singer to the one who's currently rapping. The upbeat music fills the kitchen and she sways her hips and kicks her leg, seeming lost in the song.

I'm supposed to be going through a case file, but I'll do that later when she goes to sleep. That's when my violent silence returns and I can concentrate.

However, that might be a fucking lie, because I've been losing grasp of the word *concentration* since I made this chaotic girl my wife.

She never misses a chance to barge into my thoughts uninvited. Whenever I'm working, in a meeting, or even in court, I think about her on my desk with her legs wide apart as she moans my name and tells me she's been a very bad girl and wants me to teach her how she can be a good girl. Though she doesn't genuinely mean that, considering she's always being naughty in one way or another.

And I can't stop thinking about that, about her hidden tendencies and sweet taste. I haven't been able to stop since the first time.

Since I touched her and got a hard-on for my friend's fucking daughter.

I close my eyes to chase that line of thinking away.

When I open them again, Gwyneth is jumping to the music, screaming with the singer about silence. The same silence she's massacring right now.

She turns in my direction at that exact moment and freezes, her eyes going wide, with her spatula mic still at her mouth.

"Nate." My name comes out as a flustered sound in the middle of the loud music before she clears her throat and shouts, "Alexa, stop."

The music comes to a halt and she grimaces. "Was I too loud?"

"You think?"

"Sorry. I thought you had noise-canceling headphones or something since you've never complained about the music before."

That's because I come out to watch. But I don't say that, continuing to observe her instead. She has flour on her cheeks, which have turned red from all the singing and dancing. A cap covers her auburn strands, but a few stubborn ones are peeking through and she blows on them whenever they get into her eyes.

"I'm baking," she announces, motioning at the bowls, the flour, the butter, and the mess on the counter.

"I can see that. Cupcakes, I assume?"

"Yup. I have to make more than usual since Daniel steals them. Oh, and I'm making all the flavors, because apparently, not everyone likes vanilla."

I smile at how she pouts. She really sounds offended. Extremely so. I hope Christoph doesn't like fucking vanilla either.

"That's blasphemy, I presume?"

"It is!" She mixes what's in the bowl with gentle, graceful movements. "What's there to hate about vanilla? It's peaceful and delicious and smells good."

"It's also boring."

Her head shoots up and her chin trembles the slightest bit. When she speaks, her voice sounds clogged like when someone is about to cry. "You think vanilla is boring?"

"Sometimes."

"But why? There are a lot of things you can add vanilla to, like shampoos and shower gels and essential oils and…and…all the cakes and milkshakes and ice cream."

"That does sound like a lot."

"And there are many others, like vanilla sauce, cream, yogurt, and smoothies. Oh, and did you know it's used in many alcoholic beverages, too? Because it smooths the harsh edges of alcohol."

"And that's important?"

"Of course! There needs to be a balance, and vanilla is perfect for that."

"I see."

"Does that mean you changed your mind?"

"It takes more than that to change my mind."

"Then I'll keep on trying to convince you. One day, you'll fall in love with vanilla and you won't be able to go back."

"You think?"

She gives a curt nod. "I'm sure."

"That's good and all, but where's dinner?"

"Huh?"

"Don't tell me you forgot."

A delicate frown lodges itself between her brows. "Forgot about what?"

"When Martha asked to take the day off today, what did you say?"

"That I'd clean and cook and take care of everything."

I raise a brow and her lips fall open. "Oh."

"Right. *Oh.*"

"I…got engrossed in baking. Dinner slipped my mind."

"Do you do that a lot? Get so engrossed in something that you forget everything else?"

"Yeah, it used to drive Dad insane. Sometimes, I'd be reading a book or cleaning and he'd call my name but get no reply. Then he'd find me and call me by my middle name because he thinks it makes him sound stern, which it doesn't, by the way." She's about to smile, but her lips pull downward and I see the exact moment she dismisses it as if it never happened.

Gwyneth isn't the type who'd forget about her father just because he's in a coma. But that's what it seems like recently. She's stopped going into his room, removed her picture with him from the entrance hall of the house, and never talks about him anymore. She slipped just now by mentioning him.

"I'll fix something," I say.

"You don't have to. I'll cook pasta when I'm done."

"It'll be faster if you bake and I cook at the same time." I'm already in the kitchen, searching through the cupboard for what I'll need.

"I didn't know you could cook." She stares at me over her shoulder.

"I've lived alone for long enough to learn how."

"So it's only out of necessity? You don't enjoy it?"

"Not particularly."

"What do you enjoy then?"

"Work."

She rolls her eyes as she scoops the batter into the small cupcake liners. "Work isn't a hobby."

"It can be." I chop the tomatoes fast and she stares at me with weird fascination.

"Wow, you're good with a knife," she says because she easily gets distracted and has to express everything on her mind, then she shakes her head. "Anyway, there must be something else you enjoy outside of work."

"No, there isn't."

She pushes the tray into the oven and when she leans against the dirty counter, her top rides up her pale belly and flour smudges her denim shorts, thighs, and even down to her sneakers. She won't be happy when she finally notices that.

"How about…when you're with Aspen? What do you guys do?"

"Work."

"Really? You don't do any other activities together?"

"Aside from work, no."

She smiles a little, then says, "But that's just sad."

I throw the ingredients into the pan and add olive oil and some garlic. "That we're workaholics and have no interest in anything that wastes our time?"

"That you don't have hobbies. I'll find you one."

"No need to."

"Yes, there's a need to. Hobbies are important. Everyone I know has at least one, and some have a few."

"Everyone you know is a kid. All kids have are hobbies."

"That's not true. There's Daniel and Knox, and they like a lot of things, like sports and clubbing."

"They tell you that?"

"Yeah."

My spine jerks in a rigid line despite my attempts to remain calm. Fact is, I can't stop thinking about her having cheerful conversations with those two bastards. Yes, she's outgoing, especially with those who are nice to her. And it probably means nothing, but that doesn't negate the fact that the idea fills me with a raw feeling I've never experienced before.

An irrational feeling I don't want to find the reason behind. "Just what do you talk about with them?"

"Stuff."

"Like?"

"Nothing important."

"If it's not important, then don't talk about stuff with them."

"But I like them."

"You'll stop it and that's final."

"No."

"Gwyneth."

"I don't tell you to stop talking to Aspen. I'm being an adult, even though I hate her, so you can't tell me either."

I narrow my eyes. She's becoming more and more shrewd at negotiating and putting her foot down. But I'll deal with those two fuckers and whatever information about clubbing they're feeding her.

I pour hot water into the pot and bring it to a boil, all while she observes each of my movements. "And why do you hate Aspen?"

"Because…because she's mean."

"Has she been mean to you?"

"She doesn't even talk to me."

"Exactly. So why do you think she's mean?"

"Everyone at W&S thinks she is."

"I'm not going to dig into everyone's reason for thinking that. I'm asking about yours."

"Well…Dad hates her."

"You're not your dad, Gwyneth."

"Whoever Dad hates, I hate. It's that simple. We're one like that."

"Is that why you haven't visited him in a week?"

She jolts at that, her lips clamping shut. So, I was right. She's been avoiding him or her feelings about what happened to him.

Silence stretches between us for long moments and only the sound of the boiling water can be heard in the air.

She clinks her nails in that fast, manic way that betrays her inner turmoil.

"Answer me, Gwyneth."

"I...just got busy with the internship. I'll do it later."

"Later when? Tomorrow? Next week?"

"Just later." She turns to leave, probably to go hide in the nearest closet.

"Stop."

She flinches, her nails still clinking together, but she doesn't face me.

"Turn around, Gwyneth."

The shake of her head is so strong, so forceful, it shakes her entire frame.

"Baby girl, look at me."

At that, she does, so slowly, until her eyes meet mine. They're muted, the gray spreading all over the other colors, covering them until each eye is too gloomy, too lifeless.

"Tell me why you don't want to visit King anymore."

If it's because of me, because she feels too guilty that we're doing this while he's in a coma, fuck, I won't be able to handle it.

My guilt is fine, I can deal with it, but I can't bear the thought that she's being strangled to death by hers as well.

I'm older and have dealt with enough life situations and criminal cases to control it. She hasn't. She's still too young and inexperienced.

Despite her inability to sleep sometimes and her claims of having an empty brain, she's still innocent.

And pure.

And I shouldn't be so eager to fucking tarnish all of that.

She grabs a rag, wets it, and starts scrubbing the counter. Hard, fast, and with precise movements. But she's staying in the same area, stuck on one spot that she's scrubbing clean over and over again.

"Because I don't want to think about him being gone. Because when I go to the hospital and smell that godawful stench of antiseptic and step into his room, I know he won't smile at me or hug me or call me his angel. Because he's there, but not really. Because when I read for him and touch his hand and cry, I don't think he hears me. If he did, he'd come back. He said he wouldn't leave me alone, that he's not Mom. But he didn't keep his promise. He abandoned me like she did, and now, he's not here. And it hurts too much to think about it or him or that my parents hate me so much that they both abandoned me at two different phases of my life. So no, I won't go tomorrow or next week or next month. If I do, I'll see him but not talk to him, and I'm a little mad at him because he didn't keep his word. So I'll just think of him as if he's gone on a long business trip and will be coming back soon. That's the only way I can keep myself together."

She's breathing heavily by the time she finishes and there's a tear that has run down her cheek and is forcing its way into her mouth, but she doesn't pay attention to that as she scrubs and scrubs, faster, harsher, longer.

I slowly approach her and grab her hand. It's wet and has turned red. She also scraped her nail against the surface until a few droplets of blood came out.

She's still clutching the rag tightly, like she did that piece of glass the day I told her about King's accident.

"Let it go."

She shakes her head, her full attention still on the counter.

"Drop it, Gwyneth." I press on her wrist hard enough that she opens her deadly grip and releases the damp, bloodied cloth.

"Now, look at me."

She does, though hesitantly. Fuck. The way she looks at me is so pure and fucking trusting that I don't know why it stabs me in the goddamn chest.

"King didn't abandon you, do you understand? It was an accident. If it were up to him, he'd wake up and get back to you. He'd never willingly leave you. If you don't feel like visiting him, I won't force you to, but I think he has a better chance of waking up if you keep talking to him."

"You think?"

"I do."

She nods meekly.

"Are we good? Have you stopped thinking he abandoned you? He's not your mother. He hated that woman. Because fuck her. Do you hear me? Fuck her for leaving you in the streets and being a coward who ran into the night."

"Yeah, fuck her."

"Good."

She smiles through her tears and I love the fucking sight of it, how the green rushes back to the surface, chasing away the gray. She never gets upset for very long. She's always striving to move forward and trying her best to stay afloat.

Because she's special like that.

"Hey, Nate."

"What?"

"You didn't comment on my language."

"You get a pass."

"Fuck yeah."

"Gwyneth."

"What? You said I get a pass."

"Not twice." I inspect her finger, and thankfully, it's not bleeding anymore. "And stop hurting yourself, or I swear to fucking God…"

"What?" The word is so breathy, it's barely audible.

She has this habit of wanting to know the consequences. Sometimes, I suspect she does it on purpose, just to see my reaction.

"Or I'll eat you out, drive you to the edge, but will not let you come."

"No…not that."

"Then stop hurting yourself."

"It's subconscious."

"Then make it conscious. "

"How do I do that?"

"By practicing self-control and discipline so you never spiral out of what's expected."

She shakes her head but doesn't remove her hand from mine. As if this feels so fucking natural, like it does for me. "That's not possible, Nate. People can get out of control sometimes. It's what makes us human. If we were all perfect, it'd be like watching some sci-fi movie, which I don't really like. I prefer horror."

"Even though they scare you?"

"I like to live on the edge…wait. How do you know they scare me? I don't think I've mentioned that to you."

"King did."

A smile paints her lips. "And you remembered it."

"I have a strong memory."

"Whatever." She's still smiling as she gets on her tiptoes. At her closeness, images from two years ago rush back in.

But it's different now. So, so different.

It doesn't feel odd or fucking disturbing that she's close. Unlike then, I don't question my morals or my damn humanity. They can fuck off.

Gwyneth doesn't kiss me, not on the mouth, anyway. Her lips graze my stubble as she gets back on the soles of her feet. "Thank you for talking to me about Dad. I don't know how I would've done this without you, Nate."

Fuck.

Fuck. Fuck!

I get slammed by that tinge of possessiveness that strangles the fucking life out of me.

And this time, all I can think about are the words I told my best friend the day I visited him right after I released my beast on his daughter.

I'm taking away your little angel, King, and she won't be pure and innocent anymore, because I'm taking that away, too. I should say I'm sorry, but I'm not. I won't apologize for what I'm about to do. I don't know what exactly she is to me or where we'll go from here. But I know one thing for sure.

Gwyneth is now mine.

TWENTY

Gwyneth

Y OU KNOW WHEN YOU'RE HAPPY BUT FEEL LIKE EVERYTHING will eventually turn into an epic clusterfuck?

Yeah, that's me right now.

Because it's been so peaceful these last couple of days, so happy, so wholesome. Dad even moved his hand in mine when I went to visit him the day after my talk with Nate. He squeezed it, just the slightest bit, and I nearly fainted from happiness.

The doctor didn't give me much hope and said it was most likely a subconscious motor reaction and doesn't mean anything, but I don't believe that. I'm sure Dad wants to wake up. Besides, he was welcoming me back because it's been some time since I last visited him.

I apologized for wanting to bury him while he's still alive. I told him that I didn't mean to and that I just didn't want him to abandon me like my mom did, and at that exact moment, he squeezed my hand.

So yeah, the doctor is wrong, because Dad was listening and responded to me, so I know he's there, that he didn't leave me.

That he's not my mother.

My spirits shot up after that and I've continued to visit him almost every chance I get, telling him about my day and then working on the assignments Nate gives me.

God, he's such a strict jerk.

A gorgeous one, but a jerk nonetheless. He has no chill whatsoever when it comes to work—even though he doesn't mind ordering me around on his desk or on his sofa to *eat my pussy* as he says. It stopped being mine the moment he called it his.

But other than that, he doesn't take it easy on me. Hell, he can be difficult on purpose, because he's an asshole like that.

I know Nate's character enough to not have any misconceptions about getting preferential treatment, but the least he can do is treat me like the other partners do their interns. I don't see any of them being given a hard time like I am.

It's a bit different when we're home alone. He comes to watch me bake now and doesn't mind the loud music, *I don't think*. And I've been on a mission to find him a hobby, so over the last week we played card games, board games, and all the games I could think of. I lost every time, and Nate was like, "Next." So we watched a selection of movies and did outdoorsy activities, such as picnics and camping in the garden. I don't think he cared for any of them, but he indulged me. All while telling me to give up already.

I won't.

It's not okay that he enjoys nothing. So I'll find him something as a token of my gratitude for all the happiness he's bringing me these days.

And orgasms.

Dirty, *dirty* orgasms.

Now, if the feeling that something is wrong would leave, I'd be more at ease thinking about everything that's right. But it keeps getting worse with each passing hour. Maybe it's because I haven't seen Nate today.

Last night I fell asleep on his lap while we were watching a horror movie. As I told Nate, I've never been the type to run away from what terrifies me.

I still sometimes hide in my closet with my notebook, but I haven't done that a lot lately.

Something else I haven't had much trouble with as of late is insomnia, because I slept like a baby after I used his thigh as a pillow.

I woke up in my bed alone, and no, I wasn't disappointed. Okay, maybe a tiny bit.

Anyway, when I went downstairs, he was already gone. Martha said he went to work early this morning and when I found that he'd left me a Post-it Note that said "Eat your breakfast," I hid it in my pocket as I did just that. Not that I'm collecting his notes. Fine, I totally am.

And then when I got to W&S, he wasn't here either. Grace said he had off-site meetings today.

So maybe that's what the bad feeling is all about. The fact that I haven't seen him at all today. It's crazy to think I survived with catching glimpses of him in the past, but not seeing him for a whole day is messing up my equilibrium.

"Earth to Gwen," a male voice calls.

I snap out of my daze and focus on Chris and Jane. We're having lunch together in the IT department because we're the cool kids and don't care about the crowd in the cafeteria. And because Jane doesn't like it when there are too many people. It makes her super fidgety and awkward, so Chris and I aren't going to leave her alone.

"Finally back to the world of the living?" he asks.

"I've been here all along," I lie through my teeth.

"No, you haven't."

"Yeah, you haven't been." Jane takes a bite of her sandwich.

"Hey! Whose side are you on, Jane?"

"No one's?"

I bump her shoulder with mine. "I found you first, you know. Chris is extracurricular."

"Who are you calling extracurricular?" He steals my fries and throws them in his mouth before I can stop him.

"You!"

"Lies. You love me, Gwen."

"Maybe I'd just love to hit you right now."

"Uh...should I go?" Jane says with a straight face. "Let you guys get a room or something?"

"We're not like that," I say.

"Yeah, we're not." Chris taps his chest. "She broke my poor little heart, so I've been trying to fill it with stuff."

"Stuff like clubbing?" I ask.

"You don't have the right to judge, babe."

"Wait, you guys were a thing?" Jane stares between us.

"A tiny little thing that Gwen murdered mercilessly. Don't be fooled by the innocent look. She breaks hearts." He feigns a sad expression and waggles his brows at me. The dork.

"Yeah, I realized Chris is too good for me. But hey, I can matchmake you guys."

"What the fuck? I'm wounded, Gwen. You think I'd need your help to hit it off with Jane?"

"Maybe you need encouragement or something."

"Thanks, guys, but...my tastes are different."

We both turn toward her at the same time and she just drinks from her water nonchalantly.

"Do you veer in the other direction?" I ask, then blurt, "Sorry, I shouldn't have asked that. You don't need to answer."

"I'm not a lesbian. I just...like older men, I guess."

"Oh," both Chris and I exclaim at the same time.

Jane is actually my age, not mid-twenties like I thought. But she's a genius—graduated college early and started working here not long before I came along.

But all those details fade into the background. Only one is

important and sticks with me; the fact that she likes older men. I knew I found her interesting for a reason.

"I'm slightly wounded," Chris breathes out. "Now I need to get older fast to get on your radar, ladies."

"What do I have to do with it?" I whisper, taking a large bite of my burger.

"Come on, you have the hots for Nathaniel."

I choke on my mouthful and Jane pushes the bottle of water into my hand. I nearly guzzle it all down, but it doesn't remove the burn in my throat. I stare at Chris as if he's grown two heads. "Why the hell do you think that?"

"You look at him as if he's your custom-made god that you can't survive without worshipping at his altar."

"I…I do not."

"You kind of do," Jane confirms.

"You guys knew this all along?" I hang my head. "I can't believe I'm that obvious. I wonder how many others found out."

"They're not as attuned to you as we are, so they probably have no clue," Chris says.

"But I think Nathaniel is getting obvious," Jane says.

"Yeah, he keeps calling her any chance he gets." Chris steals more of my fries and I don't even have the will to stop him. "He has better control of himself, though. So I'd say she's the one giving it all away."

"And not so subtly either. She's all depressed because he's not around this morning."

"Right?"

"Hey! Can you stop talking about me as if I'm not here?"

"Only if you tell us when it started." Chris narrows his eyes. "It was before you broke up with me, wasn't it?"

"I don't know."

"You don't know?" Chris asks while Jane retrieves another bottle of water and drinks from it with a straw. She can act like a real princess sometimes.

"I don't. It just happened. I'm not sure if it was all in one go or gradually, but it just did, and I actually realized it when I was fifteen. I also realized it was impossible to fight it. I tried at first. I really, *really* tried. He's Dad's best friend and partner and the same age as him, so it should be wrong. It *felt* wrong, and that's why I did my best to forget about him. But I wasn't able to." And it kind of hurts sometimes. Like right now, when he isn't around and I can't call or text, because he's in a meeting and I'm not supposed to be disturbing him.

"How about him?" Chris asks. "Does he share your feelings?"

"He…he's just taking care of me until I'm twenty-one."

Chris steals more of my fries. "So it's unrequited?"

"I guess." The crush and the stupid feelings are, anyway. The physical isn't, because I can tell he wants me as much as I want him.

"That's dependency," Jane announces out of nowhere. "You like him, but he has some sort of guardianship over you. It's not healthy."

"That's not true."

"It is, in a way," Chris chimes in. "I mean, it would've also been creepy if he was banging his best friend's daughter."

"Why are you calling it creepy?" I nearly shout. "I thought you weren't judgy, Chris."

"I'm not. I'm just thinking about it from your dad's perspective. Do you think he'd be full of smiles if he found out that his best friend took advantage of his daughter when he should've been taking care of her? He's the older one. He should know better."

"He didn't take advantage of me. *I* chose this. I'm twenty and I can make my own decisions."

"Hey, calm down." Chris softens his voice. "I was just saying it from a different perspective. Sit down."

It's then I notice that I'm standing up, crushing the burger between my stiff fingers. And I hate this, I hate that I got worked up so fast and nearly lost my shit. If it was Nate, he wouldn't have acted this way. Because he's older and wiser, and maybe Chris is right. Maybe I just don't know better.

I flop back on the chair, my eyes stinging and my heart sinking in my chest. If the people who are supposed to be by my side are secretly judging me, how would others feel about it? Nate was right to keep the marriage a secret.

Once again, he predicted the future while I'm always stuck in the present. He must've known that if news of our marriage went public, people would be judgmental and then I'd overreact and mess everything up.

"It's different if he likes you," Jane says softly. "That means it's mutual and you're not chasing after the dependency."

He likes me.

I think he does.

Right?

I mean, why would he say all those things about my dad and bring me back from the edge if he didn't?

Except he might simply be playing his role of guardian.

But a guardian wouldn't touch me like that. He wouldn't talk so dirty that I need a cold shower just thinking about it.

Though it could be just that. Sex.

"So this is where you've been."

The three of us stare at the doorway, where Knox is standing, narrowing his eyes on Chris—his intern.

But he's not the one who stiffens, nearly turning into a statue.

It's Jane.

The straw is between her lips, but she's not sucking. She's staring at Knox, who's standing there with his shoulders squared. It's almost an aggressive stance—which is out of the ordinary for someone like him.

Chris gets up and offers his charming smile. "I was just having lunch. I'm finished."

"Then why are you still standing there?" Knox says in his serious voice that I rarely hear from him. He's usually outgoing around me, but he sounds like a British villain right now.

My friend must feel it, too, because he quickens his pace and leaves the IT room. Knox doesn't. He keeps staring. I thought it was at Chris earlier, but it's at the computer. Or maybe it's Jane, but why would he stare at her? No one even knows she exists. Nate calls her the IT girl and only because I talk about her. She's invisible to everyone and likes it that way.

"Aspen is searching for you, Gwen," he tells me, slowly breaking eye contact with Jane to focus on me.

"Why?"

"No clue. But you should go. She doesn't like to be kept waiting."

I stand up, resisting the urge to roll my eyes. Aspen is the last person I want to see. But I'm still an intern and interns don't go around being stubborn little bitches to senior partners.

Jane grips the sleeve of my shirt hard, so hard that she nearly causes me to fall. I stare down at her and the alarm in her eyes is loud and clear, even through the thick as shit glasses.

"Gwyneth." It's Knox and he definitely sounds impatient. I haven't seen him like this before, but I don't want to be on his bad side. Like, at all.

"Uh, one moment." I lean down and whisper, "What's wrong?"

Jane tightens her hold on my shirt for a fraction of a second before she lets me go and murmurs back, "Nothing."

I'm still unconvinced, considering the fact that she looked to be on the verge of a meltdown just now. But I also don't want to risk Knox's wrath, so I throw the remnants of my burger in the trash and step past him. I expect him to follow, but he doesn't.

Weird.

I take the elevator up and head to Aspen's office. I've dropped some files off to her before, so this isn't the first time I've been here, but I hate it just the same.

Her assistant tells me to go in, and I knock on the door, waiting for her curt "Come in" before I step inside.

Her office is large, neat, and a bit manly, even if she is the most elegant woman I know. In a way, I understand why people like Jane or even Chris respect her. She's a very hard worker and made it in a male-dominated world when the odds were against her. I should probably give her the benefit of the doubt, but I just can't.

Not only has Dad always painted her as a witch, but she also chose Nate to be the only man she's close to.

It could've been any man, so why Nate?

"You called for me?" I ask as soon as I'm inside.

Aspen looks up from the stack of files piled in front of her. "No. I didn't."

"Knox said you did… It must've been a mistake. Then…"

"Wait." She stands up and marches in my direction, then towers over me. It's on purpose, I swear. She likes being taller, prettier, and older than me. She likes having the upper hand in everything.

The witch.

She crosses her arms over her chest and I do the same. What? She doesn't get to be the only one on the defensive.

"Nate probably didn't tell you this, but I believe you should know."

A ball the size of my fist lodges in my throat. Tell me what? That he's in a relationship with her and will marry her as soon as I'm of age and he divorces me?

Calm down, Gwen, calm down.

"Know what?"

"Kingsley's accident might not have been an accident."

So it's not about her and Nate. *Phew.* "Wait. What?"

"They found a problem with his car's brakes. It's minimal, something that could have been caught during a checkup. But Kingsley hadn't had his car checked in a while, so the police ruled it as an accident."

"Yeah, so?"

"So? Do you really think Kingsley wouldn't know what's wrong with his car? That man notices everything."

"Are you saying…?" The ball tightens and blocks my breathing. "Are you saying someone messed with his brakes?"

"I don't know. Do you?"

"Of course not! But who would want to hurt him?"

"Seriously, now, Shaw? He has more enemies than the fortune

he's amassed. He might have been a doting father to you, but he was a ruthless devil to everyone else."

"And Nate knows this? He's aware of the suspicions but never told me?"

"He thinks it's nothing. We have no proof and that means we can't ask for a second investigation."

"Then why are you telling me?"

"So that you'll watch your back, Shaw's spawn. You're too out in the open for your own good. If it's true and someone tried to kill Kingsley, maybe you're next."

"I didn't know you worried about me."

"I don't." She clears her throat. "I worry about the firm, and Nate, who will be drawn into every mess you make."

"He's my husband."

"On paper."

I purse my lips. "Maybe it's not only on paper."

"What?"

"N-nothing." Shit, I almost told her our secret. Once again, my temper nearly got the best of me. I swear it's her face. It's too beautiful and too put-together and I hate it.

I hate her.

But I keep thinking about her words all day long. Like who would want to hurt my dad?

I decide to investigate on my own. Chris agrees to help me after hours and says he owes me an apology for when he was being judgy.

He drives me to the police station on the back of his Harley, and I demand to have the records of Dad's accident, but they blow me off.

However, I don't move from there until a detective from the NYPD who knows my dad lets me into his office and closes the door.

I sit on the faux leather chair and stare at Detective Ford. He's tall, lean, and has a bald head and black skin. I wouldn't call them friends with Dad since he goes against him sometimes. Seriously,

Nate is Dad's only friend. Everyone else is just an acquaintance. Oh, and Detective Ford has a strong sense of justice, so that puts us on the same side, because Dad definitely doesn't have that.

"You're not supposed to be here, Ms. Shaw."

"I just want Dad's records from the day of the accident."

"Records," he repeats with a slight narrowing of his eyes.

"Yeah. Who he talked to and everything."

"Why?"

"Because it's come to my attention that there might've been foul play."

"What's your proof?"

"He was off that morning."

"Off?"

"He wasn't acting like himself and it felt like he was on the verge of something."

"Why didn't you mention that before?"

"I didn't think it was of importance, but I do now. Please, I just want to know what you have."

"We have nothing, Ms. Shaw, since we don't think it was attempted murder. You should go back home, and next time, maybe you should send Nathaniel."

"This is about my father. I don't need to send anyone."

Detective Ford dismisses me anyway since I've taken up so much of his time. My shoulders hunch as I leave the office.

"No luck?" Chris asks when I get outside.

"No."

"Maybe you should ask Nate. He's your father's attorney, right? He'll be able to dig in with the police."

"He hid it from me. He won't magically decide to help. I have to see this for myself and find a way…oh, the dashcam! It's not in evidence anymore and I can ask the company to send the footage over."

"If it's not in evidence, it probably means there's nothing there."

"I won't know until I try."

I feel giddy by the time Chris drops me off back at home. I

just need to reach out to the car company that has the wreckage and retrieve the footage. I should probably rein in the hope, but I can't help it.

Ever since Dad went into a coma, I've felt helpless, like I couldn't do anything, which is part of the reason why I let those dark thoughts about him abandoning me fester inside me.

But now, I can.

Now, I can search for the truth. If there's someone who messed with Dad, I'll destroy them.

I wave at Chris as the sound of his Harley fills the neighborhood. They definitely hate him—and probably me for bringing him here.

I run to the stairs so I can get to Dad's office for the car company's phone number.

My feet cease to function when an ominous voice fills the air.

"What did I say about riding on that fucking bike, Gwyneth?"

TWENTY-ONE

Gwyneth

MY SPINE TINGLES AND JUMPS AND I NEARLY REEL FROM THE shock of hearing his voice.

Not only do I plaster myself against the wall, but my whole body also hums to life. From my stuttering intakes of air to the curling of my toes in my white sneakers and all the way to my heaving chest. My nipples tighten and so does my pussy.

It's just a voice, damn it, a voice among billions of others; however, it's not merely any voice. It's *his* voice. The man I'm not supposed to be crushing on, because it's a form of dependency.

It's not healthy.

And Dad will kill him when he finds out about this.

But all those thoughts blur in the background, all those don't matter, because what I'm feeling is healthy in my mind, and Dad isn't here. He still doesn't want to wake up, so I'll think about everything else when he does.

Right now, there's only Nate's voice and me, his stern voice that I can recognize the anger in. There's a slight vibration in it, so even though it sounds calm, I know he isn't. Oh, and the cursing. He only does that when he's mad or aroused. I don't think it's the latter at the moment.

Anyhow, Nate's voice should probably go on the list so I can desensitize myself and not lose my shit whenever I hear it. Because even though he doesn't sound to be in a good mood, all I can think about are the dirty words he's whispered and growled and ordered with that voice.

"Answer me," he insists, still angry, still on the verge of something.

I stare up at him, and I think Nate's face should be on the list, too. Nate's body as well and, more specifically, Nate's presence. Because that's what turns me into a bundle of hyperaware nerves. That's the actual thief that steals my breath and sanity.

But I can't stop staring at him, at his broad silhouette that's bathed in the late afternoon sun and at his gorgeous hair that's so perfect, I want to run my fingers through it and mess it up a little, maybe mess *him* up a little, too, because he's perfect and I hate that.

I hate the dependency.

"Chris and I went out." I can't tell him about the police, because he'll make sure I find nothing. He'll take away my investigation and if I insist it continues, he'll take over it.

And that's dependency, right? Leaving everything in his hands and letting him handle it all. And since I loathe the thought of it, I'll change it. Fuck that word. Fuck *dependency*. I won't depend on him anymore. From now on, I'll take care of everything myself so that no one can say that word again.

I'm adding *dependency* to the stupid *D* list that keeps growing.

"You went out with Christoph," he repeats slowly, menacingly, and my fingers shake. They shake so hard, I think he sees the effect he has on me. He sees how much he rattles me. But I don't hide it, because his eyes rage a dark color that leaves me breathless.

His reaction to my shaking is wrong. My reaction to him is even more wrong.

We are wrong.

"Yeah. We went out."

"Where?"

"Around."

"Around isn't a fucking answer, Gwyneth. Where did you go?"

"To the...uh...park." It's such a stupid, lame place to pick, but I'm not good at lying and that's what came to mind first. I should've said to his house or something to gauge Nate's reaction.

But I don't need to, because he's approaching me now, stalking actually, with his jaw set and his broad shoulders eating up the horizon, at least for me.

"You went with Christoph to the park on the back of his bike, is that right?"

"Yeah."

"And what did you do?"

"Stuff."

"What type of stuff?"

"Talking and..." I trail off, because he's right in front of me and I'm drunk on his scent and the masculine warmth that's emanating from his chest.

"And what?"

I jerk up, and my head hits the wall, but that doesn't matter. I lose sense of pain and reality when he's so big in front of me. His sheer size makes me feel so small, and I clench my thighs because I'm sure he can smell my arousal, the reaction I have because our size difference turns me on.

"Go on. What else did he do? Did he touch you?"

"W-what?"

"Did he put his hands on this face?" He cups my cheek, his skin hot. Or maybe it's mine since I'm on the verge of combusting.

"No."

He drags his palm down to my throat, to the pulse point that's about to burst and spill my heart out. "How about here? Did the fucker touch you here?"

"No..."

The hand that was just touching my face is now wrapped

around my throat. Tight. Not so tight that it cuts off my oxygen, but it's tight enough that all my attention is zeroed in on him and on the nerve endings of my jaw where his thumb is grazing it.

His other hand bunches my shirt and he pulls, tearing it open with more ease than any man should have. I don't see the flying buttons, but I hear their sound as they scatter on the stairs.

My breasts bounce out, and even though they're covered by a bra, that doesn't last for long. He pulls it down, ripping the straps on my shoulder, and I gasp, the sound so aroused, I don't recognize it as coming from me.

He exposes my pale naked breasts tipped with two hard rosy nipples that ache and harden with each passing second.

And the air hitting them has nothing to do with it.

He grabs them in his large hands, in those strong, veiny hands, and squeezes the tips together with so much force that it makes me whimper.

"Did he touch these tits? Did he cop a feel, Gwyneth?"

"No...he didn't."

"Did he try? Did you let him?"

"No..." I can't stop whimpering and moaning at the same time because he's mashing my breasts together, squeezing my nipples, and making them more tight and sensitive than I've ever experienced before.

Zaps of pleasure flood through me and cause arousal to pool in my panties, and I know he'll feel it, too. He's about to find out how much he affects me when he releases my throat and unzips my skirt, letting it fall around my ankles.

He cups me over my panties, digging his long fingers into my needy core with a raging possessiveness that makes me go up on my tiptoes.

"How about here?"

I'm struggling for a sliver of oxygen because I can't speak. I can't even think. His intensity is too raw and thick, wrapping around my throat, which is still tingling from his grip.

"Tell me, baby girl. Did he touch my fucking pussy?"

"No…"

"He didn't, huh?" He squeezes my nipples, then glides his fingers over my dripping folds and teases my opening, and even though it's only through the material, I'm nearing that edge that only Nate can drive me to.

The edge where nothing and no one else matters. The edge where it's just me and him without the world's judgment, labeling, and bullshit.

"He can't touch it," I breathe out.

"And why is that?"

"Because it's yours."

His jaw clenches and I can tell how much he's aroused now, because his nostrils flare and the possessiveness washes over me in waves. It's why I say things like that; I know they make him shed his control and turn into the powerful dominant who's able to tear my world to pieces.

And then he curses and I get wetter at the thought that he wants me so much, he can't contain it. Other men sound coarse when they curse, he sounds hotter than sin.

"What's mine?" His voice is thicker, deeper.

"My pussy. It's yours."mn

"Fuck."

"Yes, please fuck me."

He closes his eyes, and even though his jaw is in a rigid line, I think he's trying to conjure some form of patience, but when he opens them, he isn't calm. On the contrary, his eyes are nearly black with all the shadows crowding his masculine face.

"What did you just say, baby girl?"

"Fuck me." It's barely a murmur now, a bit unsure since he's pressing hard on both my nipples and my clit, playing with the tight tips, teasing and rolling them between his thumb and forefinger. And the pressure is reeling and about to take me under.

So I let it.

I let my limbs relax as the orgasm washes over me. It's long and smooth and effortless, just like everything about him.

Then he's moving me up and removing my panties, I realize in my pleasure haze, so I lift my trembling legs one at a time to help.

I'm completely naked now—aside from the torn shirt and bra—while he's still dressed in his prim suit, and for some reason, that brings up the heat a notch. To make things even more unbearable, he shoves my panties in his pocket. He must have a collection of my vanilla-colored underwear by now, and I keep buying them, the same color, over and over again.

And then his hands are back on me, one gripping me by the waist and the other slipping into my slick opening. "You're shaking like a leaf after a mere clit orgasm and you think you can take my dick up this tight cunt?"

"I...can try."

"What if you can't take it? What if you start crying because it hurts?"

"It's okay." My lips are trembling and my throat is so dry, it's uncomfortable to swallow. "Because you'll make it feel good afterward. You'll make me smile after I cry."

"You're so sure that I will, huh?"

"Yeah."

"But you said you'd be my toy, and toys break."

"Not me."

A strange look passes over his features as he releases my hip and unbuckles his pants. I can't help the small gasp that slips out of me.

He's *huge*.

I've felt his erection against my stomach, my ass, my pussy—everywhere—and I predicted he was probably big, but nothing could have prepared me for the sight in front of me.

His cock is not only long and thick, but it's also veiny and hard, so hard that my mouth waters and my pussy clenches around his fingers.

There's a drop of a transparent liquid rolling down the sides and sticking to his hand that's pumping his length. He's not gentle, even though he's slow and I'm caught in a trance by the way he touches himself. So completely in tune that I wish it was my hand, or better yet, my mouth.

"It's so big," I murmur breathlessly.

"Did you change your mind? Afraid that my big cock will break your tiny pussy?"

Jeez. He really needs to stop saying things like that or I won't be able to focus. Screw that, I'm unable to focus anyway.

Or maybe I'm *too* focused on him, on this moment, and on how that cock will fit inside me.

"I changed my mind. I think it'll break me." I bite my lip.

"It will."

"That's okay." I reach a hand to his face, not his shaft, and stroke my cold, sweaty fingers on his stubble. "Because it's you."

I can feel the muscles of his jaw tightening beneath my palm and I know he's at his limit, maybe even more so than me, because he groans. It's deep and rough and simultaneous to him pulling his fingers out from inside me.

"Now, you're truly fucked, baby girl."

I squeal when he lifts me up in the air with one hand beneath my ass. It's so effortless, as if he's not carrying a person, and I'm forced to let go of his face to wrap my arms around his neck.

Then I'm trapped between the hard ridges of his stomach and the wall. I'm a bit higher than him, looking down at him for the first time ever with my feet dangling mid-air.

"Put your legs around me and hold on tight."

I wrap my legs around his narrow, muscular waist as he glides the crown of his cock up and down my sensitive folds. The sensation is torturous and I instinctively rock my hips.

"Feel that? That's you lubricating my dick so it can fuck you later. Do you feel yourself drenching me?"

"I do…" Embarrassment heats my cheeks and neck, but I can't help getting both of us more wet, until my arousal coats my thighs and his shirt. He seems to take pleasure in it, because he keeps smearing it all over us.

"So fucking messy, my Gwyneth."

I nearly come from that, how he called me *his* Gwyneth. The humping of his cock against my folds increases in intensity and rhythm until I'm hanging by a thread. And just when I think the thread will break and I'll roll down the cliff, he slips inside. It's not hard or violent, but it's in one go.

One. Go.

Every inch of his huge cock is in me at once and it's deep. So fucking deep that I whimper and gasp, and my insides feel like they're tearing apart.

Because I think they are.

Holy shit. The sting hurts so good. It hurts better than I imagined. All the stories I've heard about this moment are nonsensical. They said it would hurt like you want to die or cry, and I do want to cry, but for an entirely different reason than pain.

Like how ethereal it feels, how full, how deep and right.

Nate doesn't seem to share my thoughts, because he freezes, like completely, even though he's breathing harshly and heavily. And his eyes, the color of darkness, widen a little as they stares into mine.

"Fuck, fuck, fuck!" His curses start low, then grow in volume. "You're a virgin?"

"I don't think I am anymore."

"Why the fuck didn't you tell me, Gwyneth?"

"I didn't believe it mattered."

"Of course, it fucking matters. I wouldn't have fucked you against the wall for your first time. I would've been gentle."

"I don't like it gentle." I stroke the strand of hair that's fallen over his forehead. "I like it exactly the way you do—rough and unapologetic."

"You don't even know what the fuck rough means." He's rocking his hips a little, thrusting slowly, and holy mother of all things, the bursts of pleasure running through me is too intense to handle.

"You can teach me. I love it when you do." I rock my hips, too, and that makes him pick up his pace a little.

"Are you in pain?" One of his hands snakes behind my back

and the other holds my hip so tight that his fingers are digging into my skin. I think he's pining for patience to not take me as hard as his cock is ordering him to right now.

"I'm not." I go down on his cock a few more times. "So don't take it easy on me and don't even think about holding back. Give me all of you."

"Fuck this."

And just like that, he does. He gives me all of him.

He moves inside me with deep, slow thrusts at first and I cry out at how good it feels, how damn full.

And then it's faster and my body feels like it would fall if it weren't for the firmness of his grip that keeps me chained to him.

Each stroke is so delicious and sensual, and I want to keep soaking it all in. His thrusts, the power in his shoulders, and even my long moans and slow whimpers.

But I can't, because I can feel the savage building of the climax about to pull me under.

"A virgin. *Fuck*." He grunts against my chest, taking a nipple into his mouth and sucking on it, then biting until I'm about to crumble here and now. "Why are you a fucking virgin, Gwyneth?"

"I didn't want to…have sex…" I don't know how I'm speaking with all the things going on inside me. Everything is just too raw and heightened.

"Why?"

"I didn't find the right one to give it to."

"You didn't, huh?"

"No." And I think, deep down, I was saving it for him. I wanted him to be the first man to explore that part of me, but I don't say that. I *can't*.

"But I came along and took it anyway, didn't I?"

"You did."

"Because it's my pussy and it's only supposed to be mine, right?"

"Yeah…"

I have no more words to say, because I'm coming. The climax

drags me under and holds me hostage, and I scream from the sheer intensity of it.

Nate lets me, he lets me scream his name and how much I love it, how much I love what he's doing to me. Usually, he stuffs something in my mouth to stop me from screaming, his fingers or a piece of clothing, but now, he doesn't even attempt to mute me.

Soon after, I hear his low, deep grunt and feel him tightening and growing even thicker inside me. My pussy walls clench around his cock, wanting him to stay there forever.

And then there's warmth. On my breasts. Because he pulled out at the last second, put me down, and came all over my chest.

No idea why a gloomy feeling that's so similar to disappointment perches on my chest.

But the low mood is short-lived. As I stand on my wobbly feet, I can't stop staring at the spurts of his cum on my pale breasts, clinging to the tips of my nipples and dripping down my stomach and onto the shirt he ripped.

Nate isn't watching that, though. He's watching my legs with a frown. I also look down and, through my unfocused vision, I make out a trail of blood gliding down my leg and to my ankle, then soaking my white sneakers red.

A long moment of silence stretches between us as we observe the evidence of my becoming a woman.

"Fuck." His curse is low, almost a whisper, as he picks me up and carries me in his arms bridal style.

I wrap myself all around him, sighing, then I kiss the hollow of his throat and surrender to a deep sleep.

TWENTY-TWO

Nathaniel

GWYNETH IS FAST ASLEEP.

I can't stop staring at her. At the delicate lines of her face, at the slight flutter of her long, thick lashes over her cheeks. At how her fiery hair frames her face.

But most of all, I can't stop staring at the blood.

Her virginal blood, because she hasn't had sex before. She hasn't let a dick inside her, and I acted like an animal and took her against the wall.

If I had an ounce of control, even a sliver, I would've stopped and carried her to a bed. I would've put on a fucking condom like I usually do. But all those thoughts didn't exist when she had her legs around me, rocking against me as if she'd waited for that moment as long as I have.

There was no thinking, period.

I should've known better. I *really* should've known fucking better.

I leave her on her princess bed, with muslin curtains and fluffy pillows, and head to her bathroom to wash my dick.

It's covered with remnants of my cum and her blood. And I can't stop staring at it. At the evidence of her belonging to me. At the proof that she didn't choose anyone else. Just me.

A wave of blinding possession grips hold of me. It's harsher than the other times and more fucking violent because a screwed-up part of me likes this.

Fuck that. I don't only like it, my dick is getting hard at the memory of tearing through her while she said those words. That she didn't want to give it to anyone.

No one else but me.

I slowly shake my head and wipe my length with a wet towel, resisting the urge to get off in remembrance of her clenching around me like a vise.

What the fuck am I? A teenager?

Why the hell would I think about sex right after I just finished?

I don't usually. It's always about getting off for me. No more, no less. I make sure the women know that, too, so they don't expect anything after a night of fucking and orgasms.

But *usually*, I don't settle for oral either. I'm all about the act itself. The fucking. However, a part of me resisted that with Gwyneth for more than ten days. I tortured my dick and myself in a fruitless attempt to get her off my fucking radar.

But with each word out of her mouth, each orgasm, and each fucking sexy sound, my resolve crumbled. The last straw was seeing her on that not-some-normal bike with that fucker Christoph and knowing she'd been alone with him.

So I had to stake my claim in the most unsophisticated, animalistic way possible. Even now, I still don't know what's come over me.

I'm not like this.

I don't fuck against walls. I don't fuck virgins. And I sure as hell don't fuck without a condom.

Gwyneth smashed all my rules to the ground. She's muddying my logic and I should stop it. I fucking should. But that's the last thing on my mind right now.

I tuck myself in, then I grab a few towels, wet them with warm water, and go back to her room. She's sprawled on her back, her arms thrown above her head in a carefree position, and only her torn shirt and bra cling haphazardly to her shoulders and torso.

And the blood. It's dried up between her thighs and down her legs to the fucking white sneakers that are all smudged in red now.

I sit on the edge of the bed, place the towels on the nightstand, then remove the scraps of clothes I savagely tore. She's like a doll in my hands, completely lost in sleep, no matter how much I maneuver her and move her around.

It's weird to see her so deep in slumber like this. She suffers from insomnia, which is why she bakes or watches horror movies late at night. I often find her sleeping upside down on the couch, her legs in the air and her head lolled to the side. I carry her to her room every night so she doesn't break her neck in that position.

After I remove her sneakers, I place a warm towel on her pink, swollen pussy. She sighs, mumbling something incoherent. She talked in her sleep when she was a kid and Kingsley used to freak out whenever she sometimes called for her mom.

He's always hated that. Gwyneth needing a mom, and the woman herself. He hates Gwyneth's mother with a passion I've never seen him have for anyone else.

He thinks his daughter only needs him, that having him is enough, but he's wrong. Gwyneth misses her mom, even though she's never met her. I became surer of that after she mentioned the abandonment thing. She's still wounded by it, and King was wrong to sweep her feelings about it under a rug. She needed to deal with it a long time ago—when she was a kid and talked in her sleep.

I wipe the blood away and it's not as much as it seems. Thank fuck, because the sight earlier made me think about driving her to the ER.

Then I take my time cleaning my dried cum from her tits,

nipples, and stomach. I want to engrave this sight into my memory so I can picture it later.

After I'm done, I cover her to her chin with the blanket, though it's a fucking shame to hide her tempting pale skin and her beautiful tits.

"Ice cream…" she mumbles, and I can't help the smile that breaks across my lips.

She has an unhealthy obsession with that. And milkshakes. And everything vanilla, basically. She's been slipping it in everything I eat or drink, trying to convert me to her side.

I reach a hand out and push a stubborn auburn strand away from her forehead, and my hand lingers there, then slowly slides down to her flushed cheek.

I know I should feel guilty. I should be beating myself the fuck up and confessing to every god on the planet for fucking my best friend's daughter and loving it. For thinking about repeating it. For being deranged and loving the fact that I'm her first.

But I'm not.

Because I'm a sick bastard and I'm not apologetic about it.

What's the point of confessing if you don't stop doing the act? And no, I surely don't intend to stop.

Not now that I've had a taste of her.

Not now when she's officially mine.

Fuck. I need to put a halt to these fucked-up thoughts, because my dick is pressing against my pants with the need to act on them.

I start to remove my hand, but she catches it in her smaller one and softly places it under her cheek, as if I'm her new pillow.

Ordinarily, I'd pull away and go to my room. I'd work out to deal with my own sleep problems, but I don't this time.

This time, I lie on my side, facing her, facing her soft face and her dreamy expression. Then my hands are on that face, and I stroke her hair behind her ear.

"Don't go…" she mumbles, and it's probably about her father or maybe her mother.

But I'm the one who says, "I won't go anywhere, baby girl."

⚖

I wake up in pain.

My dick. It's so fucking hard, it hurts.

I groan deep in my throat and open my eyes. Usually, I sleep in nothing because any friction from clothes causes this fucking discomfort.

I'm about to reach down and adjust it when my gaze lands on that colorful chameleon one. It's so bright and shiny, like the green has slaughtered all the other colors.

"You slept here," she blurts as if she's been waiting for me to wake up so she can say the words.

Fuck. I did sleep here, and it's early morning already. I don't usually sleep that easily. I don't sleep at all unless I exhaust my body in the gym first.

But I did. Last night. Even with my clothes on.

"I didn't have a choice. You held my hand hostage." I tip my chin at my palm that's still under her cheek and how she's gripping my wrist.

"I don't care. It still counts." She inches closer and I grunt when her thigh touches my raging erection.

At that, she stares down, her eyes widening. "It looks painful."

"Whose fault is that?"

She sits up and the sheet falls away, exposing her tits that my eyes automatically go to. I love how comfortable she is in her nakedness around me. She doesn't even attempt to hide from me anymore. "Mine?"

"Yes, it is. And do you know what that means?"

She shakes her head, even though her eyes are shining, still exploding with bright green.

"It means you'll take care of it."

Her teeth sink into the corner of her lip. "I will?"

"Get my dick out, Gwyneth."

She scrambles between my legs, her small hands fumbling

with my zipper, then my boxer briefs until she has my thick erection between her hands.

"What do I do now?" She stares from my dick to my face, and it's that trust again. She trusts me to tell her what to do and she'll follow through with it. No questions asked.

"Now, you put those pretty lips on it and suck."

She strokes me a few times from bottom to top, and I grunt. My dick is turning harder with each of her innocent movements. But there's nothing pure about the look in her eyes.

"I've always wanted to do this." She licks her lips. "I've practiced."

A red mist covers my vision at the image of her sucking someone else. The picture of her opening these lips to that kid with the not-some-normal bike hits me with fucking violence.

It's illogical, doesn't make any fucking sense, but it's there and it's starting a fire in my chest.

"You practiced?" I ask with a calm I don't feel.

"Yeah, why do you think bananas are my favorite fruit? But you're bigger…and…I don't think I can take you all in. But I want to." She bows her head and licks the crown of my dick and the drop of precum.

I suck in a harsh breath when she stuffs me into her mouth, taking as much of me as possible as she sucks and hollows her cheeks. Her movements are inexperienced, but that in itself is a fucking turn-on. What she lacks in experience, she makes up for with pure enthusiasm.

Her head bobs up and down as she sucks and licks, and I grab her by those strands, my hand fisting into them.

As if my hold spurs her on, her movements become longer yet out of control. She keeps her pace, on and on with her fingers fondling my balls.

"Fuck," I grunt. "I love your mouth, Gwyneth."

She quickens her pace and I use her hair to keep her in place as I rock my hips, hitting the back of her throat.

She sputters and chokes, but she doesn't attempt to push me

away. If anything, she encourages me. She opens her lips the widest possible and lets me fuck her mouth.

And I do it. I thrust forward until the friction is unbearable, until all my blood rushes to where her skin meets mine, where she's handing me the reins to use her mouth any way I see fit.

My back muscles tighten with each jerk of my hips and I can feel the orgasm ripping through my balls.

Before I know it, a growl echoes in the air as I empty down her throat.

"Don't swallow it all," I order as I pull my dick out of her wet heat.

She stares at me with those eyes that I always feel the urge to see in order to gauge her mood through them.

"Keep my cum in that mouth."

She clamps her lips shut and a trail of cum streaks down her chin. I sit up and pull her toward me by the arm and then my mouth is on hers.

I thrust my tongue inside and drink my cum from her mouth. It's mixed with her now and it tastes like vanilla. I never even thought about doing this before, but it's another thing that's exclusive to her.

The girl who's currently writhing against me, her naked tits glued to my chest as she kisses me back and lets me drink myself from her.

She lets me drink what I did to her.

And I kiss her harder, faster, long after my taste is gone, and it's all her now. Fucking vanilla and ice cream and cupcakes.

I pull away when she's wheezing, her neck red and her pulse thundering. Fuck. I was so engrossed in the act that I forgot to let us breathe.

She stares at me, her lips swollen and parted and so damn tempting. "You kissed me back."

"Huh?"

"I thought you never would. Kiss me, I mean."

"That wasn't kissing. That was snowballing."

"I love that. Snowballing. Let's do it more."

"You're not vanilla, after all."

"Not with sex, I guess."

"How do you know that?"

"I want all the things."

"All the things?"

"Yeah, everything."

I'm going to fuck her again. I can feel it. And I will.

But I need to feed her first.

I begrudgingly get up and tuck myself in. "Take a shower and meet me downstairs."

"Can't we stay in bed for a bit more?"

"No, Gwyneth. We have work and you still haven't finished the workload I gave you yesterday."

"Dictator," she mutters under her breath.

"What did you just call me?"

She crosses her arms over her chest, squeezing her tits and accentuating them. "You're a dictator, Nate. An impossible one."

"Come down. You have fifteen minutes."

"And if I don't?"

"You don't want to know. Behave."

Her lips part at that, and I leave the room before I grab her and fuck her while she's still sore.

I go to my room, and after I take a shower and put on my clothes, I go to fix breakfast. Martha gives me a look when she sees me. She's probably figured things out about us, but she doesn't say anything.

King knows how to hire staff who know not to meddle in affairs that are none of their business.

She offers to help me and I tell her I can take care of it, so she leaves to carry out her other chores.

By the time Gwyneth comes to the kitchen, I'm almost done.

"Sit down," I tell her without turning around. "I'll be finished in a bit."

Her arms wrap around my waist from behind and she rests her chin on my back.

I pause frying the eggs. "What are you doing?"

"Hugging you because you look sexy as hell preparing breakfast in your suit and apron."

Two polar opposite feelings slash through me at the same time. One is pride and a weird sense of joy I've never experienced before. But the other is red fucking alerts.

I might have miscalculated something.

Like Gwyneth's habit of staking her claim on everything whenever she goes after something.

And I need to make sure that's not the case here. That no "all in" is involved.

I turn off the stove and face her. "Are you having inappropriate thoughts about me?"

"Yeah, it's a problem."

"Only inappropriate thoughts, right?"

A delicate frown appears between her brows. "What do you mean?"

"Are there feelings involved that I should know about?"

"No," she says quickly, without thinking, and something shreds in my fucking chest. That's the answer I wanted to hear. So why the fuck do I want to grab her by the shoulders and shake her?

"Good, because I don't do that."

"You don't do feelings or you don't do attachment?"

"Both, and you know that."

"I do." Her coy little smirk falls for a moment, and then it's back in full bloom. "Don't go having feelings for me either, I'm just using you for sex, Uncle Nate."

I grind my teeth. "Why the fuck did you call me that?"

She steps back, giving me a sweet smile. "You are, aren't you? Uncle Nate."

"Stop it."

"I like it, though."

"Gwyneth."

"What, Uncle Nate?"

I grab her by the throat and her fake sweet smile drops. "Say that again and I'll fucking punish you."

She goes still, but her lips tremble and there's more blue in her eyes than the ethereal green from this morning. There's an un-natural brightness, too, almost like moisture gathering in them.

I glare at her and she glares right back, her gaze defiant and filled with so many things unsaid.

A commotion somewhere in the house breaks up our glaring session.

Martha's voice reaches us first. "Madam, you can't come in."

Before I can fathom what's going on, the woman I could've gone a lifetime without seeing again barges into the kitchen. The woman who shouldn't know about my arrangement with Gwyneth.

Her expression is snobby as she clutches her precious pearls. "Oh my God, Nathaniel! What are you doing?"

I release Gwyneth with a sigh. "Hello to you, too, Mom."

TWENTY-THREE

Gwyneth

NEVER THOUGHT MUCH ABOUT THE MEETING THE PARENTS part, because Nate and I aren't like that.

This whole thing is for convenience. There shouldn't be feelings he has to be aware of and I'm only using him for sex.

The asshole.

The fucking asshole.

I hate him so much sometimes, and okay, calling him Uncle Nate was probably not the best way to get revenge, but he hurt me. He cut me in half after giving me the best night and morning of my life. He turned me into a woman, took care of me, and slept beside me. And he didn't leave like he usually does.

He stayed.

Not to mention, he was nice and playful and took me to heights I didn't realize were possible. Then he crashed it all to the ground.

And I had to hurt him back. That's what Dad told me; if someone punches, you don't stand there and take it. You punch back, the hardest you can, with all your might and with twice the aggression.

So I did that and said I used him, and then I called him Uncle Nate because I know he hates it. He might've wanted me to call him that before, but that's not the case lately. There's been an unspoken rule about how he'll never refer to me as kiddo and I'll never call him Uncle.

But I said it to hurt him, not that it worked. He doesn't feel the same things we mortals do, because he's a god whose heart is made of stone. I can touch it, but I can never breathe life into it.

And now, there's another person with us, and I can't even touch his stone of a heart, because suddenly, there seems to be walls surrounding him. No, they're not mere walls.

They're forts.

Tall, solid ones that not even armies can bust through.

The reason is the person. The intruder. Debra Weaver. I know her, I've seen her countless times at the events I attended with Dad. Not to mention on TV. She's the second half of the Weaver power couple, Senator Brian Weaver's wife and a kickass woman.

At least, that's what I used to think.

Before I felt how Nate surrounded himself with a rigid exterior in her presence. As if she's the army closing in on his forts.

She doesn't look like an army. If anything, she appears classy and elegant in her tailored beige dress and her black high heels. Her golden hair is gathered in a neat twist and her light eyes have a serene look. She also looks way younger than she's said to be. I mean, Nate's older brother who died a long time ago was way older than him, ten years or more—if I remember correctly. So that makes Debra approximately in her late sixties, but she looks to be in her early fifties.

Anyway, she doesn't seem amused right now as she flicks her gaze between us like she's a merciless teacher and we're the two insolent kids in her class.

"I'm sorry," Martha tells Nate, but she peeks at me. "I couldn't stop her."

Why is Martha looking at me as if she pities me? I'm fine. I no longer feel like going to visit Dad and crying beside his bed because those feelings of abandonment are hitting me out of nowhere.

I don't hear the clinking emptiness in my half-full brain or feel the need to jot a million other words on my list.

I *don't.*

"Stop me?" Debra clicks her tongue. "This is my son's house and I get to come whenever I want."

"It's okay, Martha," Nate tells her in his usual calm tone, and she scurries away, bowing her head.

"It's not your son's house, it's my dad's," I correct her. Because it is, and I won't allow anyone to take anything of Dad's. Even with words.

Debra narrows her eyes on me, and holy shit, since when did they become so judgmental? They look so calming on TV and at events. "What did you just say to me, little girl?"

"I'm not a little girl. I'm twenty. And I said this is Dad's place."

"Go to the firm, Gwyneth," Nate coldly lashes out his order, and I internally flinch at the apathy in his tone. Is that how he's going to treat me now? As if I'm someone he can order around?

In that case, he has another thing coming.

"No, we have a visitor, so I'd like to stay." I flop onto a chair by the counter, where my cupcakes, my vanilla milkshake, and my boiled eggs are laid out because Nate remembers these things. He knows what I like to eat and drink and even look at. He just doesn't know how to be a fucking human being and has no trouble cutting me open. "You can join us for breakfast if you want."

I don't mean that as I stuff my face with a cupcake, but Debra approaches us, or more likely she's heading toward Nate, who's still standing where I left him, behind me.

"I can't believe this. This must be a distasteful joke." Debra sounds horrified.

"What are you doing here, Mom?" Nate is still in his usual unaffected mode, but there's tension at the end of his words.

"You weren't answering or returning my calls, so I had to come and see for myself."

Nate doesn't pick up his mom's calls? Now that I think about it, he rarely appears in public with his parents anymore, even though he's their only child now.

"When Susan told me you got married, I thought it was to that other one. What was her name again? Right, Aspen. Even though she has no origins, she at least has made a name for herself and I could work on her. I could make an image for her. But you married this…this…little girl? Kingsley's daughter? What were you thinking?"

I nearly swallow down all my milkshake and I don't bother with a straw either, but it doesn't quench the fire spreading in my throat. All her words make me burn. The fact that she was fine with him marrying Aspen. That Aspen is the right choice for him. That I'm a little girl.

God, I hate that and my age, and I think I hate Debra, too.

And—oh, Susan. I fucking despise her. Of course, she'd go tattle to Debra because she didn't get what she wanted.

"It's to protect the firm and King's assets," Nate says in that disturbed calm, the one that seems to be at the edge.

"It's still registered, Nathaniel. People will find out and I'll have to take care of the rumors and speculations. Do you know what they'll say about you? They'll say you wanted a kid, that you were attracted to her when she was underage and growing up before your eyes. They'll call you a deviant, a pedophile, and a damn predator!"

I flinch with each of her words. I flinch so violently that I spill some of my milkshake onto the counter and I'm clinking my nails. Hard. Fast.

Oh my God. She's right. That's what the press will say. They'll tear either me or Nate apart. They'll say I seduced him or he preyed on me.

And they'll definitely go for the latter because he's Nathaniel Weaver. The prince of the Weaver empire and a senator's son. So they'll want to bring him down and will try every trick under the sun to do it.

Every ugly trick.

The press loves his family. They stalk them. They write articles about them all the time.

Sebastian brought his girlfriend of Japanese descent to an event one time and they went nuts about the couple. They even wrote disgusting articles alleging that he's with her for publicity because having an Asian girlfriend makes him look good.

But anyone who's seen them in private knows how much Sebastian worships that woman. He loves her with a passion that could be sensed in the air and tasted with the subtle yet possessive ways he touches her.

They're one of the most badass couples on earth and no one would convince me otherwise. Definitely not the rotten media who spew lies for their own benefits.

Anyway, the Weavers are in the limelight all the time. And the press wouldn't hesitate to bring Nate and his family down. His parents will have to disown him to keep their image intact and—

"She's twenty years old and not an underage kid. Stop looking at her or treating her as a clueless child, and you know what? Fuck the press."

A breath I didn't know I was holding whooshes out of me. It's so long that I feel the burn in my lungs and the ashes of the fire settling at the base of my throat.

I stare back at Nate because I'm thankful. He didn't need to say those words, but he did, and now, I can finally breathe.

"Nathaniel!" Debra clutches her pearls. "This is serious. I will not allow you to endanger how far your father and I have come."

"I'm also serious, Mom. If you see it as a problem, prevent it beforehand or afterward with your media play. Otherwise, I don't give a fuck. Gwyneth is old enough to make her own decisions and neither you nor anyone else has a say in it."

Debra twists her lips.

Me, however? I want to hug him, but I can't, because he's an asshole and I can't have feelings for him.

Because even though he's standing up for me, he's doing it in a way a guardian would. In a way where I'm just under his care.

Where I *depend* on him.

"I don't approve of this, and neither does Brian," Debra announces. "You need to divorce her."

"With all due respect, I couldn't give a fuck about what either of you think."

"Nathaniel! How dare you speak to me in that tone?"

I sense it then, the hardening of his walls. They're turning into pure metal with each second and I want to stand and check on him, make sure he's okay, but his demeanor stops me. This Nate is kind of scary, and it's not the type of fear I'd jump straight toward. This type is darker and causes my spine to jerk into a line.

"Leave, Mom," he grinds out through his teeth. "And don't come back here again."

"I'm not moving until you promise to do the right thing."

"The right thing? What's that, Mom? Is it throwing me at the staff to raise me? Or maybe it's trying every trick under the sun to get rid of me when you were pregnant with me. You even took the very drugs you look down your nose on, right? But I was stubborn and insolent enough to come to life. So you decided neglect was the next thing you'd use to kill me. Nick was already there, so my presence wasn't needed, but I lived and he fucking died and that's not the right thing. It should've been the other way around. I should've been in that crash. Isn't that what you told Dad back then? Why did Nicholas die? Why not Nathaniel? Why did it have to be Nicholas?"

Slap.

The sound reverberates in the kitchen after Debra slaps Nate on the cheek.

I lose it then. Because the fire is burning me now. The thought that his parents treated him this way makes me stabby on his behalf and I want Debra gone. I want her to stop hardening his walls and turning him into a stone.

Even though his words were calm, I can sense the frosty coldness behind them. I can taste it on my tongue, and it stings.

So I practically jump from my seat and step in front of him, facing her. "Get out of our house. *Now*."

"You, shut up."

"No, *you* shut up. And get out before I call the police to arrest you for trespassing. I don't remember inviting you in. And believe me, a trespassing charge won't look good in the press."

She purses her thin lips together into a line, then releases them. I don't stop glaring at her the entire time, my arms crossed and my sneakers tapping on the floor.

"This isn't over," she announces before she spins around and leaves, the sound of her heels echoing down the hall.

I breathe out a puff of air and release my arms as I slowly turn to face Nate. I didn't expect him to be proud of me, but I didn't think he'd have a frown etched deep in his forehead either.

"Don't ever, and I mean ever, talk to her again."

"Yes, I will. I won't allow anyone to hurt you."

"That's not your fucking place, Gwyneth. My relationship with my mother or anyone else is none of your business."

"You're such a jerk."

"Now that you know that, stop meddling and go to work."

"If you keep pushing me away like this, you'll have no one left."

"I'm fine with that."

"I really hate you right now."

"I don't give a fuck. Now get your ass in the car and go to the firm."

He's breathing harshly, I realize, his chest muscles stretching his shirt and the apron with every move. And it's like he's on the verge of something—what, I don't know. I shouldn't care either, because his words have dug a deep, black hole in my chest.

Is it too late to add his name to the negative words list?

Because I desperately need to be desensitized to him. I need to stop hurting because he got hurt by his parents. I need to stop being in pain because he's cold and frigid and his tall forts are closing in on me, crushing me in the middle.

So I grab my bag and storm out of the house, and I drive so recklessly, it scares me. Maybe this is how Dad was that day. He knew something was wrong and got into an accident.

That ominous thought makes me gulp and I slow down, way down, and put on a mash-up playlist of Twenty One Pilots and NF because they calm me. They're special, like I am.

Special people are misunderstood and that's okay. Special people get hurt and that's also okay. Because we're special that way. No forts would destroy us or keep us out.

After a while of soaking in the music, I'm ready to get engrossed in something different than the clusterfuck of this entire morning. But I don't go to the firm straight away, I head to the car company, where I have to sign some paperwork and show ID to prove I'm Dad's next of kin so that I can get the dashcam's files.

Then I drive to the firm and snuggle up beside Jane in IT to enjoy the peace away from Nate's watchful eyes. He has a meeting with the other partners anyway, so I'm safe for a little while.

Jane offers to help me sort through the files' different dates.

We both sit with headphones on, listening to the recordings and watching the feeds. I choke on my own tears the whole time. Seeing Dad talking, driving, and alive forms a ball in my chest. It expands with each second and I don't think it'll ever deflate. Or maybe I'll have some sort of a heart attack. Panic attack. Or any attack.

I pause when I see the last person I expect get into Dad's car. Aspen. She yanks the door open and flops into the passenger seat.

"Get the fuck out," Dad barks at her, and even I wince at it.

I often forget that he's not the same person around other people as he is around me.

He might have been a doting father to you, but he was a ruthless devil to everyone else. Her words come back to me as a reality.

"You need to stop being difficult for no reason, Kingsley," she tells him, her tone as hard as his.

"I have my conditions and they're final."

"*Nonsensical* conditions. You can't possibly expect them to accept those conditions."

"They will do it peacefully and settle or we'll go to court and make them. Either way, I will win."

"You don't even want it done the peaceful way, do you?"

"Peaceful ways are boring. Now, get out. I've spoken to you enough for this decade."

She flips him the finger as she steps out of the car.

"Fucking witch," Dad mutters under his breath and drives away.

I'm left skeptical about the entire exchange, but I push on and listen to his phone calls, which are mostly with his assistant about work and court. Many are with me, asking what I want for dinner.

Moisture gathers in my eyes when I watch the easing of his expression whenever he talks to me. I took everything for granted. His love, his attention, his presence. And now, I have none of those.

Jane taps my shoulder and I stare at her, removing my headphones. She gives me hers and points at the laptop. "I think you should listen to this."

I plug in the headphones and hit Play. The image on the screen is of Dad driving. He's wearing the suit from the day of the accident, and he has those dark circles under his eyes.

An unknown number flashes on the dash and Dad answers with, "Tell me you found her."

I lean closer in my seat, but I can't hear what the other person is saying, because Dad is listening through an earpiece. However, I see the change in his face, the way it turns to granite, and his knuckles tighten on the steering wheel.

"That can't be..." His voice is low, almost a murmur. "She can't be Gwen's mother. Look again."

He ends the call, throws the earpiece down, then hits the

steering wheel a few times in a row. I can almost feel the rattling of the dashboard in front of him, because it's inside me, too.

I didn't hear it wrong, did I? He said Gwen's mother, right? Does that mean Dad was looking for her?

According to what I just heard, he found her. He did, and then the accident happened.

The whole thing can't be a coincidence, can it?

TWENTY-FOUR

Nathaniel

"I THOUGHT YOU WOULDN'T SURVIVE MRS. WEAVER."

I glare at my nephew as he slides on top of the conference table, facing me. The other partners left, but he stayed behind to play the bastard role.

"You knew she was coming and didn't tell me?"

He raises his hands in the air. "Hey. I only got the call after she left. A furious one at that in all of Mrs. Weaver's snobbish glory. She kept asking if I knew and then said of course I did and that I should bear the consequences if this becomes public and all that fun stuff. But most of all, she was royally pissed that "the little girl" kicked her out. Gwen really did that?"

"Gwyneth. The name is Gwyneth." And she did. She kicked out my mother even though she's not the type who shows rudeness without a reason. Despite her smart tongue and sass, she's not an antagonist. But she has a strong sense of justice and that's what pushed her to talk to Mrs. Weaver that way.

I've been in a gloomy mood ever since she left this morning.

I'm surprised I was able to handle this meeting with enough reasoning.

It shouldn't be this way. It shouldn't feel empty, harsh, and unyielding, as if something inside me is lifeless. As if her hollowness is now with me and I couldn't get rid of it even if I tried, because that emptiness is restricting my breathing, no matter how much I loosen my tie.

And because she transferred her hollowness to me, there's an urge to go find her, to fucking talk some sense into her so she stops having girlhood dreams. Because that's all they are, girlhood fucking dreams and misconceptions and everything in between.

But even if I do talk to her, she'll make those dreams shine harder and brighter. Gwyneth is the type of person who thrives on small gestures yet plummets hard because of them as well. And I can't let her tow that line.

"She's more like King than I thought." Sebastian grins with amusement and I want to wipe it off of his face. I don't want him or any fucking one amused by her. I'm the only one who should be afforded that luxury.

A few months back, he never would have grinned or acted amused. But ever since he got back with his girlfriend, Naomi, I see more of his old charming self shining through and it's a relief. I hate the grouchy, grumpy person he became after she was gone. But that doesn't mean I'll let him have fun at my expense.

"If you're finished, go back to work."

"I'm far from finished. You still didn't tell me what you'll do."

"About?"

"Mrs. Weaver."

"I don't care about her or anyone else."

"But she could be right. The entire situation could backfire."

"And I'll take care of it accordingly when it does."

"That doesn't sound like you, Nate."

I stare at him, even though I understand what he's saying. I'm not the type who moves without counting my steps or the possible effects. Despite the hasty decision of marrying Gwyneth, I studied the outcome. I knew there could be complications, because I don't trust Susan and her destructive ways. Even though King's father was smart enough to have Susan sign an NDA that forbids her from slandering his family, King and Gwyneth included, in the press or she'll lose any right to his money, I know that's not a guarantee. I even have a press statement ready just in case.

But those precautions suddenly don't feel like enough. Because at that point, I didn't count on going this far with Gwyneth.

I didn't count on tasting her and becoming addicted. I didn't count on being so fucking entangled with her that I can't see the light at the end of the tunnel anymore.

"I'll handle it when it becomes a problem," I tell Sebastian, who's still waiting.

"Do you have something prepared?"

"Of course."

"How about Gwen?"

"She has nothing to do with this."

"Hello? She's your wife. Of course she does."

I like that. *She's your wife.* Everything else he said, however, doesn't have the same impact. "She's staying out of this and that's final, Sebastian. Don't even think about bringing it up to her if things get ugly. I don't want her involved. Got it?"

He nods slowly but watches me as if we're meeting for the first time. "You're different."

"Different how?"

"A few weeks ago, I swear you would've made her stand in front of the press with a carefully written statement and you would've prepared her to recite it with the right emotions and body language that would seem innocent but would actually be calculated. You'd make it into a sob story, because that's what you do best, isn't it? You use your clients' goals as a motivator to turn them into actors and win cases. It's how you've gotten this far."

It is.

That's how large and limitless my ambition is. I win cases to use them as stepping stones. I win cases, not because I have a sense of justice, but because I'm plagued with an insatiable need to go somewhere.

Anywhere.

Like a train.

"She's not one of my clients. She's my best friend's daughter."

"Is that all?" He's smiling again.

"What the fuck is that supposed to mean?"

"Don't get too defensive, Uncle. I'm just asking an innocent question here. Is she only King's daughter to you?"

"Fuck off."

"Annnd I got the answer I need."

"Why do you sound so happy? I thought you were against this marriage."

"That was when I thought she was caught in one of your webs and would be another stepping stone, but turns out that's not the case. Maybe it hasn't been all along." He hops off the table and taps my shoulder. "Best of luck, Nate."

"With what?"

"Being caught in someone's web for once."

And with that, he strolls out, humming a happy tune.

His words keep playing at the back of my head all day long, refusing to shut up or disappear.

When it's time to go home, I'm ready to stop trying to ignore Gwyneth's presence. She's spent the whole day with the IT girl, according to Grace, and I know that's one of her peaceful places, so I didn't call for her. She gave my assistant all the work I asked of her anyway, so I didn't have a reason to.

Now, I do.

Now, I need to sit her the fuck down and tell her about all her options. The ones I talk to my clients about so they have no rosy thoughts about what's waiting for them in the real world.

I never wanted Gwyneth to be on the receiving end of that, but I need her to be prepared. I need her to be able to stand tall, even if she becomes a target.

She's not in the IT department, though. And her silent friend isn't there either. My jaw tightens when one of the engineers tells me she left with Jane and Christoph.

Of course, it's fucking Christoph again.

I retrieve my phone and call her as I head to my car, but she doesn't pick up.

My fist wraps around the steering wheel so tight, I nearly break it from its hinges.

Then I dial her again as I drive out of W&S. Still no answer.

I loosen my tie as I hit the gas and reach the house in record time. She really needs to learn how to answer her fucking phone.

When I go into the house, however, no loud music fills the air and there's no sound of her off-tune singing and chaotic dancing.

It's quiet.

Lifeless.

Empty.

Just like the hole she fucking left me with.

Martha has left for the day and it's just one giant, silent house. This would've been my haven not so long ago. This is what I prefer, after all—silence, order, and complete discipline.

This is what I work for, what I like to come home to. But now, that same silence sounds violent and so fucking wrong.

I call her again and yank my tie when she doesn't pick up.

My head crowds with images of her with Christoph and I nearly break the phone that continues ringing in my ear.

I'm on the verge of breaking other things, too.

My mind is going to ugly places where he has his hands on her, where his hands are on her fucking body. The same body that belongs to me and shouldn't be touched by anyone but me.

But what makes me really lose it isn't only that he's touching her physically but that he's also reaching her emotionally. That he's in places I would never fucking be.

That drives me into an obsessive thought process that I wouldn't allow myself to spiral into under normal circumstances.

But these are anything but normal.

I decide to focus on work since it usually clears my mind.

Not tonight, though.

Because I keep staring at my watch, at the minutes and hours ticking by.

I keep thinking about her barging in to confiscate my coffee and replace it with vanilla flavored green tea. In her words, tea is better for my health and she can't have me getting sick.

"I'm, like, the protector of W&S right now. Imagine if the mighty Nate Weaver gets sick? Nuh-uh, that can't happen," she said the other night when she put the tea on my desk. She was wearing one of her countless pairs of tiny denim shorts and a tank top that fell off her pale shoulders, and her damp hair covered the small of her back. Due to being too impatient, she never properly dries her hair.

"For the thousandth time, I prefer coffee, Gwyneth."

"Coffee doesn't let you sleep at night. Trust me, tea is better."

"And I should take your word for it?"

"Yup. As your personal caregiver, I know what I'm doing."

"Personal caregiver, huh?"

She grinned, flipped her hair, then cleared her throat. "Yeah. That's me."

"I don't remember giving you the title."

"I volunteered. It's not about you, Nate. It's about W&S's and Dad's legacy."

"I see."

"Yeah, so you kind of have to roll with it."

"Is that so?"

"Uh-huh."

"Tell me something, is my personal caregiver supposed to be wearing that?" I tipped my chin to her top that said "Good Fucking Girl" in capital letters.

Without breaking eye contact, she grabbed it by the hem, pulling it down until it molded against her breasts. She wasn't wearing a bra, because one of her rosy nipples peaked and showed through. My dick strained against my pants at the tease.

"Aren't I?"

"Aren't you what?"

"A good girl."

"You're fucking distracting, that's what you are." I tapped my desk. "Come here."

"Why?" She stretched her tank top until I could see the peak of her other nipple. "Are you going to make me a good girl?"

"It'll be the exact opposite. Come here. Now."

She did and I showed her just how bad she was while she was only wearing that tank top. And then she fell asleep on the couch in my office, and I was even more distracted all night long.

But that doesn't compare to how distracted I am right now. It's late and she hasn't come home yet, not to mention that she's still not answering her phone.

Just when I'm thinking about going back to the firm to get Christoph's number from HR, my phone vibrates in my hand.

My hopes crush when I find Knox's name flashing on the screen.

I answer with a, "What do you want?"

There's a low humming of music from his end, like he's outside somewhere loud. "Hello to you, too, Nate."

"It's after-hours, in case you haven't noticed."

"I have, which is why I'm calling." Then I hear the rustle of clothes and the shuffling of feet. "Hang on."

"Mmmm." It's a female mumble or a moan beside him, but I can't tell for sure.

"Don't tell me you're screwing someone and calling me in the meantime?"

"I'm more professional than that. I'm just…checking on something…now stay quiet for me, beautiful."

"I'm still waiting for the reason behind your call, Knox."

"Oh, right. Aren't you Gwen's new guardian or dictator or whatever? I thought you should know she's drunk enough that she can't stand up."

I jerk to my feet so fast that the rolling chair slams against the wall. "She's with you?"

"Not technically."

"Knox, tell me that's not her voice I heard just now or I swear to fuck…"

"It's not her. Jesus Christ, calm down, Nate. I ran into her when I came into the club."

That's where she's been all along. The fucking club.

I bark at Knox to send me the address, but I can't keep my cool, because all the anger and tension from today are on the verge of exploding.

And she'll be the one to bear my wrath.

TWENTY-FIVE

Gwyneth

I'M NOT DRUNK.

Yes, I'm swaying and my body feels light and hot, but it's only because of the music.

And the dancing.

I don't usually like electro, but the buzzing of energy keeps me on a high. I dragged Christoph and Jane with me and even called Jen and Alex to join us. Jen couldn't, but Alex is a party guy so he showed up soon after.

They're all party people, actually. I'm usually the fun-ruiner. The one with a words phobia and a general phobia of the outside world.

But maybe I'm drunk, after all, so it doesn't really matter.

Alex is a few steps behind me, jumping to the upbeat music. He's a bit taller than me, but he's lean and fit because of all the cycling he does. Chris is dancing with me, letting me use his hand to twirl, even though he said we should go home an hour ago.

He repeats it again, shouting over the music, "You've had too much to drink, Gwen. I'll give you a ride."

"No! I'm not druuunk," I slur. Okay, maybe I am. But only a little.

"Gwen, come on." Chris tries to grab hold of my arm, but I pull myself free and plaster my back against Alex's front.

"You go home. I'm staaaying." I shake my ass against Alex and he wraps his arms around my waist and we sway to the music together. "Alex is so much fun."

He's fun because he's laid back and loves weed, but he doesn't care about anyone enough. That's why I've always preferred spending time with Chris. People like Chris who appreciate that I'm a bit crazy, a bit different are rare to find. But that's the thing, I don't want to be crazy or different tonight. I want to be like Alex. I want to forget about what I saw and heard today.

From Debra to Nate to Dad. I want to forget that my father was searching for my mother and when he found her, he had a deadly accident.

Because abandoning me wasn't enough, so she had to take Dad away from me, too.

Moisture gathers in my eyes and I wipe it away with the back of my hand. I'm grateful it's dark enough in here that no one can see my weakness.

The darkness is soothing sometimes.

Tonight is to forget. That's why I bought a slutty dress that's too tight, barely covers my ass and shows half of my back, and then I drank more shots than I can remember.

But it's like I'm floating in a different place than the dance floor. Yes, I'm in the midst of writhing bodies, upbeat music, and violet lights, but I'm not. I'm roaming inside that emptiness again, letting it fester and rot me to the bones.

Usually, I'm able to fill it, to somehow push it away by repeating the words *hollow*, *empty*, and *void* in my head. Not tonight, though. Tonight, it hurts so much that I'm unable to desensitize anything.

"Where's Jane?" I ask Chris while Alex and I move to the rhythm of the music.

Even though I convinced her to put on a dress and come with us, she was anxious out of her mind because there are a lot of people here and she dislikes them more than I do on my empty days.

She refused to dance or drink or anything, just sat down with an energy drink in the corner of our booth, but she's not there anymore.

"She probably left," Chris shouts over the music. "It's time you do, too, Gwen."

"Why are you being sooo difficult?" I run my fingers under his chin.

"Yeah, dude." Alex moves his hands up and down my side, feeling me up. "Chill."

"Maybe we should teach him." I grin and while I'm still swaying against Alex, I grab Chris by the cheeks and pull him close so that he's glued to my front.

Then I rub my ass and stomach against their erections, feeling them get hard all at once. Grunts and groans fill my ears and I lick my lips, so intoxicated on the feeling of having them both so turned on by me.

"This isn't you, Gwen," Chris whispers in my ear, arousal evident in his tone.

I glide my breasts against his chest and my ass against Alex's growing erection. "Maybe it is."

We're not dancing anymore. In a few seconds, the scene has turned into full on grinding, and I ride it out. I let the wave consume me because they want me, both of them, and if I let them, they'd have me at the same time.

But when I close my eyes, it's not Chris and Alex who are engraved so deep into my soul that I see his face as if he were here.

There's a frown there, a tension in his jaw because he doesn't like this. He doesn't like me grinding my body against two guys who aren't him. So I do it harder, I take it to the next level until their hard-ons are poking against my dress, and they're the only things I feel.

You hurt me first. This is what it feels like to be hurt, asshole.

It doesn't matter that I want to believe those words, to believe that I could hurt him by giving myself away to someone else, because my body and soul and even my mind hate that idea.

And my heart. It's currently clenching and squeezing and clawing at me to stop.

This isn't what I want. These aren't the hands that make me feel safe, like I could let go at any time and still wouldn't crash to the ground.

"What the…"

I hear Alex's dazed voice before that same strong hand I just thought about is wrapped around my wrist and I'm pulled out with a force that steals my breath.

Please don't tell me my imagination is running wild enough to conjure something that isn't real.

When I open my eyes, I gasp at the sight in front of me.

I'm pressed up against a body all right, but it's neither Alex nor Chris. This one is harder, taller, broader, and so masculine, it should be a crime.

He should be a crime.

Because I'm always tempted to commit this particular crime, to take that step that will push me off the edge, even if I know that I will hit the ground at some point. Even if I'm sure it'd be the last step I'd take.

I guess that's what criminals feel. They know they might get caught, that they'll be punished, but they still go for it anyway. Because the crime is worth it.

And I'm staring at one right now. At my own crime, and that emptiness doesn't feel as damning anymore, nor is it lethal. It's just lurking in the background, unable to manifest into anything.

Nate had always had that effect on me. His presence is so sharp and imposing that it eats up any hollowness.

"Let her go." It's Alex who speaks, sounding drunker than me.

I'm not really focused on them, because my wrist is being held hostage by Nate, and my soft curves are glued to his hard muscles, and he's glaring.

God, even the way he glares is hot. My thighs clench and my nipples harden, and it has nothing to do with the not-really-dancing I was just doing.

From my peripheral vision, I can see Chris shaking his head at Alex while rubbing the back of his neck.

Alex, however, steps toward us—or, more accurately, staggers. "Who the fuck are you?"

"I'm her husband. Put your hands on my wife again and I'll break them." And just like that, Nate pulls me behind him and pushes through the crowd.

It's impossible to keep up. One, I'm drunk—so drunk that I see double and can't feel my legs. Two, I think Nate just told them he's my husband. He broke his own rule and told my friends that we're married.

Holy shit.

I think I'm drunker than I thought, because I'm unable to sort through all of these things.

When I keep tripping over my own feet, Nate picks me up bridal style. My arms automatically wrap around his neck and I squeal, but I don't hear it through all the noise and chaos.

Once again, I'm caught in a trance by how easily he carries me, how effortless the act is, as if he's not lifting a person in his arms. Not just any person. Me. His wife. That's what he said, right?

Put your hands on my wife again and I'll break them.

I wiggle in his hold but not so he'll put me down, just to feel him more. To feel the strength of his taut arms wrapped around my back and under my legs. To soak in the hardness of his chest against my side and to breathe in his scent that's more intoxicating than alcohol.

He's not paying any attention to me, though.

Nate never watches me, not like I watch him. He doesn't stop to see me as I see him.

The emptiness I shoved to the background jostles and rears its ugly head, and I don't have the strength to push it back down.

I don't have the strength to fight it.

The night air hits us and I shiver as he strides toward the parking lot. I don't even focus on the onlookers who are watching us.

They don't matter.

They never did. People don't understand. People judge.

He doesn't. Nate's never judged me, even when he acts like an asshole with multiple jerk tendencies. He's strict but never judgmental.

He's practical, but never narrow-minded.

"Nate…" I whisper his name in the silence of the night, and I sound so drunk and emotional because he's still not looking at me.

"Shut the fuck up, Gwyneth. I don't want to hear your voice right now." The harsh anger of his words is like a slap to my face, a hard one that springs tears. They're gathered in my lids now and I don't get the chance to wipe them away before he opens his car door and drops me in the passenger seat.

After he fastens my seatbelt, he yanks off his jacket and throws it on top of me. It smells like him—spices and woods and damnation. That's what he is and always will be.

My crime and my worst damnation.

Another word on my *D* list.

By the time he's in the driver's side, I'm clenching the jacket tight against my hammering chest.

He pulls out of the parking lot and drives down the streets in silence. There's no radio or words, and the more time passes, the tighter my grip on his jacket gets.

"Aren't you going to say something? Anything?" I try not to slur but do so anyway.

"I said to shut your mouth, Gwyneth."

"I don't want to shut up. I want to talk, okay?" It's probably liquid courage—or stupidity or whatever—but it's there and I'm taking the bull by the horns. "In case you didn't notice, you ruined my evening."

"What the fuck did you just say?" He fixates me with a sideways glance and it pins me to my seat so forcefully, I hiccup. Or maybe that's because of the alcohol.

"My evening, Nate. I was having fun until you showed up." I'm feigning nonchalance and lying through my teeth.

No, I wasn't having fun. I was miserable and headed down a path I didn't like even in my intoxicated brain.

"You were having fun grinding against those kids and I ruined it, is that what you're saying?"

"We...were dancing."

"I saw your ass and stomach rubbing against their fucking dicks, Gwyneth. There was no fucking dancing involved."

"Maaaybe."

"Did you like it?" His voice is calm, but his entire body is tight, especially the hand on the steering wheel. That strong, veiny hand that I dreamt about when he wasn't there.

"Did I like what?"

"Humping them, gliding your body against their dicks and turning the two of them so fucking crazy with lust that they would've taken you on the dance floor. Did you like it?"

"Maybe I did. Maybe I'm a slut." I throw his jacket to the side, still high on the alcohol-induced adrenaline.

I remove my seatbelt and close the distance separating us, pressing my breasts against his shirt-covered arm.

"What the fuck are you doing, Gwyneth?"

"I'm showing you how much of a slut I am." I press my lips to his hot neck and trail my hand from his chest to his erection. It jumps to life under my touch and I squeeze it as I continue kissing down his collarbone.

"Get back to your seat. Now." He's ordering me, but I'm too far gone to listen. His body is tightening against mine and I rub my breasts down his arm, hardening the tight buds until they're painful.

"My nipples didn't get this hard earlier, you know." I take his free hand and slip it under my dress until he's sinking his fingers against my folds. "I wasn't this wet either. Do you know what that means?"

He doesn't look at me, his entire attention on the road, but he doesn't remove his hand from my pussy either. "What?"

My lips meet the shell of his ear and I whisper, "It means I'm only a slut for you, Nate."

The change is barely noticeable, but it's there in his flaring nostrils and the tic in his jaw. His fingers tighten on my core and I moan, feeling my wetness drenching my panties and messing up his hand and my thighs. That's all I've ever been for freaking five years.

A mess.

And it's one of the most beautiful messes to have ever been created.

One that he made. One that he keeps nurturing.

"No, you're not." He removes his hand from me and the car comes to a halt. We're already home, but I couldn't care less about that right now, because he stopped touching me.

"What? Why?"

His eyes meet mine, and I think I liked it better when they hadn't, because there's a strong current there that's about to sweep me under and bury me in its depths.

"You're not my slut if you let other people touch what's fucking mine. Get the fuck off me."

I do the exact opposite and awkwardly tumble forward until I'm sitting on his lap. My legs stretch wide on either side of him so that I'm able to sit down. But I don't sit anywhere. I lift my dress and lower myself onto his erection, so his cock is nudging against my soaked panties.

My core clenches in remembrance of him inside me and the image turns me delirious as I glide myself against his bulge.

"Gwyneth, stop."

I shake my head frantically. "I lied. I didn't like it, not really."

"You didn't like what?"

"Grinding against Alex and Chris."

"Then why the fuck did you do it?"

"Because…" I wet my lips. "Because I wanted to forget."

"Forget what?"

"You…among other things. But it didn't work. All I could think about was you." I bite my lower lip because his hard-on is growing against my swollen folds and I can't help rocking against it. Back and forth until I'm so wet, my thighs are soaked with the evidence.

His strong hand wraps around my waist, under the dress that's now bunched to my stomach. He jerks his hips up as I go down and I whimper. "You thought about me, huh?"

"Yeah."

"What did you think about?"

"Your strong hands and hard chest. I thought about your cock, too, and how big it is." I'm dry-humping him now, my movements turned frantic by his thrusts.

"What else?"

"I thought about how much my pussy wants you. Not anyone else, you."

"Because it's my pussy?"

"Yeah. It is."

"And you're a slut. *My* slut."

"I am." He didn't ask, but I'm answering anyway. I'm sliding up and down, fucking myself on his bulge and I'm getting close, so close that my legs tremble.

"Is my slut going to let anyone else but me touch her again?"

"No…no…I won't…"

"That's right, because if you do, I'll fuck up their lives, Gwyneth. I mean it."

I come then. It's so harsh and intense that I scream. I scream loud and uncensored, not caring that someone might pass by and see me becoming his slut.

That someone could see me screaming and panting and moaning Nate's name.

Actually, they should.

I really wish someone would see me shattering all over him.

His words shouldn't make me this horny. I shouldn't come at the promise of him hurting people because they touched me, but I do, and it goes on for such a long time that I don't think I'll ever come down.

The alcohol in my blood makes my head buzz as I stare at him through droopy eyes, still rocking back and forth against him. At some point, both of his hands wrap around my waist and now it feels like everything is complete.

There's something in his dark gaze. I don't know what, but it's there, and it's filling me with so many emotions at once.

I lean in to kiss him. My mouth is a few inches away from his lips, the same lips I've fantasized about since I was fifteen and got my first taste of when I was eighteen.

The forbidden lips that I shouldn't have wanted to kiss in the first place but couldn't help myself.

But before I can touch them, he pulls away and opens the door, and I jerk back, my action delayed because of all the alcohol in my bloodstream.

I don't hear it, but I feel when my heart splinters to pieces.

What was I thinking anyway? Men don't kiss their sluts. Even if they make them their wives.

I ease off of him, as awkwardly as I planted myself on his lap, and he gets out first.

He waits for me in front of the car, probably to carry me, but I run ahead of him to the house. I'm hot.

Too hot.

And my steps are wobbly and incoherent. But I'm burning, and that needs to go away. That and the fucking breaking that's currently happening in my chest.

My feet come to a halt at the edge of the luminous pool. Water.

I unhook my zipper and push the dress down my body, then yank away my panties so that I'm completely naked.

"Gwyneth, don't," Nate calls out in the distance, but I'm not listening. Because he's the cause of this burn. He's the reason I have to do this.

Taking a deep breath, I jump in.

Shock ripples through me, but the burn doesn't go away. Is there water for internal fire? Because I'm about to explode from it.

My lungs burn and I realize it's because I haven't been breathing. That's when I realize something else, too.

I can't move.

TWENTY-SIX

Nathaniel

"**F**UCK!" I KICK MY SHOES AWAY AND RUN TO THE POOL. Where Gwyneth just jumped in because she wasn't thinking and she's drunk as fuck. If she had access to her brain, she would've remembered that she doesn't know how to swim.

She's the type who always has some sort of a crutch, even when she's in the shallow end of the pool. No matter how much King tried to teach her, she never learned to swim.

The seconds tick by like a damn lifetime the more she doesn't resurface. She's not even flailing around like she usually does when the crutches are taken away.

I curse under my breath as I plunge in after her, diving deep into the cold water.

The more time I spend getting to her, the harder my fucking heart beats. It doesn't slow down even after I grab her by the arm and haul her to the surface. She splutters for breath, coughing and choking on water.

Her legs circle my waist and she uses me as a lifeline. Her entire body is wrapped around mine as I swim to where I can stand.

I grab her by the shoulders, shaking her. "What the *fuck* were you thinking just now?"

"I...wasn't thinking..."

"Why the fuck weren't you thinking? Do you want to die? Is that it, Gwyneth?"

"No, it's just..."

"It's just what?"

"It burned. I only wanted it to stop burning," she slurs, blinking away the water from those fucking eyes. They're bluer now, reflecting the surface of the water.

"What burned?"

"Everything." Her shoulders slump in my hold. "I thought the water would fix it."

"The water you don't know how to swim in."

"Oh."

"Right. Fucking *oh*. What would've happened if I hadn't been here?"

She flinches but says nothing.

"Answer me. What the fuck would've happened if you'd been on your own, Gwyneth?"

"I...would've drowned."

Her softly-spoken words stab me in the fucking chest and I have to close my eyes for a second to chase away their impact. The thought of her drowning, gurgling and choking on water with no one to save her is like the monster I feared as a kid.

Turns out that monsters can show up at any time in your life. I just never thought that this damn woman would be the cause of it.

And then as I open my eyes and look at her bloodshot ones and the strands of her hair sticking to her face and neck, I realize it's not only about the possibility of her drowning.

It's about her being hurt in any way and my not being there.

It'd kill me.

Even if I'm mad at her, even if I'm still seeing red from when I caught her drunk and grinding against two guys. Fucking *two*.

All my self-control was used up at that moment, because if it were up to me, I would've claimed her in front of them and showed the world who she belongs to.

I would've fucked her in front of them, then blinded their fucking eyes.

But that anger and violent possessiveness are nothing compared to the fear that she could've died if she'd been here all alone.

That her reckless behavior I once thought was adorable could've taken her away from me.

"That's right. You would've fucking drowned." I dig the pads of my fingers into her shoulders. "This nonsense will never be repeated. Understand?"

"Okay."

"And you're not drinking again until you're twenty-one, and you know the meaning of drinking responsibly."

A delicate frown etches in her forehead and she slurs, "Stop talking to me as if I'm a kid. I hate that."

"Then don't act like one. And for the last goddamned time, answer your phone when I call you."

She bites her lower lip but doesn't say anything.

"I mean it, Gwyneth. You can't disappear without notice again."

"Why?"

"What do you mean why?"

"Why would you care whether I disappear or not? Whether I answer your calls or not?"

I grind my jaw, but before I can say anything, she tightens her legs that are wrapped around my waist. "Is it because you're my husband?"

"Yes."

"You told Chris and Alex that. You said you're my husband and I'm your wife."

"You are." I never thought I would like saying those words out loud, but there was a weight that lifted off my chest the moment that statement was out in the open.

"And you care about me."

"I do."

"Like your wife or like your best friend's daughter?"

"Both."

She scrunches her nose at that, but she plants a palm on my cheek. "But it's only sex, so I'm, like, your trophy wife."

"You can't be my trophy wife when you own as much as I do, Gwyneth."

"True. But it's still just sex."

I don't say anything, but I don't need to, because there's something other than water glistening in her gaze and the gray is warring with the green and the blue, slaughtering them to take complete control.

She releases my waist and I think she'll make the short trip to the edge of the pool, but she dives underwater.

Is she going to be reckless again? Gwyneth and alcohol are clearly not the best of friends and I need to keep her far away from it in the future.

Just when I'm about to go under and shake the fuck out of her, she grabs my hips with both hands and unbuckles my belt.

What the…?

My dick, that's been semi-hard since she dry-humped me in the car, thickens and hardens when she frees it with her tiny hands. Then she's on the surface again, holding on to my shirt.

The water contrasts against her pale skin, the rosy tips of her tits hardening. I grab one of them and squeeze, making her moan.

"What are you doing, Gwyneth?"

She wraps her arms around my neck, using the water to lift herself up so that she's at my eye level. "Fuck me, husband."

My muscles tighten and my nostrils flare at her sure yet playful tone.

"You're drunk, wife."

"I can take you."

"Are you sure you can fit my cock up that tight pussy? Last time, you said it was too big."

"It's okay if it hurts a little. I like it." She wiggles around, pressing her tits against my chest. "Fuck me and make it hurt."

"Why do you want it to hurt?"

"Because it means you're giving me your all. And I'll take it." There's a challenge in her eyes, a pure fucking fire that's blazing in the middle of the water.

"You'll take what?"

"Everything you have to offer and everything you don't."

My fingers dig into the flesh of her hipbone and it's neither gentle nor soft. It's rough and unapologetic because the challenge in her words is still burning and has to be put out.

"You need to learn your fucking place, Gwyneth."

She runs her fingers through my hair and murmurs against my ear, "Make me."

I back her up against the wall of the pool and she gasps when her back hits it.

"Are we going to have sex now?" Her voice is a bit low, but it's sultry and throaty.

"We're not going to have sex. I'm going to fuck you, wife."

Placing both hands under her ass cheeks, I part them and lift her up, then bring her down until I'm fully inside her. In one fucking go.

She whimpers, shaking around my length as her cunt clenches, swallowing me in.

"See? You can't take me."

"I can..." she whispers.

"How about this?" I start rocking and thrusting into her with minimum lubrication due to the water. Then I part her ass wider, giving my dick more access so that I'm in her deeper than before.

"Oh, fuck..." Her head rolls back.

"Language."

"But I...uh...it feels so good." She rocks her hips, thrusting her tits in my face and I suck a nipple into my mouth, nibbling on it until she's trembling and her incoherent noises of pleasure echo in the air.

Seeing her so pleased, so lost and unable to take the onslaught of sensations is the most gratifying thing I've ever experienced.

Her nails sink into my shoulder blades as she holds on to me for dear life when I pick up my pace. I release her nipple and bite on the creamy skin of her breasts, causing her to cry out and dig the heels of her feet into my ass.

My lips, tongue, and teeth take a journey up her breasts and neck, leaving giant red marks behind. Then I hold her ass with one hand and grab a fistful of her hair, pulling her back to feast on the sensitive flesh of her pulse point. I devour her and leave the biggest mark of all. The one people will see and know that she fucking belongs to me.

I marked her. I claimed her. She's mine.

After I release her hair, I grab two handfuls of her ass, squeezing. "Is this hard enough for you, baby girl?"

"More." She's panting, rolling her hips to meet mine and partially failing. "Please...I want more."

I thrust up her tight channel, pull almost all the way out, and drive back in again. Then I lift her up so she nearly lets me go and bring her down on my length. She moans, then whimpers and holds on to me with all her might.

"Does that mean I shouldn't take it easy on you?"

"No. Don't. I like it this way."

"What way?"

"Rough. Out of control." Her eyes shine with tears. "I like *you* out of control."

That makes me lose all my inhibitions and I drive into her with a speed that makes her bounce, her tits temptingly close, so I take one of them in my mouth and nibble and suck. I make her writhe and shake so hard that there are waves around us due to our explosive joining.

Still parting her ass cheeks, I slip my thumb inside the opening and speak against her nipple. "I will claim this ass soon, baby girl, and it's going to be filthy and dirty. It's going to hurt, too. Worse than when my dick made your pussy bleed."

"Yes…please…" She strangles me, her cunt choking me as she comes undone.

There are masterpieces and then there's Gwyneth's face when she's having an orgasm. Her head rolls back and the darkest of greens overwhelm her irises as her eyes droop and her skin flushes red. She trembles, her whole body going into a shock reaction as a translation of the sensations plaguing her body.

Her lips drop open, begging for something to be in them or on them. Like my own lips.

It takes everything in me not to give into the urge. A fucking dangerous one at that, and so I fuck her harder instead, pushing my thumb all the way into her ass until her tight ring of muscles swallows it and she's full of me.

Until I'm the only one she can see, think of, or feel.

Only me.

"You're not going to go around boys again, do you understand?"

"Yes, yes…" she chants, her nails dragging down my back and bicep muscles.

"No one will touch you but me."

"Mmm…yes!"

"Now, say it."

"No one will touch me but you."

"Because you're mine."

"I'm yours."

Those words and her overwhelming heat lure my own orgasm and I crush her to me, attempting to pull out.

Because I didn't use a fucking condom. Again.

A part of me wants to fill her with my cum and my baby, but that part is a fucking asshole. She's still so young and there's no way in hell I'm making her relive her mother's story.

"I-I'm on the…shot…" she pants, sinking her nails into my shoulders and her feet into my ass. "D-don't pull out. I want to feel it."

"Fuck, fuck, fuck," I curse as I come inside her long and deep until my balls are spent.

We're both breathing heavily with my thumb and cock inside her and my mouth on her nipple.

Gwyneth stares down at me and the fire that I meant to quench is still there, alive and fucking determined.

She has the type of fire that can't be put out by water. If anything, it's out to evaporate the water.

And that fire is now directed at me.

I release her nipple after one last bite that causes her to moan. Then her fingers are sliding up and down the back of my neck. "Hey, husband."

"What, wife?"

"I think we should have sex again in the shower."

"You mean I should fuck you?"

"Yeah, that." She grabs a handful of my hair and runs her fingers through it. "I love it when you do that. Fuck me."

"Then I'll keep doing it until you're satisfied."

"What if I never am?"

"Then I'll up my pace."

Her eyes shine bright at that. "You will?"

"Whatever you like, wife."

"I don't think you'd do what I really like." Her shoulders hunch, but she gives me a mischievous, contemplative smile that's filled with her earlier fire, the fire that refuses to be put out. "Yet."

Fuck.

This woman will really be the death of me, won't she?

Not only did I let exceptions creep in because of her, but now, my brain is also bringing up the questions I never wanted to be answered.

The what-if kind.

TWENTY-SEVEN

Gwyneth

I'M IN A COURTROOM.

I mean, yes, I've been inside one before when Dad takes the lawyer mic. He's a witty but very sharp lawyer, the type whom everyone pays attention to when he speaks.

But I haven't done it since I became Nate's intern. He said I wasn't ready back then, but today, he just stood beside my desk and said, "You're coming with me, Shaw."

It's kind of hot when he calls me by my last name at work. They still don't know we're married, because I kind of begged Chris after I apologized for what I did to him and Alex that night a week ago.

He totally spilled it to Jane, though, albeit accidentally. She looked at me weird, but she promised to keep my secret, too. Now, I feel a bit more at ease that I can talk freely with them without feeling like I hold the keys to some intelligence stuff.

Chris still doesn't understand why I even have feelings for

Nate, but Jane does, and that's okay. It's also okay if no one else understands, like Nate warned me.

The morning after the hot drunk pool sex, he sat me down, put my comfort drink in my hand—my vanilla milkshake—and told me that his mother is possibly right and that this whole thing will backfire. He said I should be prepared for that and that he won't let me take the fall.

Nate said he'll let them paint him whichever way they wish, because he couldn't care less what they think about him.

I heard what he wasn't saying, though. That he cares about what they say about me. He doesn't want them to come near me and even has a press statement ready, which is very stern—like him—and doesn't touch my name even one bit.

Nate doesn't know this, but things won't go his way if—when—our relationship becomes public. For the millionth time, he and everyone else will learn that I chose this and I'm old enough to make my own decisions.

There are a lot of things that I want to shout at the top of the world. Like how much Nate and I are compatible and how much we can easily do an activity together without clashing. I want everyone to see that I belong with him, that I never felt as peaceful as when I'm lying in his arms.

That I never felt as beautiful as when he fucks me like a madman.

Sometimes, I take sneaky pictures of him; of his nude back when he cooks naked—yes, he totally does that sometimes, and he sleeps naked, too, because clothes bother him, or more accurately, his cock. My perverted side kind of wished I knew that information before.

But I digress. Slightly.

Those aren't the only pictures I take of him, though. I'm a collector of everything Nate, remember? That means I have a collection to keep alive and happy. So I sneak a selfie here and there when I'm lying on his lap and others when I sleep on his chest.

My personal favorite, however, was when I woke up and he

had his hand around my throat. I was so wet that my fingers shook when I took the picture.

"Are you posting any of these?" he said in a half-sleepy voice while his eyes were still closed.

I startled, throwing my phone under the pillow. "W-what?"

His eyes met mine and there was so much light in them considering how dark they are. "The pictures you take religiously, Gwyneth. Do you post them?"

"You…knew?"

"Of course, I knew. You're not exactly subtle."

My cheeks and ears burned. "And here I thought I was being sneaky."

"Not enough." His hold tightened on my throat. "You still didn't answer my question. Do you post anything?"

"Maybe you should get a social media account and see for yourself."

"Gwyneth." His voice hardened, taking on a warning tone. "If I find an inappropriate picture of you anywhere…"

"I wouldn't do that. Besides, there's something we do now that's more fun than inappropriate pictures."

Her narrowed his eyes and I could tell he was getting impatient by the way he held me by the throat. "And what is that?"

"Thirst traps."

"The only thirst trap you'll be posting is my hand around this fucking throat."

I don't remember the rest of the conversation because he mounted me and fucked me hard and fast—without releasing my throat.

Despite my big talk, I never posted any of our pictures together, though. Not only am I paranoid about the press hurting him in any way, but I'm also kind of selfish. I don't want to share anything Nate with the world.

Sue me.

Anyway, I'm now at a hearing where he's the attorney in a civil lawsuit and I'm sitting a few seats behind him because he already has one of his associate lawyers with him. That's okay, though. I'm here, and I'm watching Nate be a lawyer. That's such a rare occasion nowadays since he deals with large corporations behind the scenes.

So seeing him in his sharp suit in the middle of the courtroom makes me a little giddy. Okay, a lot. I helped him put on that suit this morning—the tie, to be specific. I might have an unhealthy obsession with it.

And all of him, actually.

He's been fucking me more than anyone should and in positions I didn't even know existed. Sometimes it's on the kitchen counter when I'm trying to bake cupcakes. Other times, it's in the shower, where he'll come in unannounced and take me against the wall. Oftentimes, it's in his office, on his desk, on his sofa. Anywhere, really.

I'm as unsatiated as he is, because whenever he's not touching me, I act like a brat just so he'll order me to sit on his lap or bend over on his desk.

It's a high and I don't want to reach the peak. But it's not only about the sex. It's how we eat together, cook together, and he indulges in all the activities I come up with to find him a hobby.

He doesn't even tell me the music is loud anymore. He just stands there and watches me dance before he scoops me up and fucks me.

And it's not fair that my favorite band is now associated with him. Whenever I hear my playlist, I think of Nate fucking me. Whenever I eat my ice cream or drink my milkshake, I think of him bringing them to me.

He hasn't only robbed my body and attacked my soul, but he's also coming after my heart. My stupid vanilla heart that loses flavor every time he doesn't kiss me.

I try to pretend it doesn't bother me and that I'm completely fine with just sex and companionship.

It doesn't matter, okay? I'm using him as much as he's using me.

Lie.

You're a damn liar, Gwen.

I squash the voice and focus on Nate because he's talking now, and holy shit, how can he sound even more authoritative than normal? Everyone's attention is zoomed in on him and I'm definitely not the only one who's hardly blinking. No one wants to miss a moment of his show—that's what it feels like right now. A one-man show and we're all witnesses.

He's always had the type of blinding charisma that makes it difficult to look away.

Still, I force myself to open my notebook and take notes. I jot down points in his speech, the way he cross-examined a witness. One day, I'm going to be the one up there and he'll be out here watching me. With Dad. When he wakes up.

Because he will.

I don't care what the doctors say, he squeezes my hand when I talk to him. My dad will come back and tell me why he was looking for my mom.

After what I learned from the dashcam, I tried broaching the subject with Nate.

"Do you think Dad was searching for my mother?" I asked him once while we were watching a horror movie together. We do that now, watch movies and swim together—or he does while I hold on to him. I guess he's insistent on us doing activities together since sex is always part of the equation.

But we weren't having sex at that moment. We were merely watching a movie and making fun of how clichéd it was while I had my head on his lap and my legs up in the air, against the back of the sofa.

He stared down at me for a moment, then narrowed his eyes. "Why are you asking that?"

"I was just curious."

"Don't be. Whatever King has going on with your mother is between the two of them."

"Umm, hello? I'm what came out of their union, so I think I have a say in it, thank you very much."

"You don't, and drop the sarcasm before I fuck it out of you."

He totally did that, fucked me, but the sarcasm isn't completely out.

So yeah, Nate isn't my ally on this. The only person who can help me is probably Aspen since she's the one who told me about the possibility of the actual cause of Dad's accident. But I haven't gathered enough courage to talk to her. Besides, she wouldn't know about my mother. Aspen and Dad don't actually sit down and share stories about their lives.

The judge informs everyone present that the trial will continue next week, and we're done for the day.

I leave with Nate and the others from the firm, but I remain in the background while they talk in the elevator about a press conference and so on and so forth.

When we're in the parking garage, Nate tells his associate lawyers to leave first.

I lower my head and go to the passenger seat of his car. I could've driven here myself, but he said I should come with him.

Nate gets in and I beam at him. "You were awesome in there."

"And you were fucking distracting." He leans over and pulls the seatbelt over my chest.

"I…was?" He didn't even look at me, *I don't think*. How could I be distracting?

"You were. Very."

He's still there, leaning over me, so his face is mere inches away from mine, and I'm breathing him in. God, when am I going to be desensitized to him? Ordinarily, I'd be over my reaction to certain words by now, but it seems that it's getting worse, not better, when it comes to him.

But then again, Nate has never been a word. He's a whole damn book.

"Does that mean I've been a bad girl, husband?"

"Extremely, wife."

It's a game of ours that usually means he's going to fuck me until I'm spent and then start all over again.

"So let's go home. You have nothing this afternoon. I checked with Grace."

"You want me to go home early so I can listen to your loud music and watch you dance?"

"You can join in or whatever. And don't call the loves of my life *loud* music."

"The loves of your life?" He raises a brow.

"They are. Don't be jealous."

He is. Very. And possessive, too. He's usually on the verge of losing his cool whenever I'm being touchy or friendly with any man, especially Chris. But even Sebastian, his own nephew who's in a committed relationship, is a target as well.

I'll never tell Nate this, but I love that side of him. It means he cares, in his own way.

"Why would I be jealous when you're fucking mine, wife?" His hand trails down and he cups me through my pants. "My pussy agrees."

My eyes bug out as I stare out the windows. "Nate! We're in public."

"So?"

"We...we can't. If they find out, everything will be compromised and then...then they'll attack you and my dad. I can't take that...I can't..."

"Hey..." His hand is no longer on my core, because he's cupping my cheeks. "Fuck them, okay? Now, breathe. Relax. I won't touch you in public if it freaks you out."

I'm sucking in air as I wrap my hand around his. "It doesn't freak *you* out?"

"No."

"I wish I was as confident and assertive as you."

"You are, baby girl. You're strong. If anyone tells you otherwise, I'll fuck them up."

I can't help but smile at that. "Does that mean you're my personal caregiver as well?"

"Isn't that a given?"

"Like my guardian?"

"Like your fucking husband, Gwyneth."

I bite my lower lip, then release it. "Okay."

"Okay?"

"Yeah, okay."

"Promise?"

I smile again. For someone who has asshole genes, he can be nice. "Promise. Now, let's go home."

"I have better plans."

My heart skips a beat because Nate rarely has plans for us. Yes, we live together, cook and eat and fuck and sleep and fuck again together, but that's all in the cocoon of the house.

And I don't dare think that he'll take me out. Otherwise, we'll get caught.

But he has plans now.

"What type of plans?"

"I'm going to sweep you away, wife."

TWENTY-EIGHT

Gwyneth

NATE TAKES ME TO THE MIDDLE OF NOWHERE.

Well, not literally, but close to it. We're heading to a cozy cottage Nate owns that's situated on a mountain out of state. We drove for an hour to get here and now, we're having to hike for the rest of the way, something I've been grumbling about for half an hour.

Even though both of us are wearing hiking clothes and boots, every step feels like torture. I'm not good with physical activities, okay?

Nate must know that, too, because he sighs, picks me up, and carries me on his back. All discomfort is forgotten and I release a small squeal as my body plasters itself to his. I'll always be in awe at the ease with which he holds me, as if I weigh nothing.

"I feel like such a princess," I speak against his ear, eliciting a muscle jump in his jaw.

"You do, huh?"

"Look at me having someone to carry me. Am I lucky or what?" I rub my breasts against his back.

He tightens his hold on my leg. "Stop it."

"Stop what?" I feign nonchalance.

"Stop grinding against me or I'll fuck you against the tree and you'll have to walk the rest of the way."

The fucking part is tempting, but the walking on my own part, not so much. As a compromise, I wrap my legs around his waist in a tight grip, even though he's been holding them while carrying our bag. Nate is strong that way. He can lift me and a bag and still hike like nobody's business.

I also stroke his face with my arm looped around his neck. Usually, he'd stop me—or he's stopped me in the past. But now, he's given up. Like he gave up trying to have me sleep in my own bed. I either fall asleep on his lap or in his bed. He also gave up hating loud music—I'm converting him to a Twenty One Pilots fan as we speak. NF, too, if I get a say in it. I told him once that it's such a lovely coincidence that he and NF share the same name, but he just glowered. He's jealous that way, even about singers, and I might like that a bit too much.

Anyway, coffee is on the list of things he gave up, too. Yeah, he loves my green vanilla tea more now. Soon, he'll also love vanilla.

I've been slowly but surely changing his mind about things. Whenever he says, "No, that's final and not up for discussion," I just reopen the subject until he listens to me.

Like the Susan thing. There will be a trial soon and he said I shouldn't testify, but I put my foot down and insisted. Aspen sort of agreed with me, which was a first, but we're two-to-one now, so I'm totally testifying.

Maybe if I'm determined enough, I'll change his "no feelings" rule, too, though I don't have any misconceptions about that. Deep down, he's a hard, cold man and I don't think I have enough stamina to climb over the walls of his forts.

But I can build that stamina.

Yes, I hate physical activity, but I'm all for endurance.

We finally arrive at the cottage. The outside looks like a scene from a horror movie with all the old wooden pillars and all, but the interior is...cozy.

The wood flooring shines under the late afternoon sun and the curtains cast a yellowish glow on the small living area. There is a colorful sofa and chairs. Even the carpet is a mosaic of joyful colors and shapes.

Nate helps me slide off his body and there's barely a drop of sweat on his gorgeous face. My husband looks sharp and handsome in a suit, but he's mouthwatering in hiking clothes that stretch across his chest and hug his strong biceps like a second skin.

He could've been a bit less perfect, but then again, gods like him don't have flaws.

We're removing our hiking boots at the entrance when I say, "You didn't decorate this yourself, did you?"

"How did you know?"

"It's not your style."

"And you know my style?"

"Of course. I've been to your place before and it's all gray and stuff. You wouldn't touch colorful things with a ten-foot pole."

He wraps his arms around me, pulling me flush against his body. "I touch you, don't I?"

"I'm not colorful."

"You're the most colorful fucking thing I've ever met, Gwyneth."

I nearly hiccup at that and turn into the fifteen-year-old who hid whenever she saw him because he was too bright to look at.

He really needs to stop saying things like that, because my heart will start misunderstanding it and then we'll have a huge problem on our hands. Like me falling for him.

As if you haven't already, Gwen.

I shoo that idea and get away from him because I'm totally not desensitized to having his hands on me. I didn't put them on the list and I don't want to.

Walking around the cottage, I touch the small figurines of

anime characters lined up by the TV. "You definitely wouldn't have these either."

"This used to be my and Nicholas's hideout. He brought me here during the summers to get away from our parents and the city for a while."

I grab a pink-haired girl figurine and turn around to face him. His features have sunken at the mention of his brother and the walls of his forts are going up again.

Oh, God. How could I not have thought of this after Debra's visit? It's not just about his parents, is it?

"Were you guys close?"

He gives a vague nod, then heads to the kitchen area and disappears behind the counter. "I'll make dinner. Go take a shower."

"I'll help." I slide to his side.

There's no way in hell I'm letting him build forts again. I hate them. His forts and his coldness, and his wounds that no one ever looked into. He's too cold to allow anyone in, and people are usually too scared of him to try.

Not me.

Well, I might have been a bit scared in the past, when I was young and clueless, but not anymore.

I bring out some of the vegetables we brought and start washing them under the faucet. "What type of person was Nicholas?"

"The heir to the Weaver clan."

"Not your brother?"

"That too, but his most important role was as the promised prince and he was treated as such."

"What about you?"

"What about me?"

"You're a member of the Weaver family, too."

"Only in name. I was never as good as Nick at anything, whether it was studies, sports, or even existing. He aced them all and I was meant to be number two."

"You're not number two, Nate." *You're my number one.* But I don't say that, because it would get emotional and messy. That's what feelings are. Messy. "Did you hate him for being your parents' favorite?"

"Sometimes it felt that way, but I could've never really hated Nick."

"Why?"

There's a small smile on his face as he chops the vegetables. "Because he was my parent. Being ten years older than me, he stepped into the role so easily. He's the one who made sure I was taken care of, that I ate and slept well. He's the one who spent all-nighters by my side when I got sick, because my mother didn't give a fuck. He taught me what a father should teach his son. Again, because my father was too checked-out to pay me any attention. It's thanks to him that I know what the world is all about."

"He sounds so cool."

"He was. Nick was also a natural leader, which is why it made the most sense for him to follow in my parents' footsteps. They had great plans for him and had his political career all mapped out ever since he was a toddler. But he threw it all away by marrying a middle-class woman my mother didn't approve of. They started a fucking drama about it, especially my mother. She was vicious and hurt Julia, Nick's wife, by demanding he divorce her."

Jeez. Debra is a bitch who only likes her sons divorced. Or married to the women she picks, I guess. "You mean like she did to you?"

"Her reaction to me was nothing compared to how she acted with Nick and Julia. She was an absolute nightmare and used her influence to have Julia fired from her job and basically blacklisted her in New York City."

"What did Nick do?" I stop pretending that I'm focused on helping him prepare the ingredients and lean against the counter to face him.

"He fought it at first, but it was too much drama and daily fights and he was caught in the middle. But then he gave my parents a choice—either they leave Julia alone or he'd burn all the plans they had for him. They threatened to disown him, and I never saw my brother as relieved as he was in that moment. As if he'd been carrying a load since he was born and he could finally get rid of it. He chose to be disowned, took Julia, and left the country. Just like that. A few years later, he and his wife died in an accident and Sebastian came to live with us."

I see it then. The pain. It's in the way his shoulders hunch and his movements turn stiff.

The reason he's been building the forts isn't because of coldness, it's due to pain.

"You hate him for it, don't you? You hate that he left you alone with the parents who never cared about you. He abandoned you."

"I was old enough. He didn't abandon me."

"You were what? Ten when he left? You weren't old enough, Nate."

"He did what he had to do. I don't blame him for wanting out of my parents' clutches. I would've done the same if I were him."

"No, you wouldn't. You took care of Sebastian after his parents died and never left him in his grandparents' clutches. Not once did you turn your back on him, not even when he was acting up a few years ago. Because you didn't want him to be like his father or you, right? You wanted him to have all the options so he could pick his own future."

"He deserves that."

"And you deserved not to be abandoned back then by both your parents and your brother. They're assholes."

He pauses chopping. "No calling Nick an asshole."

"But he was. He knew you'd be all alone and still left anyway because he was selfish. Like my mother. People like them don't care about who they leave behind and then pick up their lives as if we never happened, and that's wrong, okay? It's messed up and hurts on empty days because I keep thinking, was I not good enough? Was I just a stone in her life that she so easily kicked away and moved on with her life? Was I unnecessary?"

"Hey." He grabs me by the shoulders and the warmth of his big, strong hands seeps under my skin. It's a safety net, one I can hold on to with all my might and not worry that it'll break and let me go.

"You're not fucking unnecessary, Gwyneth. Do you hear me?"

"You're not unnecessary either, okay? Fuck your parents for only realizing your worth after losing your brother. I want to punch them. Especially your mother. She's the worst ever. At least my own mother decided to disappear from the get-go; Debra was there but did nothing to earn the title of a mother. I'm going to tell her all of this when I see her next time."

"You will, huh?"

"Yup, and I will metaphorically punch her, too. I can't do it physically or she'll sue me for assault and then will tell a sob story to the media, and they'll believe her. Yikes."

"That's smart." He glides his thumb under my eye and I realize I have moisture there and he's wiping it away. "Though she won't have a chance when I'm your lawyer."

"Hell yeah, she won't. You're the best lawyer I know. Aside from my dad."

"I am?"

"You're the best, Nate. You must hear that from everyone every day."

"Not from you."

"And that's important?"

"It is."

"Like when I love it when you praise me?"

"When you behave, which is a rare occurrence."

"Oh, please. You like it when I'm a bad girl."

"Do I, wife?"

"Uh-huh." I wrap my arms around him because I like it. I like how he looks at me as if he'll have me instead of food, and I like how he touches me. I like how his veiny hands stroke my face and grab me so tight that I become so small in comparison to him.

But what I like the most is him, and I want to engrave him in every cell of my body, take everything he has to offer, and make him all mine.

A mortal trying to trap a god.

Don't all of those stories end in tragedies? Everyone says it's impossible for two different worlds to collide. They need to stay separate, watching from afar.

But I've already touched him and he's touched me. And I don't only mean physically. There's an ease to our relationship now, and it feels peaceful, normal while still being exciting and fun.

It's full. That's the type of effect Nate has on me—he makes me full and I want that fullness. I fucking need it.

And it's not because I'm dependent on him. It's not because I grew up watching him being a god among humans.

Those aren't the reasons why he fills me up. It's because he's Nate. The cold, stern Nate with a broken side. The one who has forts so tall, but he still opens them for me to steal a peek inside.

The protective, possessive Nate who wouldn't allow anyone or anything to hurt me.

Even if he does it himself sometimes.

Even if his knife stabs me deeper with each passing day that his lips refuse to meet mine.

Once upon a time, I thought I'd gotten over him.

Turns out, I'm still waiting for him to kiss me back.

TWENTY-NINE

Nathaniel

GWYNETH SAID SHE DOESN'T LIKE HIKING.

Then she wakes up early this morning, puts on her clothes, and says, "Take me hiking, husband."

So I did exactly that, then fucked her against a tree to teach her how to behave and not be a flirt. Although, in her case, that only makes her act out more.

Over the weekend, hiking has grown on her so much that she doesn't even need me to carry her on my back anymore. I've done it anyway because her tiny body wraps all around me and she plays with my hair and face and neck and anywhere her hands can reach.

She's a touchy person. One who needs physical contact to feel connected. But she doesn't go around touching everyone, just her inner circle that she deems safe.

At the moment, I'm in the middle of that circle and it's a fucking wild ride.

Any time spent in her presence is. Even when she's sleeping, she stretches her body out all over me and hides her face in my neck. Or she lays her head on my lap and flings her legs in the air.

Like right now.

She was reading her negative words list and telling me how she worked hard to desensitize herself to them. Not only is Gwyneth a storyteller, but she's an entertaining one at that, which is why I know she'll make a good lawyer, especially for civil cases. She'll be able to spin her own stories and capture the audience, and that's what makes the best lawyers. Even those who only chose law due to having a grudge against the system, such as Knox, can succeed as long as they're good storytellers.

"Dad never knew about this," she says in a sleepy voice, then closes her eyes.

As if King wouldn't know anything about her.

He's the one who put her in therapy because he's so attuned to her and her needs. She thought he did it because of her sleep-talking, but it was also because she showed signs of depression. She started showing them after she accidentally learned that her mother threw her away without looking back.

I slowly pull the notebook from her fingers, not wanting to wake her up. Her insomnia has gotten better lately and she sometimes sleeps through the night.

Still keeping the notebook in hand, I slowly put her legs down. She doesn't open her eyes as she climbs into my lap, wraps her arms around my shoulders, and hides her face in my neck.

Her breathing slowly evens out and she sighs into the hollow of my throat. The small puff of air makes my dick fucking hard and I release a breath through my clenched teeth.

Gwyneth makes me a sex addict, unable to get enough, no matter how much I take her. No matter how much I feel her warmth and hear her moans, I need more. And it is a need. One I can't fucking stop or restrain.

I'm about to close her notebook and carry her to bed when the page flips to the letter *M*.

My chest squeezes when I see the first word there. Gwyneth

says she categorizes them by colors. The red is for the hardest ones to get over.

And the first word under the letter *M* is written in a thick red marker. A word that shouldn't be in the negative words list in the first place.

Mom.

It has several red lines underneath it—bold, messy, harsh— and I can imagine her furrowed brow and stiff movements when she did this. When she decided *Mom* is the worst word under the letter *M*. Like she thinks *death* is the worst word under the letter *D*.

"You've never gotten over her even though you've never met her, have you?" I ask her sleeping form, stroking her auburn strands away from her forehead.

This must be why she's been asking if King was searching for her. Does she want to find her? She's never expressed that before, neither to me nor to her father.

It's understandable in King's case since he's the founder of Gwyneth's mother's anti-fan club, but she's never talked to me about it.

Or maybe I wasn't listening.

She stirs, moaning softly in my neck, before she pulls back and stares at me, then at the notebook that's still open on the letter *M*.

All sleep whooshes away from her face as she startles and snatches it from my fingers. She staggers to the other side of the sofa, pulling it close to her chest.

"It means nothing." She smiles, but it's with effort and barely-there. This woman can't fake a smile to save her life and it's weirdly endearing.

"Do you want to find her?"

"No!" she says too fast, too defensively.

"Hey, this is me, not King. You don't have to lie or hide to protect his feelings."

She winces. "Was I that obvious?"

"Kind of."

"It's not that I want to find her because I want a relationship with her like Dad thinks. I just want to ask her why, you know? I want to know why I meant so little that she threw me away and didn't care whether I lived or died."

"I understand."

"You do?"

"I'm sure King understands, too, even though he doesn't want to admit it or admit that he can't erase her from your life."

"He wanted that?"

"It's one of his goals, aside from crushing Susan."

She gets on her knees and inches closer to me. "Please tell me, Nate. Was he looking for her?"

"He was." I didn't think she needed to know this before, but if she's still this entangled in her mother's story, then she deserves the truth. Or as much of the truth as I can give her without making her hate her father.

"Why?"

"To keep her away from you so you'd never meet, even by coincidence."

"Oh."

"I told you. He takes protecting you to the next level."

"Did he manage to find her?"

"He was getting close, but I'm not sure if he did."

"He...did."

"How do you know that?"

"I...uh..."

"What did you do, Gwyneth?"

"I got his car's dashcam and watched some footage. I think he was speaking to a PI, but I couldn't get his number to call him. Anyway, Dad said, 'She can't be Gwyneth's mother. Look again.' So that must mean he thought he'd found her. And that whole thing happened the day of the accident. Isn't that too much of a coincidence?"

Jesus. I keep her out of my sight for a second and she goes playing a dangerous detective game. She really has no sense of self-preservation sometimes. "Why the fuck did you even get the footage?"

"Why is that important right now?"

"Answer the question. What pushed you to watch it?"

She remains silent, biting her lower lip and staring at me through her lashes. At my harsh stare, she blurts, "Aspen said she suspects that Dad's accident wasn't an accident."

Fucking Aspen. I'm going to have a word with her about planting these seeds in Gwyneth's head when we don't even have concrete evidence.

I'm almost sure it was an accident. If there had been foul play, the detectives would've told me as much, or I would've sensed it myself.

"Since when are you and Aspen friends?"

"We're not, but after she told me that, I saw that Dad found my mother on the day of the accident, so what if she's the one behind it?"

"That's a reach."

"But what if it's true?"

"That possibility is slim to none, especially since we're not one hundred percent sure that the accident was premeditated. You need to stop this train of thought."

"As long as the possibility is there, I won't give up."

"Gwyneth, you need to move on."

"I will after I see this to the end. But here's an idea: I'll be able to move on faster if you help me."

"Nice negotiating skills."

"I learned from the best. You teach me a lot of things, husband." Her voice turns breathy and she lets her notebook fall to the sofa as she inches toward me.

The strap of her oversized shirt falls off her creamy shoulder. She's not wearing shorts today, just the shirt.

"Like what?" My voice is thick as my whole body tightens, responding to the bright look in her eyes and the way she keeps approaching me until her heat mingles with mine.

"Like how to be full."

"Full?"

"Yeah, it's a thing. I like being full."

"What else do you like?"

"Being your slut."

I grunt but it's not only because of her words, but also because of the way she crawls on top of my lap, parting her legs until her shirt rides up her thighs.

My hand grips her tiny waist and she wiggles against my rock-hard dick. "So you're my slut?"

"I am."

"Only mine?"

"For now."

My chest burns at that, and I hate the sensation so much that I dig my fingers into her side. She moans when I reach under her shirt and it's met by my grunt when I grab her bare cunt.

"Were you ready for me, wife?"

"Maybe?"

I bunch a fistful of her shirt and lift it over her head. She's braless, too, my bad girl.

Instead of pulling the piece of clothing over her arms, I lay her on the sofa and tie her wrists with the shirt that was covering her.

"What…what are you doing?"

"Stay like that."

"Why?"

"Don't ask any questions, got it?"

"O-okay." The breathlessness in her tone makes my dick strain against my shorts.

So I stand up, push them down, and remove my T-shirt as she watches me with those huge eyes that have turned into a myriad of bright colors, all mingling and mixing the more she watches me.

I shouldn't feel fucking proud that she looks at me like that, like I'm the only one who exists in her world, but I do.

And it feels fucking euphoric.

"Now, I want you to open your legs in the air, baby girl, like what you do when you sleep upside down."

Her face turns a deep shade of red, but she does, lifting her legs and opening them, giving me the perfect view of her glistening pussy.

I position myself on my knees at her opening and glide my dick up and down her soaked folds.

Her legs tremble in the air and she moans, then groans. "Nate..."

"What?"

"Aren't you going to fuck me?"

I push two inches of my dick inside her pussy, then pull out, then thrust in again and out so that I'm coated with her arousal. "Not in this hole, no. Tonight, I'll claim your ass."

She trembles, her eyes doubling in size.

"Did someone touch this ass, Gwyneth?"

She shakes her head frantically.

"Use your voice."

"No..."

"Is it because you were saving it for me, too? Like you saved your virgin pussy?"

Her channel tightens around my cock, swallowing me in, and she lets out a long puff of air. "Yes...for you. I've always been yours, Nate."

A harsh current of possessiveness grips me by the balls and it takes everything in me not to fuck her as savagely as my cock demands. "After tonight, every inch of you will be mine and mine alone."

Her lips part open and her leg droop.

"Keep them in the air, Gwyneth." I part her ass cheeks and slip a thumb in. I've been preparing her by always fucking her pussy while there's a finger or two in her ass, but she's tight as fuck.

So I gather her natural lube and smear it on her back hole, teasing her clit in the meantime until she's writhing, her nails digging into the heels of her palms.

Then I push the first inch of my cock inside and stop. She's closing her eyes and strangling me.

"Relax, baby girl. I've got you."

Her eyes slowly open and she does relax, her breathing slowing a little. I rock for a few moments, then push in the second inch while thrusting a finger inside her pussy.

She moans and opens up for me, so I push more and add another finger into her inviting warmth.

By the time I'm fully sheathed inside her ass, we're both panting. "You're so fucking tight, wife."

"Mmm."

"Does it hurt?"

"It does, but it's the good kind of pain. Oh, and…and it's full…so full…" She opens her legs farther in the air, giving me more access, and I start thrusting into her, slow at first, as I pound my fingers into her pussy.

She writhes on the sofa, her back arching and her legs unable to stay still.

So I bend them and push them back until her knees are at either side of her head and my face is inches away from her neck.

The position gives me more depth, both in her ass and pussy, and my thrusts go deeper. She feels it, too, because her moans are higher in pitch.

"Do you feel my cock claiming your tight ass, wife?"

She nods frantically.

"This ass is now mine, too, isn't it?"

"Yes!" She lets out a breath as she tightens around me and starts shaking. My fingers soak with her arousal when she comes undone, her limbs trembling and her lips falling open.

My pounds get even deeper and sharper, and she takes it all, still whimpering and trembling.

It's impossible to control my pace as it mounts and spirals out of control. Usually, I can, but I'm a fucking animal when it comes to Gwyneth.

It's that inability to get enough. The inability to stop even when I know I should.

My lips latch onto her neck and I suck the soft skin in as my balls tighten and I shoot my cum up her ass.

Her pussy clenches around my fingers and I pump them more, making her leak arousal and scream another orgasm.

By the time I pull out of her, she's dazed, her eyes half-droopy, even as a little smile grazes her lips.

I stroke the sweat-soaked strands out of her forehead. "Are you in pain?"

"A little, but it feels good."

"It does?"

"Yeah, so maybe you should fuck me in the ass more often."

"Is that so?"

"Uh-huh"

"Are you sure you can take it?"

"I can take anything you offer, Nate." She smiles and I can't help mirroring it. Lately, I noticed how easy it is to smile around her.

"Come on, let me take care of you."

"I love that. When you take care of me, I mean."

I carry her in my arms and take her to the shower, where I fuck her slower in the cunt while I clean her. Then I wash her hair with her vanilla shampoo. She kisses me on the neck for having remembered to pack it.

We spend more than an hour in there, fucking and cleaning and messing everything up again, especially after she gets on her knees to clean me and ends up sucking my balls dry.

Once we're done, I wrap her in a towel and carry her back to the bedroom to dry her hair.

"It'll dry on its own," she grumbles, staring at me through the mirror.

"That's not healthy. Stop being lazy." I run my fingers through her strands and inhale her scent. The scent that should be boring but is now growing on me more than anything. Then I turn off the hairdryer and brush the strands back.

"Hey, Nate?"

"What?" I ask absentmindedly, too focused on her hair.

"Why do you never kiss me?"

I pause, meeting her gaze in the mirror. It's cautious, expectant, and on the verge of gray.

"What's with that question all of a sudden?"

"You never do. I just thought it was weird."

"I don't kiss."

"You just fuck?"

"Correct. I just fuck."

"What if I want to kiss?"

"Gwyneth, I told you…"

"This is sex only, no feelings," she repeats, mimicking my tone before she slips back into hers. "I know that. But this is about kissing, not feelings."

"Kissing is related to feelings for me. That's why I don't do it."

She stands up abruptly and faces me. There's a soft halo around her face, a tension in her neck, and she's clinking her nails over and over as if she can't keep them in one place.

"Even now?" she asks in a low, haunting voice that fucking guts me.

Though, no. It's not the voice that guts me, it's the expectation in it, on her face. It's practically shining through the green of her eyes.

But I can't allow her to have rosy dreams. I can't let her build her life on expectations.

She said I make her feel full, but it's the fake type that holds no meaning.

After all, how could I cure her emptiness when I'm hollow myself?

"Even now," I say.

She flinches as if I've slapped her. There's a tremble in her chin before it spreads to the rest of her body.

"Screw you," she whispers, and storms out of the room.

I don't follow after her, because it'll just get ugly. She probably needs to cool off for a while before we talk again.

I spend some time checking my emails, then I go to the living room to find her sleeping with her head on the table and her notebook between her fingers.

It's open on the letter *N*, where she's been scribbling in bold red letters.

Nate.

My jaw tightens and it takes everything in me not to rip up the thing. Does she really think she'll get rid of me by just writing my name in a notebook?

She obviously doesn't know the heights I'd reach to make sure she remains fucking mine. I warned her and she didn't listen, so all she can do is bear the consequences.

I carry her to the bed and when I'm covering her, my phone vibrates on the nightstand. It's the hospital.

My fingers flex. They wouldn't call at this hour if it wasn't something important. I take my phone and step outside to answer it.

"Nathaniel Weaver speaking. Is everything all right with Kingsley?"

"Yes." There's glee in the nurse's voice. "Mr. Shaw just woke up."

THIRTY

Gwyneth

DAD WOKE UP.

Dad. Woke. Up.

I still can't believe it and keep mentally shaking myself during the entire ride to the hospital.

I think I'm dreaming.

That's what I did when he first had the accident, I slept upside down and dreamt about Dad tilting his head and telling me that sleeping in that position isn't healthy.

Then I woke up and he wasn't there, but there were tears in my eyes.

So that's what I think during the entire ride. I think that this is a dream—I'll eventually wake up and Dad will still be in a coma.

My nails clink together and I dig them into my skin. Pain means it's not a dream and that the call Nate got was real.

That my father is back.

We don't talk the whole way. I just listen to my NF and

Twenty One Pilots playlist and count the minutes until we get to the hospital.

Anytime he opens his mouth, I raise the volume until he gets the memo and stops trying to speak. I don't want to talk to him, I don't want him to spout more words that will cut me open. Because you know what? Fuck him.

Fuck his coldness.

Fuck his assholish tendencies.

Fuck it all.

I know about his history and what turned him into a hard man, and I get that. I do. I was abandoned, too, so we're similar in that way. We understand what it's like to be left behind by the same people who should be there for us. We understand how those feelings shape who we are. I have an empty brain, a notebook, and use unhealthy obsessions to cope, but I don't go around hurting others.

I don't go around telling them that, no matter how much they try, I'll feel nothing for them.

Being hurt doesn't give him the right to hurt me.

Before, I bided my time and stupidly believed that he'd come around. That one day, he'd feel a sliver of what I feel for him, but I've only been chasing a void.

An impossibility.

So yeah, fuck him. Now that his name is officially on the list, I'm going to be desensitized to him.

Or that's what I tell myself.

Anyway, I just need to focus on Dad and the fact that he woke up.

When we reach the hospital, however, the doctor, an older man who has a clean-shaven face and a dimpled chin, tells us Dad is unconscious again.

My legs nearly give out, and I wipe my sweaty palms on my shorts. "But...but...the nurse said he woke up."

"He did," the doctor says. "He responded to my commands and stayed awake for twenty minutes and tried to talk. Recovering from a coma is gradual, which means that he will gain awareness over time."

"Does that mean he'll wake up again?"

"We believe so, yes. Mr. Shaw didn't have a severe score on the Glasgow Coma Scale and we're confident that he'll make a full recovery. Your father is a very strong-willed man."

"I know. He is." Tears gather in my lids again and I wipe them away with the back of my hand. "Can I see him?"

"Of course."

I storm to Dad's room even though my limbs barely carry me. Nate doesn't follow me and I think it's because he wants to talk to the doctor.

There's a nurse moving Dad's arm so he doesn't get bedsores. Ever since his bruises and broken bones healed, he just looks asleep.

When it got to be too much and I missed him so badly, I used to sit beside him and joke that he doesn't fit the Sleeping Beauty role. It was either that or crying whenever I came here.

"I'll do it," I tell the nurse, and she lets me, even though she stays to watch. I learned how to move my father, to wash his hair without much water, to clean his body, and make him as comfortable as possible.

"Dad…it's me, Gwen," I announce my presence before I lift his arm and stretch it out. He lets out a sound, a grunt or a moan, I don't know which.

I stare at the nurse, bug-eyed, and she nods. "It's because you're stretching his arm."

"Am I hurting him?"

"No. I believe he's probably reacting to your voice. Keep talking to him."

My attention slides back to him. "Dad…I came as soon as I heard. I'm sorry I wasn't here when you opened your eyes. But I'm not leaving your side, okay? It's us against the world, right? And I can't go against the world if you're not in it. Also, also…I'm working hard in my internship and I'm confident that I'll kick ass in college this fall. And did I tell you that I have a new friend? Can you believe that? Me, making friends? Jane didn't even know you were my dad in the beginning, and she might have thought you're a bit egotistical, but I changed her mind and she's totally a member of your fan club now. I want to introduce her to you since she joined the IT department after your accident. They called her Plain Jane there and I totally put them in their place. I had to use your name for it—sorry about that—but I promise it's for a good cause."

I stroke his hand in mine and sigh. "I also went ahead and broke my own heart, because I gave it to someone who doesn't want it. I think I have vanilla dreams and I need to get rid of them, so, Daddy, please wake up and tell me how."

He squeezes my fingers, and before I can freak out about it, his lashes flutter and his eyes slowly open.

I nearly have a heart attack, my fingers pausing on his arm as the blue-gray color of his irises shines under the lights. The color I haven't seen in weeks. It's muted now, exhausted, but it's staring directly at me.

He blinks slowly, but his gaze remains on me.

"Oh my God, Dad…"

His fingers squeeze around mine and he mumbles something. At first, it's incoherent, but then I get close and the word he croaks fills my lids with moisture. "…Angel…"

"Yeah, it's me, Dad. I'm here."

He blinks again, says something unintelligible and slowly closes his eyes.

"What…what's wrong?" I ask the nurse.

"It's normal. He'll be slipping in and out of consciousness a lot before he regains complete awareness. He's just sleeping now."

"You've slept for long enough, Dad. Sleeping Beauty really doesn't suit you, so you have to wake up now." I try to scold him but sound tearful instead.

He squeezes my hand again, but he doesn't open his eyes. I remain by his side long after I finish moving him. It's very early in the morning, and I should be sleeping, but I can't. What if he wakes up when I'm asleep?

The door slides open and I think it's the nurse, but Nate walks inside with a vanilla milkshake in hand.

He places it between my fingers. "You should go home and rest, but I assume you won't move from his side now."

I dig my nails into the cup. Why does he have to be so good at reading me but not know how painful his actions are?

He shouldn't be this attuned to me if it means nothing.

He shouldn't know things about me and bring me those things because they're what keeps me at peace.

"The nurse said he opened his eyes and talked to you?" he asks.

I just take a slurp of my milkshake. Yes, the asshole bought it, but it's not its fault and it should be consumed.

"Gwyneth." There's a warning in his tone because he's a god, and gods don't like being ignored.

They don't like being defied.

Well, too bad for him because I'm in the mood for anarchy.

"Look at me."

I don't.

"Gwyneth, I said look at me."

When I refuse again, he steps in front of me and grabs my chin with two fingers. They're strong and powerful and so warm, it feels as if I'm being set on fire.

His size eats up the horizon as he stares down at me with disapproval. As if he has the right to disapprove right now.

I jerk my head away from him. "Don't touch me."

A muscle tics in his jaw and his brown eyes rage in color, darkening. "What did you just say?"

"I said, don't touch me, Nate."

"You're my fucking wife. I will touch you whenever I want."

"Not when you intend to keep this physical only."

"You were fine with physical before. What changed?"

"Me. I changed, Nate, and I'm not going to let you hurt me every time I wait for you to kiss me and you don't."

"So that's what this is all about? A fucking kiss?"

I jerk up and nearly spill the milkshake. "It's not about the kiss, it's about what comes with the kiss. The feelings you don't want."

"You didn't want them either."

"Are you serious? Do you really believe I don't want feelings? Why the hell do you think I kissed you two years ago? I've had this burn for you since I was fifteen, Nate! Since you told me the emptiness isn't my reality and I can't fill it up but it's okay to feel empty sometimes. I realize now that was because you understand what it means to be hollow. You were abandoned, too, you were left behind, too, and there's a void that remains, like the one my mother left in me. I didn't know that before, that you were empty, but I understood it deep down. That's why I was able to connect with you, that's why I had a burn that would become all painful and hot whenever you were around.

"I fought it at first, you know. I really, really did, because it was wrong, right? You're eighteen years older than me and Dad's best friend, and it killed me to hurt him or be the reason that you guys grew apart. So I hid whenever you were around. I ran to my closet and closed the door. I used the trees as camouflage to be out of sight. But you know what? I kept watching you through the opening of the door and from behind the trees. Because the burn wouldn't stop. If anything, it kept growing and heightening until it became a volcano. That's why I kissed you on my eighteenth birthday—the volcano erupted and I couldn't stop it anymore. But you turned it to ashes when you rejected me and I gave up. Or I tried to, anyway. But the thing is, that volcano was never dormant. It's been slowly resurrecting, especially since I became your wife. And now it's about to erupt again, and you're turning it to ashes. Fucking *again*. So no, Nate, it's not that I didn't want feelings. Feelings are all I have. I'm empathetic. I feel, and I feel deep and hard. I agreed with your stupid no-feelings rule to get whatever I could from you. I believed you'd change with time, but that's not the case, is it? You'll always turn my volcano to ashes, won't you?"

His body tightens during my outburst. His nostrils are

flaring and his chest nearly bursts from his heavy breathing. When he speaks, his voice is calm but tight. "What are you saying, Gwyneth?"

"I'm saying that you don't get to touch me unless you're willing to give me more."

"I don't do feelings and that's fucking final."

"Then I won't do sex. That's also final."

"Gwyneth," he growls.

"What, Nate? What? If you want a whore, go pick one off the side of the street."

He grabs me hard by the shoulders and shakes me. "Don't you ever—and I mean, *ever*—think of yourself as a whore, do you hear me?"

"That's what you make me feel like!" My voice raises and I hate it, because that's not true. He doesn't make me feel like a whore, not when he always takes care of me and makes sure my comfort comes before his.

But that's what I'm supposed to think, right? If he doesn't have feelings for me and doesn't intend to, then how am I any different from a whore?

Nate releases me with a shove and I flinch from the gutting harshness in his expression.

"I see." He turns around. "I'll be outside if you need anything."

And with that, he's out of the room.

I fall to my seat, and the milkshake hits the floor and spills all over it. And with it, my tears.

Because I know, I just know, something just broke between us and there's probably nothing that can fix it.

THIRTY-ONE

Gwyneth

"WELCOME HOME."

Dad smiles as he steps into the living room. He doesn't even need me or the crutches anymore. He only needed some physical rehabilitation, but zero mental.

In ten days, he was able to walk, talk, and when Daniel and Knox came to visit, he even scolded them for cases they almost lost a few days before his accident.

He remembers everything.

The doctor said it's because he didn't have severe damage to his brain, which is why he was able to make a fast recovery.

And just like that, I have my dad back.

I still can't believe it as we walk together into our home. Even though he's wearing his shirt and pants, he doesn't fill them like before. He's lost weight and often appears wary, as if there's something heavy perching on his shoulders. So I massage those shoulders, hopping now and then because Dad is really tall.

His critical gaze roams over the place, taking in every nook and every surface as if he's searching for something.

Or someone.

I stop my hopping and step in front of him in an attempt to distract him. "How does it feel to be back home?"

"Different."

"Different how?"

"It smells different."

A ball the size of my fist gathers in my throat. *Shit.* It's Dad's weirdly sensitive nose.

I predicted he'd detect anything that's out of the ordinary, so Martha and I scrubbed the house clean after Nate moved out. He left a few days ago when the doctor confirmed that Dad would be able to come home. Hell, I washed some of Dad's wardrobe and sprayed my perfume and my father's cologne everywhere. He can't possibly smell him.

I'm just being paranoid, right?

Because if Dad finds out about Nate and me this soon, it'll get ugly. The entire situation is already ugly. I don't want it to be even uglier.

"It must be the cupcakes I made yesterday."

"It's not those."

I swallow and link my arm with his. "Do you want some?"

"Sure, I missed your cupcakes."

We go to the kitchen and he sits on the stool as I busy myself behind the counter, putting the cupcakes on a plate.

"I'm telling you, Dad. These cupcakes became a hit at W&S. I've been getting clingy texts the past couple of days because I was with you and didn't bring any."

"Who are the assholes who dare be clingy to my angel?" Dad takes a bite of a cupcake and a small smile twitches his lips. "Chocolate. I thought any flavor other than vanilla is blasphemy."

"It is, but apparently, chocolate is popular."

"Apparently. Presumptuous chocolate."

"I know, right?" I lean over on the counter to watch him closely.

I've been doing that a lot lately, watching him, making sure he's actually awake and right in front of me.

The thought of losing him again keeps me up at night.

After he finishes the cupcake, he sniffs the air, or more like, me. "That smell again."

"W-what smell?" Shit. Damn it.

Dad's eyes narrow on me the second I stammer. My heart thunders and the ball in my throat grows bigger until it's blocking my breathing.

Oh, God.

Oh, God.

He knows. No clue what exactly he's aware of, but it's there in the dip in his forehead and how he's flexing his fingers on the table as if stopping them from balling into a fist.

"Is there something you want to tell me, Gwen?"

"No."

"Are you sure?"

Oh, God. There's a full frown in his forehead now and he looks to be on the verge of breaking all hell loose.

When I first married Nate, I wasn't scared of Dad's reaction, because I was doing it for him, to protect this house and his assets. However, that was before I gave Nate my virginity and my stupid heart that's hardly beating right now.

That was before I really wanted the marriage.

So I don't know how to bring it up. Nate told me not to say anything and that he would take care of it. And that was on the few occasions we talked after Dad woke up.

He went back to his workaholic life and I took care of Dad. He brings me whatever I need, leaves me milkshakes in the morning, stocks the fridge with ice cream, and asks me if I need anything.

But that's all.

He's never tried to touch me, not even by accident, and he's kept his distance, even during the time he spent here before Dad came home.

And it hits me then. He seems content with the way I cut off our physical relationship.

He seems content with being Uncle Nate again.

Those thoughts have kept me awake at night—aside from my concerns about Dad—and no amount of lying upside down has helped me sleep.

Because even now, as I get swallowed in Dad's severe gaze, I can feel the pieces of my broken heart digging into my ribcage as I choke out, "Yeah, I'm sure."

"Why are you clinking your nails then?"

I flatten my sweaty palms on the counter, but that gets me more narrowed eyes from him.

"It's nothing, Dad. Really."

"When I was in a coma, I heard voices."

"Voices?" Holy shit. Does he remember everything I talked about while he was in a coma? While I didn't mention Nate's name for fear of agitating him, I did talk about us and about how much of a jerk he is and how much I love being in his company. Not to mention the conversation Nate and I had the night he woke up.

"They're still chaotic up here." He taps the side of his head. "But I'm organizing them."

"You don't need to. They were probably nothing."

"On the contrary, I believe they're important. So if there's anything you have to tell me, do it now before I find out on my own. And I will find out, Gwen. I always do."

Shit. *Shit.*

My hand goes to my bracelet and it's like I can feel Nate through it. As if there's a presence there. He said he'd take care of it and I believe him. Even if I hate him right now.

"There's really nothing, Dad. Come on, let's take a walk."

He doesn't protest, but there's tension in his shoulders and stiffness in his strides.

After lunch, he goes to take a nap in his room. He does that now, napping, and the doctor said it's normal.

I kiss his forehead, then I hurry downstairs to keep from having an epic meltdown in front of him.

The ball in my throat grows bigger and harder as I pace the edge of the pool, my sneakers slapping against the concrete with each step.

I'm clinking my nails again, and my palms are sweaty and cold. A million thoughts about how this will be disastrous sneak into my head, crowding it with my dark ones.

What if Dad will never forgive me? What if I lose him because of my stupid crush that ended before it even started?

"Don't tell me you're thinking about jumping again?"

I come to a screeching halt and whirl around so fast, I nearly fall backward. A strong hand wraps around my wrist and pulls me forward.

My sneakers make a squeaking sound as my head bumps against a solid chest. The same chest I hid in when I slept. The same chest I think about when I try to fall asleep and fail.

His scent hits me hard, its masculine notes of spices and woods turn my head dizzy and seep through my bloodstream so that it's the only thing pumping in and out of my heart.

It must be because it's been some time since I felt this or him. It's been a long time since he's been this close, surrounded me with his warmth, or touched me.

God. His hand is on my wrist. And it's like a blazing fire is about to spread all over my skin.

It doesn't, though, because as soon as I can stand on my own, he releases my wrist and steps back. There's always some sort of safe distance between us now.

And I hate the distance.

I hate space.

But what I hate the most is the man standing in front of me, looking as handsome as ever in his dark suit, with his hair styled, and his face as hard as granite.

It's because of him that I gambled with my heart and failed.

Or maybe it's because of that stupid vanilla heart that's still trying to revive itself back to life at the mere sight of him. Hearts don't understand, do they? All they care about is staying alive, even if it hurts.

Even if it's being slashed open in the process and all that's left is blood with his scent mixed in it.

Then it hits me.

Nate is here.

Dad is also here.

Oh, shit.

"What are you doing here? Dad's upstairs and you have to leave before he wakes up. He asked me if there's something he should know about and he even said something smells different. No idea why he has that sensitive nose, but he does, and I nearly lost it and he knows, Nate. He knows something's wrong, because he's Dad. He knows things and I can't lie to him. I can't do this—"

"Hey. Deep breaths."

I inhale, then exhale harshly, staring at him from beneath my eyelashes. "I…I'm scared. I'm scared of making him mad or losing him after I've finally got him back. It's a miracle that he's home and has recovered so fast, and I can't…I can't think of losing him."

"You won't. I'll make sure of it."

"Really?"

"Have I ever made a promise and not kept it?"

"No, you haven't."

"Then trust me one final time."

"Are you…going to talk to him?"

"It's about time I do. I waited for him to recover, but I need to be the one who tells him before he goes back to battling with Susan and finds out on his own."

"Yeah, okay. I get it."

"We're going to be realistic here, Gwyneth. He's probably not going to take it well."

"Oh, God. He's…he's going to be so mad."

"He will. But I'll take the heat of it."

"How…how are you going to do that?"

"I'll say I convinced you to go ahead with this marriage and you only went along with my plans."

"But that's not true. I agreed to this and I'm able to take responsibility for it. I told you to stop treating me like a damn kid, Nate."

"It's not about that."

"Then what is it about?"

"You can't afford to lose him. He's your father and your only family."

That brings tears to my eyes because the meaning behind his words hits me straight in my barely-beating heart. He knows how much Dad means to me, so in order for me not to lose him, he'll risk losing him.

He'll risk being tossed aside for me.

He'd rather be abandoned again than have me go through it.

And that hurts. Because he's not supposed to take the fall for me when he doesn't do feelings. When he stopped touching me instead of trying to fight for me.

"I'm going to take responsibility for my actions, Nate. You don't have to sacrifice yourself for a fuck buddy."

A muscle jumps in his cheek and he tightens his jaw. I can tell he's pining for patience, because he breathes heavily before he speaks. "That's not what you are, so stop using those fucking terms, Gwyneth."

"That's what people my age call a sexual relationship. Fuck buddies. Isn't that what we were?"

"If you were my fuck buddy, I wouldn't have honored your demands whenever I saw you. I would've pushed you on all fours and fucked you. So no, you're not a fuck buddy."

My core tightens at the image he's planted in my head. I swallow because my heart is taking it as a fake sign to get back to life.

My body is definitely joining in because I've missed him. I've missed being fucked by him and sleeping in his arms.

But my brain is smarter, because it's in control and it won't compromise anymore.

"Then what am I, Nate?"

"The most infuriating person on earth, that's what you are."

"Infuriating because I won't let you touch me?"

"Because you want fucking feelings. Why would you? From me? You know how broken I am. I'm empty, too. Like you said, I don't like people to get close, because they leave. They fucking leave, Gwyneth. That's why I don't do feelings. So you're not supposed to want them from me."

"Don't you understand? It's because it's you that I want them, idiot. We're the same, you and I. That's why we care about each other's opinions. That's why we sleep in each other's company despite the insomnia. It's because that emptiness isn't allowed to make noise anymore, and it's peaceful and right. Have you been sleeping lately? I haven't. The emptiness has been so loud and harsh and I've missed you, but I've hated myself for it because you don't miss me, too."

"I do." His voice is low, barely audible.

"What did you just say—"

Any other words disappear when he grabs me by the face, his strong hands cupping my cheeks as he slams his lips to mine.

A kiss.

He's kissing me.

I'm so stunned that I can't think straight. I can't think about anything except that his lips are on mine. They're firm and demanding and I open with a moan because he's feasting on me, his tongue claiming mine while one hand is at my throat and the other is fisting in my hair, pulling it back so he can deepen the kiss. So he can reach places in my soul that I didn't think existed before.

This is what it feels like to be kissed by Nate. He's the one who erupts the volcano but doesn't allow it to turn to ashes.

He's the one who revives my vanilla heart and lets it breathe properly.

Freely.

With no restraints.

He bites down on my lower lip, and I whimper as he plunges

his tongue inside again and pulls my body so it's flattened against his front.

And I think I can die at this moment.

With him kissing me, claiming me, touching me in the way I always wished he would.

Like he cares.

Like he doesn't want this to end either.

There are groans and moans and I don't know whose they are, but I don't care, because I'm too far gone to come back to the world of the living.

My hands are all over him, too, bunching in his shirt and hair. I kiss him as hard as he kisses me, not like the pure, innocent girl I was two years ago.

That girl with the measly crush is gone. She's a woman now who's not afraid to go after what she wants.

And now, I want this man with everything I have.

I show him that, kissing him back with the same fire he uses to claim me.

And then Nate's suddenly pushed off me and I shriek as Dad punches him, sending him flying into the pool.

THIRTY-TWO

Nathaniel

THE SPLASH OF WATER IS LOUD, BUT IT ISN'T LOUDER THAN Gwyneth's shriek.

It's the first time I've heard that sound from her. The terror in it tears through my chest and clashes against my bones.

Fuck.

I don't want her scared, terrified, or any of the negative emotions she's written on her list.

But now this has happened, and in hindsight, I shouldn't have touched her when King was around. Even if he was napping, because he's a fucking hyena and if he's suspecting something, he won't sleep. He'll be roaming and digging around like a fucking lunatic until he gets what he wants.

But I couldn't stop it. And it's not for lack of trying.

I gave her the space she demanded, even though I hated it, because it was the right thing to do. I wasn't going to drag her into my mess or give her hope that doesn't exist.

However, every day I spent without her was absolute fucking hell. Concentration? Zero. Sleep? Nonexistent.

And it's not about her body or how perfect she feels in my arms. It's the little fucking things, like how she sleeps with her face tucked in my neck or how we cooked together while she danced to her music.

It's her light.

It's her energy and cheerfulness. It's the fucking meaning she gave to my life when I thought I didn't need such a thing.

And I couldn't stop thinking about that. About her presence, about that meaning I didn't ask for but was there anyway, which opened wounds I thought were long healed.

So I had to kiss her.

I had to claim her for all the times I've wanted to kiss her since she stole that kiss on her eighteenth birthday.

That was the exact moment she stopped being my friend's daughter and became her.

Gwyneth.

Just Gwyneth.

And now, said friend will kill me for it. Because he jumped after me in the water and the moment I resurface, he grabs me by the lapel of my jacket and punches me in the face.

My head snaps to the side from the force of it. Fuck. His punch is still as strong as when we were teens, if not harder. And here I thought he was recovering and didn't have enough strength.

"Dad, stop!" Her shrieks from the side of the pool bring out the temper lurking inside me.

Yes, I was prepared for King's reaction and wrath, but not in front of her. I don't want her to see his ugly side—or mine.

Because this is heading straight in that direction.

"I'm going to fucking kill you! Your life will end today, you motherfucking asshole." He enunciates every word with a punch to my face, my neck, my chest, everywhere.

I don't stop him or punch back, not even when blood explodes in my lip or when my ribs sting with every breath I take.

"Dad, please!" She's flat out crying now while perching on the edge of the pool.

"King, stop it," I grind out. "Gwyneth is—"

He shuts me up with a punch to the mouth and it almost sends my teeth flying. *Motherfucker.*

"You don't say her fucking name. That's my daughter. My fucking daughter, Nate!! What type of fucking death wish did you have when you touched my fucking daughter?" *Thwack!* "Are all the other women not enough for you so you went after her?" *Thwack!* "Have you fantasized about her since she was a toddler? Were you touching her behind my fucking back?"

I raise my fist in a huge splatter of water and drive it straight into his face. I didn't mean to punch him, but I do it because he's saying shit he shouldn't be saying. "I would never do that and you know it, but you're being a fucking dick right now. She was never a woman to me until recently."

"She's not a woman. She's my baby daughter, you motherfucker!" He grabs me by the hair and pushes my face into the water, then locks my legs with his to stop me from moving around.

He's going to drown me.

The motherfucker is really intent on drowning me.

I grab his arms and push, trying to remove his hold on my head, but he has brute fucking strength that keeps me pinned in place. How can it be that this crazy asshole was in a coma and is still recovering?

The fucking idiot. If he kills me, he'll go to jail and no one will be there for Gwyneth.

That's when I hear her hysterical cries for her father to stop, but he's too far gone to listen to her.

Or anyone—aside from the demons in his head.

My lungs burn and I swallow the chlorinated water in my attempts to get some air. My grip loosens from around his arms and black dots fill my vision.

Ah, fuck.

I thought he'd try to kill me. But not that he'd actually succeed.

Still, all I can think about is Gwyneth's tear-streaked face and how she'll probably lose both of us now.

Me to death.

King to jail.

Then she'll be all alone again.

The pressure of King's hand disappears from my head and I think I'm crossing over to the other side, but then soft palms grab me by the cheeks and lift me up from the water.

I gulp in a sharp intake of air and splutter water as I cough up everything that I swallowed. The scratch and burn in my throat don't disappear, but none of that matters.

Not when Gwyneth is holding my face, wet strands of her wild hair sticking to her temples and tears streaming down her cheeks. "Nate? Can you hear me? Are you okay?"

I can't talk, and it's not only because of the grogginess in my throat. How the fuck did she get in here? She doesn't know how to swim.

I stare behind her and find that King has her by the waist to keep her afloat even when his face is tight and murderous, and he definitely still has plans to kill me.

Fuck me. This brave woman jumped in the water, despite not knowing how to swim, because she knew her safety is what King cares about above anything else. She risked drowning to save me, my Gwyneth.

"He'll be dead in a second." King tries to push her to the edge of the pool, but she wraps her legs around my waist, her sneakers digging into my back. Her arms circle my neck, and that forces King to bring us both to the edge.

Then he climbs up and reaches his hand out to her. "Come here."

"Not until you promise you won't hurt him."

"You don't want to talk about him, Gwen. Let him the fuck go."

She stares into my eyes and I nod before I speak in a scratchy voice, "I'm fine. Get out of the water."

That's not what she does, though. Instead, she uses the back of her arm to wipe at my face, probably the blood, and sniffles. I wince when she touches the bruises her father left behind and that causes tears to slide down her cheeks.

Ever since she was young, Gwyneth was always the type who felt other people's pain and discomfort before her own. When King noticed the signs, he stopped her from becoming a people pleaser early on, but he could've never tamed the wild emotions that run through her.

It's what makes her a unique person who's not a copycat of her father. She's special that way even though she's prone to get hurt easily, like right now.

Being the reason behind her pain is the last thing I want to do, which is why I try to tamp down my reactions as much as possible.

King, however, glares down at us, a muscle tightening in his jaw. "Gwen. Come out. *Now.*"

She flinches and starts trembling uncontrollably. He's my friend and her father, but I'm about to punch him hard enough to send him into another coma.

He's scaring her right now. I know it. I see it in her eyes, where the gray has staked a claim.

Since she's his daughter, she doesn't know him to be cruel or a bully. She doesn't know how brutal he can get, but she's seeing it now, and I can tell she doesn't want to go.

She doesn't want to face that tyrannical part of him.

But I nod again, because if she doesn't, he'll turn the crazy up a notch.

She hesitantly places her hand in his and he pulls her out of the water in one sweep.

I take a breath and start to climb out. When I'm halfway there, he jams his foot against my chest and shoves me back into the pool again.

Motherfucker.

"Dad!" I hear Gwyneth's shriek when I resurface, coughing

from the water again. At this rate, I'm not getting out of here. But hey, it's better than being drowned.

I swim to the edge and he's waiting up top with a dark expression on his face, probably ready to push me again.

But I climb out anyway.

Before he can act on his plans, though, Gwyneth steps in front of him, holding her hands wide apart. "Stop it, Dad. Please, stop."

"You stay out of it. I'm going to deal with you later." He starts to push her away, but she keeps her feet planted long after I'm out of the pool, dripping all over the ground.

"I can't stay out of it, because this is about me, too. I chose to be with him. I chose to marry him. No one forced me to."

"You fucking what?" He nudges her away and starts to lunge toward me. "You married her? You fucking married my daughter, you sick fuck?"

I'm ready for him to throw me into the pool and actually drown me this time, but he stops mid-step when frail arms wrap around him from behind. "Daddy, please…please stop. I'm scared. Stop."

He's breathing so heavily that a few blood cells have exploded in his eyes. His fists are clenched at his sides, but he doesn't make a move toward me.

The reason is attached to him. He's feeling her tremble against him and he's hearing the fear in her voice, the same fear he spent his entire life protecting her from. And now, he's the reason behind it.

He breathes harshly through his nostrils. "Get the fuck out of my house."

"No. We're going to talk."

"Nate…leave before I murder you."

"No."

He must sense the determination in my tone and see it on my face, since he throws one last glare my way and pulls Gwyneth inside.

I wait for a few minutes beside the pool, wiping the water out of my face and grimacing when I touch a cut. The crazy mother-fucker went for my looks, even though we have a rule against that. Not that I blame him, but still.

After some time has passed, I go through the back entrance of the kitchen and grab a towel and some dry clothes from the laundry room. It's King's clothes. Gwyneth has been on a high ever since he woke up and washed some of his clothes, so they're fresh.

He'll kill me for this, too, but he shouldn't have ruined my Italian suit.

I quickly dry myself, then pull on a pair of King's khaki shorts. I put my arms through the shirt sleeves and wince when my ribs ache. I stare at my chest and find a violet spot forming. Fucking King and his fists.

Sometimes, it feels as if he's still the delinquent from school who dealt with everything by using violence.

I'm about to button up the shirt when I hear a slow tapping of shuffling feet. Sneakers.

Sure enough, Gwyneth slips in as if she knew I was here all along. She's changed into one of her long shirts and her hair is still wild and wet, barely dried with a towel. A shadow covers her tiny features and it's accentuated by the warring of the gray and blue in her eyes.

She runs toward me and stops a breath away. "Are you okay?"

"I'll live."

Her fingers touch the cut on my brow and I wince. Tears glisten in her eyes and she starts to remove her hand, but I grab it, flattening her palm against my cheek. "I'm fine. I expected this."

"I hate this. I hate Dad like this. He almost drowned you out there… You almost died, Nate."

"I would've done the same if I were in his place, except the killing part, because that will land him in prison."

"Nate!" She pushes at my chest, straight on the bruise, and I groan.

"What's wrong?" She starts to inspect my chest and gasps at the view. "Oh, God."

"It's nothing." I button my shirt and she helps me, her fingers trembling when they reach the top. "Hey, this is nothing. We had worse fights than this when we were young."

"Maybe you should leave, Nate. For now, just go and I'll talk to him—"

"No, you won't. I will."

"But—"

"I've known him longer than you have and I can deal with him."

"What if he hurts you again?"

"He won't. I can protect myself."

"Promise?"

"I promise. Now, where is he?"

"In his office, I think." She digs her nails into my shirt, not wanting to let me go.

So I lower my head and claim her mouth. I suck on her bottom lip until she opens with a moan. My hand fists in her wet hair and I feast on her taste, a mixture of vanilla and whatever she's feeling at the moment. Right now, it's despair. And I take that for myself so she doesn't have those negative emotions anymore.

I never liked kissing. Never engaged in it either, but I want to keep kissing her until I'm out of air and she's the only oxygen I breathe.

I want to keep feeling her body clinging to mine, her softness molding against my hardness and her moans filling the air.

Those moans and sounds are for me.

Only me.

I almost died because I kissed her not so long ago, but I will still repeat it. I will still risk death for her.

But I don't want her to risk anything in case King sees us again.

So I begrudgingly pull back, relinquishing her sweet lips.

She's panting, her eyes darkening with a bright green color, but she doesn't look to be on the verge of a breakdown like earlier.

"Be careful," she whispers and lets me go when I coax her to step aside.

"I'll be fine," I tell her and stride out of the kitchen without a look back. Because if I do, I'll be tempted not to leave her side.

If I do, I will take her away from here and give King the middle finger.

But that's just not the smart thing to do in a situation like this.

I take the stairs slowly because my ribs ache with each step I take. The crazy fucker probably bruised some of them.

I barge into said asshole's office without knocking. Because fuck him and his crazy ass.

When we were teens and I decided to fight him, everyone told me not to challenge the "King." That it was stupid and reckless and I'd get my ass whipped.

But I did. The best way to become a king is to slaughter one.

And I was out to do just that.

Yes, he used me as a punching bag the first few times, but I didn't give up until the king himself fell at my feet.

Until I became his worst friend and best enemy.

And right now, it feels like we're back to those times where he's the king and I'm out for his throne.

He's sitting in the chair at his window that overlooks the front pool. This is probably where he was when I was kissing Gwyneth earlier and decided to use his fists.

But now, he doesn't look like he wants to touch me, because he has a gun in his hand.

"That's smarter," I say, locking the door behind me so Gwyneth doesn't have the chance to come in. "Better than your clear jealousy of my looks that you tried to ruin."

"Explain yourself before I fucking kill you."

I might have lied to Gwyneth just now. I don't think I'll be fine.

THIRTY-THREE

Kingsley

PEOPLE SPEND THEIR ENTIRE LIVES AVOIDING CRIME—OR try to.

Not me.

I knew that I'd do it one day. That at some point, the crazy genes, as my father and his bitch of wife called them, would catch up to me and I'd snap.

That's why I chose law. It definitely wasn't out of a warped sense of justice. I just had to learn law to get around it and apply self-restraint so that I didn't end up murdering someone accidentally.

Or intentionally.

It's been easier with Gwen around, because I have someone to focus on, someone not to get caught for. I had to raise her, to be the parent my own parents weren't. I had to be the person who protected her from the world.

But I couldn't protect her from my motherfucking friend.

Ex-friend because I'm going to blow his brains out in about five minutes.

I always knew I'd kill. I just didn't know it'd be the man I considered a fucking brother.

Nate and I didn't start our friendship the conventional way. We were rivals for way too long, then we saw similar traits in each other. So for the sake of our ambitions, we decided to put our differences aside and partner up.

And with time, I realized he was the only person I could call a friend.

Not anymore, though. Because he's going to die.

Said asshole flops onto the chair in front of my desk, running a hand over his battered face—the face I should've punched a few more times and erased its expression. He dares to sigh as if he's the wronged one, as if he's the one who was stabbed in the fucking back.

He places both his elbows on his knees and leans his chin on the backs of his hand. "I know you're upset—"

"Upset?" I storm in front of him and tighten my hold on the gun. "Try enraged. Try fucking murderous. That girl is my daughter, my flesh and blood, my fucking second chance at life. And I left for one second, one fucking second, and you swooped in and ruined her. She's become a stranger who stands up to me when she never has before."

He purses his lips as his dark eyes stare up at me. "She never stood up to you, because she respected you. Now, she's fucking terrified of you, King. She's seeing a person that she doesn't recognize in you. What the fuck is wrong with you? Do head injuries make you act like a monster?"

"A monster? That's rich coming from a motherfucking predator."

At that, he stands up and grabs me by the collar of my polo shirt. "Don't ever, and I mean, *ever*, repeat that. Respect your own fucking daughter."

I slam the gun on the desk and choke-hold him by his shirt.

"Did you respect her? When you put your hands on her, did you think of respect? Of *me*?"

"Of course, I thought of you. Why do you think I avoided this place like the fucking plague over the past two years? It was because of her, King. Because she kissed me on her eighteenth birthday and I could never see her as your little girl anymore. Because you were her father and I couldn't take it any further. Because you're my fucking partner and best friend and I didn't want to lose you."

She...what?

A red haze covers my vision and it's all I can do not to self-combust. Did he just say my Gwen kissed him—as in, she went after him first? No, he must be fucking lying and making excuses for himself. If she had a thing for him, I would've noticed it...

Images of her flushing red whenever he was mentioned or dropped by slash through my mind. She hid away, too, almost always when he was around. It started about five years ago and I didn't think much of it then, because it didn't mean anything.

It *doesn't* mean anything and Nate is a fucking liar.

My glare falls on his battered face. "It's so obvious that you didn't want to lose me, because the moment I was out of the picture, you pounced on her."

"Watch your fucking language. I didn't pounce on her."

"Oh, right. You *married* her. That makes it all fucking better."

"We had to because of all the damn wars you have going on with Susan. She would've taken this house, which you fought for tooth and nail, mind you. She was suing to own shares in the firm and make our lives hell. We didn't know if you were ever going to wake up and Gwyneth wanted to protect your assets. She did this for you while she grieved your loss, because she thought you'd abandoned her like her mother did."

He shoves me away and I hit the edge of the desk. My hands ball into fists and my breathing comes harsh and fast. I didn't stop to think about what Gwen must've gone through because of my accident.

I'm her only family, and she knows how much this house means to me. She wouldn't have thought twice about protecting what I left behind, because by doing so, she was also protecting me.

Because my little angel isn't so little anymore.

But I don't want to think about that. I don't want to believe that she's all grown up now and doesn't need me anymore.

"Let's say you married her for my and the firm's sake. But it should've been on paper only."

"It was."

"Oh, really? Then did I imagine your tongue at the back of her throat just then?"

"You can curse and hit and punch me all you want, but you need to watch your fucking language when you talk about her. And yes, it was just on paper at the beginning. To protect her and the firm and you, but it became more."

"More, like what? Like you were fucking her under my own roof? Did you perhaps do it in this very office? Was it a fantasy of yours that you harbored for years, you sick fuck?"

He raises his fist and punches me in the face. He doesn't hold back and my head snaps to the side from the force of it.

"I told you to watch your language, King."

I drive my fist into the cut of his mouth and revel in the sight of the blood that explodes from his lips as I grab him by the collar. "Do you think I want to talk about my own daughter like that? It makes me sick to my stomach thinking that you touched her, that you had your fucking hands on her and used her."

"I didn't use her, King. Never."

"Oh, come on, I've been on your side for over two decades and I know you use women for sex."

"Not her. She's different."

"Heaven could fall and you wouldn't change, Nate. It's in your fucked-up genes, right? Because your parents didn't like you, because you were always second to the same brother you couldn't hate, because he took care of you. But even he didn't like you very much, no? Otherwise, he wouldn't have left you without giving it a second thought. Because you were jealous I had a life, a fucking family, so you went ahead and destroyed it. You went ahead and stained my little angel with your darkness because you wanted to take the one thing that made sense in my fucking life."

He loses it then and starts punching me. I punch him back and we roll to the ground, hitting and kicking each other until we're both bloodied, him more so than me. I can tell he's holding back.

In the past, Nate was never the type to hold back, not for any reason. But right now, he's lessening the blow of his punches, no matter how much I hit him, and I don't think it's because I'm still recovering from the accident.

The same damn accident that caused me to leave Gwen alone with him and the fucking woman who gave birth to her.

When we're finally spent, I roll to sit against the chair while Nate winces and leans against the wall, his legs outstretched in front of him.

He wipes his face and grunts. "Fuck you, King. Fuck you for being a goddamn motherfucking dick."

"And fuck you for stabbing me in the back. She's a fucking kid. She hasn't lived yet and you ruined everything."

"She's not a fucking kid. She stopped being that a long time ago, but you keep overprotecting her to keep her with you forever. She's strong and knows how to take care of herself, and you need to start getting used to that."

"Shut the fuck up. You don't get to tell me how to treat my own daughter. You will stay away from her, you hear me? I'm going to file a restraining order."

"You can't do that on her behalf. And stop being a fucking dick. I care about her, okay? I care about her like I've never cared about any woman in my life. Hell, like I never cared about any person. This is serious. I'm serious about her, King."

Fire like never before rises in my veins and images of him with my beautiful little angel, my Gwen, nearly cuts me open. Nausea clogs my throat and I want to fucking kill him.

So I stagger to my feet and grab the gun, then point it at him. "You shouldn't have touched her, Nate. Best friends don't touch their friends' kids."

"Don't you think I tried not to?"

"You should've tried fucking harder." I approach him with the gun and put it to his forehead.

"Put it away, you idiot. If I die and you go to prison, she'll have no one."

When I don't make a move to comply, he grabs the gun and throws it on the sofa.

"I'll find a way to kill you without getting caught then. Now get the fuck out of my house and don't ever show me or my daughter your face again."

"That's impossible since you're my partner and she's my wife."

"Like fuck she is. You will divorce her."

"No."

"What the fuck did you just say?"

"Unless she wants the divorce, it won't be happening." He staggers to his feet, grabbing his ribs that I fucked up—good, maybe that way, he can feel a sliver of the pain I feel from his betrayal.

Maybe that way, he can understand what it feels like to be a horrible father for leaving my only daughter on her own.

If I hadn't had that fucking accident, if I hadn't made that call, I would've stopped this. I wouldn't have allowed him to prey on my daughter.

Or allowed him to be near her.

I would've prevented this whole mess.

He pats my shoulder. "Get some rest. We'll talk later."

"You get some rest and sort out your will, because I'll kill you later."

He says nothing as he struggles to open the door, then steps out. I follow after him because Gwen is waiting right outside. I saw the shadow of her feet as she kept pacing.

As soon as she sees him, she gasps, hands covering her mouth and tears glistening in her colorful eyes.

"Oh my God, Nate." Her voice is brittle, chin trembling as she reaches a hand out for him.

"Gwyneth, come here. Now." I don't usually order her this harshly, and she knows that, too, because she startles, her hand falling to her side.

Nate nods at her and waits until she comes to me while he uses the wall for support to remain standing.

Gwen keeps staring at him, but I pull her inside and slam the door in his face.

Her gaze is shifty and she's clinking her nails manically. Kids avoid their parents' gazes when they've done something wrong, but Gwen has never been like that. She tells me head-on about her wrongdoings. She only ever avoids eye contact when she's in pain and doesn't want to show it.

Because it'd hurt me, too, and she's said she never wants to be the source of my pain.

Until that fucker Nate played with her mind.

"I'm sorry, Dad."

"What are you sorry for?"

"Hurting you. I didn't mean to, I didn't want to, but it's not like I could choose, you know?"

"This isn't your fault. It's his for using you."

Her head snaps up and the green in her eyes rushes forward. "No, Dad. No. He didn't use me. Never. If anything, I made the first move, okay? I kissed him on my eighteenth birthday because I had this major crush on him that wouldn't go away, no matter how much I told myself it was wrong. I even wrote the word *crush* on my list, but I couldn't desensitize myself to him. Still, I tried, I really tried, Dad. I dated and went out. I forced myself to think of him less, but it became more. My feelings were unrequited for such a long time that I hated myself for having them. But you know what? I'm not going to apologize to you or him for the way I feel. I love him and it's none of anyone's business. It's mine and I choose to have these feelings, Dad. I chose to love him. No one made me do it."

She's breathing heavily, chest rising and falling in a frantic rhythm, and a tear slides down her cheek.

Fuck. Fuck. *Fuck!*

She's too far gone for the motherfucker—whose death I will make the most painful possible.

"Gwen, Angel, listen to me. Those feelings could just be a manifestation of sentiments of your dependency because you only had him around when I was gone."

"Can everyone stop using that word? It wasn't dependency or neediness or a ruse of the moment. I've liked him since I was fifteen and those hormonal little girl feelings transformed into more. I liked him since I knew what liking someone means and it only grew deeper with time. I know what I feel more than anyone else, more than you and him, because unlike both of you, I'm not scared of my feelings. No matter how strong they are, no matter how overwhelming they get, I own them and wear them as a badge for the world to see. So don't tell me I'm mistaking anything."

My fists clench and I have this need to punch someone, Nate preferably. But I release them because she's watching my hands with wild eyes.

The motherfucker was right. She is scared of me.

"I would never hurt you, Angel." I try to soften my voice.

"You already did by hurting him, Dad."

"So you're taking his side now? First, he betrays me, then he touches you and now he turns you against me? What will it be next?"

"No, Daddy." She wraps her clammy, trembling hands around mine. "I'm on both your sides. It kills me that you're fighting. I can't take it."

"You can't be on both our sides."

"Dad…"

"You won't be with him, Gwen. It's not up for discussion."

"But why? Didn't you say you'd only let me be with someone I love with all my heart? That someone is Nate, Dad."

EMPIRE OF DESIRE | 301

"You think he is, but you're too young to know for sure. You still haven't met the right person."

"It's him. I know it. I've known it since I was eighteen, and stop using my age as a deciding factor. It's just a number. I'm old enough to make my own decisions."

"I'll never approve of you with Nate, Gwen. It's either him or me."

A sob catches in her throat and she shakes her head frantically. "Daddy…don't do that, please. Please don't make me choose."

"Him or me. You can't have both."

"I thought you would never hurt me, Dad."

"I'm not. I'm protecting you. I don't want to lose you, Angel."

"No, you're breaking me right now. Because I'll never be happy with either choice. If I choose him, I'll be unhappy and eventually hate him for coming between us. And if I choose you, I'll hate you for taking away the one person who not only accepts me for who I am but also understands me and likes me for it. So congrats, Dad. You'll lose me either way."

She fumbles with the door handle and storms out of the room, but her hiccups and sniffles stay with me long after she's gone.

I run a hand over my face and expel a large breath. Seeing her cry is like being sliced open from the inside out.

Even when she was a baby and had to cry now and again, I did my best to stop the flow of her tears. It fucks me up even more now that she's an adult.

When I woke up, she told me that she didn't let anyone touch what was mine, but she let Nate touch the most important thing.

Her.

So even though she's in pain, I won't console her like I usually do. I won't bring her tea and joke around until she smiles again. This is out of necessity. To protect her.

Which reminds me that I need to protect her from her fucking mother, too.

The snake who couldn't just fucking disappear like she did the night she threw her own daughter away.

THIRTY-FOUR

Gwyneth

DAD CAME UP WITH A PLAN.

Or more like expulsion.

He told Nate to go to the Seattle branch of W&S; it's been around for a couple of years and has been growing noticeably. That way, he can stay away from me.

It's not that Dad cares about the Seattle branch, it's that he wants to separate us with everything he has.

Over the past week, he's been setting things in motion for the separation of property and threatened Nate to shred the power of attorney agreement. Nate did it because he's been mostly placating Dad. Besides, he doesn't need power of attorney now that all properties legally belong to my father.

Then Dad insisted that he divorce me, and that's when Nate said no. He also said no to leaving because, "Fuck you, King."

Those were his exact words the other day.

I don't see him much anymore, because Dad has kicked up the overprotectiveness a notch. Obviously, I intern with him now and he takes me everywhere, including to his ruthless showdowns with Susan that he usually doesn't want me to witness. Then we go home together and he keeps watching me with that cold stare of his.

Something changed in Dad after the coma.

At first, I thought it was because he found out about me and Nate and lost it, but there's something else.

There's a troubled look in his gaze and agitation in his soul that seems to be consuming him. He's harsher now, more ruthless than I've ever witnessed before. Though he was probably like this to the outside world before, he'd never directed it at me. It's not that he's stern with me—he's still my dad, in a way, but he's also become merciless.

His weird sense of smell has kicked up to higher levels, too. The other day, I crossed paths with Nate in the hall and we touched hands, since that's all we can do now, and Dad smelled him on me. No kidding, he said, "Why the fuck is the bastard's cologne on you?"

So yeah, something is up.

It's almost like that time before his accident when he was disheveled and out of sorts. Fear that events will repeat themselves again keeps me up at night, roaming the house like a ghost. Especially with the way he dismissed foul play to be the reason behind his accident.

He said it'd been a while since he'd had maintenance done on his car, but the tone of his voice was wrong.

Everything is wrong now.

Not only do Dad and I have a gap between us, but also Nate and I keep growing apart.

With each day, the empty hole inside me grows bigger and deeper, and soon enough, it'll swallow me whole.

"Maybe they just need time," Jane tells me while we're having lunch with Chris in the IT department.

"I don't think time will fix it." I glide my fry in the ketchup but don't eat it. I've lost my appetite lately. "He asked me to file a restraining order against Nate. He won't stop."

Chris steals a fry and throws it in his mouth. "That shouldn't be a surprise, though."

"Don't you dare say I told you so." I give him the stink eye.

"I'm just saying, Gwen. Fathers don't like anyone fucking around with their daughters, especially overprotective ones like yours."

Jane gulps at that and clears her throat. "I still think it'll be fixed with time. They're best friends, right? That should mean something."

"If by something, you mean that he keeps threatening to kill Nate, then sure, it means something. You know, I always heard stories about my dad and his coldness, but this is the first time I've witnessed it firsthand and it's terrifying. I want my dad back."

Chris steals another fry. "You know the only way to do that is to separate from Nate, right?"

Moisture gathers in my eyes as I nod. Because Dad is making me choose anyway. No matter how much I've begged him and told him my feelings for Nate, he doesn't believe them.

The thought of separating from Nate leaves me breathless, with insomnia, and so hollow that I hear its cracking sound sometimes.

I leave all the fries for Chris and jerk up. "I'm going to get some air."

"I'll come with you." Jane stands and interlaces her arm with mine.

Chris, however, takes all the fries and tells us to go without him.

"You're strong, Gwen. Really." Jane rubs my arm when we're in the elevator, heading to the parking garage. "I wish I had your strength and wasn't so much of a coward."

"You're not a coward, Jane. You just hate people, which is okay. You're okay."

Her gaze gets lost in the distance, staring at nowhere and

nothing. "I don't hate people. I just don't know how to deal with them, so I choose to stay away because…I'm good at that. Running. Staying away. It's how I survive. Truth is…"

The elevator dings as the doors open on the second floor, and I feel Jane stiffening even before I lift my head to see Knox standing there. A hand rests in his pocket and a blank expression covers his features.

"Come out," he orders, his accent even more prominent.

I think he's talking to me, but it's Jane who jolts, and her nails dig into my arm. It's the second time she's done this in his presence. Or is it the third? I think I saw him that night at the club when Jane disappeared on us.

"I said, come out, Jane."

She slowly releases me and steps out of the elevator. She faces me and murmurs, "Talk to you later."

"Uh, okay." I catch Knox's lips twisting in a cruel smirk as the elevator doors close.

That was weird.

I'm still thinking about that scene when I get off in the parking garage. A hand wraps around my mouth and I shriek into it, but the sound is muffled, then it dies out when I recognize his warmth. The warmth mixed with spices and woods and belonging.

Nate drags me to a supply room and slams me against the shut door.

We're both breathing harshly, and our chests are glued together so that we feel each other's heartbeats. The bruises Dad gave him have faded to yellow and the cuts are slowly healing, but he's still the most handsome man I've ever seen. The only man my heart would skip a beat and try to escape its ribcage for.

I run my fingertips over the line of his jaw and the cut on his lip. He closes his eyes, those beautiful, *beautiful* dark eyes that I don't wake up to anymore. And probably never will again.

"Are you okay?" I sound emotional, heartbroken, and Nate must sense it, because he opens his eyes.

"Aside from missing the fuck out of you, I'm fine."

"I miss you, too. I…it hurts, Nate. Everything hurts."

"I'll make it better. I promise."

"But Dad—" The words come to a jolting halt when he places a finger to my mouth.

"Don't mention him when I'm about to fuck you."

A wildfire erupts in the bottom of my stomach and I gulp as he slowly removes his finger from my mouth and replaces it with his lips. I open up with a moan, reveling in how my nerve endings erupt to life.

I've been dead for so long and my resurrection to life hurts in a bittersweet kind of way.

For someone who doesn't do kissing, Nate is the type who swallows you whole with the mere act. There isn't an inch of me that doesn't belong to him right now. And the dominant way he grabs me by the hair and neck to deepen the kiss turns me delirious.

As if that's not enough, he trails his lips to my neck and sucks on the skin of my collarbone. I hiss in sharp intakes of air, feeling the hickey already forming.

"I've fucking missed your vanilla scent."

"I thought vanilla was boring," I breathe out.

"Not on you."

I'm so delirious, that I barely register when he places two hands under my ass and lifts me up, then places me on a surface after he knocks everything off of it.

My skin tingles and catches fire when he pulls my skirt up and cups me through my panties.

"I see you're wet for me, baby girl."

"Only for you."

"Fuck. Say that again."

"I only get wet for you, husband." I reach for his belt, but he shakes his head.

"Not so fast. Let me take my fill of you."

"Nate…please… Don't you miss me?"

"Oh, I fucking do. But you'll be my good girl, won't you, wife?"

He pulls down my panties and slips them in his pocket. I trap my lip between my teeth as I watch. I've missed that, him confiscating my panties.

"I didn't hear an answer."

"I'll be your bad girl, too."

"You will?"

"Mmm."

He wraps an arm around my waist and pulls me to the edge. My fingers splay out on his shoulders and then I'm kissing him again because I love it. I love how his tongue toys with mine and how he nibbles on my lips, letting me know who's in control.

And he is, because I completely let go and I still feel powerful as fuck. He makes me feel it with the way he worships my body, the way his hands are all over my breasts, my waist, and my thighs as if he can never get enough of me.

He makes me feel powerful by wanting me with a ferociousness that turns him animalistic, and I get off on that.

I get off on how he wants me, not caring about the consequences or what the world thinks of us.

While he's still kissing me, he frees his cock and lifts me slightly off the table so he can drive inside me.

"Oh, God," I mumble against his lips, my eyelids slowly closing.

"No. Look at me while I fuck you, wife."

I open my eyes and our gazes lock as he thrusts into me slow and long and deep. So deep that he hits a place I didn't think existed.

With each roll of his hips, he not only fills up the emptiness, but he also engraves himself into that large space in my heart that he's been occupying for years.

The space that kept growing without my permission and wouldn't stop.

His lips find my forehead, my cheek, my nose, my collarbone as he whispers, "You're so fucking beautiful. So fucking addictive. So fucking mine."

308 | RINA KENT

And then he claims my mouth, his tongue emulating the same depth of his cock. They both pick up speed, his tongue and his cock, making the table hit the wall with each powerful rock of his hips.

He kisses like he fucks, with maddening urgency and impeccable control. He kisses like he never wants to separate his lips and tongue from mine. And I'm a goner for his possessive dominance, for the way he handles me with sure command, for the way he knows every inch of my body.

I don't last long under the assault.

My head turns and my vision becomes hazy, but I don't close my eyes as I shatter around him. I want him to see me, to see the feelings that he provokes in me and how uncontrollable they are. I want him see me, not his friend's daughter, not the girl who's eighteen years younger than him, but the woman who's so irrevocably in love with him, she's slowly dying at the thought of losing him.

A grunt spills from his lips as he empties himself inside me, the warmth making me moan against his mouth.

And then he's kissing me again. It's harsh and unyielding as if he's also telling me something.

What, I don't know.

When we finally break apart, a line of saliva forms between us and he licks it off my lips, ripping a shudder out of me.

"I don't want to go out there," I whisper, wiggling so I can feel him inside me.

"We can stay here."

"Forever?"

"If you want."

We remain like that for a moment before he pulls out of me and uses some tissues to clean me up. And then he's between my legs as we fix each other's clothes like we're an old married couple. That puts a smile on my face as I adjust his tie.

"What are you smiling about?"

"This. Us spending peaceful time together."

"We always did that when we used to live together."

"Yeah, we did. I miss those days."

He lifts my chin with two fingers. "We'll go back to those days soon."

"How can you be so sure?"

"I have something on King."

"Are you…are you going to hurt him?" Yes, he's difficult and we've had our differences lately, but I'd never let anyone harm Dad. Not even Nate.

"Of course not. He's your father. I would never hurt him, even if he deserves it."

"Then what?"

"I'll tell you when I have further proof."

"Why don't you tell me now?"

"I don't want to raise your hopes for nothing." He kisses the top of my head. "Go out first and I'll follow after in case there's someone outside."

I wrap my arms around him, burying my face in his neck. I breathe him in and it's so soothing and right. Why can't Dad and the world see just how right this is?

Why can't they understand that I've never wanted and needed someone as much as I do Nate?

"Gwyneth."

"Just a moment. Let me recharge."

I feel the vibration in his chest as he groans before his strong hand wraps around my head.

We stay like that for minutes, just hugging and feeling each other's heartbeats. It's peaceful, but just like any peace, it has to come to an end.

Because wars have to happen. Because they're more permanent than peace, no matter how much I like to think otherwise.

Nate begrudgingly releases me. "Go before he notices you've been gone for too long. I don't want him taking it out on you."

"Will you kidnap me again like this, husband?"

"Absolutely, wife."

I smile, kiss his lips, and carefully slip out of the supply room.

I tiptoe to the elevator—thank God my sneakers don't make a sound—while watching my surroundings.

The parking garage appears haunting, its blinding white lights turning me anxious despite myself. Then something else kicks up my jittery insides a notch.

The very familiar voice talking somewhere.

Dad.

Shit. Shit.

If he smelled Nate on me after a mere brush of fingers, he'll have a heart attack now.

I crouch behind one of the cars and watch through the windows. A frown forms between my brows when I see who my father is talking to.

It's…Aspen.

My dad is talking to Aspen and for the first time since I met her, she's shaking.

Flat out shaking, like when I'm about to have some sort of a meltdown.

I should probably leave, wash up, and pour perfume all over my body, but curiosity gets the better of me. Using the cars as camouflage, I slowly move toward them while still in my crouching position.

Jeez. This is harder than I thought.

I'm finally a car away and can hear them—or more like, hear my father. He sounds cold, not enraged like when he was with Nate, but there's still that terrifying edge to his voice. He's flipping his lighter on and off at a fast pace.

"You will leave. I don't care where, but you'll remove yourself from here."

She shakes her head. "No…I didn't even…I can't leave…"

He grabs her by the elbow. "Listen to me, you fucking witch. You forfeited your parental rights the moment you left her at my door twenty years ago and never looked back. You were never a

mother to her. You're a *nobody* to her. And now you'll disappear quietly like you did back then before I fucking break you."

My chin trembles as I stare from him to Aspen. The *her* he's talking about is me, right? No one left another baby at his door twenty years ago.

And…did he say a *mother?*

Aspen?

Mother?

My fingers dig into the metal of the car I'm hiding behind and it burns.

It burns so hot that I release it with a jolt and jump up. I do it so suddenly, so violently, that both of their attention jerks toward me.

Life as I've known it so far seems like a big, giant lie.

And I've been the joke all along.

THIRTY-FIVE

Nathaniel

KNEW SOMETHING WAS WRONG THE MOMENT I SAW GWYNETH sneaking up behind a car.

Then came King's fucking loud voice, because he doesn't know how to stay quiet.

Then Aspen's full-body shudder as she barely remains upright.

But the only person I care about is the girl who's standing in front of them, her mouth falling open and her nails clinking against each other fast, as if she's on a mission to injure herself.

I step to her side, holding her elbow because she's on the verge of something, and it's not something good.

Her gaze slides to mine and it's a myriad of confused, muted colors as she gulps. "Nate…they said…Dad…called her my mother. It's not true, right?"

I tighten my jaw, then glare at King, who's clenching his fists because he knows he fucked up. He couldn't just keep quiet. No, he had to make a scene and have her find out this way.

He hasn't been subtle at all since he woke up from the coma.

Even I could see that his animosity toward Aspen was uncalled for. She hit back as hard as she could, but he's been going as far as sabotaging her cases, which isn't like him. He never did that in the past, no matter how much he hated her.

But after he hit his head, he started going after her like he does to Susan, ruthlessly and without pause, which means it's a personal grudge, not just some differences in ideologies.

That's when I dug deeper—met with his PI, got him drunk, then asked him a few questions that he answered like a parrot. And my suspicions were right. He did find Gwyneth's mother for King and told him about it the day of the accident, which is probably why he lost control of his car in the first place.

"Can you believe he's been searching for her for years when she's been under his nose all this time?" The PI laughed, then went on with a grandiose speech to show how smart he was in connecting the dots of the timelines they met. He even performed a secret DNA test by stealing Aspen's toothbrush from one of the hotels she stayed at and using a sample from Gwyneth that King willingly gave him.

That's what I was going to hold over his head and wouldn't have hesitated to use so he'd stop trying to separate us. But it's all null and void now that Gwyneth knows.

"Right?" she repeats, staring at her father now. "Tell me it's not true, Dad."

"Angel…" He steps toward her, but the moment he reaches for her, she jerks into my hold.

He pauses, flicking his lighter on and off, but it's not in the slow, steady pace that he's used to. He's doing it as manically as her nail-clinking.

"It doesn't make sense." Gwyneth shakes her head slowly. "She can't be my mother; she's only thirty-five. When did she even have me?"

"I was fourteen when I found out I was pregnant," Aspen says quietly, but for the first time in the years we've known each other, her voice shakes.

She's not the type who shows her emotions. Like me, she doesn't even get emotional. That's why we got close in the first place.

Right now, though, her put-together front and aloofness are gone. Maybe that's been a façade, too, just like with me, because she's crossing her arms over her chest to stop them from trembling.

Like Gwyneth does sometimes. Now, that I know they're mother and daughter, I can see the similarities. She has her nose and a darker shade of her hair.

And that heterochromia? It's a mixture of King's blue-gray eyes and Aspen's hazel ones.

"You should've left your age in the note when you threw me in front of Dad's house then. That way, I wouldn't have felt abandoned by the woman who gave birth to me." There's so much venom in her voice that she trembles with it.

Aspen jolts, but instead of stepping backward, she starts toward us. "Let me explain."

"No, no, no! You had twenty years for that. Twenty damn years of me crying on my birthdays because they remind me of the mother who threw me away on that same day."

"Just hear me out. Five minutes, no, three is enough."

King blocks Aspen's way. "She said she doesn't want to talk to you. So fucking disappear."

"You shut up, shut up! You ruined my life, you fucking asshole, and you don't even remember it, so don't stand there thinking you're better than me. You're not."

"Oh, I don't just think I'm better than you, I am. It's a fucking fact. I didn't throw away a few hours old baby in the cold, not caring whether she lived or died. I raised her, I took care of her. I became both her father and mother when you were living your life with not a care in the world. So go back to that life and leave us the fuck alone. You vanished once. Surely you can do it again."

"I didn't vanish. And who the hell are you to judge me? Were you there when I carried her in my womb when I was a fucking kid? When I couldn't sleep at night, terrified something would happen to her?"

"No, but I was there for the following twenty years when you fucking weren't, witch. And I will continue to be there when you're gone."

"I'm not going anywhere."

"Yes, you will."

"You can't make me, Kingsley."

"Fucking watch me."

Tears are streaming down Gwyneth's cheeks and I wipe them with my thumb. The more she watches them arguing and on the verge of hitting each other, the harder she cries.

I'm used to this from them—not to this violent extent, but similar. Gwyneth isn't.

"Stop," I grind out, making them shut up as I hold Gwyneth tighter. "Stop being fucking selfish, this isn't about either of you. It's about her."

"Angel, you don't have to worry." King takes her hand in his. "I'm going to make sure the board removes her from the firm, then she'll disappear like she never existed."

"There's no reason for the board to remove me, and I swear to God, Kingsley, if you try any underhanded methods, I'll sue you and take away your money. Oh, also, even if I'm out of W&S, I won't leave the city."

"Don't listen to her, Angel. I'll definitely get rid of her and we'll go back to being the two of us."

"No, Dad. No. I can't just forget she exists because you tell me to. I have feelings and there are many of them. I can't just erase them or pretend they're nonexistent like you do."

"Gwyneth…" Aspen stands beside King. "I…"

"This doesn't mean I want to talk to you. Not after you abandoned me."

"I didn't. I would never do that."

"All these years would testify otherwise"

"I thought you were dead!" Aspen cuts her off, her voice

316 | RINA KENT

breaking before she inhales a sharp breath. "They put a dead baby in my hands and said she was mine. They...told me she didn't survive childbirth and I thought...I thought that was you. All this time, I was mourning you."

"Then how did I end up in front of Dad's house?"

"It was my uncle and his wife. They wanted me to get rid of you since they found out I was pregnant, but it was too late at the time and no clinic would do it. They abused me, hit me, pushed me down the stairs, and kicked me all the time so you'd die. But you didn't; you were a fighter. Until you weren't, or so I thought. For twenty years, I believed you died because I couldn't protect you properly. Because I was so young and clueless and didn't know how to keep you safe."

Gwyneth sniffles as if she could feel the pain behind Aspen's words. She's an empath that way, so even though she hates her, she can still allow her emotions to seep inside her. After a moment, she murmurs, "Why didn't you go to Dad?"

Aspen scoffs and glares at him. "We didn't know each other."

"Jesus Christ." King runs a hand over his face.

"What is that supposed to mean?" Gwyneth asks, and when he avoids her gaze, she squeezes his hand. "Dad, tell me. Don't hide anything from me."

"I don't remember her and she doesn't remember me. The night...we conceived you, I was drunk as fuck and so was she. It was dark and messy, and I have barely any recollections of it or her, except for waking up in my friend's house and knowing that I'd had sex."

"I went to a party with a friend," Aspen continues. "And I didn't know my own tolerance, so I drank more than I should've. I remember this jock coming to me and we talked. He said he was seventeen and I lied and told him that I was sixteen, and then we were drinking together and...that's it. I really don't have much recollection of him or that night. I remember leaving while it was dark because I had exams the following day, and I was still a little tipsy."

"Nine months later, you showed up at my door, Angel."

"But how?" Gwyneth stares at Aspen. "I thought you said you didn't remember my dad."

"I didn't. I tried to find him when I realized I was pregnant, mainly to protect you from my aunt and uncle, but I had nothing to do with it. My aunt and uncle must've dug deeper and gone asking around about the night of the party, because they clearly planned to leave you with Kingsley. You have to believe me, I would've never...never left you like that if I'd had a choice."

"But you did leave me." Gwyneth wipes her eyes. "I spent twenty years without a mother and that can't just be erased simply because you're back in the picture again."

Aspen's shoulders hunch and King doesn't hide his sadistic smile.

"I...want to be alone." Gwyneth strokes my hand and I slowly let her go.

She doesn't look at any of us as she jogs to her car.

Everything in me screams to follow her, but I don't, not yet at least, because I need to talk some fucking sense into these two idiots first.

King flicks his Zippo open, then closed. "Go to Seattle and take the witch with you, Nate. You two can continue your fuck buddy relationship and leave me and my daughter in peace. Incidentally, you fucked both mother and daughter, you sick motherfucker."

Before I can punch him, Aspen raises her hand and slaps him across the face, hard. So hard that he reels back from it.

She's about to continue, but I pull her back by the arm, pining for patience myself. "You need to watch your fucking mouth, King. Aspen and I never had sex."

He runs a hand over the cheek that she slapped but smiles in his manic fucking way. "You'll pay for that."

She struggles against me and points a finger at him. "I'm not leaving."

"She doesn't want you. No one does."

"Maybe you're talking about yourself, Kingsley. Your daughter doesn't respect you anymore and you already lost your best friend. Congratulations for winning the shitty person of the year award." And with that, she leaves.

"I'm going to fucking break her," he says in a low, dark tone.

"Leave her alone."

"What? Protective of your fuck buddy?"

"I told you we never had sex. And you need to bring down the psychosis a notch if you don't want things to get uglier. Aspen is Gwyneth's mother whether you like it or not. The decision to have a relationship or stay as acquaintances is only up to them. Stay the hell out of it."

"Or what?"

"Or you'll lose Gwyneth. She's already scared of you because of me. Stop micromanaging her, stop being the boss of her, just stop all the crazy and save it for when you deal with Susan. Don't make your daughter lose all respect for you, motherfucker."

He flicks his lighter open, then closed, and I don't like the expression on his face one bit. "Do you still care about Gwen?"

"I never stopped."

"Good. In that case, you'll do something for me."

THIRTY-SIX

Gwyneth

NATE IS GONE.

He disappeared the same day my life shattered to pieces after I learned I've had a mother all along who didn't know I existed.

The same day my dad threatened to remove her from my life again.

The same day I cried until there were no tears left, then instead of going home, I went to Nate's apartment because I needed him. Not anyone else, just him.

He's the only one who's able to chase away the chaos and make me feel at peace.

He's the only one I think of when my world splinters to pieces. It's not that he mends it together—he's not my fixer. He's just the other half who helps me in being me.

In fighting away the emptiness.

But he wasn't there and his phone was turned off.

So I called Sebastian and he said he had no clue where his

uncle was. He still doesn't. Because Nate left nothing behind and the perpetrator is my father.

I could feel it deep down in my heart that Dad had something to do with it. Not only did he drive Nate away, but he also made him the devil and said he's no good for me.

"This is what people like Nate do, Angel. Once they get what they want, they leave without a word."

I didn't want to believe him. I still don't most of the time, but it's been two weeks. Two whole weeks of not sleeping or eating properly, because every time I do, his face comes to mind. Vanilla milkshakes, ice cream, and cupcakes don't taste the same without him.

They're flavorless.

Just like my life.

Dad denies sending him away, saying that it was his choice and he can't make Nate do anything. I agree, he can't. He wasn't successful in forcing him to divorce me, so how did he make him leave me?

And now of all times. When I needed him more than anything.

At first, I didn't believe it, so I searched everywhere. I checked at every W&S branch in case he changed locations, but he's at none of them. Then I was mad at him for leaving without notice, then I fell into that empty hole that has no way out. I'm in that phase right now.

The sadness. The damning sadness with no end in sight.

Nothing makes sense anymore and I'm waiting for a change that won't happen. An end that won't come.

Every day, I come to the firm and stare at his closed office door, and sometimes, I just sneak in there and take a nap on his sofa. The same sofa where he fucked me and whispered dirty words to me.

The same sofa that he told me to sit on and behave so I wouldn't distract him, but I ended up being a brat anyway.

That's where I'm lying right now. On his sofa, hugging my knees to my chest and breathing him in, because I don't have much of his smell left. It's been disappearing over time and soon enough, it'll vanish just like he did.

Soon, I'll go back to that hollowing emptiness with no change in sight.

The door clicks open and I jump to a sitting position, thinking it's Dad. I could swear he saw me come out of here the other day, but he didn't comment on it. Maybe that was a one-time thing and he won't let it slide this time.

I really don't want to fight with him. We barely talk at home and that's painful enough as it is.

But it's not him who walks inside. It's Aspen.

My mother, Aspen. I still can't wrap my mind around it, so I don't. It'll just go away with time, or that's what I'd like to believe.

Every time she sees me, she tries to talk to me, but I just bolt or hide because I can't face her. Because I hated her, was jealous of her for very illogical reasons.

And now that I've learned about our biological relations, it's even harder to come to terms with my previous feelings for her.

Despite knowing her reasons and that she didn't really abandon me, that she was so young when she had me, I'm unable to beat those facts into my brain.

So I opt to run again, avoid her again. Maybe Dad was right and I can pretend she didn't happen.

But that's a lie, isn't it?

She was always there, at the back of my mind, and during every birthday where I cried because she didn't want me.

Turns out, that was never the case.

I mourned you. She said. *Every year, I mourned you.*

She appears flawless in her dark blue pantsuit with her red hair falling to her shoulders. As always. She's the most elegant, classy woman I've ever seen.

"Please don't go." She stops a safe distance away, not attempting to take a seat. "I just…want to talk to you."

"We never talked in the past. You hated me and I hated you."

"I never hated you. I just…hate your father, and you were an extension of him, in a way, but not anymore. You're an extension of me, too."

"No, I'm not. I told you, I don't want anything to do with you."

"I know and I understand, but I just want a chance, no matter how small, just one chance to prove that I care, that I always have. A few months ago, I got drunk while visiting the grave that I thought was my daughter's, but now, I know it isn't, and I'm so thankful for just being able to watch from afar and making sure you're well. That's all I ask for. But if you still can't give me that, it's fine. I understand. I just want to tell you I'm sorry."

The stupid feelings that I can't stop flood my insides and I start clinking my nails. "For what?"

"For not being there all these years. I'm so sorry."

"You didn't know."

"I still lost you for twenty years. You still felt abandoned and cried on your birthdays like I got drunk on them."

"You mourned me for twenty years?"

"I did."

"I think I mourned you, too, even thinking you abandoned me, I still mourned you."

"I'm sorry. So, so sorry."

Clearing my throat, I try not to let the tears loose and lift a shoulder. "I had Dad. Though he can be too much sometimes."

"I'm sorry your father is giving you a hard time about Nate. He's a jerk."

I jump to a standing position. "Do you...know where Nate is?"

Dad has been insinuating that Nate and Aspen have always had a thing going on, and I know what he's doing. He's trying to make me feel as if Nate would choose her over me because she'd fit him better.

He knew I harbored such thoughts myself and in a typical Kingsley Shaw lawyer move, he played on them to make me give up. And he almost succeeded.

However, Aspen didn't leave with Nate. She stayed, and I think that's partly because of me. And anyway, Nate would never hurt me that way, and she wouldn't either. I felt her words just now. The pain in them is so relatable to mine that I can sense it slashing my chest.

Her shoulders droop a little. "No, I don't."

"You do. You always know about things. If you want me to give you a chance, tell me where he is."

"I would if I knew, but I really don't. I know one thing for certain, though."

"What?"

"He would never give up on you. I've been with him long enough to know he doesn't allow himself to get attached. He's not the type to care about anyone very much, but he does care about you. He looks at you like he never wants to look away."

"But he did." I fight the emotions in my voice and fail. "He left."

"Because of King."

"Dad said he left of his own volition."

"Your dad is skewing truths with lies. He does it all the time. Believe me, he's the one behind all of this, so if you want to find Nate, you need to strike there."

"He wouldn't just tell me where he is if I ask."

"I agree. He won't. We need to think of a solution." She appears thoughtful for a while, her eyes bright and the most focused I've seen them.

"Why…why are you helping me?"

"Because you're my daughter," she says it with ease as if it's a given.

"Aren't you supposed to hate me? Everyone thinks you have a thing with Nate. Maybe you did, or still do."

"Nate and I were never like that. If sex had entered the equation, we would've lost each other a long time ago. In case you're not aware, he stops seeing the women he sleeps with, since they're a complication he doesn't want to deal with. That's how I know you're different."

"And you're okay with that? Us being together, I mean." I shouldn't care about her opinion, but I do. Deep inside, I really do.

"Why wouldn't I be?"

"Because he's eighteen years older than me and I'm still young."

"You're not young, you're a woman. And women have the right to make their own choices."

"Dad doesn't think the same."

"Your dad is an asshole."

I wince.

She grimaces and clears her throat. "Sorry. Sometimes, I forget he's your father."

"He's not that bad, you know."

"Yes, he is." A sheen covers her eyes and they darken before she blinks it away. "Anyway, do you want to bring Nate home?"

"Of course."

"In that case, I have an idea."

THIRTY-SEVEN

Kingsley

"I'M PREGNANT, DAD."

I choke on the water I've been drinking, the splatters scattering on the table.

There are only a few things that can make a father lose his shit. Having my baby daughter, my little angel, telling me this news nearly sends me back into a coma.

We're having dinner and she just blurted it out as if she's talking about how much vanilla ice cream she needs for the week. No, it's worse. She's dead serious when she talks about vanilla ice cream. Now, she's just apathetic—meek almost.

My little Gwen has left and there's only the shadow of her that is left behind. She hasn't been eating or sleeping well, and she's constantly in this daze that I haven't been able to reach inside of.

And it's not for lack of trying.

I've been preparing her favorite green tea with vanilla, but she gets teary-eyed whenever she sees it. She barely touches any of her vanilla stuff anymore.

She didn't even eat ice cream for a week. That's when I knew something was really wrong. It's possible to get a drug addict of decades to quit, but it's not possible to separate Gwen from her vanilla obsession.

After my coughing subsides, I clear my throat. "You're what?"

"Pregnant. I have a baby inside me. You're going to be a grandfather."

Whoa. Okay.

When they said I'm the best at working under pressure, they didn't fucking mention this.

They didn't include the little tidbit where my daughter would be fucking pregnant. At twenty. By my lowlife of an ex-friend.

I slam my utensils on the table. "That's it. I'm going to kill that fucking bastard."

In fact, I should've killed him when we first met. That way, this would've never happened.

Ordinarily, when I threaten Nate's life, Gwen would get up and stop me. She'd hug me and hold my hand because she knows she calms me, but she doesn't move from her spot and continues pushing the ham around on her plate.

"Then you'll just leave me a widow and a single mother. Not to mention. your grandkid will be fatherless."

My fists tighten on the edge of the table and I regret not having my Zippo with me, because this is a fucking perfect time for it.

"Is Nate the father?"

She stares up at me then, fire igniting in her eyes. I always loved that part about her, the determination and the fight. I thought she got it from me, but now that I look closely, it's like I'm staring in her mother's eyes.

Fuck Aspen.

Fuck her existence and for being the mother of the most precious thing in my life.

I can't believe I fucked her once upon a time. Young me was a goddamn idiot for falling for that witch.

A hot witch, but I digress.

"Of course, he's the father. Do you think I was two-timing him or something? You raised me better than that."

"I didn't mean it that way." Though I fucking wish she did. At least then I could cut him off in a nice and simple way.

Now, it's complicated.

My life is taking a sharp turn for the second time because of an unplanned pregnancy.

Or maybe it's planned.

I narrow my eyes on Gwen. "How long have you been pregnant?"

"Five weeks."

"When was your last period?"

"About six weeks ago."

"You were on the shot. Why aren't you anymore?"

"The date expired and I forgot about it."

"You don't usually forget about the date. You're not the forgetful type."

"I had so much on my mind, like your accident, how you almost died, and Susan coming after me. I forgot about the appointment."

"How many tests have you taken?"

"Three."

"How about the doctor?"

"I went to an OB-GYN."

"Can you repeat what he or she did and said?"

"He ran a blood test and said I'm five weeks pregnant, because they detected the pregnancy hormone but I forgot its name." She sighs. "Now, are you going to stop interrogating me like I'm a witness in court?"

I stagger in my seat, still narrowing my eyes. Usually, people can't withstand my rapid-fire questioning. It's how I crush my opponents since, for normal people, it takes them a long time to think of a lie.

I've never used it on Gwen before, but she could've known about it. Did she come prepared for my reaction?

"So?" She lifts her chin.

"So what?"

"Are you going to do the right thing?"

"The right thing would be to abort the baby and divorce Nate so you can live your life."

"No!"

"Gwen, listen to me—"

"No, you listen to me. If Mom had aborted me, I wouldn't be here, I wouldn't have known you, and I wouldn't have been born as your daughter. She was fourteen and had every right to want to get rid of me. She was younger than me, a damn kid, and look at how far she's come. This is my life, my body, and I have the right to decide whether or not I want to have a baby now, ten years from now, or never. I decide what's right for me, not you or anyone else, Dad."

"Fine, come here." I walk to her and pull her up by the shoulders because she's shaking. Fucking hell. Nate was right. I am scaring her; I'm scaring the only person who's ever meant something to me.

She starts crying as she holds on to me, and that fucking shitty feeling resurfaces.

The feeling that I might have screwed things up as a father. That when it mattered, I wasn't there for her as I should've been.

"Angel, stop crying. You know I hate it."

"I can't."

"Gwen…I only want what's best for you."

"Daddy, can't you see?" She lifts her head and stares at me with those expressive fucking eyes that stab me in the soul.

I've been taking care of her for such a long time that I didn't realize she really isn't a kid anymore.

She's a woman now, my Gwen, and she has feelings—lots of them, as she said.

Fuck.

When did she grow up this much? It was easier when she was young. When she used to cling to me and tell me she didn't really need superheroes because she already has me—her own superhero that she doesn't have to share with anyone else.

And for a long time, I truly believed I was the only one she needed, but I'm learning the hard way that she has another superhero now. One I didn't see coming, though I really should have.

I should've suspected something when she started hiding and blushing around him and he tactfully avoided coming to my house.

I should've suspected something when she started collecting his things and forbidding anyone from touching them. I thought she only idolized Nate, I could've never guessed that her feelings for him would grow so deep that she'd be in physical pain due to being separated from him.

"See what?" I ask.

"He's the best thing that's ever happened to me since you, and if you weren't so blinded by your anger, you'd see it, too."

"So now you're replacing me?"

"You're my father. He's my husband. Neither of you can replace the other. So please, please stop hurting me, Dad. I beg you."

Well, fuck.

THIRTY-EIGHT

Nathaniel

KNEW THIS WOULD BE HARD, BUT I DIDN'T THINK IT WOULD be this fucking unbearable.

There's always been an emptiness inside me—it comes with all the baggage of being an unwanted child. But I've managed it well through the years.

Or, I thought I had.

Turns out, I was only numbing it with no way to effectively deal with it. Which is why I'm here, in the middle of nowhere.

On the mountain.

I've done a lot of hiking and thinking, mostly about her.

The girl I left behind without a word because her dick of a father is testing me.

"Stay away for a while and take the time off as an overdue vacation," he told me that day. "If she's really serious about you, she won't move on. But if she does move on, you will fuck off from her life."

He also wants ten percent of my shares, which will give him

the majority in W&S. We agreed to never sell our shares to out-siders or each other in order to keep an equal power balance. But he's using the circumstances to twist my arm.

I agreed anyway. Fuck the shares and the firm; they don't mat-ter compared to her.

His other conditions included never letting her know where I was, talking to her, or even giving her any type of an excuse. The fucker wants her to be angry at me for ghosting her and hopes that will eventually make her forget about me.

But he sometimes forgets that she's as headstrong as he is.

If she wants to leave me, she'll do it on her own terms, not because of whatever the fuck he's doing.

That doesn't deny that the current situation is pure fucking torture. Being cut off from her bright smiles, easy laughter, and cheerful presence is similar to dying slowly. It's different from when King first found out. At least then, I could see her at the firm and make sure she was all right.

Now, it's a blank slate.

Now, I hang on to scraps of my memories of her and how she felt in my arms. I think of the colors she injects into my life and try not to let them darken like my soul.

It's fucking hard, though. And on bad days, like today, it be-comes almost impossible. The black ink I carefully locked inside me is spilling onto those colors and smudging them.

I take a swig of my water as I hike down from the peak. That's all I've been doing lately, hiking and thinking about her. Then get-ting hard and fucking my hand to the memory of her tight heat.

Then I go through her social media like some sort of fucked-up stalker, just to make sure she's all right. But she hasn't posted anything for two weeks. Not even any fangirling updates about her favorite Twenty One Pilots or NF song of the week. Not even a throwback picture of when King took her to their concerts for her sixteenth birthday.

There's nothing.

Only radio silence.

And maybe that's what's been darkening my mood even worse than being separated from her.

My feet come to a halt in front of the cottage. The last person I expected to see is sitting on the steps, flicking his lighter on and off. He stands out in the cozy setting with his black suit and menacing eyes.

"What are you doing here, King?" I remove my backpack and throw it to the side.

"Gwen said she's pregnant."

I stride toward him, my muscles tightening. "She is?"

"No, she lied to me so I'd bring you back. I confirmed it later, after I saw the doctor's fake report. This has that witch Aspen's fingerprints all over it since Gwen would've never lied to me on her own accord. That woman is already corrupting my little angel."

I lean against the rails of the wooden stairs. "If you're not here because of that, then why did you come?"

"Because she wouldn't stop crying and that fucks me up. I don't want to be the cause of her tears, even if I still want to fucking murder you."

"Does that mean you approve?"

He stands up on the stairs so that he's towering over me and flicks the Zippo shut. "She said you're the best thing that's happened to her since me, that she needs you in her life as much as she needs me. I don't really have a say in the matter now that you've made your mark all over her. Besides, you're my best friend. I know you better than anyone and I'm well aware that when you care about someone, it's for life."

"I'm serious, King. I would never hurt her."

"Fuck right you won't. If she cries because of you, I will kill you. For real. This place gives me inspiration for a good burial site."

"I see the head injury didn't reduce the crazy."

"Fuck off." He sits again, flicking his lighter, and I drop down beside him. He doesn't kick me in the nut, so that's a good sign.

"How is she?" I ask.

"Depressed. I knew shit was hitting the fan when she wasn't

eating her vanilla ice cream for a whole week. Can you believe that?"

"That's a record."

"I know." He leans back on his palms and stares up at the sky. "I can't believe I'm giving you my daughter, motherfucker."

"I'm better than the kids who wouldn't know how to appreciate her."

"That's true… Still, *fuck*. Thinking about you with her makes me all ragey."

"It'll get better with time."

"Fuck you. I swear to fuck, Nate, I'm going to kill you if you hurt my little girl. I mean it."

"Thanks."

His head tilts to the side and he narrows his eyes. "I'm threatening to kill you and you're thanking me?"

"I'm thanking you because you put her before you. You're selfish as fuck, but not with her."

"It was either that or lose her. And go fuck yourself, dick. I'm not selfish. You are."

"I might have been once, but I'm not selfish when it comes to her. Even when I was an asshole, all I ever wanted was to protect her."

"Yeah, no. We're not going to have a heart-to-heart talk and paint each other's toenails."

I laugh and it's the first real laugh I've had with him in a long time. "Instead of painting toenails, how about an actual match, not one-sided like the other time."

"Prepare to be defeated."

"I'm not holding back just because things have changed."

"I'll still kick your ass."

"Like fuck you will."

"Hey, is that any way to speak to me now that you're my son-in-law?"

"It's the only way to speak to a dick."

He smiles a little and I smile back. We remain like that for a few minutes, watching the sky and listening to the birds.

It's our modus operandi. Silence means more than words. He might be loud and a general asshole, but King also knows how to use and appreciate silence.

Despite his sharp words, he's giving me a chance. And while he means it about killing me if I hurt Gwyneth, I can tell he's also slightly relieved.

He'll probably never tell me this, but deep down, he's glad it's me. King never thought anyone would be good enough for the daughter he sacrificed his youth for.

"Keep the shares, Nate. I was only testing you with them." He flips his lighter closed. "I have one condition, though."

"What?"

"You'll make something up and have the board remove Aspen from W&S. If I do it, Gwen will hate me."

"And you think she won't hate me? Also, there will be no removing Aspen. She's a senior partner and the best we have. Stop thinking with your dick."

"I'm not thinking with my dick."

"Yes, you are. I've been with you for over two decades and I know how obsessed you were with finding Gwyneth's mother. Sure, you didn't want her to be Aspen, but she is and you need to accept that."

"Fuck no."

I shake my head but don't say anything.

King and Aspen aren't my main focus. All I can think about is getting Gwyneth back.

She must be so angry at me.

THIRTY-NINE

Gwyneth

THE DAY NATE CAME BACK, I COULD FEEL IT.

I got out of bed early on a Saturday for no reason at all and made lots of cupcakes that I won't be eating, then I told Dad to go jog without me.

I sat on the edge of the pool clutching a vanilla milkshake, removed my sneakers, and dipped my feet in the water.

Sometimes, it's calming because I remember when Nate and I had hot sex here. But other times, all I can think about is when Dad tried to drown him.

I shake that image away and grab the milkshake, then stare at it in the sun. "What's wrong with you, buddy? Why are you tasteless?"

"Are you really talking to a milkshake?"

Ever since I got up this morning, I had a feeling, but having that feeling and the actual reality is entirely different.

Because the sound of his voice after such a long time is like a shockwave and it's now spreading through me, lighting up all my nerves.

God. His voice, that rich depth in it, clutches me in a tight noose.

His face blocks the sun as he stares down at me. If hearing his voice put me in a loop, seeing his strong features nearly sets me on fire—the entire pool wouldn't be able to put it out.

It's only been a couple of weeks since I last saw him, but it feels like years. Maybe decades, even.

My eyes take in his entire face—the lines in it, the handsomeness of it. His stubble has grown thicker and his shoulders are broader somehow. So broad that they hide the sun and the world beyond them. They block everything except for him.

The man who once stomped all over my vanilla heart but still made it feel loved and appreciated anyway.

The man without whom I can't sleep, because he's the peace that makes my brain stop shouting.

"You're here."

"Looks like it."

"Why… Where did you go?"

"To the cabin for a mandatory vacation ordered by King."

The fact that he's back, that he's really here and I'm not dreaming, sends a jolt of excitement through my bones. I want to jump up and hug and kiss him until I can no longer breathe.

I don't, though.

The volcano that's been turned to ashes by his disappearance bursts back to life and the fire nearly consumes me.

And him.

I jerk up to a standing position, leaving my milkshake on the side of the pool. "And you couldn't tell me that? How could you just leave?"

"King wouldn't let me say anything. He was testing me."

"Then why are you here now?"

"Because he finally approves."

He…does?

Oh, God. Is that why he smiled at me and hugged me before he went out this morning? Because he knew Nate was here and he approves?

I know I should be happy, and I am, but it's shadowed by the bitterness that's exploding at the back of my throat. "What if he'd never approved? Would you have stayed away for years?"

"Fuck no. I was just letting him cool down for a while by putting some distance between us."

"I don't like that word. *Distance*. I hate the letter *D*."

He cups my cheeks with his hands. "I would never leave you willingly, Gwyneth. You're the person I never thought I needed, but ever since you got close, my life feels incomplete without you."

"Because I'm a little crazy?"

"Because you're special. And also because you understand me more than anyone ever has. I meant what I said. I don't do feelings, never believed in them, not when my own parents didn't want me. Like you, I despise my birthdays because they remind me that my existence doesn't matter. But what I didn't say is that my perceptions have changed ever since you went on your tiptoes and kissed me on your eighteenth birthday. I wanted to grab you by the fucking waist and kiss you back, and I don't even do kissing."

My heart jolts and my eyes grow in size, not believing my ears. Not believing what Nate just said. "You wanted to kiss me?"

"More than I've ever wanted fucking anything, but I couldn't, because all I could think about was that you're King's daughter. That's why I avoided you these past couple of years. I wanted to push you away, but you just wouldn't budge."

"Yeah, Dad taught me to never give up. Especially on those I care about."

"Then I should be thankful to him."

"For teaching me not to give up?"

"And for being a drunk idiot and having you when he was so young."

"Yeah, me too."

"I'm a lucky bastard to have found you."

"Even though I'm empty sometimes?"

"I'm empty sometimes, too."

"That's okay." I reach a hand out and glide it over his stubble. "We can fill each other up, because that's what love is, Nate. There are bad days and good days. Yes, the bad days can be hard and have a lot of empty bursts, red markers, and negative feelings. But that's okay, too, because we're there to catch each other when we fall. We're there to turn the bad days into good ones because we can. I don't know about the rest of the world, but you and I can totally do it. Do you know why?"

He grabs my hand that's on his cheek and strokes his thumb on the back of it, eliciting tiny shudders from me. "Why?"

"Because we're a team, Nate. Just you and I."

"You're a fucking gem, did you know that?"

"No, so you'll have to tell me that every day."

"I fucking will. Remember when you were trying to find me a hobby?"

"Yeah."

"You don't have to look anymore. I already found it."

"Really? What is it? Oh, is it board games?"

"No."

"Then what is it?"

"You."

"M-me?"

"Why do you think I kept agreeing to do all of the things you planned?"

"I thought you were only placating me."

"I'm not that unselfish. I did it to spend more time with you, and the longer I did, the deeper you drew me into you."

"I'm glad I was persistent."

"I'm glad, too." He brings my hand to his mouth and kisses the palm so delicately, I melt. "I know we agreed to divorce when you're twenty-one, but I can't bear the thought of being away from you. The last couple of weeks have been enough torture for a lifetime."

"I can't stay away from you either, even if Dad is against it."

"So you'll stay my wife?"

I bite my lower lip. "People will talk."

"Fuck them."

"Does that mean I get to call you my husband in public?"

"Always." He breathes heavily, the shirt of his suit stretching with the depth of his inhales and exhales. "I love you, baby girl. I'm in love with your colorfulness as much as your emptiness."

"I love you, too, Nate. I think I've been in love with you for years."

"I think I've loved you ever since you kissed me, and I'll show you how much I love you for the rest of our lives."

"Oh, Nate." I get on my tiptoes and just like that day two years ago when he fell in love with me, my lips find his.

EPILOGUE 1

Nathaniel

Three years later

S OMETHING'S WRONG.

I can tell because Gwyneth has been avoiding me.

She never avoids me.

Not even when she says I'm being a jerk and drive her mad sometimes. Instead of turning her back to me or sulking, she jumps onto my lap and makes me teach her how to behave.

But now, she's been avoiding me.

For two days.

She's also been staring at her negative words list before bed, which she rarely does. These past three years, she's been working more on herself and has a better grasp on her emotions. She even has a positive words list that makes her smile and laugh and puts her in a bright mood.

However, the list she's been looking at is the negative one. And she's done it two nights in a row.

"My angel finally realized that being with you is a mistake," King said when I asked him if she'd told him anything. "Now, she can divorce you and come back to me."

"Fuck you, King."

"Hey, is that any way to speak to your father-in-law, motherfucker?"

Needless to say, he's of no help. Even though he's not as opposing to our relationship as when we first got together, he has this way of getting on my fucking nerves, which, of course, I pay him back for in full.

So I asked Aspen if Gwyneth had mentioned anything, but she wasn't of much help either.

I'm even contemplating calling Sebastian, but fuck that little rascal, all he does is tease me whenever he gets the chance.

My nephew and I are mostly out of my parents' influence now, no matter how much they try to lure us back into the Weaver clan.

When news of my marriage to Gwyneth first broke out, the media was all over it, but King, Aspen, and I had a plan. The moment King announced that he was all for it, the story became boring and they moved on to the next hot thing.

I'm glad Gwyneth wasn't brought into the middle of it, because my fucking crazy wife would've stood there and told them, "Yeah, I love him. Why the fuck is that any of your business?"

She told me so herself around that time. That she'll give the middle finger to anyone who judges us.

We still get looks sometimes, but it doesn't really matter to us since we've always lived in a world that's secluded from the rest.

We spend weekends hiking or pissing King off. We rarely work together, because she's focusing on family law, but we talk cases all the time. She's passionate, my Gwyneth, and I could spend the rest of my life listening to her talk about the subjects that interest her, which are usually law, me, and fucking.

She never gets enough and my dick loves her for it. I've never been so sexually compatible with anyone as I am with my beautiful wife. It's not even about the act itself, it's about the feelings that come with it. It's about the fucking belonging that I'm a lucky bastard to have found.

Every day, I try to make her feel that. I try to prove in action instead of words how much her presence means to me.

And since we're each other's world, it fucks me up all day when she avoids me.

So when I get home, the one we bought together after we had an actual wedding ceremony three years ago, I'm ready to get to the bottom of this.

I place my briefcase on the island. "Gwyneth? Where are you, baby girl?"

"Surprise!" She jumps in front of me, her eyes glimmering with all the colors, and a wide smile paints her face in a glow.

My gaze follows her every movement, from how her dress stretches over her breasts and falls to her knees and to how her white sneakers are a bit undone.

"What's the surprise?"

She jumps me, her arms going around my neck and her legs circling around my waist. I stagger backward before I plant my feet on the ground and wrap an arm around her back.

"Me. I'm the surprise."

"Hmm. Does that mean you'll tell me why you've been avoiding me?"

"I wasn't avoiding you, I was planning your birthday party, and yes, I know you don't like your birthdays, but you made me love my birthdays again and I plan to do the same. I'm going to do something good during your birthday so that you don't remember that your parents didn't want you, and instead, you'll remember me. Just like I remember that kiss from when I was eighteen."

This fucking woman will be the death of me. "Then why were you staring at your list?"

"Because of the word *anxiety*. I was so sure you'd figure me out."

"I didn't, but you kind of just told me everything."

"That's because you get me as your early birthday present."

"I do, huh?"

"Yup, I'll be your good and bad girl tonight."

"What if I tell you to behave?"

"Too late." She bites her lower lip and murmurs, "I'm wearing nothing beneath this, husband."

I groan, wrapping my arms tighter around her. "I'm going to fuck you like you deserve, wife."

"Yes, please."

And then my lips are on hers as I carry her to the bedroom, and when I put her down, she stares at me with those colorful eyes that see straight into my soul.

I always thought I loved the look in her eyes, but it turns out, I love how these mesmerizing eyes only look at me.

EPILOGUE 2

Gwyneth

One year later

"Don't cry…I'm here…" I croak, patting my hand on a chubby chest and holding another chubby bottom so she can suck on my breast.

Only…I'm not holding anything. I'm not sitting down either and I'm only touching the mattress.

I startle, my eyes flying open.

Our bedroom comes into sight with the pulled-down curtains that make it dark even though the clock on the wall reads ten in the morning. I fumble for the baby monitor, my heart beating so loudly, I hear it in my ears.

Holy shit.

Shit.

Where are my babies? I clearly remember falling asleep breastfeeding Lily and rocking Logan back to sleep around two in the morning.

Did I lose them somehow? Nate spends one night working late in the office, *one night*, and I lose our twins?

They're three months old—I think I got pregnant that day before Nate's birthday a year ago. As soon as we found out the news, I was ecstatic, but that can't be said about everyone else. Dad wondered if I was going to be fine with law school and everything, but I told him that if he could do it, so could I.

Besides, Nate never let me do anything on my own. He took care of me more than before and even tolerated my brat attitude more than ever. I was an emotional mess in the first trimester and cried over the stupidest things, but Nate just wiped my tears and hugged me.

Then he proceeded to fuck me because that totally helped with the hormones—or that's what I told him, anyway.

He rubbed my swollen feet and held my hand through the whole delivery process. Though, I'm pretty sure both he and Dad threatened to sue the doctor and the hospital because they wouldn't ease my pain.

Being doted on by one protective man is one thing, but having both Dad and Nate can be a nightmare sometimes.

Only sometimes, though, because I'm a lucky girl to have the best father and the best husband in the world.

A husband who enables me every step of the way. Just because I decided I want kids now doesn't mean he let me slack off law school or put it on the back burner. He knows that it's my dream and it's important, too.

Which is why he takes care of our newborns most of the time, even though there's a nanny. He reminds me of Dad, who didn't trust them around me when I was younger and always watched them through cameras and such. He often reminded them of the legal action he could take against them, too, because he can be extra like that.

Nate is similar with our children, but his methods are more subtle. He doesn't threaten anyone, but he can get his point across with his normal manner of speech alone. That delicious, stern manner that I can't get enough of.

Our twins, Logan and Lily, are a handful to say the least, but Nate successfully puts them to sleep. Last night was the only time he was going to spend an all-nighter at the firm since their birth.

And I obviously screwed it up because there's no sight of them.

Tears sting my eyes and I'm about to have a meltdown of epic proportions, but I notice a Post-it Note on my upper arm.

I command Alexa to turn on the light, and all the breaths I've been holding instantly deflate out of me when I read the words written in Nate's beautiful, distinctive handwriting.

The twins are with me and King in the garden. Sleep in and don't worry about anything.

P.S. Happy birthday, baby girl. I have plans for us as soon as I kick your father out. In the meantime, I left you an early birthday gift on the bedside table.

All fear about my babies' safety vanishes and it's replaced by furious warmth for their father. Just how the hell did I end up with this man? Every day, I wake up more in awe of him than the day before.

My gaze falls on the box on the bedside table and when I open it, I find a photo album inside. The first page has a picture Dad took of me and Nate while we each held one of the twins. My face is filled with happy tears and Nate is kissing my forehead.

Our first family picture.

Before I can get all emotional, I spot a folded piece of paper on the album's jacket. My fingers are a bit unsteady as I open it and instantly recognize his handwriting.

Gwyneth,

I met you the day you were born.

King freaked out when he found a baby at his doorstep and thought it was a good idea to call in his nemesis for crisis control.

Truth be told, I planned to make fun of him and his carelessness, but when I got to his house, you were crying your head off and he was flustered until I told him you were probably hungry.

He pushed you in my arms and flew to the kitchen like a madman. It was the first time I held a baby and it was pretty awkward at best, but then something happened.

You stopped crying.

Just like that.

You stared at me with those colorful, inquisitive eyes that somehow pierced through my chest.

Since then, you have always held a special place in my life. I might not have been a doting uncle, but I believed that I cared about you as much as King did. Which is why I made sure no one bullied you or gave you a hard time. Sort of like I did with my nephew.

But you ruined that six years ago.

When you kissed me on your eighteenth birthday.

When you got on your tiptoes, ignored all common sense, and crashed your lips to mine as if you've been waiting your whole life to do it.

In that single moment, you demolished every picture I had of you. Instead of being like my nephew, you planted other images in my head. Images I shouldn't have entertained for my best friend's much younger daughter.

I shouldn't have thought about lifting you up in my arms, slamming you against the nearest object and kissing you until you could only breathe me.

But I did.

And I hated you for it.

Not only because I lost the easy relationship I had with you, but also because no matter how much I tried, I couldn't think of you as King's daughter anymore.

Those two years were pure fucking torture, baby girl. I struggled so much between doing the right thing and taking you anyway. It's why I avoided being in the same room with you; I couldn't trust myself not to fuck up everything and hurt King. Especially since I had no idea how deep my feelings for you were.

However, once you became my wife, my self-control spiraled out of control. I blame your lively energy that I was never allowed to have and your determination that can break stones.

Even one as solid as me.

You didn't only break me in, but you also mended all the broken parts together again. You did it carefully and with so much love that I can't imagine my existence without you anymore.

Without your cheerfulness.

Without your empathy.

You added colors to my life that are as bright as the ones in your eyes. Every day I wake up to those eyes and your contagious smile, I feel like the luckiest bastard alive.

Thank you for choosing me.

For not giving up on me.

For being my wife and the mother of my children.

Love,
Nathaniel

A tear slides down my cheek by the time I finish reading.

Is it possible to fall in love with someone all over again? Because I think I just did. I'm so irrevocably into this man that it scares the shit out of me sometimes.

He said he can't imagine his life without me, but it's no different for me. I can't picture a world where he isn't in the middle of it.

I can't picture a world where he's not my husband and the father of my children.

Carefully tucking the letter into the photo album, I place it on the nightstand and get out of bed. I do a quick work of freshening up and wearing the first pair of shorts, tank top, and sneakers I find, then I run outside.

I find Nate holding Lily while standing up, and Dad sitting down, rocking Logan as he sucks on a baby bottle.

The view of my babies never gets old. I think I fall in love with them more every time I see them. They're so small and innocent and I want to give them my life.

And the reason I have them is right there, appearing larger than the world, as always.

Nate is wearing black slacks and a white button-down that accentuates his muscular frame. I swear the man has been getting even more handsome over the years. It should be illegal for someone in their forties to look so deliciously attractive, but I'm not really complaining.

He's still the most beautiful man I've ever seen and he will always be.

I jog to him, wrap my arms around his waist, hugging him and Lily, then I get on my tiptoes and kiss him. He holds our daughter with one hand and pulls me to him with the other, deepening the kiss.

My senses skyrocket as I melt in his embrace, and I get lost in his addictive taste. No matter how much he kissed me, the intensity never disappeared. In fact, it feels earth-shattering as that first time he claimed my lips by the side of the pool.

He's been kissing me for years, but it still feels as if he's kissing me back for when he didn't kiss me on my eighteenth birthday.

He's been kissing me for years and I can't get enough.

I probably never will.

"Morning, husband," I breathe when we break apart.

A dark gleam of desire shines in his eyes as he speaks low, "Morning, wife."

"Thank you for the birthday gift. I love it and you."

A clearing of a throat comes from behind me before Dad appears by our side, carrying Logan and glaring. "I'm over here, in case no one noticed."

"Hi, Dad." I kiss his cheek.

"So now you have a dad?"

"Your jealousy is showing, King." Nate smirks at him.

"You shut up, daughter stealer."

"Dad." I grab his arm, laughing, and he just shakes his head.

Since he's overprotective, it's impossible to have him stop throwing jabs at my husband anytime he gets.

Even if he loves how much Nate takes care of me.

"And stop your PDA in front of my grandchildren. Give me Lily." My father basically snatches her and holds each of the twins on an arm as he speaks to them. "You two prefer your grandfather anyway, don't you?"

I smile as he takes them back to the house, but it's interrupted when Nate wraps his arms around my waist from behind and rests his chin on my shoulder.

"Have you slept well?" His words against my neck draw a shudder out of me.

"Yeah, and I just had the best morning." I turn around to face him and flatten my palms against his chest. "Thank you for the photo album and that letter. I will cherish it until I die."

"You don't have to."

"Too late. Already learned it by heart."

He smiles and I'm trapped in it. In how easily he does it around me. Sometimes, it feels like I'm the only reason he smiles and I selfishly love it.

I love that I'm his world as much as he's mine.

"Happy birthday, wife."

"Happy anniversary, husband."

A small frown appears between his brows. "Anniversary?"

"For the day you fell in love with me." I stroke his cheek. "It was a few years after me, but it's okay. You're stuck with me now."

"That's where you're wrong, baby girl. You're the one who's stuck with me."

And then he flings me close to his body and kisses me with a passion that seals my fate.

Our fate.

I'm his and he's mine.

Probably ever since I was born.

THE END

Next up is the standalone book that features Knox Van Doren, titled *Empire of Sin*.

Curious about Sebastian who was mentioned in this book? You can read his story in *Red Thorns*.

WHAT'S NEXT?

Thank you so much for reading *Empire of Desire*!
If you liked it, please leave a review.
Your support means the world to me.

If you're thirsty for more discussions with other readers of the
series, you can join the Facebook group,
Rina Kent's Spoilers Room.

Next up is the long-awaited book, *Empire of Sin*, that will
feature Knox Van Doren who was a supporting character in
Royal Elite Series. His leading lady will be a surprise to many!

ALSO BY RINA KENT

For more books by the author and a reading order, please visit:

www.rinakent.com/books

ABOUT THE AUTHOR

Rina Kent is a *USA Today*, international, and #1 Amazon bestselling author of everything enemies to lovers romance.

She's known to write unapologetic anti-heroes and villains because she often fell in love with men no one roots for. Her books are sprinkled with a touch of darkness, a pinch of angst, and an unhealthy dose of intensity.

She spends her private days in London laughing like an evil mastermind about adding mayhem to her expanding universe. When she's not writing, Rina travels, hikes, and spoils cats in a pure Cat Lady fashion.

Find Rina Below:

Website: www.rinakent.com
Newsletter: www.subscribepage.com/rinakent
BookBub: www.bookbub.com/profile/rina-kent
Amazon: www.amazon.com/Rina-Kent/e/B07MM54G22
Goodreads: www.goodreads.com/author/show/18697906.Rina_Kent
Instagram: www.instagram.com/author_rina
Facebook: www.facebook.com/rinaakent
Reader Group: www.facebook.com/groups/rinakent.club
Pinterest: www.pinterest.co.uk/AuthorRina/boards
Tiktok: www.tiktok.com/@rina.kent
Twitter: twitter.com/AuthorRina

Made in the USA
Coppell, TX
05 June 2024